CW01454865

The Compass Line

By

D A Millington

Copyright © 2022 D A Millington

British Library Cataloguing in Publication Data.
A catalogue record for this book is available from the British Library

ISBN 978 0 86071 862 8

A Commissioned Publication Printed by

MOORLEYS
Print, Design & Publishing
info@moorleys.co.uk · www.moorleys.co.uk

Synopsis

Emilie Weston is expecting to become the Mayor when circumstances take an unexpected turn and she discovers that not every man (or woman) can be master of their own destiny.

About

This is a work of complete fiction, a yarn if you will, set amidst a world as it unfolded during the course of the twentieth century. Whilst the historical occurrences portrayed are routed in some fact, (I say *some* fact since I imagine professional historians may dispute the minutiae) the protagonists are entirely fictional, borne from nothing more than the imagination of the author. Any likeness to any individual whether alive or dead is purely coincidental. The exceptions to this, Sonny Bono, Frank Sinatra, John F Kennedy, The Earl of Ancaster, to name but a few, are obvious and are included to set a scene.

Acknowledgments

This book would not have been written but for the Covid crisis, its subsequent Lockdown and a wish of the writer to, for the most part, remain in a state of sobriety and do something other than binge watch whatever Netflix had to offer. To Stephen, for picking up the domestic flack during the writing process; to the first readers of the manuscript, L Bettany, A. Kind and K. Arnold, I thank you. To Chris Page for inspiring me to stop talking about writing and to just get on and do it. To Microsoft spell checker, don't know what I'd have done without you. To John Boyes and his excellent book on Project Emily, you got me started. The Royal Children's hospital Melbourne, the Council on foreign relations, Newscientist.com and MIT Student cable, all who had excellent online resource material, there were many others, I offer eternal thanks and gratitude.

CHAPTER 1
EMILIE

May 7th 1998

'If someone could tell you what was going to happen before the end of the day, the week, the month, the year; would you want to know?'

Before Emilie Weston had time to consider the prospect, she drove her car over the dropped kerb and onto the suburban driveway of the place she called home. She put the car into neutral, applied the handbrake and switched off the ignition, silencing the radio and the presenter who had posed the question. Home was a modern brick built detached house under a tiled roof, much the same as the other houses in the street with large picture windows and a glazed vestibule. Emilie shared the house with her husband Will and their two sons, Sam who was nearly fourteen and Miles who was ten. Home was her sanctuary from the world, her haven of tranquillity, her pride and joy. It is often said that an Englishman's home is his castle. No less is true of the modern English woman. This sentiment was evident along the length of the street with each neighbour having made their individual attempts at fortressing their red brick and slate castles behind an array of wrought iron, stone walling, wooden panelled fencing and impenetrable hedging. The developers of the most recent dwellings had adopted a convention of open plan when it came to front gardens, presumably to cut building costs. Only time would tell whether this newly adopted openness to the world at large would continue or whether the fortress mentality would prevail. Will and Emilie had provided for both options; open plan but with the addition of a series of high sturdy black wrought iron gates that could be secured to prevent trespassers or unwanted visitors. In practice the gates were

1

never closed so as to facilitate easier access and egress with the cars. The Weston's were a two car family. It was only a matter of time before two cars would become four. Emilie collected her large satchel handbag from the passenger foot-well and climbed out of the car. She noticed the house was fully illuminated despite it not yet being dark, with a light on in every window. Will's parking space was ominously empty. The sound of footsteps approaching caused her to turn around. Philip Morgan, a journalist for the Nottingham Post who lived down the street, was walking by. He had a habit of quoting what she said in Chamber out of context to fit his own narrative. As a result, she tended to be guarded in his presence and didn't engage in conservation much beyond that of neighbourly civility.

'Hi,' called Emilie.

'Hi,' he replied. 'Are you on your way to the Town Hall?'

'Soon. I just need to freshen up and collect the troops. Will I see you there?'

'Nah, not tonight. I've seen the agenda. There's nothing that interests me. It's a quick visit to Ladbroke's to place my sure fire bet for the weekend, then a beer and an early night. See you around'.

'Yeah, bye' Emilie replied as a vision flashed into her mind. She was standing at the back of a commuter train. She could see the platform clock through the window. It ticked over to 08:06 and she was moving out of Paddington station. She sensed the sway of the carriage as the train crossed to an adjacent line and then crossed over another. A signal appeared ahead, mounted on an overhead gantry. SN109. The bright sun was hanging low in the sky, casting a blinding glare. She couldn't make out whether the light at SN109 was red or amber. The train accelerated. It must have been amber. Suddenly she sensed an almighty jolt. Unbalanced, she steadied herself against the side of the car only to be enveloped by the sensation of intense heat accompanied by the unmistakable stench of diesel and scorched hair. She checked her attire for signs she might be on fire, she wasn't, before looking around. Nothing was untoward. The disturbing vision dissipated.

Emilie rushed into the hall, dumped her bag on the floor at the foot of the stairs and made for the noise emanating from the kitchen. The siblings were arguing as usual. Sam, who was the older brother at thirteen, had become a loud insolent adolescent, who always wanted his own way and who generally got it. Miles, who was ten, was the polar opposite; quiet, introverted, kind and caring.

'Where's your Dad?' she asked over the petty squabbling.

'He just called to say he's running late' said Miles. 'Something about a car smash on the Motorway and the traffic's backed up. He says he'll be here as soon as he can.'

'That's all I need tonight' said Emilie. 'What does this say?' she asked, thumping her fist on a notice stuck to the door of the large refrigerator.

'Spaghetti bolognaise' replied Sam.

'Then why haven't you started it? You both know how to make spaghetti bolognaise. Have you forgotten tonight's my big night? I'm running late and I haven't got much time.'

'You're always running late' Sam retorted.

'So why haven't you put the dinner on?'

'We've been busy' replied Sam.

'Doing what?'

'Just stuff. We have lives too you know.'

'Have you done your homework?' she asked accusatorily, guessing what the answer was going to be before either of her reluctantly studious offspring could respond.

'Haven't got any' said Sam.

'I don't believe you.'

'Look, we'll do it later ok.'

'No we won't' interrupted Miles candidly. 'Layla and Phoebe are coming over. They want to watch TV so we're gonna chill out.'

'Chill out, great. I wish I could chill out once in a while. Can't they watch TV at their own house?' asked Emilie.

'No, their Dad wants to watch the match and you know they've only got one TV.'

3

'I assume you won't be accompanying me to the Town Hall this evening then?' asked Emilie disappointingly, indignantly thumping the frying pan onto the halogen hob. 'It's not every day your Mother becomes the Mayor. I thought you said you'd be there to support me.'

'Look Mum, it's not really our thing.'

'What do you mean it's not really your thing?'

'Politics, it's boring as hell and we're just not interested ok. We'd rather stay here.'

'Well thank you for your support, it's touching' she replied, emptying a pack of minced beef into the pan and thrashing it with a spatula so as to remove all doubt the poor cow that produced it was dead. 'Remind me to be as supportive to you two sometime.'

'You can be this weekend.'

'I can be what?'

'Supportive, a group of us want to go paint balling on Saturday' said Sam.

'I thought we decided on Karting' interrupted Miles.

'Ah, we can go karting next weekend. Phoebe and Layla are paint balling this weekend so we're going paint balling, ok?

'I suppose so' said Miles reluctantly.

'I'll go and call them, say we can make it on Saturday.'

'While you're up there turn off all the ruddy lights' Emilie shouted after him. 'It's like Blackpool illuminations in this house, electricity doesn't grow on trees.'

Sam had already disappeared without acknowledging her request so she guessed her words had fallen onto deaf ears.

'Give me a hand Miles, there's a good boy, I'm really up against the clock tonight. Put the pasta on will you please?'

Emilie chopped frantically at a clove of garlic and then did the same with the first unsuspecting onion from the fridge.

'You really shouldn't let him bully you like that. You need to be more assertive, stick up for yourself a bit. He always gets his own way. You give in far too easily.'

'I know, but he's a tosser, he can't help it.'

'Well that's not exactly how I'd have put it but I know what you mean' she smiled sympathetically. 'Perhaps you need to work on your vocabulary though and opt for better choices of adjectives; it's really not very nice to refer to your big brother as a tosser. Right, I'll be upstairs' she announced, emptying a can of tomatoes into the pan and adding a generous sprinkling of oregano followed by a pinch of salt and pepper. 'I need to change. When this boils, turn down the heat and give it a stir. I'll be back to dish up in fifteen minutes.'

When Emilie came back down, having changed into a navy pinstriped suit and stiff white collared shirt, Layla and Phoebe had already made themselves comfortable at the breakfast bar. Miles was serving bolognaise onto four plates. Sam was at the blender pureeing the last of the fruit from the fruit bowl into smoothies.

'Dad and I aren't eating here tonight' she said. 'There will be a buffet after the ceremony we'll grab a sandwich then.' She thought better than to voice her contempt at the loss of the fruit she'd intended to serve with breakfast the following morning.

'I know' said Miles. 'It's not for you. Layla and Phoebe are having dinner with us.'

'Where's your Mum tonight?' asked Emilie.

'She had a row with Dad so she's gone to the Bingo' responded Phoebe, averting her attention for just a second from the TV. An episode of the sitcom *Friends*, now in its fourth season, was being broadcast for the first time. Emilie had noticed that no one liked to admit they watched it but that everyone must do since, whilst her colleagues at work belittled its long running presence on the screen, they were all able to name the six main characters, had a favourite and were usually able to recount the current storyline.

Emilie glanced up to the screen to a close up of the English character Emily, walking down a makeshift aisle amidst a multitude of twinkling candle lights to marry her soon to be fictional husband Ross.

'He'll say Rachel' exclaimed Emilie.'

'No, he's not marrying Rachel, Mrs Weston. He's marrying Emily' informed Layla.

5

'Yes I know, but he'll say *I take thee Rachel*, you see if he doesn't' said Emilie disappearing into the hall to look for a suitable pair of shoes from where the volume was loud enough to hear the scene.

'I Ross, take thee Rachel....'

The girls were sat open mouthed when Emilie returned to the kitchen.

'How did you know?' asked Phoebe.

'Know what?'

'How did you know Ross would say *Rachel* when he should have said *Emily*? You can't have already seen it, it's new. How did you know?'

'It was obvious I guess' shrugged Emilie.

'Not to me it wasn't' scoffed Layla. 'He'd be a dead man now if I was Emily' she scorned. 'I'd definitely have to kill him. A man would only embarrass me like that once.'

'Where are you going Mrs Weston?' asked Phoebe.

'The Town Hall, I've got a Council meeting.'

'But I thought you said you were going to a ceremony' Phoebe replied.

'Well yes, I'm being promoted to the position of Mayor of the Borough but that's just part of the meeting. That part is called a ceremony I suppose. Not that there's much else on the actual business agenda other than the issue of free tampons.'

'Free tampons?' Phoebe enquired.

'Well not just tampons, free sanitary products generally.'

'We don't want to hear this Mum' groaned Sam.

'Yes we do' interrupted Phoebe. 'What about free tampons?'

'Well since you ask Phoebe, we shall be moving a motion that if successful, will mean all girls of school age will have access to free tampons.'

'How come?'

'To avoid something that has come to be known as period poverty.'

'What's period poverty?'

'It's when you can't afford to buy the products you need for your time of the month.'

'I can't afford products. Does that mean I'll get poverty tampons?'

'What do you mean you can't afford products? I find that hard to believe.'

'It's true, I can't. I've never got enough money for all the stuff I need.'

'What kind of stuff do you need?'

'I needed some new earrings last week and some new trainers, the week before I needed new jeans.'

'I think you might be confusing things you need with things you'd like to have Phoebe.'

'No I'm not' she contested. 'If I hadn't have bought my new jeans I'd have been utterly miserable. It's important to have new things when you want them, me Mum says so. When are we going to get them, the free tampons?'

'That depends, probably not for a good few months, maybe a year or so, that's assuming the motion is approved. I have a horrible feeling the opposition are going to say it doesn't go far enough and will move an amendment that the provision should be extended to all unionised women, but I won't agree to that.'

'Why not? Layla asked. 'Me Mum's a dinner lady. She's part of a union, why shouldn't she get free tampons?'

'Well Layla, I suppose because unionised women are paid a fair wage, thus quite capable of buying their own tampons whereas school girls don't have their own income. The two are not comparable. Not to mention the unfairness to non-unionised men and women who wouldn't receive the same benefit in spite of them being the tax payers who'd ultimately have to pay for it through extra taxes.'

'Don't worry about it Sis' said Phoebe 'We'll just get more than we need and let Mum have the surplus.'

'The hell we will. No, we'll get more than we need and sell em to Dad at a knock down price for him to give to Mum. We can make some money out of this if we play our cards right.'

'How entrepreneurial of you girls, if somewhat an abuse of privilege.'

'Privilege?' scoffed Layla. 'It's hardly a privilege bleeding out every month.'

'Oh yeah and what about shaving?' intercepted Sam.

7

'What about it?'

'You think it's fun having to shave every day?'

'You don't shave every day' argued Layla.

'Well I will do soon. Are the tax payers gonna pay for my razors and gel? No they're not. We're reduced to accepting shaving products as Christmas gifts every year, for which we're supposed to be grateful. You can ask my Dad if you don't believe me. I bet you don't have to have tampons for Christmas do you?'

'I didn't think you were interested in politics' said Emilie.

'It's hardly politics' retorted Sam. 'Politics is about whether we go to war.'

'And how we go about keeping the peace' added Miles.

'But it is politics' argued Emilie. 'Everything you do is governed by politics, not just decisions about war. It'll be a political decision that changes the current position with regards to providing girls with free sanitary wear. It's a political decision because it will change who will be responsible for paying for it. You can't shift liability for something from the individual to the state without politics. Now give your Mum a kiss you two' she pleaded, tapping her freshly rouged cheek with her index finger. 'Wish me luck and tell your Dad to meet me at the Town Hall as soon as he gets home. The ceremony starts at seven thirty we'll be back around ten thirty and do your homework. I'll be checking your school diary when I get home.'

A shiver ran down Emilie's spine as she opened the car door. The hairs on the back of her arms stood up. *Someone has just walked over my grave* she thought. A footstep in the gravel behind her caused her to turn around to see who was approaching. There was no one there. She brushed it off as a cat having walked by and climbed into the driver's seat igniting the temperamental engine with the key.

The gritty voice of Cerys Matthews and Welsh band Catatonia was playing on the radio; *you and I know, it's all over the front page, you give me road rage, racing through the best days ...* Emilie turned up the volume, checked the rear view mirror and reversed out of the drive for the short drive to the Town Hall.

CHAPTER 2
IVY

August 26th 1899

'It is time' called Sister Edith, fumbling beneath her long pristine white scapula and removing a clean cotton handkerchief from the pocket of her white tunic. She wiped away the stinging beads of salty perspiration that were dripping into her eyes. She longed to rip off her suffocating veil, the heat was blistering. Instead, she silently scolded herself for considering such impudence. Age and its associated infirmities were beginning to take their toll on the once youthful and rebellious nun.

'What can I do to help Sister?' asked Sparrow who was just seventeen and a novice to the Order. Sparrow had only been with the Sisterhood a month and although unknown to Edith and the other Sisters, Sparrow had already begun to doubt her suitability as to her chosen vocation, with its strict adherence to regimental conventions.

'Ah Sparrow, good you're here. I need you to take this list over to the Sisters of Saint Dominic and bring everything on it as quickly as you can. Report to Sister Hamble. She will know what to do.'

'Very good Sister.'

'And be sure to wear your cappa magna when you return.'

'But Sister Edith, it's so hot today' moaned Sparrow. 'Must I?'

'I'm well aware of how hot it is' replied Sister Edith curtly, clutching the sodden handkerchief in her sweaty palm. 'Now go child, quickly, there's no time to waste.'

Edith waited for the sound of the door closing. Satisfied she was now in solitude; she fumbled for the row of rosary beads on her belt, knelt on the tiled floor and sat in silent prayer.

***

The journey to the Abbey where the Sisters of Saint Dominic had taken up temporary lodgings was some three miles away. Sparrow lifted her long tunic which had a tendency to trail on the floor and trip her up, unless she was walking in the rigid head up, shoulders back position, favoured by Sister Edith. Sparrow assumed Edith's strict adherence to the correct and proper stature was due more in part to the fact her tunic had been sewn too long, rather than anything to do with being closer to God. Edith had been prepared to neither alter it nor spare the sewing thread needed for Sparrow to alter it herself, so she continued to trip a lot. Sparrow made haste across the grounds of Grace Dieu Manor, pausing at the Warren Road before heading across the scrub and into Cademan Wood, a short cut she had made a number of times in recent weeks since arriving in the sleepy rural hamlet. The shade provided by the canopy of the trees was a welcome relief from the ferocity of the midday sun which felt like it was burning a hole into the top of her head through the black veil. When she was certain she was out of sight, Sparrow paused and removed the veil to escape the suffocating confinement before continuing onward toward the Abbey. Her long tunic caught in a stubborn branch of a large prickly shrub and tore a hole. Lifting up her tunic and scapula to the knees, she scurried on until she reached Oaks Road, stopping to replace her veil, lest she be spotted by a passer-by, who would no doubt report her infringement to Sister Edith and then she'd have to deal with the sack cloth again. She continued for thirty minutes before turning at the stone farmhouse for the final leg of her journey, up the long tree lined avenue, to rouse the Sisters of Saint Dominic into action.

Sparrow was met by Sister Hamble, a short stout woman of senior years with a round friendly face.

'What's all the hurry?' enquired Sister Hamble.

'It's time, the baby is on its way' said Sparrow breathlessly. 'We are to make haste. Sister Edith has given me a list of provisions we must deliver to the manor. It's taken me so long to get back here, I'm afraid we'll be too late.'

'There's no need to panic' replied Sister Hamble. 'Babies don't arrive at the drop of a hat. I'm sure we have plenty of time. Sister Edith knows what she is doing. Give me the list and I'll prepare the necessities. While I'm doing that, you go and find Sister Agnes and together see if you can find Brother Hipwood and ask for the use of a carriage.'

'Right away Sister' said Sparrow before hurriedly disappearing along the corridor of the abbey.

Sister Hamble had already prepared what she expected would be needed. She opened the scrap of paper to check Sister Edith's requirements. Removing a pencil from the pocket of her tunic, she began ticking off the items on the list.

two fresh bars of carbolic soap
sixteen clean rags cut into one foot squares
a bottle of Lysol
a bowl of lard
twelve lengths of satin ribbon one yard
one new unused shaving blade
one enema kit disinfected
one pair scissors disinfected
one clean nightdress
one clean petticoat
eight clean muslin or cotton towels
four thimbles ergot powder
one vial chloroform
two vials scopolamine
two vials Godfrey's cordial
two vials morphine
two vials chloral hydrate solution
one pestle and mortar
forceps
one straightjacket
one reel suture thread
two needles disinfected
two swaddling sheets

Sister Hamble realised she had not second guessed all of Sister Edith's requirements. The list continued over and above those items she had already packed into two suitcases that were waiting in the hall.

one pen with ink and well

11

sixteen pennies in readiness to be paid to the village postmaster for sixteen Mulberry Penny Pinks

three shillings in readiness to be paid to the village Postmaster for six twelve word telegrams

five pennies in readiness to be paid to the postmaster for two overseas letters

two sheets of fine writing paper

Lynne Blackburn, the wet nurse, is to be retained. Four shillings will be required.

The Sisters of Saint Dominic had no money to speak of. God's work didn't require them to carry cold hard cash. The good will of others usually sufficed. Sister Hamble made her way to the Chapel to look for Brother Hipwood for some assistance with the money. It was a most irregular request by Sister Edith, who had been delivering babies for many years without the need for so many shillings and pennies.

Brother Hipwood was not in the Chapel but Sisters Agnes and Sparrow were, giggling like parlour maids.

'Where is Brother Hipwood?' asked Sister Hamble.

'He's gone back to Grace Dieu Manor to raise his Lordship's horse and carriage as the abbey doesn't have one' replied Sparrow. 'We are to wait here and he'll return as soon as he can. We thought we'd brush the floor while we were waiting.'

'I didn't see any evidence of brushing when I came in but never mind that, come and help carry the cases to the door. As we have some time, we should eat. Lord knows when we'll have the chance again.'

The Sisters produced the remains of a loaf and small block of cheese from the cold store and sat at a large table in the centre of the scullery.

'Bless us, O Lord, and these, Thy gifts, which we are about to receive from Thy bounty. Through Christ, our Lord. Amen' said Sister Hamble, blessing the meal with the sign of the cross.

***

It was past two o'clock when the Sisters, who were squeezed in to the back of the carriage, arrived back at Grace Dieu manor. They made their way to the Gardeners cottage and went straight in.

The small stone cottage belonged to the Grace Dieu Estate and was home to the Head Gardener William Newlove and his young pretty wife Summer. The door led into a small but inviting sitting room with

12

a cast iron fireplace, inset with blue and white tiles, on the back wall. Above it hung a large ornate mahogany framed mirror which reflected a mahogany bureau that stood on the opposite wall. Two comfortable blue winged back chairs straddled the hearth. A small heavily buttoned cream sofa nestled into a bay window which overlooked the extensive garden. A large patterned rug, depicting flowers and birds as would be found in an English country garden, sat with mathematical precision in the centre of the tiled floor. The walls were decorated in an intricate William Morris design wallpaper of bluebells and snowdrops into a repeating damask pattern that invoked in the observer a peaceful serenity. Sparrow couldn't imagine anyone being anything but profoundly happy here. It was certainly a far cry from the bare stone walls, the cold hard floors and the functional furnishings of the abbey. There were certainly no soft furnishings to be found there, except for the thin straw mattress. A tinge of sadness welled in her and she stifled a tear. How she missed her creature comforts.

William Newlove appeared in the doorway, his grubby fingers fumbling with his cap.

'Is Summer alright?' he asked nervously. 'Brother Hipwood says the baby is on the way. Can I see her?'

'Absolutely not!' Sister Hamble exclaimed. 'The birthing room is no place for a man. Look at you, you're filthy. Be off with you. I assure you when there's something for you to do, you'll be the first to know.'

'It's going to be a while yet' interrupted Sister Agnes. 'Perhaps by suppertime, there may be some news. You go about your business now. Brother Hipwood will come and find you when the baby arrives.'

'Alright, if you're sure, although I'm not sure I will be able to keep my mind on my work today. You will send for me the minute the baby arrives?'

'Yes' snapped Sister Agnes, closing the door abruptly.

'Sister Edith' Sparrow called upstairs.

'Thank the Lord' exclaimed Sister Edith 'I didn't think you were ever going to get here. Up here as quick as you can.'

The youthful Sisters, Agnes and Sparrow, each picked up a suitcase and followed Sister Hamble up the steep narrow staircase. Summer

Newlove was on her knees on the crumpled bed. The beautifully embroidered eiderdown had been removed, folded neatly and placed on the floor underneath the window, alongside two pretty pillows. Summer let out a fearful shriek and her head disappeared as if she were trying to bury it into her swollen breasts.

'How much longer?' she cried. 'I don't think I can take much more. It hurts, it really hurts' clenching her fists and pounding the mattress.

Sister Edith opened the first suitcase on the dresser.

'Take this' she said, offering a freshly wrapped bar of carbolic soap to Sister Hamble. 'Downstairs, ensure the range is lit and each of you, wash your hands and arms, up to your elbows in water as hot as you can stand. Use plenty of soap, we don't want childbed fever, I need you clean. Remember, cleanliness is next to Godliness. Then bring up a bowl of hot boiled water. Sparrow you can prepare a teacup of boiled water please.'

The three Sisters disappeared leaving Sister Edith to rummage through the suitcase. She removed a small brown leather box and placed it on a small table at the side of the bed.

'What's that?' asked Summer.

'Necessary' replied Sister Edith. 'You don't want to spoil your lovely marital bed for your Husband and its important your baby comes into a clean world, free of dirt and germs. The cleanliness is not only important for your baby, it's important for you too, otherwise you risk coming down with Puerperal Fever and then you might die. I've never lost a Mother to Puerperal Fever yet and I'm not about to start today, so you just do as I say and soon you'll have a beautiful baby daughter.'

'How can you be so sure I'm going to have a daughter?'

'Trust me when I say that God will bless you with the gift of a daughter.'

Labour pains began again and the expectant mother buried her face into the mattress to stifle her cries.

Sister Edith checked her pocket watch.

'The birthing pains are coming at five minute intervals. We should prepare for the delivery. I want you to slip into these' said Sister Edith, placing a white cotton petticoat and nightdress onto the bed.

'Freshly boiled.'

Summer waited for the contraction to pass and slipped into Sister Edith's nightclothes. The cotton felt stiff and rough against her skin, quite unlike the silk gown she'd just removed. Sister Edith took two lengths of ribbon from the case, sat on the bed and parted Summer's long flowing auburn hair. The comb refused to go through her matted locks.

'We should have done this earlier' said Sister Edith, tugging at a particularly stubborn lug. She made two tight plaits and tied each one securely with the ribbon.

'There, that's better.'

Another contraction took hold. Summer fell to her elbows and howled, her head shaking frantically from side to side as if she were trying to shake off the devil himself. Sister Agnes appeared with a large porcelain bowl of boiled water and placed it on the dresser next to the suitcase.

'Good' said Sister Edith. 'Now take this' handing her the bottle of Lysol and a clean rag. 'Clean everything thoroughly. The table tops, the bed head and anything you think you might touch. It's imperative everything is impeccably clean.'

'Yes Sister.'

'Now I want you to pull up your petticoat Summer. That's right, a little further. Now spread your legs.'

Summer reticently pulled her ankles towards her buttocks. Sister Edith rummaged in the suitcase and took out the second fresh bar of carbolic soap and a cut-throat razor.

'What are you going to do with that?' asked Summer.

'Wider' ordered Sister Edith, jabbing at Summer's knee. Wider please. Wider. Just let your knees fall to the side. It's a little late to be coy now, don't you think?'

Sister Edith worked the soap into a lather.

'Will you fill that jug with water please' said Sister Edith to Sister Agnes. 'And hold it. I need two hands.'

Sister Edith worked fastidiously between Summer and the jug until all her pubic hair had gone. Spots of blood dripped from where the razor had nicked the skin, soiling the fresh petticoat. Sister Edith blotted the spots away. Another contraction and Summer wailed.

'Now roll onto your side and bring your knees up. That's it. This might be a little uncomfortable.'

Without warning, Sister Edith inserted the enema pipe into Summer's anus. Summer instinctively recoiled and Sister Hamble pressed firmly on her hip to hold her still. The water flushed unnaturally inside her. The silence in the room became deafening. Summer closed her eyes, and prayed for the indignity to be over.

'The bedpan if you please Sister Agnes. I'm sure it won't be long.'

Sister Agnes felt under the bed to retrieve the bedpan, poured in a generous amount of Lysol and wiped it with her damp cloth before placing it on the bed.

Sparrow appeared with a blue and white china teacup and saucer.

'Ah about time, thank you Sparrow. Put the cup on the dresser please. Sister Hamble, will you locate the Ergot please. I think it's time.'

Sister Edith took the packet and measured a thimble of powder which she stirred into the hot water.

'Now drink this.'

'What is it?'

'My, you ask a lot of questions. It's Ergot tea. It will help stave the bleeding.'

'But I'm not bleeding.'

'Not yet perhaps.'

Another contraction, much stronger than before ascended. Summer's forehead erupted in perspiration. When it had finished, Summer's bottom lip was soaked in blood. Sister Agnes mopped her fevered brow.

16

It was four o'clock when Summer announced she needed to use the bedpan. Five o'clock came and went. Six o'clock came and went. At seven o'clock Summer was screaming for it to be over.

'Please let it be over' she wailed. 'Please just kill me. No more. I'm sorry God. Whatever I did, it won't happen again. I'm sorry, please make it stop.'

'Chloroform Sister?' asked Hamble.

'I think so. Still only three inches dilated. I'll do it. Summer, I'm going to give you something for the pain. Would you like that?'

'Oh yes, a million times yes yes yes, I beg you.'

Sister Edith administered three drops of chloroform onto a rag.

'Here now, I'm going to hold this over your face, just breathe naturally.'

The next contraction came. Summer was quieter and less frantic.

'That did the job' sighed Agnes. 'I wish we'd used it earlier.'

By nine o'clock, the frantic, helpless wails had returned.

'Don't you think it's time for the twilight sleep Sister?' asked Agnes.

'No, not yet' answered Sister Edith.

'But the girl is in severe distress.'

'She's having a baby. Of course she's in severe distress.'

'But the pains have been coming every two minutes. If not now, then when?'

'Sister Agnes' scoffed Sister Edith 'if God had intended childbirth to be free of pain, then he would have made it so. Cheating the pain is tantamount to cheating God and I'm not about to allow this child of God cheat her creator before she's yet out of the womb.'

'Then why did you have me bring the scopolamine and the morphine?'

'Sister Agnes, you have seen what happens when we use it. This child needs to retain the wear-with-all to be able to push when the time comes. I suggest you calm yourself, go downstairs and make us all a pot of hot tea. Then and only then, will I reconsider administering the twilight dream.'

The twilight dream was a concoction of the opioid morphine and scopolamine from the nightshade family. The Sisters had been introduced to it whilst attending a recent birth in Germany. The drug's effect was to supposedly result in a pain free birth. Sister Edith disputed the claim, maintaining the birth had not been pain free at all, but had simply brought about amnesia in the Mother who couldn't remember her pain. The sight of the mother, thrashing about in a state of delirium to the point a straightjacket was needed to prevent her harming herself, left Sister Edith with reservations about the use of the twilight dream again.

At eleven o'clock, Sister Edith decided it was time for Summer to start to push.

'Fetch the lard please Hamble, let's get her as comfortable as we can. I need you to lie on your back and open your legs Summer. This won't hurt.'

Sister Edith smeared a large dollop of lard between Summer's legs and massaged it into her crevice.

After an hour of pushing, Summer Newlove gave birth to a quiet baby girl. Sister Edith cut the umbilical cord, administered a slap on the babies bottom and she wailed into life.

'Well done Summer' chirped Sparrow. 'You have a beautiful baby girl. What name are you going to christen her with?'

'Ivy' replied Summer.

'It's not quite over yet my child' interrupted Sister Edith. 'You still have to push again, one last time now, as hard as you can.'

The bloody placenta spewed from Summer's vagina, showering Sparrow's scapula with blood.

'Well done Child' praised Sister Edith. 'Now I want you to drink this.'

'What is it?' asked Summer.

'Something to help you sleep.'

'But I don't want to sleep I want to hold my baby.'

'There's plenty of time for that. You must rest now. Your baby will need all your energy tomorrow. Tonight you must sleep.'

18

Summer took the cup, swallowed and fell back into the soft feather pillow. Within a matter of minutes she had fallen into an exhausted sleep.

'We'll take it from here Sister' whispered Hamble. 'You go and do what you must do. Sparrow will bring you a cup of tea.'

'Someone needs to inform the Father he has a child' stated Sister Edith.

'Oh let me tell him' chirped Sparrow, turning on her heals to dash downstairs in search of Mr Newlove, who still hadn't been allowed back into the cottage.

'No, come back here at once' called Sister Edith after Sparrow.

It was too late, Sparrow had already flown.

'I don't know where she gets her energy from' said Hamble. 'I'm quite exhausted.'

'Don't let him come up here' shouted Sister Edith down the stairs. 'Mrs Newlove needs to rest. He can make up a bed in the sitting room tonight and he can see them in the morning.'

CHAPTER 3
THE GROUP CAPTAIN

November 1958

An unseasonable blizzard had gripped the country. Heavy snowfall had rendered visibility close to zero. The hedgerows which usually delineated the road from the fields, had become invisible under a thick undulating blanket of snow, making it impossible to tell where the tarmac finished and the drainage ditches began. The car's inadequate heating system caused the windscreen to fog. The condensation had to be continually cleared by both the driver and the front seat passenger. The windscreen wiper blades were proving to be worse than useless and the frozen virgin snow on the road ahead, unmarked by the lack of traffic having passed before, made for a treacherous journey. At last, the car slowed and signalled right. The gate as expected was locked. The driver engaged the hand brake, got out and removed the padlock before opening one gate fully. He climbed back into the car.

'Get out' he said, looking over his shoulder to the back seat incumbent. 'Stand at the entrance and signal the second car. I don't want them to miss the turning.'

He disengaged the handbrake and teetered forward slowly, staying in first gear before parking to wait for the second car. When he saw through his rear view mirror that the second car had entered through the gate, he climbed out and replaced the padlock. The second car was instructed to follow. They drove a short way until another gate blocked their path.

'You can do it this time' said the driver, throwing a small bunch of keys to the front seat passenger. When both vehicles were inside the compound, the passenger replaced the padlock. They drove at a snail's pace for another few minutes until the driver stopped, engaged the handbrake once more and switched off the engine. The frigid blizzard was unrelenting.

'Where the hell are we?' asked Bob Halford, lifting the collar of his coat to shield his face from the icy chill.

'For those of you who don't already know me, I am Group Captain Mulberry Montgomery. I'll take questions when and only when we get out of this goddamn weather. For now, I want you to listen. Follow me.'

Four men dutifully followed, trudging through the deep snow. Montgomery stopped midway between two thick L shaped concrete structures. The walls of which were a good six feet thick.

'I think we'll start here' Montgomery shouted, trying to make himself heard over the roaring wind.

'We are at a redundant Royal Air Force base. You are standing on what is to become a launch emplacement for an intermediate range ballistic missile. This launch emplacement is one of three launch emplacements at this site. These structures are blast walls. You don't need me to tell you which side of the wall you should be on when the missile is launched.'

'Don't you mean *if* the missile is launched Sir?' Tom Summerfield asked.

'Quite right Mr Summerfield. This site will be the headquarters and the airhead. It will serve an additional four satellite sites' Montgomery continued. 'There will be four additional airhead sites at different coastal locations with their own satellite stations. These American manufactured missiles are enormous in both size and destructive capacity thus they present a number of logistical challenges. Sixty four feet long, eight feet in diameter, they have a range of one thousand five hundred miles and if deployed, will carry a 1.44 megaton nuclear warhead. That hollow in the ground over there, which I appreciate you cannot currently discern very well due to the snow, will contain the Liquid Oxygen tank system. That hollow over there will contain the kerosene fuel tank system. I appreciate none of you are Chemists, so I will simply state that on no account, must these fuel sources be stored

21

together. That hollow just there will provide an emergency water supply. Each of these fuel systems will be served via a pipeline, the trench for which is currently empty so please, do not fall in, watch where you put your feet. Now gentlemen if you will follow me this way.'

The five men trekked tentatively on through the snow, being sure to keep close to the footprints Montgomery had made, until they came to a large empty hangar. Montgomery unlocked the door and opened it just sufficiently to slip inside.

'Does anyone have any questions?' asked Montgomery.

'Yes, what the hell are we doing here?' asked Halford.

'I'll get to that in good time gentlemen. This is hangar number three and it is in here the missiles from the satellite stations will be brought on a low level transporter to be serviced and maintained. The maintenance will be carried out initially by United States Air Force personnel and then by Royal Air Force personnel. You will not be required to involve yourself with these maintenance procedures but you will need to have knowledge of them. Each of you will therefore be given a comprehensive manual which you are expected to digest until you are familiar with the processes involved. Now, if you'll follow me again please.'

The group followed Montgomery back outside and onward for another two hundred tentative feet.

'Launch emplacement two is over there' pointed Montgomery 'and number three is over there.'

He unlocked another door into a single storey brick building. The group followed him in.

'This will be the communications and administrative block.'

One door led to another room which in turn gave way to a series of ante rooms.

'It will also house the medical centre.' He kept walking. 'The dining room, the kitchen, the Sergeant's Mess and in here'; Montgomery paused to unlock a door, 'is what will be known as the decontamination room.'

The decontamination room was another series of empty rooms with further ante rooms off.

'This door is to remain locked at all times and through here, is where you will be working.'

'With the greatest of respect Captain you still haven't told us what we are doing here' repeated Halford.

'You're here because you are going to pose as officers of 144 Squadron.'

'But we're not airmen; we're scientists' said Halford.

'No Mr Halford, I'm sorry to disappoint you but I'm afraid you're labouring under a misapprehension. You *were* scientists' Montgomery exhorted. 'At the present time, you are merely academics without funding. The Government has cancelled your budget. They don't think your project has merit.'

'It had merit three years ago' argued Harry Holbrook. 'What's changed?'

'Another team has beaten you to it. Their technology is already being employed with some success in the field.'

'Which team?' Holbrook asked. "As far as I knew, we were the only team working with this technology".

'I'm afraid I am not at liberty to disclose that information.'

'But you can disclose details of the deployment of nuclear warheads?'

'By virtue of necessity, yes I can, although I haven't yet told you anything we don't expect the press to put into the public domain before the end of the year. This will change however, secrets will be divulged, so if anyone wishes to walk away and seek employment elsewhere, now is the time to do it.'

Each man had his own reasons for needing to stay. They'd each invested three years and to date, had diddly squat to show for it. Loss of funding was a grievous blow.

Bob Halford was a future materials and technology man. He'd spent his formative years at Cambridge and had recently digressed into real estate. This digression wasn't going according to plan. There had been problems with the planning authorities and the scheme had been

23

hampered with delays as a result of public opposition to his proposed project. His plan was to build an unprecedented number of homes in an equally unprecedented small amount of space, by building up and not out, as was the norm. The delays meant that all his investment actually consisted of was a very large and very useless, overpriced piece of unproductive land. He was in hock to the bank for the loans he'd taken out to secure its purchase and the interest was mounting up. Now was not a good time to turn his back on a regular income.

Harry Holbrook was first and foremost a medical practitioner who, for the last three years, no longer practised medicine. Funding for his neurology research hadn't increased in the manner he'd been led to believe it would, severely hampering his ambitions. Consequently, it had been easy to lure him away from the post he had occupied, with promises of improved personal wealth, greater professional credit, notoriety and the gratitude of a nation. Ultimately, Holbrook didn't need the money. His family had money, far more than they could ever hope to spend over the course of a lifetime. He wanted a Knighthood and he side stepped his way out of medical practice and onto the path he'd been promised paved the way to him getting it.

Tom Summerfield was a quiet, mild mannered man who found great satisfaction immersed within the intricacies of the logical and practical applications for the new wonder of the age, the computer. He wanted very little out of life personally except to keep his wife happy. She was a large domineering woman with a predisposition to long expensive lunch's at the most prestigious restaurants. She insisted on drinking only the finest wine, eating only the finest food and frequenting only the most exclusive tailoring establishments where she held accounts. Summerfield soon discovered he had married a woman who was impossible to please and pandered to her demands like a frightened puppy at the hands of a cruel master.

Dick McDermott was a womaniser, a petty thief and a charlatan. At least that was how Montgomery described him, adding that McDermott would have sold the soul of his own mother for the merest whiff of personal gain. Blessed with the gift of the gab, somehow McDermott always came up smelling of roses and managed to avoid the attentions of the long arm of the law. Whilst not actually qualified to do anything in particular, in practise he could turn his hand to most things given the right incentive. With humble origins from the docks of Liverpool, McDermott wanted the high life and intended to have it. His predilection for the charms of both the Bookmaker and the Casino however, conspired to keep the high life he craved firmly at bay.

The four men stood firm, exchanging sideways glances, but otherwise kept quiet. If any of the four harboured any doubts about what they were being asked to commit themselves to, the doubts remained unspoken. Certainly no one announced the time had come for them to walk away. They were all too heavily invested with three hard years of toil, graft, disappointment and gritted determination to succeed. The groundwork had been done and they were on the verge of implementing biological trials.

'Good', said Montgomery. 'Now that our Prime Minister has confirmed his intention to climb into bed with Eisenhower and whistle the tune of the star spangled banner, it gives us a unique opportunity. We expect to be able to proceed with our project, unhindered I might add, by the interference of the target driven pen pushing bureaucrats at the Ministry. Fortunately for your team, there are men in the new Ministry of Defence who disagree with the decision the Prime Minister has taken to cancel your funding and terminate your contracts.'

'So our funding isn't being withdrawn?' asked Halford.

'Yes and no. The current funding arrangements are terminated, of that you can be in no doubt.'

'So there's a new source of funding?' asked Holbrook.

'Yes, but the conditions are quite different. It is my duty to inform you that if you wish to continue with your work, it will have to be conducted with the utmost secrecy under the new rules.'

'What new rules?' Summerfield asked.

'The project will become a covert operation, carried out under the radar of the Government. You will not, under any circumstances, discuss your work outside this group and that includes with representatives of the Ministry of Defence or any other Government Department. There will be no official acknowledgement of the existence of this team, the work it does, or any result it produces or fails to produce.'

'It sounds to me like you're inviting us to commit treason' ventured Harry Holbrook.

'Absolutely not' replied Montgomery. 'We simply need to ensure that Ministers retain an element of plausible deniability in the event that information we don't want to be released, falls into the public domain before we are prepared for it. It's politics, pure and simple.'

'Why isn't Ambrose Mortimer here?' asked Holbrook. 'I'd have expected him to have been here. He's an integral part of the team.'

Mortimer was the Chemist of the group.

'We weren't sure that Mortimer would be on-board with a covert project so he's been kept out of the loop for now. That's why Mr McDermott is here. He will be replacing Mr Mortimer and will be your go-between from now on.'

'I don't see why. I don't mean any disrespect to Mr McDermott but Mortimer has signed the Official Secrets Act just like the rest of us.'

'Yes, but we are moving from a confidential project of some sensitivity, to a Top Secret covert classification. We have to be sure all protagonists on-board are quite clear about the differences. Mr Mortimer hasn't always given us confidence in this regard. Any more questions before we move on?'

'Yes' said Dick McDermott. 'How exactly is this new arrangement going to work?'

'The project, its aims and outcomes, will be as it's been from the beginning. They won't change. What will change is the place you will work from and how your work will be funded. You will now be working from here, under the auspices of the new official government sanctioned programme that will operate from this base, project Emily. As I have already explained, the United Kingdom has entered into an agreement with the United States Government to play host to a number of Intermediate Range Ballistic Missiles. Three of the sixty missiles will be operated from this site, with three missiles at each of the satellite sites.'

'So there are twenty sites in total?' asked McDermott.

'Your grip on mathematics is astounding' said Montgomery sarcastically.

'So is this a US Air Force base?' asked Holbrook.

'No. It's fair to say the American's would have preferred to use existing U.S bases for obvious reasons but many were deemed to be unsuitable.'

'So will the Americans or the British control the new sites?' asked Holbrook.

'The first operational airhead and its satellites will be in the control of the Americans initially, until such time as British Forces have received the necessary training whereupon responsibility will be divided between the British and the Americans.'

'So who will control this site?' asked Holbrook.

'The British will maintain operational control of this base as they will all the bases. You have seen the hangar that will receive and inspect the missiles and carry out servicing and maintenance. Maintenance will be carried out by British personnel once training has been undertaken and British forces will be responsible for launching the missiles. You will shortly be leaving for the Vandenberg Air Force Base. I have arranged for you to receive the same training that other members of the squadron are receiving. After the period of training, Mr Halford will stay on for two more weeks and travel south to meet with our new contacts in the Silicon Valley.'

'So if the British are responsible for the servicing, maintenance, operation and launch, what exactly are the Americans responsible for?' asked Holbrook.

'They are supplying the missiles. The technology is theirs.'

'And the warhead?' Holbrook enquired.

'The Americans will also supply the warhead. In addition, they will retain dual responsibility for the decision to fire.'

'So the Americans can veto us launching?' asked Holbrook.

'Yes, a launch can only happen with the bilateral agreement of both Britain and America.'

'Will the British have a veto as well?' Holbrook enquired.

27

'Yes. Arming the missile will require two keys. The British will hold one, the Americans the other. Without both of these keys, the missiles cannot be launched.'

'Why are we reduced to accepting American missiles when we have our own programme?' asked McDermott.

'Programme?' Montgomery enquired.

'Blue Streak' replied McDermott.

'Take it from me Mr McDermott, whilst it may not yet be public knowledge, Blue Streak is dead in the water. The Americans are years ahead of us in terms of technology. It makes much greater economic sense to use their missiles. Not to mention the political importance of repairing the special relationship we have with our American friends after the Suez debacle. There are a lot of transatlantic fences to mend and the powers that be would appear to believe this is how that process should begin. Now, if there are no more questions, we must press on. Follow me please.'

Montgomery led the way back out into the snowstorm and headed off at a pace across the compound, stopping five minutes later at the entrance to a long circular topped Nissan hut. He unlocked the door and stepped inside, stamping his feet at the entrance to loosen the snow from his boots. It was as cold inside the hut as it was out.

'Welcome home gentlemen.'

Seven single size bed frames without mattresses sat at equidistance along the length of both walls. Next to each bed stood a full height locker adjacent to a small chest of drawers. An unlit fire stood at the far end of the hut.

'It's not The Ritz I agree, but this will be home until we can find suitable alternative lodgings in the village.'

'What about my wife?' asked Summerfield. 'I can't see her agreeing to this standard of accommodation.'

'As I say, alterative accommodation is being sought but it is in short supply. Married men will be given priority as soon as housing becomes available.'

'There are fourteen beds' noted McDermott. 'Who will be occupying the other nine?'

28

'Nine?' Montgomery queried.

'Yes, nine. There are five of us which leaves nine. Who are we being expected to share with?'

'You will have ten room mates' informed Montgomery. 'I have been secured a house in the village, so it will be the four of you in here plus ten others. They'll be Non Commissioned Officers of 144 Squadron when they arrive.'

Four groans of disapproval punctuated the frigid air.

'Orwell was right' complained Halford. "We're all equal, but some of us are clearly more equal than others'.

'In the lockers' Montgomery continued unabated, 'you will find a uniform. You will be expected to wear it at all times when on duty.'

Montgomery took a piece of paper from his inside pocket.

'Harry, you are assigned number one, there. Bob you are at number two, Dick you are three and Mr Summerfield you are at number four.'

Harry Holbrook opened the number one locker, took out the blue grey uniform and inspected it.

'Three stripes' he said checking the insignia on the arm. 'By my reckoning, that makes me a Wing Commander.'

The others did likewise and removed their suits from their allotted lockers.

'I'm also a Wing Commander' Bob Halford exclaimed. 'I like the sound of that.'

'Check again' said Montgomery.

'Three stripes' repeated Halford.

'Two wide stripes and a centre narrow stripe Bob. That's not a Wing Commander, it's a Squadron Leader, so it looks like I outrank you old man' Holbrook jeered.

Dick McDermott checked his. 'Two stripes, so what does that make me?' he asked.

'My bitch' laughed Halford.

'A Flight Lieutenant' answered Montgomery.

'Mine hasn't got any stripes' announced Tom Summerfield. 'What does that mean?'

'Look again' Montgomery hollered.

'I am looking. There's no insignia' he said, studying the lower arm of the jacket.

'Here is the insignia' Montgomery gestured, stabbing his finger at a single chevron on the upper section of the sleeve. It means you're a non commissioned Lance Corporal, which means that when on duty, you salute your senior officers and refer to them as Sir. Do you understand?'

'I understand Sir' said Summerfield, studying the four stripes on Montgomery's lower sleeve, 'but it's hardly fair. I'd like to request the uniform of a Wing Commander or a Squadron Leader.'

'Don't be an imbecile Summerfield. You can't all be Squadron Leaders. You're a non commissioned Lance Corporal and that's an end to it.'

'Then make Halford the Lance Corporal and I'll be the Squadron Leader. I don't think Mrs Summerfield will approve of my being a Lance Corporal when Mr Halford gets to be a Squadron Leader.'

'Sir!' Montgomery bellowed. 'I am your Group Captain. I outrank you, therefore you address me as Sir.'

'Then make Halford the Lance Corporal and I'll be the Squadron Leader, Sir' Summerfield grudgingly repeated.

'No, I am making the decisions here *not* Mrs Summerfield. You will appear as the rank you have been given and that is final. Have you been listening to anything I've said?' Montgomery continued. 'You are not to discuss anything that goes on here and that includes your allocated rank, with anyone outside the group and that includes those you share a pillow with. Am I understood Mr Summerfield? Is that clear?'

'Yes Sir, quite clear, Sir' Summerfield replied 'although I wasn't suggesting I'd share the information with someone with whom I shared a pillow.'

'Relegated to the spare room again eh Summerfield?' teased Halford. 'What heinous marital crime have you committed this time?'

'I cancelled her account with the milliner. I mean really, how many hats does one woman need?'

CHAPTER 4
TO BE OR NOT TO BE

May 7th 1998

Emilie Weston pulled out of the cul-de-sac, turned right along the narrow Victorian street, giving way to the oncoming traffic. She manoeuvred slowly along the road, in and out of the parked cars. The neighbourhood had been built long before the herald of the motor car and the concept of on-street parking. She applied the handbrake when she reached the queue of traffic at the junction with the main road. Fifteen minutes passed and just three cars at the head of the queue had fought their way into the onslaught of traffic. She checked the clock on the dashboard. Six thirty became six forty five. Six forty five became seven o'clock before her vehicle was first in line to make its way out into the rush hour. The main Wilsthorpe Road was gridlocked as far as the eye could see, in both directions. A driver flashed his headlight, signalling for her to pull out left to join the convoy. By seven fifteen Emilie had still not passed the Tavern, less than four hundred metres hence. She fumbled for her mobile phone and pressed speed dial 7. It rang until it went to voicemail. She cut the call and called the Town Hall switchboard but was met with an automated *we are closed* message. She scrolled her address book and called the incumbent Mayor. Voicemail again. The traffic edged forward opening up a car's length. She discharged the handbrake and crept forward another fifteen feet before scrolling through her address book again. Angela Gentley answered.

'It's Emilie. I'm stuck in traffic. I'm not going to be there for seven thirty.'

'Well don't panic. There aren't many people here yet as it happens. I guess everyone has the same problem. Just get here as soon as you can' said Angela. 'It's not as though we can start without you is it?'

Her mobile phone bleeped an incoming text message at seven thirty five. *Meeting postponed until 8pm.* At five minutes to eight, another message advised the postponement would be until eight thirty.

At eight o'clock she was inching torturously slowly along the Derby Road, one building at a time. She passed the accountants office, the physiotherapist, the dentist, the vet, the marital counselling service, another accountant, the day nursery, another accountant, the hairdresser, the green grocer, the sandwich bar, the coffee shop, the sports bar, the ambulance chaser, the convenience store, another accountant, the bookmaker, the wedding dress boutique, the jeweller, the kebab shop, the bargain booze shop, the newsagent, the barber shop, the trophy shop, the double glazing shop, another accountant, the art shop, the music shop, another accountant. Who knew there were so many accountants?

It was eight thirty when Emilie finally pulled into the Town Hall car park. Unusually, there were still some spaces in the lower sector and she swung into one of them. Scooping up her papers from the passenger seat, she ran like the wind, into the Town Hall. She was both surprised and relieved to see hordes of folk milling around the reception like spare parts. She made for the reception desk to sign in before heading down the passage towards the Mayors parlour, looking for Will as she went. She couldn't see him anywhere.

Emilie burst into the parlour, nearly knocking over the Chief Executive who moved out of the wake of the door just in time. Emilie raised her hand in silent apology as all eyes turned in her direction. The ominous silence put Emilie ill at ease immediately.

'Was it something I said?' she jested, in an attempt to lighten the heavy atmosphere, so thick she doubted you'd have got a knife through it. The outgoing Mayor was sat behind a desk in the long red and faux ermine robes of office. The trusty tail coated Mace Bearer Sam Carpenter - bin man extraordinaire by day, guardian of the Council's constitution, reputation and ceremonial mace by night - approached her.

'Councillor, there's been an accident' he said.

'I should say. Have you seen the traffic out there?'

Road accidents occurred often. When they did, due to the geography of the town, situated midway between two junctions of the motorway, the town suffered with tremendous congestion as travellers destined for the motorway, sought different routes. Gridlock was by no means a new phenomenon. One soon learned to build a small contingency into every journey to allow for it. Tonight's gridlock was extreme even for accepted standards. Not all accidents were serious of course. Most were merely minor inconveniences, as motorists stood by their dented bumpers, tending to nothing more serious than wounded pride and the vigorous refusal to give away the slightest hint of liability lest their insurance premiums might be hiked the following year.

'Emilie, you'd better sit down' Sam continued, gesticulating toward the sofa.

'No, I'm OK Sam. What's going on? What's up?'

The Chief Executive, Jazz Malinski, stepped forward.

'It's OK Sam. I'll deal with the Madam Deputy Mayor. Would you go and see if Councillor Coxstable needs anything, please?'

Sam left the parlour.

'Councillor, I'm afraid I have some rather bad news' said Jazz.

Emilie surveyed the room for a glimpse of Will. There was no sign of him. Her heart began to pound violently. A feeling of terminal dread, such as she'd never experienced before, washed over her. Overcome with nausea and light headedness, a sudden rise in body temperature presented itself and perspiration began to seep from every pore. The Chief Executive realised her sudden change in demeanour and helped her onto a chair.

'I'm so sorry, I don't know what came over me. I must be hungry, perhaps I should have eaten something before I left home.'

'Are you feeling better?' Jazz asked.

'Yes, thank you' she lied.

'As I was about to explain, I'm sorry to have to inform you of this but we've just learned that Councillors Constance, Flatliner, Hopkin and Wallmichaels were all killed this evening. It also brings me great regret to have to tell you that the daughter of Councillor Coxstable, Dana, I believe you know her?'

'Young Dana, yes, we met at a fundraiser for the local school last year. She's my protégé, I'm training her up to be Mayor one day, lovely girl.'

'It appears that Dana was also in the car and is amongst the dead.'

'Oh Dear Lord' Emilie exclaimed. 'Where's her poor Mother?'

'Councillor Coxstable has been taken to my office. She's in the care of a female Constable and a Doctor has been called. For some reason, Councillor Coxstable was travelling separately from her Daughter.'

'So it was a car accident?' asked Emilie.

'Yes.'

'How many cars?'

'As far as we know, just one. It appears the deceased were all travelling together in a single car. The details haven't yet been made available.'

The Council had been encouraging a Car Share policy for a number of months to reduce omissions given off by vehicle exhausts, in a bid to improve the air quality of the Borough. The policy had been proving to be more successful than had been anticipated as members of the Council sought to lead by example.

Emilie was many things, consummate politician with a head for simple mathematics, being among her many attributes.

'But that means we don't have a majority' she ventured.

'You are correct' said Jazz.

'Then tonight's session must be postponed or we risk the opposition running ragged with our proposals.'

'We are looking into that option Councillor.'

'Option? Why is it an option? Just cancel the session.'

'It's not quite that simple I'm afraid. Mr Turnkey is going over the Council Constitution at this very moment to try and find a clause that will permit us to cancel.'

Ivan Turnkey was the Council's Chief Accountant. He held one of the three statutory positions within the Council, as its Section 151 Officer. This statutory safeguard existed so that his job, as part of the Council's senior management team, was protected in the event of a sudden controlling political party change. The safeguard provided an assurance that the three protected officers couldn't be sacked summarily if, or when, the balance of political power shifted. The Chief Executive held the first of these protected positions; the 151 Officer occupied the second.

'Surely that Barry's job to be scouring the constitution' said Emilie. 'He's the Monitoring Officer.'

The Monitoring Officer was the Council's chief Solicitor and arbiter on all legal matters. His was the third protected position.

'Perhaps Madam Deputy' answered Jazz 'only Barry is of the opinion that a clause doesn't exist in the Constitution that we can invoke to suspend the session.'

'That's preposterous' responded Emilie. 'This must be an unprecedented situation. Surely out of respect we must postpone.'

'I agree and that would have been my recommendation' he said, crossing the room through the bustle of invited civic guests. He beckoned her to follow.

'May I?' he asked, taking a paper copy of the Council Constitution from the Mayor.

'This is our problem. Article 16.02. *The Articles of this Constitution may not be suspended.*'

'But what about article 16.03?' interrupted Emilie. '*The ruling of the Mayor as to the Constitution or application of this Constitution or as to any proceedings of this Council shall not be challenged at any meeting of the Council.* The Mayor can simply announce the meeting is postponed and her decision can't be challenged.'

'I'm afraid it's not quite that simple. Accepted convention dictates that clause 16.03 applies when, and only when, the Council is in session. For clause 16.03 to apply, the Council needs to be in session. The clause can't be invoked before the session has actually begun.'

Emilie looked toward the Mayor. 'Do you agree with this?' She asked.

The Mayor shrugged her shoulders. 'I don't like it any more than you do but I'm afraid I'm at odds with the Monitoring Officer. If we refuse to go into session the Leader of the Opposition is talking about Judicial Review to challenge our refusal. It could be a costly decision to the Council and to achieve what? There's very little on the agenda.'

Aside from the Mayor Making ceremony Emilie had to agree, the business agenda was very light and could be done and dusted in less than half an hour. The issue of whether or not to provide free tampons was hardly worth the financial risk to the Council of being brought before the High Court in a Judicial Review and losing.

'Then let's go into session and have the Mayor postpone before the business starts' Emilie suggested.

'Think about it Emilie' said the Mayor. 'Two hours ago, we had a small majority in Council. We have just lost four of our members. We no longer have a working majority. I've already spoken with the Leader of the Opposition. They've made it quite clear they will, once the session is open, move under Article 14 that a motion without notice be brought to continue the session if we attempt to move to suspend it. Without a working majority to vote against their proposal, we will be powerless to invoke a suspension. I'm really sorry Emilie, but they've also told me they intend to field their own candidate for the office of Mayor. Without a majority we won't be able to stop them.'

'Then I don't get to be the Mayor' said Emilie dejected.

'It's looking that way. I'm so sorry I know how disappointed you must be and how much you've been looking forward to it.'

Emilie was not yet beaten.

'Look at this mayhem' she said. 'Are we sure the opposition have a working majority? Perhaps they have members missing themselves.'

Jazz called to the Macebearer. 'Find Mrs Gentley please.'

Sam disappeared into the mêlée outside, returning a few minutes later with Angela Gentley.

'We're wondering whether it's possible to convene the Council session and immediately postpone it' Jazz told her. 'Do we know which Council members are not yet present?'

Angela referred to her clipboard. 'It appears we're still missing Councillors Carr and Dexter from Soarlea. The remaining Councillors from Gritty Hectare have just this second arrived.'

'I don't think that helps Angela but thank you.'

Councillor Carr was an independent member. He'd not been affiliated to any one political party for years since he fell out with the Labour Leadership and resigned his membership. In practise though, Councillor Carr always voted with the Socialists, always had and always would. Councillor Dexter was the lone Liberal voice. His influence was so small that in practice, a single Liberal vote rarely made any difference to an outcome.

'So even if we wait for Councillors Dexter and Carr and we can get Dexter on our side, his vote will be cancelled out by Carrs' the Mayor reconciled. 'It won't make any difference. The opposition will still have a working majority.'

'Then I'm screwed' exclaimed Emilie. 'Has anyone seen my tardy husband?'

CHAPTER 5
THE COMPASS LINE

August 29th 1899

Sister Edith, who was displaying signs of fatigue after a long day, instructed Agnes to find Brother Hipwood who in turn was to bring Mrs Blackburn from Grace Dieu Manor post haste. Mrs Blackburn had been waiting patiently at the manor since being placed on alert earlier in the day. She was to act as wet nurse to the Newlove infant and the baby needed to feed.

Mrs Blackburn had endured three stillbirths, miscarriages too numerous to count and remained childless. She did however, have a good supply of milk following her most recent final trimester stillbirth. This supply had been utilised by numerous ladies across the County who paid handsomely for her nursing services. It was an arrangement that worked for all parties, not least the new well-to-do mothers, who found the prospect of having a child suckling at their breast far too troublesome and irreconcilable a prospect, given the fashionable whalebone corsets of the day. For Mrs Blackburn, who now believed she was not destined to be a mother herself, the chance to provide such a service afforded her some minor comfort. The constant demands placed upon her energies by that of a hungry child, went some way to stifling her grief. Lady Noel, of Grace Dieu Manor, had made a contract with Mrs Blackburn, to retain her services for three months for the Newlove baby although this agreement had not been communicated with the new mother, Summer Newlove.

Sister Edith instructed Sparrow to deal with the bloody sheets and towels, of which there were many and then to boil the soiled rags and petticoats before packing them away to be used at the next birth. After

38

gathering the soiled items together into a sack, Sparrow covered her own blood soaked tunic with the clean cappa magna Sister Edith had insisted she brought with her earlier in the day. She now realised why Sister Edith had instructed her to bring an extra layer, on what had been the hottest day of the hottest year anyone could remember. The intense heat had mercifully dissipated and there was a refreshing breeze in the air. Sparrow threw the sack over her shoulder and made off for the long walk back to the laundry at the abbey.

Hamble was to take charge of the equipment for sterilisation and dispose of the placenta. She carried the bedpan, still full of urine and shit, downstairs to the washroom. She returned to the bedroom and placed the placenta into the clean bedpan. The practise of cooking the bloody raw organ for hours on the stovetop like a stew, to serve to the new mother for her next meal, as Hamble had done on numerous occasions in her youth, had thankfully been terminated. Instead, she ventured into the garden towards the manor house to find the dogs, who were asleep in the kennels. She tossed the placenta into the compound and left the dogs to it. She then collected the empty vials, the enema kit, the razor, the unused forceps, clean rags and the Lysol and placed them in the porcelain water bowl to begin the rigorous cleansing process in the scullery.

When Agnes returned from taking a breath of air, she was instructed to watch over the sleeping mother and baby. The baby stirred and Sister Edith peered into the crib.

'I think it's time to have a proper look at our new charge' she said, lifting the infant from the crib.

Agnes brought a jug of water, testing the temperature with her middle finger and declaring it just right. Sister Edith lay the baby on the dresser top and gently unwrapped the tightly bound swaddling sheet. She removed the soiled cotton diaper and wiped away all traces of dirt.

'Does she have it?' asked Agnes.

Sister Edith gently pulled the babies left leg up and out to the side.

'Yes she has it' whispered Edith. 'See for yourself.'

'I see it' gasped Agnes. There was a raised red brown star shaped birth mark tucked away inside the skin folds of the baby's groin.

'She has the secondary mark too' said Agnes, stroking the underside of the middle toe of the infant's tiny right foot. 'I can feel it.'

Sister Edith put the sleeping baby in a fresh diaper, fixed it with a pin and wrapped the tiny infant back in the swaddling sheet before placing it back into the crib.

'I'll be in the study at Grace Dieu' announced Edith, replacing her scapula over her soiled white tunic and checking her watch. It was well past midnight and there was much to do before the morning.

'Your writing materials are in here' said Agnes, handing over a small case. 'I was only able to acquire two shillings I'm afraid.'

'No matter' replied Edith. 'His Lordship will no doubt avail me of the remainder.'

Mrs Blackburn arrived just as Sister Edith was leaving.

'You can leave the bathing of the child to Sister Agnes' said Edith. 'You only need to concern yourself with feeding.'

'Right you are Sister' replied Mrs Blackburn. 'All is well with the mother and the child?'

'All is well' replied Edith.

Edith walked briskly across the gardens towards Grace Dieu manor. Her footsteps on the gravel alerted the dogs to her presence and they started to bark. She hurried on in the darkness, her path lit only by the presence of a quarter moon which hung above a cloudless sky. The new lawn, laid earlier in the spring, had taken a beating from the drought conditions of an unusually hot and persistent summer and was almost bare in places. So as not to disturb it further, she kept rigidly to the path.

It had been many decades since she'd last been at Grace Dieu. A new wing had been built to the east. It blended seamlessly with the existing Victorian stone mansion with its perpendicular stone mullioned leaded windows and sixteen chimney stacks protruding like miniature castles onto the skyline. The house enjoyed its own chapel to the west and the building had been completed with its own external clock and bell tower. It was without doubt the finest house for many miles.

She heard the creaking of a door and a gaslight appeared in the blackness.

'This way Sister' called Brother Hipwood. 'His Lord and Ladyship are waiting for you in the library. Follow me please.'

Edith quickened her step and followed Brother Hipwood into the mansion house. Lord and Lady Noel were sat either side of a large stone fireplace although the fire wasn't lit. They both stood up from the fashionable new winged chairs of gold brocade as she entered.

'Sister Edith' implored Lady Noel. 'Please come and sit with us. You must be exhausted. Brother Hipwood will prepare you a hearty warm supper.'

Edith sat in the chair offered by his Lordship and he collected another for himself.

'The infant is well?'

'Yes, very well. The birth was a drawn out bloody affair, as they all are, but without too many difficulties.'

'And the mother?' asked Lady Noel.

'Sleeping like a baby' replied Edith. 'A good doctor in Germany recommended a concoction which I've found to be highly satisfactory.'

'That's good' said Lord Noel. 'Still, there isn't much time to decide what's to be done. I took the liberty of retrieving the manuscript from the bank vault this afternoon, the moment we received word that Mrs Newlove had started with the birthing pains. It's on the table. In lieu of this most special of occasions, I also made arrangements for a case of wine to be shipped from France. I'd like us to partake of a small drink by way of a celebration. I hope you will join us.'

'I'd be delighted' replied Edith.

Lord Noel stepped away and poured three glasses, passing the first one to Lady Noel and then to Edith. He returned with his own glass and the remainder of the bottle, handing the bottle to Edith. She studied the label. La Grace Dieu, Saint Emilion.

'I thought you might appreciate this' he said.

Edith stifled a tear, taking a large sip in a bid to ward off a second. The wine was like nectar to her lips.

'Good yes?' he asked.

'Very good.'

A pregnant pause ensued, broken only when Edith asked 'do you have word of my daughter?'

Lord Noel slipped a hand into his inside breast pocket. 'Perhaps you might like to read this. It arrived with the shipment of wine and I hope it will give you some peace of mind in order that we may move swiftly on to the matter in hand.'

Edith took the letter and tentatively opened the fold.

Dear Sir

I am most humbled by your enquiries as to the health of my family and wish to report that all are well. Angelique continues to thrive with her newfound responsibilities at the Ministry for War. She remains a lone female advocate in an otherwise male dominated environment but exercises her duties both quietly and with fastidious efficiency. Her influence on those she serves remains honest and robust. Any reservations initially surrounding her appointment appear to have subsided.

Her Husband continues to be a great support to her and she to him. It delights me daily to witness the success of the matrimonial match. Their Daughter Celeste, now 10, is being schooled in literature, philosophy and music. She appears to be developing her gifts and is displaying great skills in the art of diplomacy. She has developed an interest in moving pictures since our visit to the Grand Café on the Boulevard des Capucines in Paris where she received a demonstration of a new cinematographe machine by Auguste Lumiere. On the return journey, the young and excitable child, declared with all certainty, that a star had just been born of a certain Augustine Boyer from Figeat who had given birth to a child Celeste insists will go on to make both his name and fortune in moving picture stories. I find it hard to believe that moving picture stories will ever be an impetus to the good name of a man let alone his fortune and I expect moving picture stories to remain firmly a pastime for those possessed of nothing more than idle curiosity. Time will tell whether she or I will be correct.

I do however feel I must report that, in spite of the aforementioned, Angelique has in recent months suffered a somewhat melancholic state of mind following her introduction to Madame Lucy Dreyfus, wife of the disgraced Captain Dreyfus. I'm in no doubt you will be aware of this grave miscarriage of justice since it has been reported widely, not only across France but across the world. I regret to say that the matter has ignited an anti-Semitic movement in the city and there have been riots. Angelique is most fearful that proposals by a new political movement, who call themselves the Zionists, will do nothing to improve the situation for the Jewish community in the long term. This movement, led by one Theodor Herzl, seeks to re-establish a Jewish state in Israel. Angelique fears that such a countenance will produce no lesser unrest than the current demonstrable failures of assimilation into the gentile community here. The matter has caused her great distress such that the melancholy has caused her to take to her bed, sometimes for days at a time, since she is unable to envisage or establish in her own mind a satisfactory solution for the troubles of our Jewish friends.

There is one matter which brings out a great optimism in her spirit, that is, she expects newspaper editor, failed politician and divorcee George Clemenceau, to become Prime Minister, which she states gives her much hope for the future of France. Monsieur Clemenceau brought himself to national attention last year by allowing his newspaper, L'Aurore, to use its front page for the publication of an open letter written by the literary Dreyfusonian Emile Zola, to President Faure. The letter concerned the fate of Captain Dreyfus who has, in spite of having spent five years in solitary confinement on Devil's Island, been found to be demonstrably innocent of the crime of Treason for which he was found guilty at a Court Martial. Aside from this notoriety, Monsieur Clemenceau's foray into public life has thus far been less than impressive to say the least, having lost his seat in the Chamber of Deputies. It appears he brought unpopularity upon himself by disagreeing in the strongest terms with the provisions in the

Franco-Russio Treaty being extended to Germany. Were it not for the unwavering confidence in which the predictions of The Compass and their assured correctness are held, I as a reasonable man, would not stake my reputation on Monsieur Clemenceau reaching the highest echelons of public office again. Nonetheless, as a result of Angelique's prediction, he is now to be given all possible assistance in political spheres of influence and a future Senate seat has been muted. A commune in the Var district of Draguignan has been mentioned in certain circles. Perhaps you would like to keep yourself abreast of the situation?

I remain as always, your eternal friend, confidante and ally,
Head Guardian of the Compass,
Monsieur Francios Lobari

Edith folded the letter and handed it back to Lord Noel who replaced it into the pocket of his waistcoat.

'So I'm technically a Grandmother' said Edith, staring at Lady Noel. 'For ten years, no less. Why did no one tell me?'

'Don't do this' said Lord Noel.

'But you could have told me. Someone could have told me.'

'How?' he asked. 'How could we have told you? You haven't been here for twenty five years.'

'You could have written. You receive the modifications for the manuscript. You knew where I'd been.'

'Precisely, we knew where you'd been, not where you were. You know the rules Edith. We couldn't send a letter lest it be intercepted after you'd moved on.'

'Don't torture yourself again' pleaded Lady Noel. 'You can see from the letter that Angelique is thriving and so too is your Granddaughter.'

'I disagree' said Edith. 'Melancholic was the term I think Monsieur Lobari used.'

'Clearly the melancholy is very recent, brought about by Angelique's sensitivity. It will pass. The Lobaris have always been nurturing Guardians. What's important is that she and Celeste are using the gifts God gave them. They are fulfilling their destiny.'

44

'Their destiny; war and moving pictures, that's what I gave up my beautiful child for is it? War and moving pictures?'

'I've no doubt the work being done at the War Office is as much about preventing war as it is perpetuating it' said Lord Noel in a reassuring tone. 'You must also take reassurance from the fact that Angelique appears also to be moving in diplomatic circles. She has clearly been well placed to bring great influence to bear within the French corridors of power and Monsieur Lobari is of the opinion she is most hopeful for the future.'

'You are right of course' Edith reconciled. 'My selfish gene has no place here.'

'It's not selfish to miss your family' Lady Noel comforted. 'What you did was a wonderful thing. It must have been very hard to give her up.'

'You'd think so wouldn't you? But it wasn't. Not at the time anyhow. It's only as the years have unravelled, that I have come to regret my decision. No, regret is not the correct word. I've never, not even for a second, regretted the work I've undertaken with God's blessing. I have proved myself a dutiful and obedient soldier of faith time and time again. I've endured the hardships of a nomadic life and have borne them with all the grace and humility I have at times, found it hard to muster. What pains me is that, despite having been present at the birth of almost thirty healthy Compass children, across all the continents of the world, when it came to my own daughter producing a child, my services were not called upon. No one thought to tell me. I didn't even know Angelique had given birth to a child.'

'The Lobaris had their reasons for not involving you. Perhaps they wanted to spare you the pain and anguish they thought it might bring' said Lady Noel.

'I'm an obedient soldier of God Lady Noel, certainly not averse to the world's pain and anguish I assure you. So Celeste is being raised by Angelique is she?'

'It would appear so' replied Lord Noel furtively.

'I hadn't realised the Compass Policy regarding guardianship had changed' said Edith.

45

'It hasn't' replied Lord Noel. 'The Policy is still to separate Compass babies from their mothers to ensure the security of the line. It does appear to be the case that the Lobaris have circumvented the policy.'

'So I could have kept my own child?' Edith scorned.

'You couldn't have entered the Order with a child' said Lord Noel defensively. 'My influence didn't extend that far.'

'I know, I'm sorry, I don't mean to be such a bitter and cantankerous old woman. It's been a long day and I'm very tired. I know you are a good man and that your heart has always been in the right place. Your father and his father were good men too. I also know that everything that was done was done only to protect Angelique so she could fulfil her destiny in the world. I'm just a stupid old woman, overcome with the emotion of the day. What's done is done. We aren't here to cry over spilled milk. Perhaps we should turn our attentions to the matter in hand. The Newlove baby.'

'I think that's a jolly good idea' said Lord Noel 'The Lobaris continue to make excellent wine no?' replenishing first his own glass then that of Lady Noel.

Edith refused a second glass. She would savour the first one and in so doing, Celeste, the granddaughter she doubted she'd ever meet would be fixed in her heart forever.

Brother Hipwood came in with a plate of ham, eggs and boiled potatoes.

'Perhaps we can move to the table' suggested Lady Noel. 'I'm sure Edith won't mind eating as we talk.'

Brother Hipwood placed the plate on a large oak table situated in the centre of the room.

'Perhaps you would like to join us Father?' Lord Noel asked. 'We'd very much like you to share in our decisions this evening.'

'Very good your Lordship, I'd be honoured' Brother Hipwood replied, taking a seat at the foot of the table closest to the wall. Behind him stood a wall of substantial carved oak bookcases, each one stacked to the ceiling with encyclopaedias, dictionaries, poetry, guide books, journals, periodicals, atlases, maps and works of fiction stretching back centuries.

Edith hadn't realised how hungry she was, having not eaten since dawn and she quickly devoured the feast.

Lord Noel began the proceedings, taking charge of the manuscript bundle.

'I will make the additions to this version of the manuscript if Sister Edith can advise the other guardians of the amendment.'

'Yes, I am happy to do this. There is the small matter of money. I will need a further four shillings to pay the postmaster for the postage stamps.'

'Of course.'

Lord Noel took a small key from the pocket of his waistcoat, walked across the room to a small desk and unlocked the top drawer before returning with four bright new shillings which looked fresh from the mint.

'Then there is the matter of the wet nurse. Another four shillings will be required to pay Mrs Blackburn.'

'That's already taken care of dear' called Lady Noel. 'I have already paid her an advance and will settle the balance at the conclusion of her service as arranged.'

'Now, as we already know, it has been the convention in recent years, to separate the Mother from the new Compass child.'

'I don't think that's a good idea' stated Edith sternly.

'I appreciate separating mother and baby is not without its problems but.....'

'I agree' interrupted Lady Noel. 'Separating them is inhumane. We can't do it.'

'But the mother need never know' contended Lord Noel. 'I have taken the liberty of finding an infant who shall we say, is superfluous to its mother's needs. A boy in Loughborough who was born yesterday.'

'And this women is content to simply give up her child?' asked Lady Noel.

'The mother is penniless, unwed and illiterate. She is without work or prospect of finding work due her idle character and is currently residing in the Doss-house. Another mouth to feed is the last thing she needs. She has by all accounts taken no interest in the infant and a Matron is currently providing for the child's needs. What life will that child have?'

'Perhaps the mother's prospects will improve.'

'How?' Lord Noel enquired. 'She's just as likely to drown it the first chance she gets to be rid of it. The Newloves by contrast, can give him a safe and comfortable, nurturing home from which he can receive an education. Doctor Holbrook assures me there will be no problem with the paperwork. Records will not be kept and the mother will never know where her child has been placed. The mother simply wants to be rid of the responsibility.'

'Forgive my husband's curtness Edith. He makes himself sound unkind and heartless but that is neither his intention nor his true feeling.'

'I've known your husband for long enough to know he is neither unkind nor uncaring' replied Edith.

'His relationship with the Workhouse has suffered a recent…' Lady Noel fumbled for a way to convey the end of the sentence, 'breakdown you might say.'

Lord and Lady Noel's attempts to improve the wretched lives of the unfortunates who fell unto the workhouse's mercy, were well known across the county. William Newlove had been a malnourished, ragged boy of just five, who'd been confined to the Workhouse after the death of his mother, when Lady Noel first came upon him, during one of her weekly visits to educate the younger children in reading and writing. Six weeks after their initial meeting, William was adopted by the Noels. Thereafter, he received all the privileges the Noels could provide.

A weekly visit to the workhouse by Lord and Lady Noel became twice weekly, once Lady Noel gained the confidence to teach the older children and this in turn became thrice weekly, when her teaching extended to the adolescents who hitherto, had never been given the opportunity to learn how to read or write. Lord Noel would deliver a selection of books each week, as chosen by his wife, from the extensive collection in the Grace Dieu library. At the same time, he would collect the finished titles from the previous week. He would then laboriously re-file them into their correct place to be referred to at a later date when willing new students emerged. A year ago, Lord Noel had arrived at the Workhouse to find the books he was due to collect being burned in the yard, despite an abundance of coal being available, which he also supplied at no cost, to keep the stoves lit. He rescued the books he could from the flames and at the request of his wife, returned with new books the following week. The same thing happened again. Lord Noel required medical attention to burns he sustained trying in vain to rescue an encyclopaedia of Botany that had been a favoured illustrated guide and source of vital information for William's interest in such things. The final straw occurred the week after that, when the same band of mindless ruffians, burst into the makeshift classroom Lady Noel had furnished. They knocked her to the ground when she tried to resist and she had lain on the floor helpless, as the ruffians destroyed the furniture, tore down pictures and paintings from the walls and forcibly removed the picture books from the hands of the youngest children, before once again, burning them in the yard. Lord Noel forbade his wife from returning after that and neither books or coal had been gifted to the workhouse since.

'I think we digress from the matter in hand' declared Lord Noel, 'namely, that we need to agree, the Newloves raise the workhouse boy as their son and the Compass child be put into the hands of approved Guardians.'

'But aren't you forgetting a minor detail my love? Summer gave birth to a girl' said Lady Noel. 'She can hardly now be given a boy.'

'Is summer aware she gave birth to a girl?' asked Lord Noel 'only I thought we agreed the gender of the baby was not to be disclosed until a decision had been taken.'

'I'm afraid so, yes' answered Edith.

'But what about our agreement?'

'I'm afraid young Sparrow let the cat out of the bag and disclosed the gender of the baby to the mother before I could stop her.'

'Why hadn't you tutored her on the importance of not disclosing the gender? Couldn't you have sent her out of the room to avoid such a calamity?'

'I'm sorry' answered Edith, her trembling voice rising in a bid to match his Lordship's obvious vexation, 'but I was busy with the final stages of labour and my immediate concern was to ensure the mother wasn't about to bleed to death.'

'No matter' interceded Lady Noel. 'What's done is done. It can't be changed now so are we agreed that the Compass baby stays with the Newloves?'

'Yes' said Edith.

'No, we most certainly are **not** agreed' argued Lord Noel emphatically. 'The convention is clear. Mother and baby should be separated as soon as practical after the birth, to reduce the risk to the security of the Line.'

'Conventions change' exclaimed Lady Noel.

'Yes, they do, with the agreement of the Head Guardians, not from a unilateral decision, taken without consultation. We have no right to make a unilateral decision.'

'Just because something was right seventy years ago, doesn't make it right today. Things change, people change, situations change.'

'The risk to the Line hasn't changed' he hollered. 'We learned that in the seventeenth century.' He stamped his fist on the manuscript. 'An entire line wiped away. Three generations of the same Compass Line gone. We have a duty to protect the remaining lines.'

He unrolled the ancient manuscript with its tattered and frayed edges and laid it out across the table. The separate paper inserts and annexed supporting papers, he placed to one side.

'See' he said. 'The lines have been reduced from one hundred and thirty six known lines to just thirty six. There are only three remaining lines in the whole of England. It is our duty to protect these remaining lines and after what happened here, we have no choice but to separate the new-born Compass from her mother.'

Lord Noel tapped his index finger to the label on the chart depicting a now defunct Compass Line.

Convention prior to the seventeenth century, had been where possible, to keep generations of the same Compass Line together. That practise had been revisited by the Head Guardians when a great fire swept through the city of London, taking the lives of the three Compasses in one fell swoop, Grandmother, Mother and Granddaughter. They all succumbed together when fire took hold of their wooden house in Pudding Lane.

'If you need a further demonstration that what I'm suggesting is the correct course of action, then, consider the fate of this line' he pleaded, once again tapping on the chart. 'Had it not have been the case that this Compass had been taken from her mother, who succumbed to the plague epidemic, that line too would have been lost forever. The Compass child was saved precisely and only because the mother and child were separated at birth and the Guardians of Eyam did what they had to do to protect the line. Once the Lines have gone, they are gone forever.'

Red faced and fractious, Lord Noel flopped back onto his chair and took a large sip of wine to calm himself.

'You seem to forget that I too, am of the Compass Line' exclaimed Edith with great consternation. 'If there is only ever to be one final occasion when my gift can be brought to bear, let it be in the here and now and I say in the strongest terms that the Compass baby should remain with the biological parents, the Newloves. I don't care what the conventions say or the whys and wherefores of the justifications for conventions existence, in this instance, the baby girl should stay at Grace Dieu.'

'It's not that I don't value your opinion Edith, I value it greatly, but you must recognise that you are not a Guardian. You do not have the responsibilities associated with belonging to the Guardianship.'

'The fact that I'm of the Compass Line and I'm telling you the baby should stay with the Mother, should be enough to put an end to the matter' Edith persisted.

'If I may play the Devil's advocate, just for a moment' interrupted Brother Hipwood. 'Who are you suggesting would take on the legal guardianship of the child, if it were to be taken from its mother?'

'The Guardians of this extinct line' stated Lord Noel, directing his audience to the line on the chart that ended over a century ago. 'They would appear to be the obvious choice. The family still have connections in influential circles, they own much land and property, are successful in business and they have a Daughter and Son-in-law who, in spite of numerous medical, spiritual and religious interventions, remain childless. The Hardinge family in New York have likewise agreed to provide a safe haven but my preference would be for the child to remain in England. With just three lines remaining in the entire country, I don't believe the preferable course of action would be to reduce that to just two if there is an English solution.'

'The security of the Line would appear to be assured with the March family' ventured Brother Hipwood. 'Perhaps the idea does at least need to be considered. Let's just for a second, remove ourselves from rights and wrongs of separating babies from their mothers and look at the Compass child and its destiny in isolation. The Compass Lines are protected at great effort, expense and dedication of the Guardians, to assure the continued dissemination of a right, just and fair influence on the future. Am I correct thus far?'

'Yes' replied Lord Noel.

Brother Hipwood glanced at Sister Edith who nodded in confirmation.

He turned to Lady Noel. 'Yes' she concurred.

'Then surely, the child should be placed where it will wield the greatest influence. Forgive me, but William Newlove is a gardener, a dedicated, able and competent gardener I'm sure, but William lacks the ambition to be anything other than an able gardener, thus his spheres of influence are, shall we say, limited.'

'Thank you for your support Brother' said Lord Noel. 'I love William with all my heart and will do everything within my power to see he lives a constructive and happy life with the woman he loves but contrast the life of William Newlove to that of the March family, who have great influence in the world of politics, religion, education, business, the law, the arts, medicine and science.'

Edith stood firm. 'The baby stays with the mother. Brother Hipwood, I am affronted that you have the audacity to bring the Devil into our sober and sombre considerations. I assure you, the Devil will play no part in this evening's proceedings.'

Lord Noel, who was about to drain the last of the wine bottle into his glass thought better of it and put the bottle back on the side table.

'A poor choice of words on my part, forgive me Sister, I apologise.'

Lady Noel turned to look at the mantle clock. 'It's already three thirty and we haven't yet accomplished anything. I suggest we take a comfort break so we can collect our thoughts. Sister Edith, would you accompany me to the scullery to help me prepare a hot pot of tea. I think we could all do with some refreshment.'

CHAPTER 6
THE TERMINATION OF
PROJECT EMILY

1962

Group Captain Montgomery slammed the telephone receiver angrily into its cradle and called Flying Officer Miller who was working in the adjacent office.

'I need you to find these personnel and have them report here at...' Montgomery checked his wristwatch, it was 5pm ... '6pm prompt' he said thrusting a sheet of note paper in Millers direction.

Miller surveyed the list.

'6pm tonight Sir?' asked Miller.

'Yes tonight, is there a problem?'

'Have we been put on a short notice alert Sir? Only today is my Wedding Anniversary and Mrs Miller is expecting me home for dinner. If it's all hands on deck I'll have to get word that I won't be home.'

At least twice a month the base went into overdrive with the advent of short alert notices. Short alert notices were dummy runs, practise for the crew to demonstrate their missiles could be deployed and ready for launch within the strategic target of fifteen minutes. The crew had grown accustomed to cancelling plans at the last minute. In spite of being an accepted part of the job, the infringements were nevertheless still a major source of frustration and inconvenience.

'No, there's no alert. It's another matter entirely, nothing you need worry about.'

Miller waited for further explanation but it wasn't forthcoming.

'Permission to take the Land Rover Sir? Only I saw Wing Commander Holbrook and Squadron Leader Halford leaving the base an hour ago so I expect they'll be in The Wheatsheaf by now. Lance Corporal Summerfield is on a week's leave, so he'll be at Silver City and Flight Lieutenant McDermott was called over to Harrington this afternoon to deal with a discrepancy in the stores and he isn't back yet. Would you like me to drive over to Silver City Sir?'

'Yes, take the Land Rover and Miller, not a word of this to anyone. If someone asks where you're going, say you've been given leave to deal with a personal matter.'

'Understood Captain.'

Miller fumbled in the desk drawer for the keys to the Land Rover, gave a cursory salute in Montgomery's direction and marched out towards the yard.

Group Captain Montgomery opened the bottom drawer of his desk. He took out a bottle of single malt whisky. He poured and downed a large measure. A telephone in the adjacent office rang, stopping after just two rings. Montgomery then heard a voice. He ventured to the door to see who the muffled voice belonged to. It was after five and he expected the office to be deserted. The room was empty aside from Ken Hickton, a twenty nine year old civilian from the village. Hickton was one of a number of villagers employed at the base. This employment generated just sufficient self-interest to stem the potential for protests by the local disarmament brigade. Hickton dealt with the administration concerned with the upkeep and the welfare of the dogs.

'What are you still doing here?' barked Montgomery. 'It's after five. You'll miss the bus if you don't make haste.'

'Oh I'm not teking the bus today Captain, I've got me a new bicycle, smashing it is.'

'Then on your bike, don't want your Mother worrying about you do you?'

'Ah she stopped worryin' 'bout me a long time ago Sir. I was coming to see you as it 'appens. I've been reconcilin' your procurement records and I appear to 'ave stumbled upon some irregularities tha' I can't explain. I thought you might like to tek a look.'

55

'Who gave you permission to do that?' asked Montgomery.

'Well no-one Captain, but I found the mistek an' I thought you should know 'bout it.

'What sort of mistake?' Montgomery asked.

'It seems someone has filed some medical expenses in the veterinary file in error and when I looked for the correct place for the record in the Personnel file, there wa' no missing record as I wa' expecting there to be. All those files were in order, with no missin' entries.'

'I'm sure it's a simple administrative error Hickton. Leave the erroneous file on the desk and I'll have Flight Lieutenant McDermott look at it when he gets back.'

'But it's not just the one file Captain. I wan't gonna be beaten by an erroneous file, so I carried on looking for where the gap in the file might be found and I discovered an 'ole 'ost of misfilings and duplications.'

'Duplications of what?' Montgomery asked.

'If you ask me, and I know it's above my pay grade, but if you ask me, someone 'as bin raising two or more invoices agenst a single procurement number and even I know, that's agenst the rules. Here's a list of all the procurement numbers where more than one invoice 'as bin raised.'

Hickton passed a clipboard across the desk. Montgomery studied it, flicking back and forth between the pages.

'As you can see there's quite a number of discrepancies.'

'Thank you Hickton, but I don't want you to trouble yourself with this; it is as you say, beyond your pay grade.'

'But Group Captain, I don't want no one comin' ta me later on and asking me questions about all the misteks, I like to do me job proper like.'

'Leave it with me' said Montgomery. 'I'll look into it tomorrow. I'm sure it's nothing to worry about. How is Sherman by the way?'

Sherman was a German Shepherd who'd been with the crew since the beginning of Project Emily and the arrival of the first ballistic missile. The veterinarian had had to be called the previous month after the guard dog intercepted an intruder trying to gain entry into the compound over the wire. Molly Sellars was a spirited young woman from the village, with an already infamous history with the Campaign for Nuclear Disarmament. She joined the campaign in 1959 and now led a posse of protestors who had made numerous attempts to scale the barbed wire encampments of bases across three counties. She finally made it over the wire, only to be met in the no-mans-land safeguarded area, by Sherman. Unfortunately for Sherman, she'd brought a lead pipe with her, which it turned out she had no qualm about using. Sherman lost three teeth and suffered a broken leg in the ensuing slaughter, before officers could rescue the wounded dog. Molly Sellars it transpired escaped unscathed and spent the next week revelling in the attention foisted upon her, when a local journalist ran her valiant story complete with her picture in the village newspaper. Sherman didn't fare so well and was removed from active duty following the incident. Following the announcement that the dog was to be put into retirement, Hickton asked if he could adopt the animal on account of its attacker having been a distant cousin and member of the Hickton clan. The paperwork was escalated and Hickton took ownership of the convalescing canine.

'Oh 'e's doing smashing' replied Hickton. 'Not walking too good, but 'e's on the mend now that the Vet 'as been able to save 'is leg. It's mighty nice of the Ministry to agree to pay all 'is ongoing veterinarian bills. I couldn't 'ave kept his leg otherwise.'

'It's the least we could do, after all those years of loyal service Hickton. Never forget, the Ministry looks after those who look after the Ministry. And what news of the infamous Ms Sellars?'

'Ah me Mum says she ain't welcome at our 'ouse no more, what with her being an embarrassment to the family an' all that. Good riddance, that's what I say, but then na matter what I say, I can't mek 'er understand the important work we do 'ere and 'ow we are keeping everyone safe from the Nazi's and the Soviets.'

'I don't think we have to worry about the Nazi's any longer Hickton. You get yourself off home to your family now. See you tomorrow, eight am sharp.'

'You know me Captain Montgomery. I'll be 'ere before eight.'

It was 6:10pm when Holbrook and Halford arrived, sporting the flushed cheeks of a good few pints of The Wheatsheaf's finest Mackesons.

'What's all the urgency Monte?' Holbrook asked.

'We have a problem' replied Montgomery. 'The bloody Government have just made a shocking announcement. I'll explain more when the others arrive.'

Montgomery poured three more glasses of Scotch, offering one each to Holbrook and Halford before downing his own.

'Who else are we expecting?'

The door swung open and in rushed Flying Officer Miller.

'Sorry for the tardiness Captain' he ushered breathlessly. 'Lance Corporal Summerfield is on his way and will be here presently. I'm afraid I have been unable to locate Flight Lieutenant McDermott. It appears he left Harrington at four thirty two but he's not at home, nor in the Wheatsheaf nor in the Officers Mess.'

'Right you are Miller. Get yourself home. Give my regards and my apologies to your lovely wife. I hope your anniversary dinner isn't spoiled.'

'You don't have to apologise Captain. I didn't marry her for her culinary skills if you know what I mean.'

Summerfield strolled in, dressed for a cricket match in all whites, aside from the grass stains to his knees. Montgomery waited for Miller to depart and for the outer door to click shut.

'Right then gentlemen, it's a shame we can't locate McDermott but no matter, this can't wait. It seems we have a problem. This afternoon the Minister of State for Defence announced in the House that funding for Project Emily is to be scrapped.'

'Scrapped?' Halford exclaimed.

'Scrapped' repeated Montgomery.

'When?' asked Holbrook.

'Over the next eighteen months. It's expected the last missile will have been repatriated to the United States before the end of next year.'

'They can't do that' exclaimed Halford. 'There's a contract with the United States Government.'

'Which expires next year, the extension beyond the initial five year contract was never a foregone conclusion. It was always intended there would be a break clause where either the Americans or the British could repudiate.'

'So why have we repudiated?'

'Technically we haven't. The Americans have. They want their missiles back. Arrangements are already underway to return eleven of the sixty four missiles before the end of the year.'

'Can they do that?' asked Summerfield.

'Technically Thor is their missile and apparently they want it to form the basis of their space programme.'

'So the British Government won't be able to continue with the project unilaterally then?' asked Summerfield.

'Apparently not, it looks like our new Defence Secretary is out to make a name for himself and we are in his line of sight. The Ministry have issued a letter that states we, that is the United Kingdom, must do everything possible to contain increases in spending, by removing anything that can be done without.'

Montgomery threw a carbon copy of the letter he'd received that afternoon across the table in the direction of Holbrook.

'There, see for yourself.'

'So we can be done without?' said Halford. 'We're dispensable are we?'

'Technically we're not dispensable. I think you'll find we're non-existent' groaned Summerfield.

'But I thought the Prime Minister was right behind Britain having its own intermediate range ballistic missile programme' said Halford. 'Why the change of heart?'

'I'm not sure it is a change of heart' replied Montgomery.

'It must be, why else would he have agreed to have missiles on British soil in the first place?'

'Perhaps because he was in a tight spot and needed to build some fences with our transatlantic friends after the debacle Eden made of Suez' sighed Summerfield.

'Eden didn't make a debacle of Suez' Halford defended.

'Yes he did' Summerfield argued.

'So you'd have just let Nasser and Egypt walk away with the canal, our canal, would you?

'That's not what I'm saying.'

'It sounds to me like that's exactly what you're saying.'

'No, I'm just saying that it could have been handled better. We should have sought the support of the United Nations and sorted the problem through legitimate legal channels before sending in the troops.'

'Bullshit. Eden was right to send in the troops. That canal was ours and Nasser had no right to try and take it.'

'The U.N didn't think so and neither did the Americans, who still like to remind us they went in to clean up the goddamn mess we'd made.'

'Gentlemen, please' interrupted Montgomery. 'None of this is helpful. You two will have to agree to disagree about the whys and wherefores of the crisis in Suez. We need to turn our attention to the matter in hand.'

'So the Prime Minister is behind the decision to scrap Emily and the Thor missiles?' Holbrook asked.

'Yes' Montgomery replied. 'The Department of Defence has its fingers in too many different pies and I understand the Prime Minister thinks a period of consolidation is called for. Bomber Command is pushing for additional investment into the Skybolt programme and the Navy; well, they won't go down without a fight.'

'Skybolt?' mocked Halford. 'What a pile of crap that is.'

'Thor was a pile of crap three years ago' said Holbrook.

'Three years?' Summerfield exclaimed. 'That's generous. Thor was still a pile of crap one year ago and for all we know, it still is.'

'What about Blue Streak?' asked Halford.

'Blue Streak won't be reinstated. Britain has neither the technical expertise nor the political inclination.'

'More crap' said Holbrook.

'Yeah well, we lost all our expertise when we got into bed with the paranoid Yanks' cursed Halford 'and now they are screwing us.'

'So how confident are you that the funding for Project Emily will be transferred to Skybolt?' asked Holbrook.

'I wouldn't go as far as to say I have any confidence in that scenario whatsoever' Montgomery replied. 'I've no doubt the Navy are pushing their own agenda. Let's be honest, they've still not recovered from the slap in the face they received when Strategic Air Command were given control of the missile programme in the first place.'

'And the Navy, they have something in the wings?' asked Holbrook.

'I've learned over the years, never to underestimate the Navy, particularly when it comes to re-enforcing their hierarchical superiority. I wager they'll whip us on the ass and kick us into merry oblivion as soon as a solid fuel propelled weapon is approved. Let's face it; Thor was always only ever going to be a stopgap until the Americans perfected their Atlas programme. Emily was always only going to last for the duration of that stopgap. If I'm honest, I'd hoped the stopgap would have given us more time. The termination of the contract at such short notice is not something anyone had planned for.'

'Where's McDermott?' asked Holbrook.

'I've no idea. He was called over to Harrington this afternoon and doesn't appear to be back yet.'

'But he should be party to this discussion' said Halford.

'I agree but he's not here and no one can find him so there's not a lot we can do about that is there?'

'So when are the crews going to be told?' asked Summerfield. 'Emily employs four thousand men.'

'Who gives a damn about the crews?' groaned Halford. 'It's us we should be concerned about, not them.'

'Well, the withdrawal has been announced publicly this afternoon' said Montgomery 'although I doubt the news will have disseminated

61

down to the crews yet. Its only just been confirmed to me by Air Marshall Cross, who I might say, is spitting feathers that even he was not consulted before the announcement was made. The information will be relayed to crews when the hierarchy deem it appropriate, so it goes without saying, until then, this conversation remains confidential. The last thing we need are teams of disgruntled operatives working on nuclear missiles.'

'So what about our work?' asked Holbrook. 'What will happen to us? The termination of Emily is going to make a difference isn't it?'

'Emily's termination gives us some logistical problems certainly' responded Montgomery. 'The chief problem, being that of funding accountability. It's too early to make any rash decisions. Much will depend on the progress of Skybolt and whether we are able to piggy back onto that budget as we have done with Emily's.'

'Is there no chance our project can qualify for open source funding?' asked Summerfield. I'd be much happier working on a project paid for with open source funding.'

'No, absolutely not' said Montgomery categorically.

'Why not?'

'Because the Government won't approve it.'

'If the government won't approve it, then should we be doing it?'

'It's a bit late to be asking that now' Holbrook declared. 'If you wanted to bail you should have done it before we started killing the monkeys.'

'Still no success?' Montgomery asked.

'No, they're all dead. We're waiting on a fresh delivery, but we'll get there.'

'I don't see why you need me' said Summerfield. 'Until you can find a way to keep your subjects alive, I'm actually quite redundant.'

'You're not bailing on us now' Holbrook boomed. 'We're in this together.'

'What exactly is it you think we're *in* Mr Holbrook? Shall I tell you? A project that as far as the world is concerned, doesn't exist, can never exist; six years of research and we still have no surviving subject, no legitimate funding and the illegitimate funding that does exist is about to be blown out of the water. If you think any of that is going to lead you into a Knighthood then Sir, you are deluded.'

'Calm down Mr Summerfield' Montgomery pleaded. 'These occasional crises of confidence are bound to occur from time to time. Let me assure you, there are men deep within the corridors of the Ministry who have every confidence in each one of you to get the job done.'

'Which men?' enquired Summerfield.

'I'm not at liberty to disclose the identities of those involved, you know that. Suffice to say, Ministers, Prime Ministers, Members of Parliament, they come and go like the wind. Their tenure is as changeable as the weather. The fickle nature of politics is the very reason Ministers can never be relied upon when it comes to long term ambition. The men who support you are as solid in their tenure as the earth on which we are standing.'

CHAPTER 7
MY WAY

May 8th 1998

The digital alarm clock rendered its incessant whine. Emilie Weston crawled to the edge of the bed and hit the snooze button before turning over and falling promptly back to sleep. Her night, as usual, had been broken with a nightmare. She had seen herself, running towards a red Vauxhall which exploded before her, scattering shrapnel a thousand feet. Shop fronts were obliterated. Roofs had caved in and electrical cables were sparking. Alarms were ringing and folk were scrambling into the field of debris screaming. A dark haired man was running towards her, calling for Martha Pope. It had been past five o'clock before she finally nodded back off to sleep. Nine minutes later the alarm sounded again. *Just nine more minutes* she thought, her head still thick with the after effects of the remnants of the bottle of gin she'd polished off the previous evening. She lay there in the dark. Will was snoring at her side. She prodded him in the ribs which brought a temporary reprieve. She thought about last night, going over the calamitous turn of events in her foggy head. She pictured her deceased colleagues and tried to remember the last time she'd seen each of them. Dana Coxstable, she'd last seen Dana at a fundraising cream tea. Councillor Constance had been making a stand in defence of a colleague, who'd been hauled before the *Standards in Public Life* committee, for a minor misdemeanour. Councillor Flatliner had been at a protest against the closure of a Care Home. Councillor Hopkin had been at a meeting of the campaign fundraising committee. Councillor Wallmichaels had attended the opening of the new gymnasium. Now they were all gone. Their tragic and sudden demise put her

64

disappointment into some perspective. She'd expected to wake up as the new Mayor and had had a full diary of events planned.

The alarm clock signalled she'd had her nine minutes more and she silenced it permanently before heading downstairs to prepare breakfast. She couldn't face anything more than a strong coffee and two paracetamol. After leaving a box of muesli, a bottle of milk and orange juice poured into three small glasses, she disappeared into the study. Taking the large diary from her overstuffed purse, she opened the page at the current week. At eleven she was supposed to be laying a wreath with the Royal British Legion as part of the annual commemoration of the Victory in Europe. The wreath lay on the floor against the desk. At one o'clock she had been scheduled to present a bouquet of flowers to celebrate the one hundredth birthday of a citizen. The bouquet sat in a vase of water on the window sill. At two o'clock she had been due to receive a group of primary school children in the Mayor's Parlour for a discussion about civic pride. The speech she'd intended to give as an introduction, lay in the out-tray of the printer. At seven thirty she had expected to be at a fundraising dinner hosted by the local hospice. The bottle of whiskey she'd bought to take as a raffle prize stood at the back of the desk, amidst the chaotic stacks of reports, minute books and papers. A copy of the evening speech lay on the top of the printer.

Sam appeared in the doorway and knocked lightly on the door.

'Do we have to bow and call you Ma'am now then, Madam Mayor?' he asked.

'No,' she replied 'because as things have turned out, I'm not actually the Mayor.'

'How come?'

'It's a long story and I only want to recount it once. Is Miles up?'

'Dunno, I don't think so.'

'Be an angel and go and wake him up. Give your Dad a nudge while you're up there. Your breakfast is out. I just need to get a few things done. I'll be out in a minute.'

'Tough night last night?' asked Will, pointing at the empty bottle of Gin on the black granite countertop.

65

'You could say that' Emilie replied. 'Where the hell were you?'

'I'm sorry babe. The new chef had a bloody heart attack. I had to fill in. The restaurant was rammed all night.'

'But Miles said you were on the way and was stuck in traffic.'

'Yeah I was, but Mel called, so I had to turn round and head back. Did you have a good night? I doubt you even noticed I was missing.'

'No, actually I didn't, I had a terrible night.'

'What time do we have to be at the hospice tonight?' he asked.

'We don't, we're not going.'

'How so?'

'Because the guest of honour at the hospice is the Mayor and as it transpires, I am not the Mayor and had you have been there last night as you were supposed to be, you would have known this.'

'I've said I'm sorry, I couldn't help it. What happened? I thought the whole evening was just a formality.'

'It should have been, at least it always has been, until last night. Four of our Councillors were killed in a road accident on the way to the Town Hall which resulted in our controlling group no longer being the controlling group. Consequently, the Socialists, when they realised they had a working majority, forced the meeting to go ahead and at the last minute fielded their own candidate as Mayor. It was a goddamn bloody fiasco.'

'So who's the Mayor?'

'Rungden, and I'm not convinced he even wanted the job, judging by the tone of his acceptance speech. The lumbering buffoon will render the Council a laughing stock. The man has the social graces of a petulant pilchard and I'm sure his mucky suits, his short shirts that barely cover his beer belly, toothless grimace and smutty jokes will go down a treat with guests at regimental and civic dinners.'

'At least you can see the funny side.'

'No I can't. I'm not even trying to be funny, not with five funerals to look forward to. So how's the new chef?'

'What?'

'Your chef, you said he'd had a heart attack. How is he?'

'Oh he's ok, in hospital.'

'Which one? I'll send a card?'

'There's no need. He wasn't working out. I was going to fire him.'

'That's charitable of you, you can't fire him now.'

'Yes I can. It's business. There's no room for charity in business or we'd all be out of business. Promise me you won't send a card, I don't think it will go down well with a P45.'

'Talking of heart attacks' said Emilie 'I see that Frank Sinatra has died.'

'I haven't heard that. Where did you read that?'

'No idea. It must have been in yesterday's paper. Las Vegas paid its respects by silencing all the gaming machines and roulette wheels and the Empire State building was bathed in blue light in tribute.'

'I don't remember reading that. Still a fitting tribute for the colossus of a man he was. So what are your plans today? I'm guessing they've changed.'

'You might say that yes. Perhaps I'll sort out my sock drawer or alphabetically file the spice rack. I do need to go to the Town Hall. I've still got the wreath and the bouquet of flowers for Mrs Harrington. Will, I've been thinking.'

'Sounds ominous, what about?'

'I might try and get my name onto the approved national candidates list.'

'Not this again' Will scorned. 'We've talked about this and we decided it's more important you're here. You have responsibilities. If you get accepted onto that list, you'll be off fighting every no hope seat in the country that's been left vacant by disgrace, de-selection and incarceration.

'Only until I get a safe seat.'

'Which will never happen. Look, I don't want to argue, we've been here before and we decided.'

'No, you decided if I remember correctly' she argued.

'That's not how it was and you know it. You're a wife and a mother. I thought that was important to you.'

'It is and I've always put you first.'

'We'll have to agree to disagree about that one.'

'And what is that supposed to mean?'

'I let you go off and fight a seat on the Council didn't I?'

'You let me?' hollered Emilie, incandescent with rage.

The vacant seat Emilie had been offered at a by-election became available when the incumbent was arrested, charged and later sentenced to a term of imprisonment, for his part in a bribery scandal at what turned out to be an illegal knocking-shop.

'Yes, I let you' Will retorted.

'Only because you thought it was a *no hope* seat.'

'You won didn't you? So what's your problem?'

'Look Will, the boys are older now. In a few years they'll be independent and you're so busy with all your own responsibilities, you're hardly ever here. I need to do something with my life before it's too late and I'm too goddamn old.'

'Then take up a hobby.'

'A hobby? Are you serious?'

'Yes. Plant herbs, you're always moaning about the price of herbs. Do crosswords, jigsaws, paint; I don't know. Only you know what you want to do.'

'You can be such a patronising bastard sometimes.'

'I'm not patronising. I just don't see why you want to change things. It's not like we need the money. Don't I give you everything you want?'

'It's not about the money and as for everything I want; we'll have to agree to disagree about that as well. It's about what I do with my life. It's about me getting to the end of my life and regretting that I didn't make a bigger difference.'

'You do make a difference. Believe me Emilie, you do make a difference. If only you knew how much difference you make.'

'To who? You? I need more than that.'

'Not just to me, to the boys. We like having you around. We like having your full attention. I'd miss you too much' he said, sidling closer and pecking her on the cheek before putting on his jacket, taking an apple from the fridge and collecting his car keys.

'You'd only miss me because I wouldn't be here to iron your goddamn shirts.'

'But you do it so well. The answer is no, you're not doing it and if you value our marriage and you love the boys, you won't think about it a second longer.'

Emilie launched the packet of paracetamol across the kitchen in Will's direction as he disappeared out of the door.

CHAPTER 8
EDITH & THE GUARDIAN

August 29th 1899

The chirping of the birds in the garden signalled the imminence of daybreak. Edith had taken refuge in the cloistered courtyard, pacing back and forth like a caged tiger. The long drooping purple flowers of the Wisteria had long since bloomed and had given way to an abundance of fresh pale green leaves.

Lord Noel reconvened his gathering and called Edith to re-join Lady Noel and Brother Hipwood around the table in the Grace Dieu library. Brother Hipwood collected Lady Noel from the scullery from where she'd chosen to take a solitary cup of strongly brewed tea.

The windowless library was illuminated by an elaborate electric light, suspended from the centre of the ceiling above the table. Edith noticed Lord Noel and Brother Hipwood had opened a second bottle of wine out of the shipment from Grace Dieu in France.

'His Lordship has made a decision' announced Brother Hipwood once Edith had settled herself at the fine long table.

The genealogical chart was fully unwound; the corners retained in place beneath four heavy cut-glass paperweights. In its unwound state, the chart extended the length of the table.

'Welcome back ladies' said Lord Noel. 'I am mindful that Sister Edith is in somewhat of a unique position in so far as these deliberations are concerned, by virtue of the fact that she is also of the Compass Line herself. The conventional norm, which has been practised throughout the last half century, has been that those of The Line take no part in the discussions of The Guardians, nor are party to

70

the decisions the Guardians ultimately reach. I think tonight, we have witnessed a demonstration of why this is the case.'

'With respect my love, I think that what we've seen tonight has been a demonstration as to the profound importance of the maternal bond' said Lady Noel.

'Precisely' replied Lord Noel 'and it has been demonstrated that a member of the Line itself, cannot hold an objective opinion on how best to secure the Line.'

'Whilst my presence may be irregular' interrupted Edith, 'you cannot deny it.'

'We are not denying it Sister' added Brother Hipwood.

'But you are going to overlook it, disregard my advice and all I have said, are you not?'

'No Sister, only a fool disregards the advice of a member of the Compass Line but beyond some sentimental intuition of misplaced maternal affection, you have furnished me with no good justification as to why the infant should remain with the Newloves. Brother Hipwood, by contrast, has provided us with many good reasons as to why the child should not.'

Edith fell silent, aware the conventions had been written and put into practice for good reason. Separating infant Compasses from their mothers had been proven to secure the Line. It did not stop her heart from breaking at the prospect of separating this mother from this child. This time it felt wrong. It wasn't that she hadn't done it before, she had. On many occasions she'd been party to the covert swapping of new-borns, always a girl taken away and replaced with another child. She'd never known there to be a shortage of unwanted babies in the world. This time she felt quite different and she wished she could put her strength of feeling into words that Lord Noel would understand. She didn't comprehend the depth of feeling herself but simply knew they were about to embark on the wrong course of action.

'You must know in your heart that what we are about to do is wrong' Edith pleaded one last time.

'How can it be wrong?' Lord Noel challenged. 'The resolutions are quite clear.'

'The resolutions were drawn up seventy years ago' Edith argued clutching at straws. 'They are out of date.'

'They were drawn up for good reason' Lord Noel argued. 'How many times must we go over this? I'm sure I don't need to remind you of the fate of the 501st Compass, or the scandal of the 821st. We are obliged to follow the conventions so as to avoid a repetition of what occurred in these tragic cases.'

Throughout earlier millennia, those born of the Compass Line had been told of their revered heritage as soon as their Guardians thought the time was right and the child was mature, educated and reliable enough to comprehend the complexities and responsibilities of their God given gift. For thousands of years, the convention of early disclosure was never questioned and its practise never wavered. Then came a series of events which changed the attitudes of the Guardians and the adopted convention of disclosure. It was two of these events that Lord Noel had just brought to the attention of the group.

The first concerned the tragedy of the 501st Compass who had been fooled into revealing her gift of foresight. A group of charlatans, on realising the accuracy of the girl's predictions, used her to determine the location of a sworn enemy. In exchange for praise sufficient to bolster her disposition and promises of improved living conditions, she happily gave them the information they sought; the whereabouts of the Knights of the Order of Saint John. Satisfied her foresight would deliver them a military victory they set sail, taking the unsuspecting Compass with them where she was imprisoned on a ship by a General loyal to the Ottoman Sultan, Suleiman. The ship reached the island of Rhodes where, as she had predicted, the Knights of the Order of Saint John were to be found. The Ottoman troops were able with her unwitting assistance, to sack the Knights, who had been given control of the island following their expulsion from the Holy land and the fall of the Kingdom of Jerusalem. The foolish Compass had already been impregnated by officers of the militia who had mercilessly used her to satisfy their masculine inclinations during the long voyage. By the time the Ottoman armada arrived in Rhodes, she was clearly with child as was evident by her swollen belly. The manner of her subsequent death shortly after the decimation of Saint John's Order, remained a matter of some conjecture but an entry in the manuscript stated a belief she had taken her own life and that of her unborn Compass child by throwing herself from a cliff onto the rocks on discovering the true intentions of the General and his troops.

The 821st Compass by contrast had not been fooled. On realising she possessed certain talents including that of foresight, she blatantly prostituted her gifts after being encouraged to do so, in exchange for personal gain. She soon amassed a fortune exploiting her skills by travelling across the globe as prospectors of good fortune laid all they owned at her door in exchange for her insights. A few years later she herself, had fallen prey to those as would do the exploiting. There was no shortage of men willing to take advantage of her power and its hold on those poor souls desperate enough to give up what little they had in a bid to improve their station. She was soon the prize attraction of a freak show, forced into obedience by the administration of copious amounts of opium. By the time she succumbed to the effects of the opium den in which she finally took refuge, the personal fortune she had amassed had been stolen away by fraudsters, thieves and corrupt apothecaries. She died destitute, in squalor and having brought the Compass Line to the brink of infamy, intrigue and ridicule.

As a result of the downfall of the 821st Compass, the Committee of Guardians called the first meeting for two centuries. It convened in London, obliging Guardians to cross great distances and jointly they made a decision that no Compass born thereafter would ever be told of their revered lineage. Guardians would continue to nurture and educate their charges, placing equal emphasis on both the written and the spoken word. They were to receive instruction in a language not of their native tongue and focus would be given to honing the skills of tact and diplomacy. The question of whether mathematics should be taught was debated at length for an interminable time. Those congregated could not agree. When the western contingent went so far as to suggest that matters of scientific principle should also be endowed into the young minds, the meeting erupted into chaos and screams of heresy were shouted by those sitting in the theologian quarter. After two days of entrenched disagreement, a vote was finally taken and much to the chagrin of the religious zealots among the group, the secular opinion prevailed. Tutors of both mathematics and scientific principle would be found. The Guardians pledged to continue to ensure protection, security and when the time was right to provide the opportunity to influence man's progress. No additional Guardian, beyond those already cited in the manuscript, would be considered a suitable Guardian without the explicit approval of twelve Guardian Heads. The Guardian Heads would ensure succession by delegating an heir. The Guardian Heads were selected at the meeting which proved to be much easier a task than defining what the right and proper education might look like. Each Guardian Head would keep a secure copy of the manuscript and each one would be responsible for ensuring the manuscript remained updated with the details of each new Compass. The final resolution confirmed that in order to protect the Lines that remained and ensure as wider influence as possible, each new-born Compass would be separated from its birth mother and given into the hands of an approved Guardian to raise in accordance with the conventions. The Order of Saint Dominic was convened and granted the responsibility to oversee all Compass births and to ensure strict adherence to the conventions.

Sister Edith had been born during this meeting of the Guardians. She came into the world just before the vote on the resolution to change two millennia of convention. She became the last of the Compass children to be told they came from a protected line, a line that had demonstrated perpetual attributes of foresight and vision, of great reasoning, unending kindness and mutual understanding, a line incapable of hatred or anger. A line that brought hope in the face of despair and certainty when there was doubt.

'So we are agreed?' asked Lord Noel. 'The infant will be placed into the charge of the March family.'

'You're making a mistake' Edith insisted. 'To safeguard the security of this Line, the baby should stay with the Newloves.'

'Why?' Lord Noel asked. 'The March family have proven themselves to be Guardians of the highest degree for hundreds of years.

I'm sorry you disagree Edith, but my decision is final. I am the Head Guardian and I have a duty to follow the convention. I might remind you that you too have a duty, to ensure I follow it.'

Edith slumped back dejectedly in her chair and closed her eyes. The vision of a carriage without a horse came into her mind. A young woman slumped forward, her head covered in blood flashed fleetingly into view then gave way to an enormous white cylindrical object spewing fire from below, as it climbed into a cloudless sky. A sudden deafening roar of thunder caused her to cover her ears with the palm of her hands.

'Are you alright Edith?' Lady Noel asked. 'Brother Hipwood, would you fetch Sister Edith a glass of water please?'

Edith fought to make sense of the visions in her head but the deafening thunder persisted, rendering her deaf to anything outside her own mind. A brilliant flash of light caused a momentarily blindness and she fought to regain her composure as her sight slowly returned. Lady Noel instructed her husband to help Edith to the couch so she could rest. Edith sank into the soft cushioning and closed her eyes.

'The poor woman is exhausted' said Lady Noel, covering Edith with a blanket. 'We should let her sleep.'

'So it's settled' said Lord Noel, returning to the table. 'I will take the carriage to the March house with the Compass infant. Brother Hipwood, I'd like you to report to this address, where you will be given the infant boy we spoke of earlier.'

Lord Noel passed a piece of paper citing the address of the workhouse where the unwanted baby would be found.

'Dr Holbrook will be expecting you.'

'I think you are forgetting one minor detail my love' said Lady Noel. 'Summer gave birth to a girl. Brother Hipwood is going to return with a boy.'

Lord Noel turned to Edith who was snoring.

'That's not a problem. Edith will have been very careful not to disclose the gender of the baby in adherence to the convention. Summer will accept a boy in lieu of the girl and will be none the wiser.'

'Mr Newlove won't' interrupted Brother Hipwood, slipping into his boots at the door.

'Won't what?' Lord Noel asked.

'Accept a boy. I heard the young Sparrow informing him he had a beautiful baby girl.'

'That's most unfortunate' said Lord Noel 'the stupid girl. No matter, I will explain the infant's testicles hadn't dropped and the naive young thing, who had never witnessed a birth before this one, was mistaken.'

'I'll report back here then shall I? With the boy child?' asked Brother Hipwood.

'Yes, as quick as you can now Brother, there's no time to waste.'

'How do we ensure Sparrow doesn't visit the Newlove house?' said Lady Noel. 'Your plan to exchange the new-borns only works provided Sparrow doesn't become aware of the deceit and lets the cat out of the bag.'

'She'll be kept busy at the Abbey' assured Brother Hipwood. 'The Sisters intend to leave for the continent in two days. Keeping her busy for two days won't be difficult.'

'You don't think we need to bring Sparrow into our confidence?' Lady Noel asked.

'Absolutely not' said Lord Noel. 'Sister Edith will enlighten the young lady when she thinks the time is right to do so. Neither the girl's maturity nor her faith is yet to be relied upon. When Edith wakes my dear, please have her take care of the business of informing the other Guardian Heads of the new arrival. I'd like the letters to be ready to take to the Postmaster before the end of the day.

CHAPTER 9
THE CUBAN IRONY

November 19th 1962

The bus bringing in the evening shift pulled into the security compound. The civilians, some in dark smart suits, others in casual slacks and sweaters gave way to the uniformed officers, who climbed down from the bus and filtered into an orderly queue at the guardhouse. What had been a sunny and balmy afternoon had given way to a chill and a light fog was already beginning to linger. Harry Holbrook stepped forward as the queue edged nearer to the security checkpoint. He noticed an increased Police presence. A uniformed Police officer approached.

'Good evening Wing Commander. Your presence is required in the Officers' Mess before you report for duty.'

'I was going there anyway, but thank you Officer.'

'What's with all the extra security? Are we expecting another ruddy VIP?'

'That's not for me to say Sir' the Police Officer replied before seeking out Halford who had joined at the back of the queue.

Holbrook flashed his badge and marched at a leisurely pace across the compound towards the Mess. Squadron Leader Halford and Lance Corporal Summerfield, who had both received the same request to present themselves to the Mess before reporting for duty, quickened their step to catch up with Holbrook.

The hangar door was wide open. A handful of officers were scurrying in and out. An empty large flatbed transporter was being reversed into position which meant that a missile, being serviced in the hangar, was about to be loaded.

The ground crew looked like they were preparing to receive an incoming flight.

The three launch emplacements were also a hive of activity. Two of the canopies that provided cover to the missiles to protect them from both the inclement British weather and from prying eyes were open. The third canopy was in the process of being opened.

'Not another ruddy short notice test' Halford complained.

'I thought the test wasn't scheduled until next week' said Holbrook.

'It isn't,' replied Summerfield. 'Something's afoot and I don't like the look of it.'

The three men continued towards the Mess. They passed United States Pilot Officer James Wingfield in the corridor. He was struggling to carry a large television set. Summerfield held the door open and Wingfield squeezed through the gap into the Mess room. He dropped the television set onto a table before plugging it in to the power outlet and affixing the aerial.

Group Captain Montgomery, holding a pint glass half full of beer, strolled across the room to meet his crew.

'Film night?' asked Holbrook.

'No, I'm afraid not. The muck is about to hit the proverbial fan I'm afraid gentlemen. I hope none of you have made any plans because I'm going to have to ask you to cancel them forthwith.'

'For how long?' Holbrook asked.

'Until further notice.'

'You don't usually ask us to cancel plans for a test. What's so special about this one?'

'What's special is that this time it's not a test.'

'It looks like we're preparing for a test. It's a right hive of activity out there.'

'What I mean is we've been placed on alert. The missiles are being readied to launch within our fifteen minute window. I'm informed the Americans could be about to move to DEFCOM2.'

'That would explain why the ground crew are running around like headless chickens' said Halford.

'I'm sorry, DEFCOM2?' enquired Summerfield.

'Don't you read your manuals Mr Summerfield? DEFCOM2 is the signal for immediate take-off.'

'Why?'

'For two reasons; To prevent their planes from being obliterated on the ground by an incoming missile and I hope, to provide us poor sods left behind on the ground, with some defence that stops us from being annihilated.'

'I know what DEFCOM2 is. I was asking why it has become necessary to instigate it.'

'It hasn't yet, but they have moved to DEFCOM3 so they are preparing to arm, fuel and pilot in readiness for a two designation.'

'Why the compulsion to watch the TV at a time like this?' Holbrook asked.

'We are about to hear from President John F Kennedy' said Montgomery, checking the time on his watch. 'Their paranoia has I fear at long last reached such a fever pitch they're about to unleash the potential for global Armageddon. I hope to God the man knows what he's doing or we're all going to hell.'

The mellow staccato tones of Elvis Presley and *Return to sender* were playing from a 33 rpm record on a gramophone.

'What's happening?' asked Halford, returning from the bar with a glass of Cola.

'It's what's going to happen we need to be concerned about' replied Montgomery.

An influx of British and American off-duty officers entered the room and gathered around the television.

'Turn that off' shouted Wingfield.

Someone lifted the needle from the record silencing the King of rock n roll.

The screen filled with an external shot of the Whitehouse. A white canopy sat atop the doorway. Bright spotlights and cameras stood ready to capture those coming and going. A dozen men mingled around, their backs to the cameras. The National Anthem played in the background. The camera moved into the Whitehouse and the monochrome figure of President John F Kennedy sporting a dark suit

79

and tie appeared on the screen from behind a desk. Dark shadows under his eyes hung like a man who hadn't slept in a long time. His high rugged cheekbones were emphasised in the shadow cast by the bright lights of the camera crew. His demeanour suggested a man with the weight of the world on his shoulders. The American flag hung limply behind and curtains on both sides were drawn. A dark screen had been positioned behind him. Two microphones sat mounted on a plinth on the desk.

'Do you think he looks that grey in the flesh?' asked Summerfield.

'You'll have to ask Mrs Kennedy what he looks like in the flesh' smiled Holbrook.

'From what I hear, if you want an answer to that, you'd be better to ask one of his interns or Ms Marilyn Monroe' said Halford.

'Turn it up' someone shouted. Wingfield obliged before retaking his seat on the front row.

'Good evening my fellow citizens' said Kennedy. 'This Government as promised has maintained the closest surveillance of the Soviet military build-up on the island of Cuba. Within the past week unmistakable evidence has established the fact that a series of offensive missile sites is now in preparation on that imprisoned island. The purpose of these bases can be none other than to provide a nuclear strike capability against the western hemisphere. The characteristics of these new missile sites indicate two distinct types of installations. Several of them include medium range ballistic missiles capable of carrying a nuclear warhead for a distance of more than one thousand nautical miles. Additional sites not yet completed appear to be designed for missiles capable of travelling more than twice as far thus capable of striking most major cities in the western hemisphere. In addition, jet bombers capable of carrying nuclear warheads are being un-crated and assembled in Cuba while the necessary air bases are being prepared. This urgent transformation of Cuba into an important strategic base by the presence of these large long range and clearly offensive weapons of sudden mass destruction constitutes an explicit threat to the peace and security of all the Americas in flagrant defiance of the Rio Pact of 1947. Nuclear weapons are so destructive and

ballistic missiles so swift that any substantially increased possibility of their use or any sudden change in their deployment may well be regarded as a definite threat to peace. Our own strategic missiles have never been transferred to the territory of any other nation under a cloak of secrecy and deception and our history unlike that of the Soviets since World War Two demonstrates that we have no desire to dominate any other nation or impose our system on its people. Aggressive conduct if allowed to go unchecked and unchallenged ultimately leads to war. This nation is opposed to war. Our unswerving objective must be therefore to prevent the use of these missiles against this or any other country and to secure their removal from the western hemisphere. Our policy has been one of patience and restraint as befits a peaceful and powerful nation which leads a worldwide alliance, but now further action is required and it is underway. I have directed the armed forces to prepare for any eventuality. It shall be the policy of this nation to regard any missile launched from Cuba against any nation in the western hemisphere as an attack by the Soviet Union on the United States requiring a full retaliatory response upon the Soviet Union. Our other allies around the world have also been alerted. I call upon Chairman Khrushchev to halt and eliminate this clandestine and reckless and provocative threat to world peace. I call upon him to abandon this course of world domination and to join in an historic effort to end the arms race and to transform the history of man. Any hostile move anywhere in the world against the safety and freedom of peoples to whom we are committed, including the brave people of West Berlin will be met by whatever action is needed. Most Cubans today look forward to a time when they will be truly free from foreign domination, free to choose their own leaders, free to select their own system, free to own their own land, free to speak and write and worship without fear or degradation and then shall Cuba be welcomed back to the society of free nations. My fellow citizens, let no one doubt that this is a difficult and dangerous effort on which we have set out but the greatest danger of all would be to do nothing. Our goal is not the victory of might but the vindication of right. Not peace at the expense of freedom but peace and freedom. God willing that goal will be achieved. Thank you and good night.'

The television screen went blank. Silence reigned such that a pin could have been heard dropping.

'Jesus Christ, the Son-of-a-bitch is going to take us to war' exclaimed Halford.

'That's not what he said' replied Holbrook. 'He's playing hard ball sure, but that's not the same as taking us to war.'

'Oh no? *Aggressive conduct inevitably leads to war* - that's what he said and then he went on to accuse the Soviets of precisely that. It sounds like a recipe for war to me and here we are babysitting Kennedy's nuclear arsenal. You don't think Khrushchev's got his warheads sighted right at us at this very moment?'

'I imagine Mr Khrushchev has had his warheads sighted in our direction the day our missiles first arrived' added Summerfield.

'That may be so, but I'm telling you, Kennedy and Khrushchev in a showdown is a sure fire way to get us annihilated. Look at who Kennedy's got advising him. I wouldn't trust that Strange McNamara as far as I could throw him, he's a raving war junkie.'

'Right gentlemen, listen up' called Montgomery addressing the crowd. 'The American military are now operating on a higher alert level. They have moved their forces to DEFCOM3 which in practise means all their aircraft are and will remain on standby, fuelled, armed and ready to go. The British Thor force will maintain a state of readiness at one-five. Maintenance technicians will restore all missiles to a condition where they are ready to be launched. All planned timing and launch exercises will be postponed until further notice. A full complement of operation, maintenance and launch crews will be expected to remain on the base. Finally, both American and British Officers with responsibility for the launch keys are to retain possession of their key at all times and remain at their station. Any questions?'

'Yes, I've got one' shouted Halford from the back of the room. 'When will Macmillan be joining us to sit here like a bloody sitting duck with the rest of us?'

'I'm sure the Prime Minister will be doing everything within his power to prevent an escalation of the situation so we never become sitting ducks' replied Montgomery.

'Should we be evacuating our families?' asked Summerfield.

'No, that's not necessary. In fact you are not to discuss this situation with anyone outside the base. Operate a *business as usual* policy. The Ministry doesn't want us to be seen doing anything that may be interpreted by the Soviets as being in any way provocative or offensive.'

'So we won't strike first?' asked Halford.

'I can't envisage a scenario where we will strike first' Montgomery replied 'but of course we can't rule it out.'

'It doesn't really matter whether we strike first or not' added Halford. 'If the Soviets strike first and we retaliate, the outcome will still be the mutually assured destruction of us all.'

'That is precisely why the deterrent works' shouted Montgomery. 'No one wants to see destruction on such a huge scale.'

'At least we won't have to worry about being unemployed in a few months' added Summerfield. 'It might be a better option than having to break that news to Mrs Summerfield.'

'I was going to ask for leave' said Pilot Officer Wingfield. 'I'm guessing it won't be granted now?'

'Is it essential?' asked Montgomery.

'It is to me.'

'Then see your Squadron Leader tomorrow he'll see what can be done.'

'I'll walk across to the lab with you gentleman' said Montgomery as the four men headed back out into the chilly evening.

'Captain Montgomery, I hope I'm not going to be expected to actually be involved in the firing of a missile should it come to it, because I don't think I can do it' said Summerfield.

'You might think differently Tom if you know there's one incoming.'

'No Sir, I'm not sure I would.'

'I've managed to keep you out of the affray so far haven't I? Still, you'd best swat up on your manuals just in case. We sent you to Vandenberg to train with the others for a reason. You may be a contingent crew but in the event of a contingency you could be called upon. You need to prepare yourselves for that.'

Holbrook led the way into the decontamination building and disappeared into his lab. McDermott was on the phone and hung up when they came in.

'We have us a live one' Holbrook called ecstatically a few moments later. 'Summerfield, at long last I think your time has come' he hollered through the door.

The four men ventured into the lab to take a look at what Holbrook was shouting about. A small primate sat in a small metal cage, was munching on a piece of banana.

'What do you think she's thinking about?' asked Holbrook.

'That's for Mr Summerfield to tell us' said Montgomery but I wager she's wondering where her next meal is coming from.'

'Wouldn't it be ironic?' said Holbrook.

'What?'

'To be bombed into oblivion just as we perfect the process of finding out what our enemies are thinking.'

'Have there been any developments with regards to our funding?' asked Halford.

'We're working on it' replied Montgomery. 'This turn of events should certainly increase our prospects wouldn't you say? Well done Dr Holbrook, very well done.'

Summerfield worked around the clock barely stepping out of the lab. His colleagues brought in three meals a day, a supply of clean shirts and messages from Mrs Summerfield, who demanded to know when she could expect her husband home as his sudden absence was playing havoc with her social diary.

The base remained on a state of alert for the next ten days as the American President played Russian roulette with the Soviets, refusing to back down until Khrushchev agreed to America's demands that Cuba be made free of Soviet missiles.

On the tenth day of the stalemate, Khrushchev agreed to capitulate. Soviet missiles and bases in Cuba would be dismantled and removed. Kennedy announced that American missiles stationed in Turkey would also be removed quid-pro-quo but not until the Cuban missiles were gone.

'I'd say Kennedy played an ace there' said Holbrook over a game of rummy in the lab with Summerfield and Halford the evening after the end of hostilities had been declared.

'It had already been decided the American missile programme in Turkey was going to be terminated just as the termination of Emily in Britain had already been decided. I can't believe Khrushchev fell for it.'

'Perhaps he didn't fall for anything' said Summerfield. 'Has it ever occurred to you the Soviets don't want war any more than we do?'

CHAPTER 10
THE VETERAN & THE
GREEN SHIELD STAMP PROTEST

May 8th 1998

Emilie Weston pulled into the car park and displayed her parking permit. She collected the wreath commemorating the victory in Europe fifty three years earlier from the back seat before opening the boot of the Alfa Romeo and collecting the bouquet. She had laboured at some length on the choice of flowers for the bouquet, eventually choosing belladonna lilies, as recommended by the florist, for their communication of pride, irises for wisdom and courage and freesias for innocence, trust and friendship. These were complimented with delicate fluffy fragrant pink and white peonies.

A crowd had gathered outside the Town Hall. She considered taking the back entrance but didn't. As she neared the gathering, she could hear a slow rhythmic chanting. *Say no to Tesco don't let them kill our High Street,* over and over, *Say no to Tesco don't let them kill our High Street.* Emilie studied the wording of a home-made placard constructed with a square of discoloured white ply board nailed onto a wooden baton. Hand painted words in black paint read SAY NO TO THE..... some attempt at over painting the last line had been made and now read in letters so narrow and small as to be difficult to read; CORPORATE BANDITS. On a closer look Emilie could see the over painted word had been BOMB. Jane Doherty, the self-proclaimed spokesperson and leader of the Markets Association, was waving a placard which read MASSACRE OF THE MARKET.

'Hello Jane' said Emilie as she tried to pass.

'Are you hear to speak on the Planning application this afternoon?' asked Jane.

'No, I'm afraid not.'

'Why not? I thought you'd be supporting us.'

'Well I did expect to have a full day of engagements.'

'I heard what happened last night. Looks like you'll be free now then doesn't it?'

Emilie realised she'd fallen into an ambush.

'I haven't been granted leave to speak and The Speakers list will have been finalised' contended Emilie. 'You don't need me Jane, you're quite capable of making your own case, I'm sure of that.'

Emilie's attempt at flattery failed.

'I don't know what we elect you people for. You're never there when you're needed' exclaimed Jane. 'They'll finish us, they won't be happy until they've killed our trade, you know it and you just couldn't care less.'

Another placard which read B*LL*CKS TO TESCO was being waved frantically. Emilie was about to ask for the offensive language to be removed when the offending plasterboard placard fell from its baton. The board struck Emilie on the back of the head wrong footing her and she toppled face first to the floor. The fall caused a hole in both of her black stockings and her grazed knees started to bleed. She gathered herself on the arm of a wheelchair and got herself back on her feet checking herself for signs of a head injury. An old man sitting in the wheelchair, sporting a host of medals pinned to the chest of his stained threadbare jacket, was doing his utmost to balance a precarious placard that read BRING BACK THE GREEN SHIELD STAMPS.

'I'm so sorry' said Emilie steadying herself. 'I think you're at the wrong protest Sir' she said, pointing up to his sign.

'I still hear em' he exclaimed suddenly, taking her by the hand. 'The machine gunners, I hear em all night long, the noise is terrible, terrible.'

'What do you hear?' Emilie asked.

'The guns I tell yer, the guns, I hear em all through the night, they keep me awake they do.'

'Are you here with someone?'

'It's the guns you know, they never stop, never.'

'Who did you come with?' Emilie asked, glancing around for a clue as to who might be concerned for him but she didn't catch the eye of anyone, so she tried again.

'Who brought you here? Who are you with? Did you come with Jane?'

'Never a minute's peace yer know, the gunners they haunt me they do, I'm haunted.'

'What's your name?'

'Bernard Radcliffe, reporting for duty Ma'am.'

'Where do you live Bernard?'

'Do you hear em?' he asked. 'The guns, do you hear em?'

'No, thankfully I don't. Do you know where you live?'

'Of course I know where I live. Do I look stupid?'

'No, of course you don't look stupid. You look like you were once a very courageous man. Where do you live?'

'In Aitone.'

'Where in Aitone?'

'In Aitone.'

'Which street?' she shouted, over the escalating protest. 'What is your address?'

'Lawrence Street.'

'What number?'

'Are you sure you don't hear em? It was terrible last night, went on all through the night. You should find em and put an end to it.'

Emilie concluded she wasn't going to get a house number from the old veteran.

'Is this gentleman with you?' she asked, tapping the shoulder of the man standing closest.

The man shrugged his shoulders. 'Nar, he wa' 'ere when we go' 'ere.'

'If you'll excuse me Sir, I have an appointment inside' said Emilie, gently squeezing the old man's arm before disappearing into the safe and tranquil surroundings of the town hall.

'Morning Joyce' smiled Emilie signing the attendance book at reception.

'I heard about last night. Tragic' said Joyce 'and what a disappointment for you. Here we all were, thinking you were gonna be the Mayor.'

'Yes, well I'm trying to keep things in perspective. My disappointment is nothing compared to the loss for some now is it? I don't mind saying I am disappointed though.'

'I bet you are. It's such a shame. We're all in shock. I really liked Councillors Hopkin and Constance, they were so nice to me and Councillor Flatliner he was so handsome, he used to make me blush he did. I didn't really get to know young Dana Coxstable, what with her Mother being new and all, but she seemed very nice. There was a Councillor I didn't like very much though. I thought he was a right bully. I was always intimidated by him but I won't name names, it's not proper to speak ill of the dead now is it?'

'Quite right' whispered Emilie leaning into the desk. 'Don't worry your secret is safe with me, I'll never intimidate you. Best not say it again though just to be on the safe side eh? You never know when Mrs Wallmichaels might walk in.'

'Oh, I never said it was Councillor Wallmichaels.'

'I think you'll find you did, not in so many words perhaps, but mum's the word.'

'Right you are Councillor. Mrs Taylor-Dunfould is expecting you, go straight up.'

'Thanks, see you later. Oh Joyce, do you know who the old man out there is?'

'Which one?'

'The man in the wheelchair with all the medals, who wants to bring back the Green Shield stamps.'

'No, I've never seen him before.'

'OK, thanks.'

Emilie took the stairs to the third floor, followed the long narrow corridor past the Legal Department and tapped on the last door before entering.

'I think you'll be needing these' said Emilie, thrusting the bouquet and the wreath of red poppies at Destry Taylor-Dunfould. Destry was head of the Civic office.

'Thanks. I have got a spare wreath or two' she said gesturing at a stack of red poppies on top of the filing cabinet.

'What happened to these?' she asked, looking disapprovingly at the dishevelled bouquet.

'A small mishap outside' replied Emilie. 'The damage isn't too bad.'

'Em, if you say so. So how are you this morning?'

'Feeling a bit redundant, if I'm honest.'

'I'll bet you are, bit of a fiasco last night. I imagine we'll make the front page of the Post and the Telegraph today. It wouldn't surprise me if we haven't taken up a few column inches in the dailies, I saw Mr Rodney running out with his notepad.'

'Has there been any more information about the accident and what happened?' enquired Emilie.

'Not really. I'm expecting the Police in a few minutes. They're with the Chief Executive at the moment. I think I'm next on the list. You can wait if you want, I'm sure they'll want to talk to everyone at some point. You could get it over and done with.'

'I don't know what they think I can tell them but I'll hang around, if only out of curiosity. While I'm here, have you got the number for the Soldier's Sailor's and Air Force Association?'

'Yes, I can find it why?'

'There's an old veteran outside wearing all his medals who I think might need some support. He just keeps ranting on about hearing the guns. I can't get any sense out of him. I think senility must have stepped in. I thought someone at SSAFA might be able to help him.'

'I thought the anti-Tesco protestors were out there.'

'Yeah they are. He's with them, waving his placard and demanding we bring back Green Shield stamps. All of life is out there, I'm telling you, all of life.'

'Green Shield stamps? Crikey, that's going back a bit. Here's the number.'

'While I'm speaking to them, can you see if you can find him on the register of electors? Bernard Hughes, Lawrence Street. I gave up trying to get the house number, he wouldn't stop going on about the wretched guns.'

'There is no Bernard Radcliffe' whispered Destry.

'Are you sure?'

'I'm sure' she scanned the register again. 'No.'

'Perhaps he gave me the wrong name, he did seem very confused. Are there any Radcliffe's?'

'No.'

'Any Bernards?'

'No.'

'Perhaps he's not registered to vote' suggested Emilie. 'He will still have a Council Tax account though, even if he hasn't registered to vote. Can we find him that way?'

'I'll call down to the Exchequer section' said Destry, picking up the telephone receiver.

Someone knocked on the door while Destry was still on the phone. Emilie went to let whoever it was in. Two Police Officers stood in the doorway.

'Hello, Mrs Taylor-Dunfould is expecting you, please come in.'

'And you are?' asked one of the Constables.

'I'm Emilie Weston, Councillor Emilie Weston.'

The Officer flicked through the pages of his notepad.

'Oh yes, Mrs Weston, you are also on our list. We'd like to speak to you when we've finished with Mrs Taylor-Dunfould if you don't mind waiting outside.'

'I don't mind waiting in here if you want to speak to us together, save you some time.'

'No, we'd like to speak to you separately, so if you don't mind waiting outside.'

'Well as you can see, Destry is on the phone, so do you want to do me first, while you wait?'

'No. We'd like to speak to Mrs Taylor-Dunfould first so if you don't mind waiting outside.'

The Constable opened the door.

'I'll be with you in a moment gentlemen' said Destry 'I'm just dealing with a matter for Councillor Weston.'

The two Constables shifted uncomfortably on their feet.

'How rude of me, please sit down while you're waiting' said Emilie clearing piles of papers from two chairs. 'Can I get you a cup of coffee?'

'No, thank you' the taller one replied.

'Exchequer have no record of him either.'

'How strange, perhaps I'll go back down and try and talk to him again.'

'Aren't you staying?'

'No, they want to talk to us alone. I'll be in reception when you're ready for me Officers.'

Emilie stepped back out into the throng of the protest. More people had gathered. She looked around. The old veteran was nowhere to be seen.

'Have you seen an old man in a wheelchair?' she asked repeatedly going from person to person before asking Jane Doherty.

'The old man in the wheelchair, have you seen him?'

'No, not for a while.'

'Did you see him go?'

'Do you mean the old guy with all the medals?'

'Yes'

'No, I didn't.

'How can he have just disappeared? He was in a wheelchair for God's sake, he can't have moved that fast. How can no one have seen him leave?'

Jane shrugged her shoulders. 'Perhaps he realised he was in the wrong place. There's a service at the cenotaph today isn't there?'

'Yes, but that's not until eleven. It's only nine thirty. Why would he have had a placard calling for the reinstatement of Green Shield stamps if he was going to the war memorial?'

'Beats me, now if you'll excuse me Councillor, *SAY NO TO TESCO DON'T LET THEM KILL OUR HIGH STREET, SAY NO TO TESCO DON'T LET THEM KILL OUR HIGH STREET.*'

Emilie walked towards the High Street across the bright civic garden displays of yellow daffodils and tulips intermixed with bright pansies and hyacinths. She crossed the busy Derby Road pausing for a change in signal at the pedestrian crossing before passing the picture window of the local estate agent with its selection of suburban houses for sale and rent. She passed the ornate terrace of tall Victorian houses that now housed the bank, the fireplace showroom and the cycling centre, pausing again to cross at Regent Street with its rows of tiny, two-up two down, terraced cottages. At a break in the traffic she took her chance and made haste to cross. Another impressive banking façade gave way to the Florist with its extensive array of willow planters, dried flowers in arrangements and fresh flowers in a staged display. The old cinema, now a home for the pigeons, was boarded up, casting its perpetual gloom. Next to the cinema, the large dirty picture window of a Victorian sweet shop. The shelves of jars, full of boiled sweets, had a resigned dusty look that suggested none of the jars had been moved in a very long time. She formed another orderly queue at the crossing in front of the bustling bread shop with its usual queue of old ladies waiting patiently outside for their soft white rolls. After crossing into the old market place where a carousel was setting up in readiness for the weekend trade, she glanced around for any sign of the old man before walking back the way she had come on the opposite side of the road. The front door of the Corner Pin Public House was closed. She glanced down the High Street where folk on a mission, armed with shopping bags, bustled about, disappearing and reappearing from shop doors. The owner of the camping shop was still in the process of displaying his wares outside. The Victorian Zionist church that once had dominated the street was long gone, having been demolished and replaced with a row of unimaginative shop fronts. She passed the Building Society, hosted in another impressive red brick Victorian double fronted building with mullioned windows and intricate lattice friezes then onward, past York Chambers, another architectural triumph of a bygone age, a hark back to a time when Aitone had come of age and enjoyed all the successes of the industrial revolution. The town's fortunes had been made following the construction of the mills and the lace making factories. She paused again at Therm House with its imposing Art Deco facade that had been raised from the ground in the 1930's for the Gas Works but was now The Oxford, a tired banqueting suite in dire need of refurbishment. The ancient Church yard of St Laurence sat tucked away behind the tall roadside buildings. Its extensive cemetery nestled under the gloomy canopy of an avenue of mature trees. In front of the church yard stood the proud war memorial, a tall old English cross in Limestone, protected behind wrought iron railings. The memorial had been steam cleaned and repaired the previous year. Emilie paused again and looked around. There was no sign of the old veteran. Vexed at not being able to find him, she trundled back to the Town Hall and forced her way through the barrage of protestors. The two Constables were waiting in reception. Jane Doherty appeared from nowhere and thrust a piece of paper in her hands.

'What's this?' asked Emilie.

'That's what you're going to say at the planning hearing this afternoon' ordered Jane.

'Oh no, you can't do that, put words into my mouth like that. I'm here to represent the interests of everyone not just the noisy few' argued Emilie. 'Besides, I've told you, I haven't been given leave to speak.'

'You have now. You're replacing Ted Soames who can't make it.'

'No Jane. I'll speak if I have to but I'll say what I think should be said not what you think should be said and you might not like what I have to say.'

'You'll say what we want you to say, that's why we vote for you.'

'But you don't vote for me, as you've made so abundantly clear in the past. *You're a Socialist through and through and wouldn't be seen dead voting for Tory scum;* I think were your exact words.'

'Aye, that may be so, but you are Tory scum and Tory scum are pro-business so I expect you to speak up for business and that includes us.'

With that, Jane Doherty turned on her heels and ventured back outside to arouse another bout of *SAY NO TO TESCO DON'T LET THEM KILL OUR HIGH STREET, SAY NO TO TESCO DON'T LET THEM KILL OUR HIGH STREET.*'

Emilie beckoned the two Constables across.

'We can talk down here where it's quieter' she said, leading the way down some steps, past the entrance to the Council Chamber and the stairs to the public gallery and into a small room with a window that overlooked the protest. She adjusted the blind and sat down behind a desk.

'There's never a dull moment' she smiled. 'Now what can I do to help you?'

The tall Officer took out his notepad. 'You were here last night?'

'Yes.'

'You were expected to be inaugurated as the new Mayor?'

'I was.'

'What time did you arrive?'

'Well, I was supposed to be here just after seven for a meeting at seven thirty but the traffic was a nightmare, the place was gridlocked, so it was probably just after eight when I finally arrived.'

'What time did you leave home?'

'Like I said, just before seven. In normal circumstances it only takes about ten minutes to drive in.'

'Was anyone else at home when you left?'

'Yes, my two boys. I had expected my husband to be at home. We were supposed to be leaving together but he called to say he was caught in traffic and was going to be late so he planned to meet me here.'

'How old are your two boys?'

'Sam is thirteen and Miles is ten.'

'Were your children home alone?'

'Yes, no, not exactly. The two children from next door had come for dinner.'

95

'Do you normally leave your children at home alone?'

The tone of the question caused Emilie to adopt a defensive demeanour which she tried to disguise.

'No, only the boys decided they didn't want to accompany us and had made arrangements for the neighbour's two children to stay with them, so I decided to cut them some slack and let them stay at home. They are sensible boys.' Emilie crossed her fingers under the desk. 'We only expected to be out for a few hours, they were going to watch TV and the neighbour was home if they had any problems.'

'And where were you yesterday?'

'In the morning I was in Keyworth and after lunch West Bridgford. I left around four thirty and went home.'

'What were you doing?'

'Bookkeeping, that's my day job. I only do this part-time. You certainly couldn't make a living from it'.

'You're a busy lady.'

'I suppose I am, although the day job is only part-time as well.'

'Can someone verify these whereabouts?'

'Yes. Do I need to have someone verify them?'

'Were you aware the five Councillors were going to be travelling together?'

'We often car share. The car parks get rammed, especially when the full Council is sitting. The Annual meeting of the Council is always the busiest of the year because there are so many invited guests. In answer to your question, no, I didn't know they were all travelling together and I don't know who was driving. Who was driving incidentally?'

Her question remained unanswered.

'Three of the deceased Councillors were past Mayors. Is that correct?'

'Yes. Councillors Coxstable and Flatliner were newly elected at the last intake.'

The tall Constable gestured to the window from where the noise of the crowd outside could be heard.

'People get hot under the collar about the decisions of Council' he said. 'As far as you are aware, were any of the deceased Councillors involved in any recent decisions that may have been contentious?'

'There's always some contention in what we do, always someone who thinks you should have done X instead of Y or thinks you should have increased spending on this at the expense of that or you should have planted red pansies instead of blue. In essence, that's about as contentious as it gets. We're a lowly District Council. We're about public conveniences, dustbins, parks and open spaces, we don't get involved in matters of war and peace, that's well above our pay grade I assure you.'

'Were any of the deceased Councillors due to speak at this afternoon's hearing?'

'Yes Councillor Hopkin.'

'In your opinion, is her absence likely to make a difference to the outcome of the hearing?'

'I wouldn't have thought so. I expect she will already have been substituted with another Council member from our group.'

'Do you know who the substitution will be?'

'No, you'll have to ask the Party Whip.'

'So there's a whip? Does that mean you are told how you must vote at planning hearings?'

'There's no party whip on matters of planning. Its evidence based on individual merit, subject to the Council's Town Planning policies.'

'Do you know how Councillor Hopkin was intending to vote?'

'No. Councillors aren't in the habit of discussing their personal opinions in public before a hearing lest they are seen to have fettered their discretion before all the evidence has been presented. That might leave a decision open for challenge on procedural bias.'

'If we can go back to the car sharing, do you share your car with colleagues?'

'Not often, no. Like you've already said, I'm busy and due to the nature of my work, most of the time I'm driving from one place to another. I often come straight in from the office and since my office changes from day to day, I can never plan in advance where I'm going to be.'

'Are you able to shed any light on why Councillor Wallmichaels was sharing a car with Councillors from Ilson in the north of the Borough and didn't instead come in with the Councillors from the south of the Borough?'

'No, I'm afraid I can't. Was Councillor Wallmichaels driving?'

'Yes. He left his home in Gritty Hectare to drive nine miles in the opposite direction to collect Councillors at various addresses across Ilson. He then drove to Dual Abbey to collect the daughter of Councillor Coxstable before driving nine miles back. Was that something he did often?'

'I don't know. I wouldn't have thought so. All the Ilson Councillors drive, or at least they did, and all had use of their own cars, even young Councillor Flatliner who I know had just taken possession of a shiny new Audi. The last time I saw him, he was proudly showing it off.'

'So why do you think Councillor Wallmichaels was driving and not Councillor Flatliner?'

'Perhaps Councillor Wallmichaels had an engagement in the north of the Borough yesterday afternoon.'

'No he didn't, he was in a meeting here all afternoon until five.'

'Then I've no idea, perhaps the families can tell you. Do you have any idea what caused the accident?' asked Emilie.

'You will no doubt be reading this in tonight's press so you may as well know. We have launched a murder investigation.'

'Murder?' exclaimed Emilie.

'Yes. All five inhabitants of the vehicle were shot.'

'Shot?' she repeated.

'Yes, at close range.'

CHAPTER 11
THE SWAP

August 29th 1899

The summer sun was already suggestive of another hot day ahead when Sister Edith, having napped for just two hours, crossed the gardens from the manor house back to the cottage of William and Summer Newlove. William was loitering at the door to the greenhouse.

'Good morning Sister' he said, beckoning her over. 'I think we are in for another fine day. You're here early this morning.'

'An hour lost at daybreak is a day wasted, looking for it' she replied curtly. 'How are you this morning Mr Newlove?'

'I'm very well, thank you. I've been propagating a number of cuttings taken from the Boston ivy on the east wall of Grace Dieu. I intend to plant them around the door of the cottage. I should have a fine choice of healthy saplings by next spring.'

'You enjoy your work in the garden don't you?' she asked.

'I do indeed. I couldn't imagine being happy anywhere else and certainly not doing anything else. I'm very fortunate to be able to do what I love. I do know that.'

'Have you never considered taking up a position elsewhere, Kew for instance? I'm sure that with your credentials and obvious enthusiasm, it would be possible to secure employment there.'

'Without my beautiful Summer? No, I'd never leave her' he said resolutely, collecting a small pot filled with compost and a small twig sticking out. 'Nor my new little Ivy.'

'You wouldn't have to leave them. You could take them with you.'

'I don't think so Sister. I'm not an explorer. I'd hate being away for months on end searching for new specimens. Besides, I'm not very fond of boats.'

'I'm sure there are many opportunities for employment that don't involve travel William. Have you been?'

'Where?'

'Kew.'

'Yes. Lord and Lady Newlove took me on the train when the gardens were celebrating the twenty fifth anniversary of the construction of Temperant House. It was very impressive. I remember it took me one hundred and fifty paces to cross from one end to the other.'

'So you won't consider it? There's enjoyable work you could do, important work even, that would bring you great satisfaction and perhaps some recognition.'

'But Summer loves it here and for that matter so do I. Besides, I've heard there is terrible poverty in London with people forced to live in overcrowded unsanitary slum dwellings, where the privies are shared with the neighbours and you have to do down to the street to use them. I hear disease is rife, the pay is inadequate for the rents the landlords charge and the only thriving enterprises are those of charlatism and crime.'

'You're very well informed, to a degree at least. The life for some people unfortunate enough to find themselves in the east of the city is just as you describe, the conditions are indeed abominable. There is great poverty, chiefly among the unskilled labourers, the Costermongers and the sweated workers. Elsewhere in the city, the conditions are considerably better.'

'I thank you for taking the time to enquire as to my future prospects Sister and I'm not ungrateful for it, but we are happy here.'

'So be it, then I'll bid you goodbye and wish you a good day William.'

'I am hoping to pay a visit to my wife and child after breakfast. I've already tried but the formidable Sister Agnes drove me down the stairs and out of the house.'

Had he have been talking to anyone but Sister Edith, he'd have added the term *old battle-axe* to his description of Sister Agnes, but out of respect, he held his tongue at formidable.

'Your wife has been through quite an ordeal, she needs to rest. Perhaps a visit this afternoon will be in order if Summer feels up to it. I'm just going to check on them now.'

'Thank you Sister. I know they are in capable hands. My Father holds the Sisters of Saint Dominic in very high regard.'

'Have you seen young Sparrow this morning?' she asked.

'No, not since the early hours when she returned to the abbey. I can fetch her if she's needed.'

'No, that's not necessary, there's work to be done at the abbey. The naive girl was rather overcome with her first experience of childbirth. I think its best she's left with mundane chores today in order that she may reflect on the experience. Now, if you'll excuse me Mr Newlove, the devil finds work for idle hands.'

'Of course Sister, I've plenty of work to be getting on with. The tomato harvest is proving to be most fruitful this year. We're going to have a tomato surplus until midwinter if the weather continues to be kind to us and we don't experience an early frost.'

'Oh, William I nearly forgot. Lady Noel would like you to tend to the Wisteria in the courtyard before lunch.'

'Is that so? I can't think why. I tied in the new shoots last month and it hasn't produced its second bloom yet. I don't usually tend to the Wisteria until October. The second flush is never as vigorous as the first, but she's still a thing of beauty none the less. I'll have a look at it when I've finished collecting the tomatoes; perhaps the main trunk has sprung a secondary shoot. I've left a basket of tomatoes by the door of the cottage to go to the abbey, you can take them if you're going back or I can give them to Brother Hipwood later.'

'Thank you William. Brother Hipwood has gone on an errand this morning. He'll collect them when he returns.'

Sister Agnes was asleep in a chair at the side of Summer's bed.

'All is well?' asked Edith after arousing Agnes from her light slumber.

'Yes Sister, she's stirred a number of times but I've managed to settle her down.'

Edith walked over to the dresser and using the pestle and mortar, prepared a solution of boiled water into which she added some crushed chloral hydrate.'

'When she wakes give her this and make sure she takes it. I'll be taking the infant to Grace Dieu shortly and then I shall be taking a walk into the village to see the Postmaster.'

Edith stepped across the landing and took up a seat beside Mrs Blackburn who was nursing the new baby from a rocking chair in the nursery.

'The Doctor would like to examine the child' Edith whispered. 'There's no urgency he won't be arriving for a few hours yet. Is the infant feeding well?'

'Yes, very well' replied Mrs Blackburn adjusting her position and removing her undergarment to reveal her second breast. Gently she turned the baby around. It latched on and continued suckling.

'Quite an appetite' smiled Edith.

'There isn't a problem is there? Mrs Blackburn asked.

'No dear.'

'It's just you said the Doctor had been called.'

'It's a new formality' said Edith. 'I've been delivering healthy babies for fifty years and now all of a sudden, the Doctors insist on involving themselves in the process. That men think they know more about childbirth than the women who have been practising it since the dawn of time only goes to demonstrate the arrogance of their gender.'

'Perhaps not all midwives are as conscientious or as capable as you Sister.'

'I'll return when the doctor arrives. Sister Agnes will continue to take care of the diaper. The Sisters will be leaving in a few days so until then, please allow us to help. Once we've left, your new charge will afford you very little time to rest.'

'Thank you Sister, you are very kind' whispered Mrs Blackburn, adjusting the baby's tiny white woollen bonnet to reveal a fine lock of jet black hair.

When Edith arrived back at Grace Dieu, having concluded her business with the Postmaster, Brother Hipwood's carriage was already outside the manor and the horse had been stabled. She tugged on the doorbell and waited to be invited in. Lady Noel appeared with a tiny bundle wrapped in a white swaddling sheet. The baby was howling.

'I can't do anything with him' said Lady Noel. 'I've tried everything I can think of. He doesn't want to eat, his diaper is fresh, he won't sleep and as you can see he won't be rocked.'

'Give him to me' said Edith, hoisting the little bundle over her shoulder as though he were a sack of coal. She rubbed the palm of her hand swiftly up and down the length of his tiny back then round and round in a circular motion before staring the process again. Eventually the baby released a loud belch which gave way to silence.

'Thank you Edith, you have performed a miracle' exclaimed Lady Noel. 'I was becoming quite agitated with the incessant screaming. I don't think I've ever heard such anger emerge with such ferocity from such a tiny creature in all my life.'

Edith passed the baby boy back to Lady Noel who hesitantly took him into her arms. 'I'll fetch the Newlove baby' said Edith. 'I've told Mrs Blackburn the Doctor is calling to examine the child.'

'What about Summer?'

'She's been given something to help her sleep so I doubt we'll be hearing anything from Summer until this afternoon, at which time she can be united with her baby.'

When Edith arrived at the cottage the infant was sleeping soundly in the nursery crib. Both Agnes and Mrs Blackburn were dozing. She lifted the baby girl out and carried her downstairs, placing her in the perambulator and covering her with a delicate white crocheted shawl until just her ruddy wrinkled face could be seen. She lifted the rain hood until it clicked into position and crossed the garden back to Grace Dieu Manor where the two babies were exchanged.

Edith was crossing back towards the cottage when William Newlove came bounding across the lawn, sprinting with such pace Edith wondered whether the Devil himself was in pursuit.

'Is this my daughter?' he asked excitedly, peering into the perambulator.

'This is your Son' said Edith 'and what a handsome little creature he is.'

William looked perplexed.

'I thought it was a girl' he said. 'Sparrow told me it was a girl. She said I had a beautiful daughter.'

'Oh dear, Sparrow, as I explained to you this morning, is a foolish girl who knows at best, very little about most things, including it would appear, the difference between girls and boys. It can be difficult to tell what with all the blood and the umbilical cord and then there's the placenta and sometimes...'

'Thank you Sister, I think I've heard enough, you can stop there.'

'The child has much to learn but her heart is in the right place. I realised Sparrow had been labouring under a mistake as to the gender of the baby but I'm afraid I had no idea that mistake had been conveyed to you. I can assure you William, your child is a most beautiful baby boy. I'm sorry if Sparrow's naivety misled you, had I realised you were labouring under such a misunderstanding I would have corrected it earlier.'

'But this morning when I mentioned my Ivy....'

'I thought you were talking about your plants, the Boston ivy, not your child.'

William accepted the explanation without argument and leaned in to take a closer look at his new offspring.

'Hello my little man. Who does he look like Edith? People say babies always look more like one parent than the other, don't they? Who do you see, me or Summer?'

'It's difficult to tell' said Edith. 'I can never see it myself. I think features change from day to day.'

'Can I see my wife now?' he asked.

'She is still asleep. I'll come and find you when she wakes up. Don't stray too far from the greenhouse and William, a word of advice, babies aren't always easy to love, people have a romantic notion that they will be, but they're not, not always. Sometimes you have to dig into a place you never knew existed to find the strength to love a child.'

'I won't ever have to dig very far for my child' he replied. 'Don't forget to come and find me.'

CHAPTER 12
SO LONG GOD OF THUNDER

November 1962

Dusk was drawing in as the Globemaster, with its four large wing-mounted propeller driven engines, appeared on the horizon. Its bulbous cartoon nose came into view as it circled overhead. The deep bellied cargo plane missed its first approach to the runway. The pilot applied full throttle to garner sufficient thrust for a go-around. The raucous engines thundered under the Herculean task and the ground crew all stopped what they were doing to look skyward. The lumbering mammoth gained altitude and banked sharp right. A few minutes later it came in for a second approach and touched down on the runway with a heavy thud, its six tyres throwing up a trail of dust in their wake. When it had come to a halt, the cargo doors below the cockpit slowly opened, like a giant pair of silver curtains revealing its empty belly.

The first of the missiles to be returned to the United States was already secured on a low loading truck outside the hangar. Captain Montgomery stood and watched as the white long bodied rocket was negotiated into the hold. He noticed Pilot Officer James Wingfield on the tarmac. He was remonstrating with another USAF Officer.

'I can't say I'm sorry to see them go' said Wing Commander Holbrook who appeared alongside Montgomery.

'The Americans or the missiles?' asked Montgomery, continuing to scrutinise Wingfield and the developing fracas. The raised voices carried on the breeze but the distance was too great to hear what was being said.

'What do you think is going on over there?' asked Holbrook. 'Someone's hot under the collar about something.'

'I could hazard a guess' Montgomery scoffed. 'The sooner the son-of-a-bitch gets on the plane the better.'

'Who?'

'Wingfield.'

'Wingfield?'

'Yes, Wingfield' snapped Montgomery.

'What did I miss?' asked Holbrook.

'It's a long story.'

'I've got all night. You can tell me about it. Fancy a pint?'

'Not until I see that plane taking off with him on board.'

'I didn't think the personnel were leaving for weeks.'

'He is.'

'How come?'

'Like I said, it's a long story.'

'I've always found him a pretty decent sort of chap. Always kept his calm when others were running around like headless chickens, knew his job, did it well, was popular in the Mess and not just with the officers, with the ladies too I gather.'

Montgomery sneered.

'I wish I had half of what he appears to have when it comes to the ladies' continued Holbrook. 'Never had much luck in that regard I'm afraid to say. Even the ugly ones with a face only a Mother could love or an ass like the back of a bus. I'd have liked to have been blessed with just half the charm Mr Wingfield appears to possess.'

Montgomery still didn't bite.

'I'm fishing here Monte; throw me a bone for pity's sake. What do you know that I don't? Why is he going back to the States now?'

'I expect they'll be late taking off now' said Montgomery, avoiding the question, 'after that bungled landing. Don't you have anything to do?'

'Is that your way of saying you want me to bugger off?'

'Yes.'

'Right you are. I can take a hint. I'll be in the Wheatsheaf enjoying a pint and a Hamburger. I don't suppose we'll get Hamburgers and Hot Dogs again, once this lot have gone. They'll probably go back to serving that ghastly Shepherd's Pie or worse still, that revolting Liver with onions. I'll miss the Americans, if only for their Hamburgers. Why do you suppose they call them Hamburgers when they're made from ground beef?'

'You've been Americanised too I see' Montgomery sneered. 'You'll be telling me you actually like Elvis Presley next.'

'Actually I do. Mrs Hart has been teaching me how to rock and roll. Well, she's been trying. Two left feet I'm afraid, all that hopping, skipping and twisting, it's all too much for me.'

'I'm looking forward to the return of some decorum in the Mess. I haven't heard the Glenn Miller records I provided played once. Didn't you say you were going to the Wheatsheaf?'

'Yes, and you're very welcome to come and join me if you want to. I'll be in till closing time.'

The closing of the cargo doors signalled an end to the theatrics of loading and the ground crew began to disperse. James Wingfield came out of the hangar with a hold all over his shoulder and sauntered in Montgomery's direction, a large cigar hanging from the corner of his mouth.

'I guess this is it then' said Wingfield inviting a hand shake. 'This is where we part company. No hard feelings Captain.'

'No hard feelings?' Montgomery seethed. 'Is that all you've got to say?'

'I understand you're a little pissed. I'd probably be a little pissed too if I were in your position, but what's done is done. It's too late now to do anything about it.'

'Do you have no honour at all?'

'I have honour alright. It's just that your opinion of what constitutes honour happens to be different to mine. Let's get one thing straight Captain. I didn't make any of them do anything they didn't want to do. They wanted a good time. I showed them a good time.'

'And now you're scurrying off into the night like a deceptive little weasel.'

'Excuse me Captain, but I thought it was as a result of your request, that I've been sent packing.'

Have you even bothered to say goodbye to her?'

'I'm no good with goodbyes, I don't see the point and since you mention deceptive weasels, isn't it you British who say *it takes one to one know one*?'

'What exactly do you mean by that?'

'I mean that when it comes to deception I think we both know that you hold all the aces. Don't think I don't know what goes on in that laboratory. I have eyes and ears you know, not that I've needed to use them. Flight Lieutenant McDermott gets very talkative when he's had one too many. Men with big mouths and secrets to keep really shouldn't drink if they can't keep their mouths shut. Don't worry Captain, your secret's safe with me. I couldn't care less what you've been up to and I happen to like McDermott, I'm not interested in seeing him arrested. He's pretty pissed with you mind and I can't say I blame him.'

'What are you talking about? Arrested for what?'

'For impersonating an officer for starters but like I said, I'm out of here, I don't give two hoots.'

'Don't take that tone with me Pilot Officer. It's not too late. I could still have you court martialled for insubordination.'

'What tone is that? Look, I came over here in good faith to shake your hand, man to man, and leave with some mutual understanding.'

'The only thing you understand is how to shirk your responsibility. If you were a man, you'd have made good your mistakes.'

'We don't know it's my mistake and it's not my responsibility. I made that quite clear to all of them. You ask if I didn't.'

'You cannot negate the consequences of your actions simply by saying that you do. Actions have consequences.'

'I don't understand. What it is you want from me Captain? You want me to marry her, is that it? Cos you know my reputation, and I'm not about to change.'

'Absolutely not. I wouldn't wish you on any woman, never mind my God daughter.'

'Good, that's settled then, because I'm an officer of the United States Air Force. I enjoy my job, I enjoy my life. I intend to continue going wherever they send me and I'm prepared to do whatever I have to do to get ahead. I'll even take orders from a trumped up little moron like you if I have to. I'm ambitious, I admit it, and I'll do whatever it takes to get me some more of those stripes you walk around with on your sleeve. If there's a bit of fun to be had along the way, then all the better; I'm a fun loving sort of guy and I'm not about to give all that up to shack up in this pathetic dreary little country with a bit of equally dreary English country skirt who couldn't wait to get her knickers off.'

Montgomery raised his fist, his teeth clenched, hatred and revulsion exploded into a single punch which knocked Wingfield to the floor.

He got up. Blood poured from his nose. He looked around. A small crowd was beginning to gather.

'I think you've broken my nose you old bastard.'

'I'd like to break a lot more than that.'

'No, Captain' shouted Bob Halford, sprinting across the tarmac from where he'd seen Montgomery lay Wingfield clean out. Halford took up a position between them to prevent either side from escalating hostilities and throwing a second punch.

'What the hell is going on with you two?'

'Nothing, Pilot Officer Wingfield was just leaving.'

'Fist fighting? Are you really reduced to fist fighting Monte? And in public, for God's sake. Get a hold of yourself man, or at least take it behind closed doors if you don't want a reprimand. What kind of example does this set to the junior officers?'

'Don't worry I'm leaving, there's nothing to see here' hollered Wingfield to the expectant onlookers who had gathered expecting a fight to unfold. Wingfield picked up his holdall, threw it over his shoulder and ambled toward the plane, pausing to say goodbye to the fellow airmen who'd remained on the tarmac to see him off. He reached the cabin, gave a final salute from the steps and boarded. The engines roared into action and the plane began its taxi toward the runway. Montgomery stood transfixed on the departing aircraft until the Globemaster became airborne and disappeared over the darkening horizon. *Good riddance* he muttered to himself.

A light drizzle began and Montgomery made his way to the lab. The administration section was unoccupied. He stopped at his own private office to hang up his great coat. The door to the decontamination room was unlocked. The light in the medical bay was on and the door was slightly ajar. The door to the lab was also unlocked. Dick McDermott was sitting at a table peering into a microscope.

'Where's Holbrook?' asked Montgomery.

'Medical bay' replied McDermott without looking up.

'I've a mind to have you arrested for treason.'

McDermott stopped what he was doing.

'What are you talking about?'

'I've just been speaking with Pilot Officer James Wingfield who informs me you've been sharing confidential information.'

'What kind of information?'

'Information about the work that goes on in here.'

'I've done no such thing. He's full of bullshit.'

'So you have never discussed the work that goes on in here?'

'No, absolutely not, why would I do that?'

'Well you wouldn't be the first to disclose national research and development secrets.'

'But why would I?'

'Many reasons; perhaps someone has been paying you for information. Political ideology; perhaps you're a Communist. The promise of improved resources for switching your allegiance; I know you're a greedy son-of-a-bitch. Blackmail, duress.'

'You've just accused me of passing secrets to an American airman. The last time I looked, the Americans were most definitely not Communists.'

'So you do know Wingfield's political ideology?'

'No, we never talked about politics, we didn't talk about much else either for that matter, but I suspect that on account of him being an American Airmen working on a ballistic missiles programme with warheads pointed towards Russian soil, its far more likely he'd be a capitalist than a Communist wouldn't you say?'

'Parity of technology' Montgomery added.

'What?'

'You asked why someone might divulge national secrets. I'm giving you another reason. Secrets have been known to have been given away simply because a traitor believes technology shouldn't be owned by an individual nation.'

'Stop, Captain, stop. That's the trouble with you military types. You're all so Goddamn paranoid about your state secrets, spies at every turn, everyone suspicious of everyone else, espionage and counter espionage, secret files and covert exchanges in the dark corners of the shadowy corridors of sinister intent. You're just as goddamn paranoid as the Russians and the Americans.'

'And we've had good reason to be.'

'Christ, not another lecture about Cairncross, Fuchs and Greenglass. I am not a Soviet Spy Captain. I'm not any sort of spy.'

'Are you mocking me Flight Lieutenant McDermott or making light of their actions?

'Who's actions?'

'Cairncross, Fuchs and Greenglass. They were traitors to this country.'

'No, I'm not making light of their actions, I agree, they were traitors. Passing atomic secrets to the Soviets wasn't cricket, but I haven't passed any secrets to anyone. If you don't believe me, then let's go and see Pilot Officer Wingfield. I'd like to hear from the horse's mouth what exactly I'm supposed to have told him.'

Harry Holbrook came in dressed in full scrubs. He lowered his face mask and removed a pair of latex gloves.

'What are you two arguing about? Some of us are trying to work. I can't hear myself think with all the noise.'

'How was it?' asked McDermott.

'It's done. Monkey's still out and will be for some time yet, but we'll need all hands on deck tomorrow, assuming it wakes up of course.'

'Any problems?'

'No, it all went swimmingly. I'm confident we managed to avoid vascular penetration and we can already see action potential spikes,

112

even in the comatose state. It's down to Mr Summerfield now to translate the output. We'll know more tomorrow.'

'Have you given any thought to my earlier suggestion?' McDermott asked.

'What, about the pig?'

'Yes.'

'I have. I think that provided the monkey survives we should probably go ahead in the next few days. We'll need to use the longer electrodes as the pig's head is bigger and the skull is thicker but they don't have the silicon carbide insulator so a second pig will be needed when longer electrodes with the new insulator is ready. We could postpone use of the first pig until the new electrodes are ready but time is unfortunately of the essence. I wish we didn't have to act in such haste but with the future so uncertain, I don't see that we have much of a choice if we're going to produce demonstrable results before we run out of time.'

CHAPTER 13
THE COHEN LEGACY

May 8th 1998

The Council Chamber was bustling with activity when Emilie Weston arrived. The public gallery on the first floor overlooking the chamber was full without a spare seat to be had. Emilie took up a seat to the right of the chamber. The Chairman commenced the hearing and led a minutes silence in remembrance of the lost Councillors. The Tesco application was the first item on the agenda. After the initial housekeeping rules, dictated by the Chairman, the Chief Planning Officer presented the case by means of a slide slow on an overhead projector. He was forced to halt the presentation on three occasions as the uproar from the assembled crowd made it impossible to be heard. The Chairman called for Order and announced the public gallery would be cleared should the uproar not be contained. The Planning Officer finished his presentation with a recommendation that the application be approved by the committee. A raucous round of booing and hissing metered out across the Chamber. The Chairman called for Order multiple times and it was only when he announced that a Constable would be called for, the groans of disapproval slowly petered out.

'I call Councillor Weston' announced the Chairman.

Emilie rose to her feet and looked around, glancing up towards the public gallery where Jane Doherty had risen from her front seat and was leaning over the balcony. A white bed sheet had been strung from the balcony railing which read simply BETRAYAL.

'Your five minutes begins now' announced the Chairman and the Democratic Services Administrator started the clock.

Emilie took a deep breath.

'It's very easy to stand here and defend the rights of the Market Traders to their fair share of trade. They do a sterling job. Whilst many of us may be fair weather shoppers, the traders don't enjoy that luxury and they turn up here three times a week come rain or shine. They stand there all day behind the shops on the High Street and suffer howling winds, freezing snow and baking heat. It's not an easy life and I'm sure there are easier ways to make a living. We've had a market in Aitone since the middle ages when the Royal Charter was granted to the town. Since then this town has been open for business. It will remain open for business provided it reflects the changing appetites of the public who use it.

Let's consider our Town Plan. This approved and adopted document states that land within the defined town centre boundary is considered suitable for retail development.

The application site has sat in dereliction for a generation since the demise of the gas works who occupied it. It sits within the town centre boundary therefore any refusal of the application would fly in the face of our own legal document. The applicant would appeal to the Planning Inspectorate against the decision of this committee and the first thing the Inspectorate would do would be to ask to see our adopted Town Plan. The land is either suitable for retail development or it isn't. We can't have it both ways and if we try to have it both ways all we will achieve is to incur settlement and legal costs in defending an indefensible position which ultimately the tax payers will pay for.

A young man by the name of Jack Cohen came home from war in 1919 and with his demob money, bought £3 worth of surplus groceries and paid to rent a market stall. It was five more years before Jack introduced his first own branded product when he purchased tea direct from T E Stockwell and repackaged it as TESCO, taking the TES from the supplier of the tea and the CO from his own surname. It was another five years before he opened his first actual store. His motto of *stack it high sell it cheap* is popular with the consumer, as attested to by the success of the brand. It's a philosophy that has helped to keep the cost of food affordable even for the most budget conscious. It's

115

been twenty years since Jack Cohen passed away but I think we'd have considered him a true entrepreneur and an asset to our Town had he have chosen Aitone in which to be open for business in 1919.

Protectionist policies are rarely beneficial to the consumer and the operation of cartels usually only serve the supply chain and are considered at odds with free and fair competition. Whilst it's not within the remit of this Council to impose competition legislation nor its responsibility to enforce it, only a fool would fail to recognise the potential for abuse of these powers when market share becomes too heavily dominated by a single player. Had policies of protectionism been practised historically then this town would never have prospered beyond its first and only lace mill and we wouldn't have the thriving, globally renowned upholstery sector we see today. Restricting new entrants to the market is not the answer. What we must do however is seek to ensure that entrants who have been invited into the market get a fair crack of the trading whip and this should extend to the market traders. I think they'd get a fairer crack of the whip if we considered the following; Footfall to the market stalls would be increased if they were allowed to trade in the original Market Place adjacent to the High Street instead of being tucked like an embarrassing secret behind the shops away from the passing trade. The Council might also consider offering some time-limited free parking, perhaps on Market days, so that traders on the High Street without the scope to create their own free car parks can compete on a level playing field.

Subject to a consideration of the aforementioned issues, I believe it is possible for the Council to be able to reconcile the needs of both its consumers who demand choice and value and have shown they are prepared to travel out of the area if we don't provide it; and the existing traders who demand a fair crack of the whip whilst welcoming Tesco with a genuine gratitude for the many jobs its very presence will create. Mr Chairman I thank you for your indulgence.'

With that, Emilie sank down into her chair and closed her eyes in order to avoid contact with the socialist Ms Doherty, who Emilie was in no doubt would be incandescent with rage. The following speakers all sang from essentially the same hymn sheet in their condemnation

116

of the capitalistic evil that was the supermarket. The market traders could never compete with its inequitable purchasing power, its endless range of discounted lines, lost leaders and loyalty schemes. They paid low wages and had unsociable working time contracts. The predisposition of customers to choose a one-stop-shop for convenience would be to the detriment of the market traders and should be denied as should the proposed free car parking. When the speakers list had been exhausted, each one determined to make the most of their allotted five minutes, irrespective of repetition, the Chairman called for a vote by a show of hands. The application was duly passed and the public gallery was dismissed. The more disgruntled observers moved towards the balcony railing hollering *shame on you* repeatedly. Someone unseen from the chamber called out something about *backhanders and brown paper envelopes*. The officers of the local press, who had been present at the back of the chamber throughout the hearing, scurried out with notepads poised, to solicit a headline quote for the next edition.

Once the furore had settled down, Emilie collected her belongings, respectfully lowered her head to the Chairman who was waiting to move onto the next item on the agenda and headed out of the swing door. She opted to take the back door to the car park in order to avoid another confrontation out front.

She arrived home and turned on the TV before rifling the fridge for the ingredients to cook a sausage and mash supper. A baby faced mopheaded blonde Telegraph journalist by the name of Boris Johnson was half way through narrating a news article from outside the picture window of an unnamed supermarket. …. *'the refrigerated cathedrals of a faithless age, run by commercial and political bullyboys. In our treacherous hearts'* he concluded *'we pretend to mourn the passing of the green grocer and the haberdasher but we wouldn't un-invent the supermarket, even if we could, because we love the convenience of the one-stop-shop.'*

CHAPTER 14
IVOR NEWLOVE & THE
DEMISE OF GRACE DIEU

August 1926

The pounding rain continued for the third day in a row casting a damp grey shadow over Grace Dieu. Ivor Newlove kicked the mud from his sturdy boots and hung his sodden coat out to dry before brewing a pot of tea which he carried on a tray upstairs.

Lord Noel lay in the old four poster mahogany bed, the blankets pulled up to his chin just where they had been when Ivor left Grace Dieu for the walk to the village newsagent to fetch the daily newspaper as he had done every day since his Grandfather became ill and took to his bed. He placed the tray on the table at the side of the bed and walked across the room to the window to open the curtains. Raindrops splashing on the panes obscured the view to the garden. The once beautifully kempt grounds so preciously attended by William Newlove had become overgrown, unloved and neglected. Thorny spines of undisciplined brambles scrambled across the grass which had all but turned to couch. The apple trees were in need of a good pruning and the apples, the result of a late bloom from the previous season were well rotten into the ground. The Rose garden had evolved into an intertwining mass of furled insect ridden leaves on coarse spindles displaying the remaining resilient rosehips.

Ivor returned to the bed and stirred the pot tapping the spoon against the china rim before replacing the teapot lid. The clinking sound alerted Lord Noel to his presence.

'I've brought you some tea Grandfather' said Ivor 'shall I pour it?'

'Yes please Ivor' said Lord Noel coughing into a handkerchief.

Ivor arranged the pillows which were in need of laundering and pulled Lord Noel up into them.

'I've taken the liberty of ordering a bronchial kettle' said Ivor. 'It should arrive in a few days. It won't cure your condition but I hope it will bring some mild relief from your symptoms. I'd like to change your chest plaster.'

Ivor unfastened the buttons on Lord Noel's nightshirt before removing the leather plaster. The beeswax softened by the temperature produced from a high fever stuck to the hairs on Lord Noel's chest as he pulled the plaster away and Lord Noel cursed with indignation.

'Don't be such a baby' Ivor teased, placing a fresh plaster into position and firming it into place with his fingertips. The sweet woody smell of frankincense soon filled the air.

'Have you brought the newspaper?' Lord Noel asked.

'Yes and there's a letter for you, airmail. Would you like me to open it?'

'Yes please and read it to me if you will.'

Ivor tore open the envelope.

My Dearest friend, confidante and ally,

I trust this letter finds you in better health and your prospects substantially improved.

It falls to me to send you news of both great joy and sadness. I regret to have to tell you that Sister Edith passed away this last winter. Her stubborn and relentless character afforded her the gift of a long life and I can report that she bore her end with such fortitude as those who knew her well would have expected. Her final resting place lays within the burial grounds of Cimetiere de la Chartreuse just a short distance from her beloved Saint Dominique's Notre Dame which doesn't have a burial ground since we know that this would have been Sister Edith's preferred final resting place. The parque Bordelais and the rive gauche of the Garonne river are close by and are the places she became accustomed to partaking of a daily constitutional stroll, which she stubbornly continued to do until just a few weeks before she died. No one is quite sure which gave out first, her legs or her will but with

119

the loss of the first came the second soon after. An appeal has been made for the addition of a suitable commemorative stone at the place of her internment should you wish to make a small contribution to this end.

I turn now to the joyous news that we have a new addition to the Compass Line and ask that you amend your manuscript to reflect this. Celeste recently gave birth to a beautiful girl who has the given name of Edith. The child will be raised by the Parisian family Calvaire who reside close to the Place du Tertre within the eighteenth arrondissement. The property stands just a few minutes' walk from the summit of Montmartre Hill in the shadow of the white dome of our recently constructed Sacre Coeur. The family are a trifle bohemian to my mind, preferring to engage in the artistic pursuits of painting and poetry rather than science and politics and I fear will not raise the child in a manner I myself would have chosen. However, that the child be placed with the Calvaire's had been Sister Edith's final wish and I felt obligated after her many trials and tribulations, to grant her this one last rite. Celeste prefers not to raise a child alone, there being no husband, so finding a surrogate child has not been necessary. Instead she chooses to spend her days at a local orphan house where there are many discarded children. Tuberculosis and Diphtheria are both rife and she spends many hours tending to their needs. She appears to strive in a constant state of exhausted satisfaction.

Angelique remains a loyal servant to France despite the circumstances of the tragic and untimely death of her husband, some ten years hence. She has never diverted from the opinion she formed in 1914, that war is much too important to leave to the Generals and she dedicates her time and energy mediating between the different departments of government. She remains greatly critical of the peace treaty signed by the allies in Versailles in June of 1919 which she maintains sought chiefly to humiliate Germany rather than offer a solution that will ensure long term peace between the nations. Neither does she have any faith in the longevity of the League of Nations to stabilise relations. One does worry about the fate of the German people and how they will fare under the imposition of such a heavy burden of reparations which can only result in the inevitable economic apocalypse for the country. The manner of her husband's death was, whilst most tragic, not unsurprising once the nature of it came to light. Under frigid and atrocious conditions, the French, unable to hold a defensive position, had been forced to capitulate at Artois. They were grossly outnumbered in both German troop numbers and heavy German artillery. Whilst the 30,000 strong French force defended a line of some eight kilometres against the 90,000 strong German force, fifty nine members of the regiment to which Monsieur Fontaine had been assigned were sent to defend the fort at Douaumont. It is believed he succumbed during the artillery barrage that ensued sometime after the 21st but before the 24th February when the Germans finally took the fort. A battle raged for three hundred days subsequently with offensives and counter offensives achieving very little by way of territory lost or gained by either the French or the Germans. By April there were over half a million French troops defending the front line at Verdun and there were great casualties on both sides with 300,000 lives lost as a result of the bloody battle which lasted until December 18th. Angelique's criticism is that Generals diverted resources to the Somme in the north at the expense of support for those charged with defending the fort at Douaumont. Both she and Celeste continue to take a pilgrimage to Verdun each February. The one lesson I have learnt from this sorry experience my dear friend, is that the path of allowing our finest young women to marry for reasons of romance and reciprocated passion is fraught with the potential for heartbreak and despair.

I remain your dear friend, confidante and ally
Monsieur Francois Lobari

Lord Noel wiped his watery eyes. A single tear escaped and rolled down his sunken pale cheek. Ivor, pretending he hadn't seen the uncharacteristic outpouring of emotion, replaced the letter in the envelope and placed it on the tea tray.

'What does he mean about diverting the resources to the Somme?' asked Ivor. 'If you were to ask me I'd say the French didn't divert enough resource to the Somme. If they had, my Father would still be here today, he's wrong isn't he Grandfather?'

'That's impossible to say Ivor. War is a terrible, miserable, dirty business and I hope you never have to find that out for yourself. I'm sure that everyone did the best they could with the information and the resources that were available to them at the time. Hindsight is a wonderful thing Ivor. It's all too easy to imagine after an event that we might have done things differently but no one can change what's been and gone. We can only do our best to learn from our mistakes for the benefit of the future. He who does not remember his errors is likely to repeat them, never forget that.'

'Who is Francois Lobari?' Ivor asked. 'I've never heard you mention him before, nor for that matter any of the other people in the letter. Who are they?'

'There's much I've never discussed with you Ivor and I wish your Grandmother was here. She would know what to tell you and how to say it in a way that you'd understand and respect.'

Lady Noel had succumbed to influenza seven years earlier. Ivor had mercifully been away at medical school during the winter of 1919 when the virulent pandemic tore through the village with as much destruction as any loaded German Howitzer. Lord Noel at the time had taken to spending much of his time at the mine as pressure for coal mounted with the onset of winter. The war effort had severely depleted both the seams and the available men to mine it and stocks were alarmingly low. By the time Lord Noel received the news that his wife was gravely ill, she had in fact already died. He drove back to Grace Dieu the following day only to discover that Summer, who had been nursing Lady Noel, had also contracted the virus. Her condition deteriorated with great speed. She succumbed to respiratory distress and by the beginning of the new decade; Summer too was dead as a result of the influenza.

Lord Noel stifled an outpouring of grief as the memory of his lost family came to the forefront of his mind. Saddened also by the news of Sister Edith whom he had been particularly fond of, despite her

122

awkward nature, he countered the anguish by invoking a deep intake of breath which provoked a fit of coughing.

'I think you should consider a place at a sanatorium Grandfather. I wish you'd let me arrange it. This expectorant medicine isn't helping and it won't cure you. There's a new procedure that is taking the world by storm. It's called a pneumothorax and it's having positive results. The affected lung is collapsed so it can be given time to recover.'

'It sounds ghastly, I don't think so' spluttered Lord Noel.

'It's not as ghastly as it sounds and it's being proven to work. Why won't you try it?' asked Ivor 'it's got to be worth a try.'

The new surgical procedure to which Ivor was referring was being carried out at a sanatorium of a colleague. Unbeknown to Ivor, Lord Noel had already made enquiries. It would however entail a lengthy stay as an in-patient which made the procedure expensive. Lord Noel's predisposition to matters of a philanthropic nature had, with hindsight, not been a sustainable virtue and he had squandered his fortune on a host of good causes, most of them at the behest of Lady Noel, the largest of which being an endowment for the building of the Abbey. The aged Brother Hipwood was now the sole remaining resident at the Abbey and lived a life of relative solitude.

The construction of the glorious Grace Dieu estate with its modern state of the art conveniences including electric lighting in every room and its own private chapel had also been a costly venture. The wage bill to staff the grandiose manor house had depleted a substantial sum and shortly after Lady Noel died the staff all had to be laid off. His Lordship took solace in that the one saving grace of his wife's sudden and unexpected departure meant that at least she hadn't lived to witness the demise of their beautiful estate.

A small fortune had been spent on the education of their adopted Son and heir, William Newlove. Despite this, his ambition never extended beyond that of tending to the extensive grounds at Grace Dieu. The gardens fell into a perpetual state of neglect the moment William was sent to fight in the Somme from where he never returned. The Noel's lavished their grandson with the same opportunities, continuing to meet his living expenses in Cambridge and by the age of twenty seven, Ivor had never actually earned a bean. The Noel's preponderance for the importance of education had also extended to the granting of numerous endowments for the benefit of children from the workhouse who they believed showed great promise. Their faith hadn't always proven to be well founded and contact was generally lost the moment the Noel's stopped paying the living expenses of their protégés.

The medical assistance scheme at the mine that Lord Noel had been proud to announce two decades earlier had proven to be yet another drain on finite resources. The scheme provided for a team of practitioners to supply a range of medical services. It also provided and an income to the families of miners indisposed with sickness or injury. Insufficient management of the scheme, corrupt practitioners and dishonest claimants had all but depleted the bank reserves.

Productivity at the mine after the war failed to reach pre-war levels, further hampering the financial position. Output per man had fallen to 199 tons per annum compared to over 300 tons a quarter of a century earlier. Lord Noel took to the mine shaft himself toiling for twelve hours a day in a bid to encourage an increase in productivity to no avail. The depleted stocks were harder to get at and the days of the mine's viability were closing in.

Promises made by previous generations of Noel's to the Alms House occupants were also a major cause for concern. The retirement homes for long serving loyal workers had been constructed at the height of the mine's success long before the turn of the last century. The newest of the houses were now forty years old and the occupants were demanding a substantial programme of refurbishment as had been promised in their lease, including a supply of electricity and a comprehensive system of indoor plumbing. The roofs of many properties were deficient. The windows barely kept out the elements. Walls were covered in black mould. The single heating sources were failing due to blocked or crumbling chimneys. Light was still provided by inadequate gasoliers and the outdoor shared privies had become nothing more than a rank and rotten festering sore compounding the risks of disease and inevitable death. Despite the high turnover of tenants, there remained a waiting list of eager retirees hoping to be granted a lease to occupy the crumbling cottages. Demolishing and rebuilding the houses was going to be less expensive than a programme of refurbishment. The collection of peppercorn rents however had not provided the necessary sinking fund from which to pay for such a scheme.

The problems at the mine were further compounded by the price of coal having fallen substantially in the export market under a strong pound which made British coal expensive. Germany had started shipping great quantities of essentially free coal to France and Italy as part of the war reparations. To add insult to injury, interest rates for borrowing increased.

The last straw came on May 3rd with the announcement of The General Strike. The miners downed tools following the Miners Federation *'not a penny off the pay not a minute on the day'* campaign in response to a national initiative to reduce the wages of miners at pits across the country whilst at the same time increasing the length of the working day. The Trade Union Council came out in sympathy and took more than one and a half million workers out on strike. Lord Noel became ill on the second day of the strike and took to his bed. Ivor travelled back to Grace Dieu after hearing of the gravity of his Grandfather's sickness and promptly diagnosed pulmonary tuberculosis.

Ivor was frustrated that the inclement weather was preventing his Grandfather from being taken into the gardens for a breath of fresh air. 'Would you like me to take you down to the cloister?' he asked.

'Not just now' Lord Noel replied. 'There is something of great importance I must discuss with you before it's too late. Under my bed is a large rolled parchment. Would you get it out please?'

Ivor took to his knees and brought out a worn embossed leather roll secured with ribbon.

'Do you mean this?'

'Yes, if you can untie it and lay it out across the bed.'

Ivor duly did as he was asked. 'What is it?' he asked after securing the corners with books strewn across the eiderdown.

'What I'm about to tell you may come as a surprise Ivor. It's about your mother.'

Lord Noel had thought long and hard over the years, particularly since Summer's passing, about what he'd reveal to the boy about his true heritage.

'Your mother was born with a special gift' said Lord Noel.

Ivor listened with interest. He never doubted it. She had indeed been the most special woman in his life. He'd found no one that came close to eliciting the affection he felt for her.

'She came from a long line of forebears, others who also shared this gift. These revered subjects, The Compass Line, have been nurtured and protected through the ages due to their perceptible abilities and honourable characteristics. This is her here.' Lord Noel pointed to the place citing her name on the chart.

Ivor studied the chart. 'Who is this?' he asked.

'That is your sister Ivy. She is also of the protected Line.'

'I have a sister?'

'Yes' he replied, opting not to furnish Ivor with the truth of the circumstances of his birth or the knowledge that no biological tie actually existed between them. Ivor had been raised as a Grandson and a Grandson he would remain.

'So where is she? Is she dead too?'

'Oh no, she lives quite happily with her guardians at the March family residence. You will find their details in this pile of papers somewhere. I'm afraid that in my reduced state I have let everything become inextricably befuddled.'

'I don't understand. Why doesn't she live here? Why has she never lived here, She can't have done or I'd have remembered her.'

'The conventions of belonging to the Compass Line dictate that a special set of guardians are appointed at birth.'

'But why? She had a special set of guardians at birth, our Mother and Father. What was wrong with them? I thought you just said my mother was gifted. How can she be gifted, yet not gifted enough to raise her own daughter?'

126

'There was nothing wrong with them Ivor. They were caring people, devoted to you as you well know. They nurtured you and gave you all the opportunities their limited resources could muster. No one could ask for more than to have been blessed with the love and affection your mother bestowed upon you or the pride so displayed by your Father with the passing of each of your milestones; the first time you spoke, the first time you walked, your first day at school. You didn't see how heartbroken he was the day you left for boarding school. But you must understand that the descendants of The Compass Line have special needs that can only be met by approved and sanctioned Guardians. You will understand when you have taken the time to study all the documents. As you can see, there are many here with the remainder in a brown leather case in the safe in the library. You must take good care of them always.'

'So am I a descendant of this Compass Line?'

'No, the gifts only extend to those born of the female line.'

'So why are you telling me this now?'

'Because I'm an old man and my time in this world is coming to a close and when it does you must carry on the mantle. It will be your responsibility to inform the remaining eleven Head Guardians of my demise and at that point you will become a Guardian for the generations yet to come so it's important you understand your duties and responsibilities.'

'What if I don't want to become a Guardian?'

'That is for you to decide when the time comes for you to be called upon but I know you Ivor Newlove and I know you will honour the time old tradition and do your duty just as I have done and all your Great Grandfathers before me have done. You will always be of the Guardian line but it will be for you to decide whether you wish to accept the duty of a Head Guardian or pass that to another. Why don't we begin now by inscribing the addition of the latest Compass child to the chart? Take the pen will you please my hands are trembling today, I'm afraid I'll blot the parchment.'

Ivor took the pen from the table and opened the small drawer to find the well of ink.

'Below Celeste's entry you need to record Edith Calvaire.'

'Only she's not Calvaire is she, she's a Lobari?'

'For the benefit of the chart, Edith is Calvaire and will be until such time as she marries and takes a husband's name at which point you will be notified and will amend the details of the chart in order to maintain a comprehensive record of the Line.'

'And my Sister, she hasn't yet taken a husband?'

'No, she's still Ivy March as you can see here.'

Ivor's eyes fell to the place on the chart identified by his Grandfather. His Sister, Ivy March.

CHAPTER 15
THE CONCEPTION OF EMILIE

November 22nd 1963

In spite of a host of recent successes, morale in the closeted lab behind the decontamination bay was at a low. Montgomery had announced the previous month the project was to be scrapped and the team were to be disbanded as soon as the last Thor missile had been repatriated to the United States. Montgomery travelled to London in a bid to convince his contact in the Ministry of the merits of their project. He was informed on arrival that his contact had retired to the country but was granted an audience with the successor. The meeting was not fruitful and Montgomery found no appetite on the part of the successor to continue funding his team's research. They'd had their chance and blown it, choosing too late in the day to opt for silicone and gold in place of germanium and alloy. Montgomery was further informed in no uncertain terms, that the ministry would be distancing themselves from any practise that might be considered acceptable in a Soviet type regime. The British did not spy on their citizens and the team had not addressed the concerns that had been raised regarding the potential for abuse should the technology fall into the wrong hands. Montgomery was ordered to destroy anything related to their work including documentation, residual stocks of implants and any live subjects containing implants. The ever present Soviet threat of Communist domination would continue to be curtailed using the more conventional tried and tested espionage tactics of agents in the field, infiltration, proven methods of surveillance and adequate due diligence when employing people into the realms of national security.

Despite the British having their own security service, the circles in which Montgomery moved considered the Americans a superior power when it came to covert operations and the control of western surveillance. Montgomery tried in vain to convince the wily civil servant that his implant was nearing perfection, ready for human trials and would give Britain a much needed edge over the Americans and their technological prowess. The stubborn civil servant maintained his stance. There was nothing to be gained by the British Secret Service in having suspected Soviet Agents who could be redeployed back into Soviet territory at any time, with implants that could be copied and then used against British agents in the field. The civil servant agreed that Britain needed to get ahead but information gathered through the use of Montgomery's surreptitious implants were not how they were going to do it. The conversation was over and so was the project.

Eisenhower's ethereal and civilian led Central Intelligence Agency was not to be underestimated. There continued to be much debate about Eisenhower's farewell speech, made two years earlier when Kennedy won the election. Eisenhower had backed Nixon but Nixon lost out to Kennedy. As a former military man and five-star general, the tone of Eisenhower's final address came as a surprise to some when he alluded to harbouring a suspicion about the power now wielded by the military industrial complex. Some thought the comments were aimed at the Generals. Montgomery was of a different opinion, believing the clandestine influence of the CIA was what troubled Eisenhower the most. He'd unleashed a monster, he'd opened Pandora's Box and the unaccountable organisation that emerged from it refused to be curtailed and put back in the box. The military regime with its transparent hierarchy and respected chain of command had given way to quiet, unaccountable men in dark suits. These clandestine figures had infiltrated the highest Executive Offices and enjoyed the confidence and faith of their paymasters. The politicians on one hand might have enjoyed a fair sway of plausible deniability in what they were actually doing, relying on the obscure chain of command that rendered it impossible to say exactly who was responsible for what. What was transpiring was a whole new level of paranoia and mistrust.

Britain was no longer a colonial super power and it seemed the Americans took every opportunity to remind the British of their fall from supremacy and her subsequent new place in a changing and technologically advanced world. What's more, the Americans now controlled the majority of allied fire power, including the production of nuclear bombs like those that had rained down on Hiroshima and Nagasaki in 1945 bringing an end to six long years of war.

Despite the British involvement in the Manhattan nuclear project, the passing of the American McMahon legislation prohibited any further sharing of technological advancements, severely hindering any desire the British had to furnish the world with their own seismic deterrent. It had been this hindrance that had partly led to the conception of project Emily and the subsequent citing of American nuclear ballistic missiles on British soil. British technology was years behind and trying to catch up was proving to be prohibitively costly at a time when the Government were trying to rebuild the nation after another drawn out and expensive war coming so soon after the Great War of 1914. Investment in the fledgling National Health Service was proving to be a vote winner. Military spending and research into the production of a bigger arsenal of more deadly weapons - a programme which would swallow up the Health budget plus some, if the bomb boffins, ambitious generals and war mongers got their way - was not. The country was suffering from war fatigue not to mention an abhorrent fear for what the scientists might actually unleash upon them next. Not everyone believed the best way to prevent war was to have the most destructive weapons stationed in their own back yards. The most vociferous campaigners against nuclear armament were the Nimby squad, *not in my back yard.* Montgomery had dealt with his share of them.

Opinion in the smoky confines of the Wheatsheaf was divided on whether folk were glad to see the back of the wretched American missiles. Whilst some vehemently believed Britain should maintain their own deterrent against mutually assured destruction, some appeared not to grasp that they themselves would be the subject of that destruction if such an affray were ever to break out. Others identified that actually having the bombs parked on British soil for all the world to see would only contribute to eventually bringing about that mutual destruction and wanted no part in it so long as the missiles were sited in their back yard. Someone else's back yard was okay, just not theirs. The few ladies present were, in the main, of the opinion that a worldwide disarmament treaty was the only viable course of action. A small group from the Women's Institute announced they were intending to march to Downing Street to deliver a request that the Prime Minister meet with President Kennedy before the end of the year to sign one. The younger contingent of ladies were, in the main, sorry to see the American officers leave, particularly the handsome ones with a friendly disposition who had proven to be very popular since they came with their own prophylactics. The contraceptive pill had recently been launched but it certainly wasn't made available to single women, not even the most liberated who demanded equality to men in all matters including sex. An unmarried man who wanted sex was one of the boys, simply exercising his legitimate biological urges. An unmarried woman was a harlot.

There was still a small but stubborn faction across the country that remained committed to the Communist Party of Great Britain, although no one in the Wheatsheaf ever admitted to being a member. The Communist Party's only two members of Parliament had lost their seats back at the election of 1950 and had to date failed to win them back. Many of its members resigned in 1956 after the uprising in Hungary which cast no doubt on the Soviet intention to communise the globe, by force and the rule of fear, if necessary. The diehard Communists that remained came mostly from the union ranks of the mineworkers and members of the Amalgamated Union of Engineering who were still in accord with the Stalinist ideology that Russia's new leader Nikita Khrushchev appeared to espouse. There were no mineworkers who frequented the bar of the Wheatsheaf so the overthrow of democracy by a totalitarian regime that would strip the people of all the freedoms they took for granted tended not to be a hotly debated topic over the pork pies and the pints of frothy headed Shipstones. One thing the locals were busy agreeing on by the end of the third pint that night was that the village was going to be less of a target for annihilation now the last of the missiles had gone. At seven thirty everyone peeled out into the street to bid farewell to the Globemaster as its deadly cargo flew over en-route back to where it came from. A round of applause reverberated as the monstrous aeroplane disappeared over the horizon.

The landlady of the Wheatsheaf declared the event was of such gravitas as to warrant a celebration and she produced two large lidded hot crock pots of liver with onions and mashed potato, announcing it was first come first served.

'That was quick' said Bob Halford, sitting with his back to the wall in the corner at a small round table in the alcove. 'It looks like we've seen the last of the Hamburgers.'

'I don't care' said Dick McDermott, 'I'm starving.'

He collected a plate from the end of the bar and joined the back of the queue.

'I don't know how he can eat at a time like this' said Harry Holbrook. 'Ten years hard graft down the swanny. I haven't had an appetite for days.'

'So close, we were so damn close' said Tom Summerfield.

'We were more than close' said Holbrook. 'We'd proven it ruddy well works and for what? To be consigned to the classified pages of some Ministerial department's aborted initiatives never to see the light of day again. Ten years wasted, I'm so angry I could spit.'

'Well don't spit yet' said McDermott sitting back down and placing a steaming plate of liver with an abundant helping of onion gravy dripping off the rim of the plate onto the table. He administered salt and pepper. 'Aren't you having any?' he asked.

'I'm not queuing' said Halford. 'I'll see if there's any left when those gannets have finished.'

'I don't want to offend the landlady again' said Summerfield 'so I'd better go and join the queue.'

'I'll get a round in' said Halford. 'Same again?'

There were nods of affirmation all round and Halford disappeared to the bar.

'I've been thinking' said McDermott, shovelling the last of the mashed potato in his mouth. 'I'm really pissed at the way we've been treated.'

'We're all pissed' agreed Holbrook.

'We know the technology works' McDermott continued. 'I think we should take it to the private sector.'

'How?' asked Holbrook. 'We've signed the Official Secrets Act remember. We're hardly likely to be allowed to wander off into the sunset with the technology. I think you'll find it belongs to the Government.'

'No it doesn't' argued McDermott. 'We developed it. It's our blood, sweat and tears that have brought it this far and the Government have made it perfectly clear they don't want it and they won't use it.'

'The Government won't see it like that' said Holbrook. 'They may not want it but I'll stake what's left of my reputation on them not wanting anyone to have it either. They don't give a damn about our blood sweat and tears. To them it's just another research project that never came to fruition along with Emily, Blue Streak and Skybolt and all the other projects the Government pull the plug on. Years of wasted time, effort and investment all for nothing.'

'It's a travesty' said Summerfield returning with a small plate.

'Then you should have got yourself a bigger plate' said McDermott.

'I'm not talking about the liver and onions you imbecile. I don't know what I shall do now. I haven't told Mrs Summerfield yet. She's got her eye on some new net curtains and she wants one of those new automatic washing machines that are appearing across the pages of the Home and Garden magazines. She's been leaving them conveniently open at the appropriate page around the house for weeks. Will there be any severance package do you think?'

'What, like demob money?' asked McDermott.

'I doubt it' said Holbrook 'on account of the fact we're not actually being demobbed. The ranks we have were only ever a cover to get us onto the base. Perhaps someone needs to broach the subject with Captain Montgomery. We'll need something to tide us over.'

'I already have' said McDermott 'and the answer is no, we're on our own.'

'Perhaps I can go back to the University' suggested Summerfield 'after all that's where I was plucked from. It shouldn't be too difficult for me to find a position.'

'Oh no?' sneered Halford 'and what are you going to say when you're asked what you've been doing for the last five years?'

'We've been working on a government research project.'

'Which government research project?'

'I can't say. It's classified.'

'Okay then, provide us with the name of the Government Minister who sanctioned the project so we can take up references there. I've already done it and believe me I finished up with egg on my face.'

'Perhaps you should have said the research was so classified that even Government Ministers aren't in the loop and directed them to Captain Montgomery.'

'I did' said Halford 'and do you know what happened?'

'What?'

'Montgomery denied all knowledge of it, of me, of us. The son of a bitch told the University that although initial discussions were had five years ago, they came to nothing because the Government cancelled the research so that was an end to it and he said he had no idea where I'd been or what I'd been doing for the last five years.'

'So Montgomery has hung us out to dry?' asked Summerfield.

'Have you asked Captain Montgomery about it?' asked Holbrook.

'Yes.'

'And what did he say?'

'He told me that since there were matters of national security at stake, he wasn't at liberty to discuss any conversation he may or may not have had. He said that for reasons of political expedience, it remains the case that Ministers must retain the concept of plausible deniability in delicate matters and that we knew what we were getting into when we agreed to continue the research under the terms that were clearly laid out to us at the time. He went on to say that he had no doubt that a man of my obvious talents, if somewhat dubious ethical character, would find suitable employment elsewhere but that a reference was not to be sought as he would have no choice but to continue to deny any affiliation with me or the work I'd been doing for the last five years.'

'Ten years' cursed Holbrook 'this is going to mean going right back to the drawing board and taking some low ranking subordinate position because who is going to employ any of us in anything other than a junior role when we can't say what we've spent the last ten years doing? We have nothing to show for it and we can't supply references. What's more, even if we could disclose what we'd been working on, the technology is now ten years old and it's been declared defunct. What use is that to anyone? We're all gonna have to go right back to the drawing board to start again.'

'Like I said, it's a travesty' said Summerfield. 'I've no idea what I'm going to say to Mrs Summerfield. She thinks I have a respectable position within the civil service and a gilt coated pension to look forward to.'

'It's only a travesty if we allow our efforts to be consigned to the annuls of history' remonstrated McDermott. 'You really are a bunch of namby pambys. I am not about to be assigned to the scrap heap. I say we take it live and find our own market. Do not ask me to destroy everything I've worked for, I won't do it.'

'Even if we were to be granted the rights to the technology, which we won't, where's the market? Holbrook asked. 'We can hardly sell it to the Soviets to be used against our own agents. We'd be shot for treason. I doubt there's an American market, the CIA have developed their own covert technologies and they're far more advanced than us in everything. Besides the Yanks might be our allies today but who knows what happens tomorrow. The Soviets were our allies two decades ago now look at them.'

'Not this' stated Summerfield. 'The Yanks don't have this.'

'It's irrelevant. We'd probably still be shot as traitors if we tried to unload it to the Americans. Its British technology developed specifically to benefit Britain by the British Government and it's been made abundantly clear the technology won't ever be utilised by anyone, anywhere, ever. It's over.'

Bob Halford, carrying a precarious tray with four pint tankards, returned.

'What are you talking about? Half the pub can hear you talking about being shot and everyone is listening with interest. I have no intention of being shot so can we keep it down please.'

'McDermott thinks our technology could be sold in another sector' said Holbrook.

'Really? That's interesting' said Halford. 'I've been thinking about the very same thing myself as it happens. It came to me the other day when I saw Ron Powell in the post office. It hit me like a bolt of lightning.'

'Who's Ron Powell?' asked Summerfield.

'You know the old soldier with one leg who sits on the park bench every morning with his dog. Well I got talking to him and he was telling me he's tried a prosthetic leg but he'd given up on it because it felt unnatural and unresponsive when he actually tried to put the action of walking into thought. What if we went back to the drawing board and reverse engineered the process so that instead of being able to extract information, we could input information?'

'I don't understand' said Holbrook.

'If it's possible to extract signals from the brain then it must be possible to input them.'

'You've lost me as well' said Summerfield.

'Think about it' Halford whispered 'prosthetics could be fitted with a chip. That chip could communicate with another chip linked to the thought processes in the brain so that when the action potential of walking was triggered in the brain, that thought would trigger the synapse to the prosthetic.'

'I don't know' said Holbrook. 'That's not what we've developed.'

'But there are a great number of old soldiers who have similar disabilities sustained in the first War. The Ministry of Defence isn't interested in our application so why don't we approach the Ministry of Health? That seems to be where all the long term investment is going.'

'And there lies the flaw in your plan' said Holbrook. 'You've said yourself they are old men, old men who have lived out their lives having grown accustomed to their reduced capacity. It's taken ten years to get our application this far. It would take years more to reverse the processes by which time most of your old soldiers will be gone. It's a noble idea Bob, but for so many reasons, it's a nonstarter.'

'Whilst I hate to be a fly in your ointment, there's another flaw in that plan as well' added Summerfield. 'The work we've been doing for the last five of our ten years hasn't technically existed. If you recall, the budget was officially cancelled in 1958. Since then we've been operating covertly in the shadow of the continued over spend of Project Emily. If we were to approach a Government department directly, the project's existence would inevitably have to be brought out into the open. I doubt any Minister would want it to become public knowledge that the Ministry of Defence has no control over its budget, doesn't know where its money is going, what it's actually being spent on or who's spending it, not to mention the fact that it has continued to be spent on a project that was expressly cancelled five years ago. Something like that could bring down a government.'

'So we go to the private sector with it' said Halford. 'We know it works.'

'By offering it to who exactly? We can't go public with it. We know and have always known its intended use was the illicit acquisition of state secrets from suspected foreign agents. Besides, we've all signed the Official Secrets Act, remember?'

'We should talk to Montgomery' said Holbrook.

'Montgomery is just a monkey, he's not the organ grinder, we all know that' said Halford.

'That's as maybe, but if Montgomery can't get our implant sanctioned for use then neither can we' replied Summerfield 'not without being in breach of the Official Secrets Act and potentially facing a charge of treason. Besides have you considered what could happen if the technology fell into the wrong hands?'

'As far as I'm concerned, there are no wrong hands' said McDermott.

'You'd want the Soviets to have it would you?' Summerfield asked.
'If the Soviets want to pay for it and I'm sure they would, why not?'
'Because we'd be arrested.'
'Only if the Government found out.'
'You're completely mad if you think you want to involve yourself with the Soviets' said Summerfield. 'I don't know about each of you, but I've no intention of putting myself on the radar of the KGB. This is dangerous talk. I don't want to be party to it and I am not going to finish up in a firing squad at the Tower of London.'
'You've been reading too many books old man' laughed McDermott. 'They haven't executed anyone at the Tower of London for centuries.'
'Is that so? Tell that to Josef Jacobs.'
'Who is Josef Jakobs?'
'He's no one since we stuck him in front of a firing squad at the Tower of London for giving our secrets to the Germans during the war.'
'We're not at war in case you hadn't noticed.'
'Not at war? I'd say we're in a perpetual state of war. Haven't we just been babysitting sixty ballistic missiles?'
'It surprises me the Soviets haven't been in contact with us' said McDermott. 'It's common knowledge there's not a single department in Whitehall that hasn't been infiltrated by at least one Soviet agent.'
'Perhaps that should serve as a reminder to us that we shouldn't be discussing this here' said Halford. 'Walls have ears.'
'I'd rather take my chances here than back at base' said McDermott 'where there's a yank everywhere you turn. I'm not just going to sit by and let Montgomery's over paid cronies at the Ministry with their expense accounts, fancy ministerial cars and gilt edged pensions throw me to the wolves. Being as none of you are enamoured by the prospect of negotiating with the Soviets and I can't keep this project going on my own, I do have another suggestion. By a show of hands, who here has heard of The Compass Line?' asked McDermott.
'That's just an urban myth' exclaimed Halford 'an old wife's tale. I thought you had a serious suggestion.'

'Ignore him, go on' whispered Holbrook.

'So you've all heard of it?'

'I haven't' said Summerfield.

'Ok, for Summerfield's benefit, it's an ancient ancestral blood line. Its members are thought to be divested with, amongst other gifts, the power of foresight.'

'How ancient?' asked Summerfield 'and how come I've never heard of it?'

'I don't know exactly, back to the time of Jesus I think.'

'And who are these people?'

'There aren't many of them left, possibly just twelve and only three are still believed to exist in Britain.'

'How do you know this?' Holbrook asked.

'That's not important?'

'It is to me' Holbrook interjected. 'How do you know about The Compass Line?'

'This is bullshit' exclaimed Halford. 'Why are we even sitting here talking about a bunch of fictional whackos and phantom fortune tellers?'

'Because I've discovered the identity of one of them' said McDermott. 'We need to carry out a human trial don't we? I've found us the ultimate human guinea pig.'

'And you think your fortune teller is going to be happy to volunteer to have a chip planted into his brain?' asked Summerfield. 'A chip we can't actually guarantee won't kill him.'

'Even if McDermott's found us a volunteer' said Halford 'there isn't time. We're going to be out of here in a few weeks. That isn't long enough to perform the surgery and carry out the necessary monitoring. It would be months before we'd have any conclusive results and to what end? What would be the point? Even if the subject survives, what would we be proving and why? We can't use the data for anything, nothing legal anyhow now our contact with the Government has pulled the plug.'

'Let's back up a minute' said Holbrook.

'I'm still waiting for you to tell me how you know of the existence of The Compass Line.'

'Surely you don't believe all this rubbish?' asked Halford 'you're a man of science not mumbo jumbo.'

'Let's just say walls aren't the only thing with ears' said McDermott. 'But if it's important and I don't want to get bogged down with this, you know that pen I gave to Montgomery for his birthday? Well it had some rather clever integral features I omitted to tell him about. Consequently, I've been able to monitor every conversation he's had since, provided he's had the pen with him of course. It turns out he's quite the dark horse.'

'That still doesn't explain how you know about The Compass Line.'

'It turns out that our Captain Montgomery is what is referred to in Compass circles as a Guardian. Not a Head Guardian but a Guardian nonetheless.'

'What's a Guardian?' asked Summerfield.

'The Guardians know the identities of these Compass people, where they are and what they're doing.'

'Even if you're correct' said Summerfield 'and Montgomery is one of these Guardians, I don't see him simply agreeing to hand one of them over to us.'

'He already has done' said McDermott. 'It was easier than I expected to convince him too. He's pretty pissed at having been given his marching orders and packed off with a meagre pension.'

'Monte's been given his marching orders?' Holbrook repeated.

'Yeah and he's right miffed about it' added McDermott. 'It seems someone shopped him for his part in the fuel transfer debacle and for aiding and abetting the cover-up of Morris' distillery.'

'Who shopped him? It wasn't you was it?' Holbrook asked.

'Why am I in the frame?' McDermott asked.

'Because you don't like him.'

'I can assure you the feeling's mutual.'

'I still don't understand to what end?' asked Holbrook. 'Why would we risk contravening the Official Secrets Act? We might not find ourselves at a firing squad as we're not actually military, but we could still be hung or spend the rest of our lives in prison?'

'By a show of hands, who reads a daily newspaper?' McDermott asked.

Three hands went up.

'And who watches the news bulletins on the TV?'

Three hands went up.

'Do you remember during the double propellant flow countdown test when Morris forgot to change the RP-1 fuel valve and seven thousand gallons of liquid oxygen spewed across the launch emplacement, then the missile couldn't be lowered back down because the metal structure had crystallized?'

There were nods of affirmation all round. It had been a memorable night.

'Do you remember the press arriving shortly afterwards, convinced that because the missile hadn't been lowered, we were actually preparing to launch it?'

Again the three men nodded. The inadvertent spillage had been a huge faux par with mistakes made along the entire chain of command for which the Squadron Commander on duty was ultimately sanctioned and redeployed elsewhere. Morris got off scot-free for his part in the fiasco. He was a popular figure with the married officers at the base on account of having an unending supply of nylons that had been produced before the war but due to a minor fault had never made it into the shops. No one ever asked how he came about them or which lorry they'd fallen off the back of. Keeping the wife happy was a far more important consideration. Morris also concocted his own distillery on site which made him a popular figure with the off-duty lower ranks who were only too happy to take advantage of his entrepreneurial generosity in exchange for their silence regarding the distillery's existence. As a result of this popularity, Morris' involvement in the potential catastrophe was played down during the subsequent investigation and as a result he kept his job. It did however, make him indebted to certain persons who had protected him from inevitable sanction.

'I recall the Press soon cleared off once they realised there was no live warhead installed' said Halford.

'Do you recall the member of Parliament asking a question in the House about it?' asked McDermott.

'I remember reading a copy of the curt reply he received from the Minister of Defence in answer to his question' answered Holbrook.

'What about when Montgomery inadvertently ordered the storage tank pressurising valve to be opened and the fuel was pumped directly into the missile instead of the tanker?'

'Yes we remember' said Holbrook 'what's your point?'

'How about the article the press published on the *arms span apart?* '

Somehow the press had got wind about a blunder with the dual key system. The launch of a live missile was a bilateral decision and there were two keys. One remained in the possession of the British the other was held by the Americans. Both keys were needed before a missile could be launched. This was supposed to prevent one country being able to arm a warhead unilaterally without the cooperation of the other, except it came to light in the press that the keyholes were so close together it was quite possible for both keys to be initiated by a single person.

'Yes, I remember it, not least because it was me who was recalled early from a spell of leave to assist with the modification to the console. What of it?' Halford asked.

'How do you think the press jumped onto each of those stories so quickly?' McDermott asked.

'If I remember rightly, they didn't' said Halford. 'Not a single newspaper published anything about the storage tank pressuring valve incident.'

'Only because the editor pulled the story at the last minute, believe me they had the story ready to go.'

'And how do you know that?'

'I know because in each case, I was the informant' admitted McDermott. 'The press they just love to be in the loop, waiting patiently on the side-lines for some juicy titbit that will differentiate their column inches from everyone else's. Journalists, they're all the same, living in hope that every story might be the big one, the one that gets them noticed, raises their profile. It's not just the press either. All ambitious men are the same, give them a bit of information that's useful to them, that helps them usurp their rivals and they become putty in your hands.'

McDermott studied the deadpan faces of his three colleagues.

'Think of it like Mrs Summerfield with her magazine subscriptions' he continued. 'Once she's seen something she likes, she takes the publication every month, irrespective of whether there might be anything useful the next month. She has the magazine delivered anyway just in case. The press are just like that, they'll keep coming back in the hope of a story. For an MP it's the prospect of discovering the right question to ask, for an opposition MP the prospect of the right awkward bloody question. Ambitious men will do almost anything for access to a repository of information that raises their profile, makes their life easier or helps them to get on. And it's not just the professionals. You'll recall the Combat Training Launch at Vandenberg when the RV sank on re-entry? How do you think that group of amateur Pod Hunters knew where to look for the sunken pod?'

'I doubt they ever found it' said Summerfield.

'That's not the point. The point is they sought out the information from the repository of the time, which happened to be me. I gave them the last known co-ordinates. Now here's our big question. What about if we had our own repository of information? For arguments sake, let's call it the Compass repository. Think of the scope, the opportunities and the potential for regular subscriptions.'

'What would be in it for the Compass subject?' asked Halford. 'There'd have to be something in it for him or he'd never agree to it. Why would he?'

'He'd never know. We implant the chip without consent.'

'What you're suggesting is wholly unethical' added Summerfield. 'The repository project was never intended to be used in such a way.'

'It damn well was' argued McDermott.

'On suspected Soviet spies yes, not on a British citizen without good cause. We were trying to curtail the threat of war. Sacrificing the privacy of foreign enemy agents was a small price to pay to avoid the possibility of an all-out nuclear holocaust. Maintaining the peace is a very different thing to the exploitation of a private individual which is what I think you're alluring to.'

'I think it's time to correct a number of misapprehensions' interrupted Holbrook. 'The Compass Line, they don't go back to the time of Jesus as Mr McDermott suggests, I've no idea where he got that information from. The line is much older than that. Their existence was first documented at around 4000BC, long before Jesus Christ ever walked the earth. Secondly, there are not three known living Compasses in Britain. There are actually five but Mr McDermott is correct when he says there are only twelve documented lines globally. It is possible there are more than are known about but since they've been the subject of much oppression and prejudice throughout the ages many known Lines have died off or Guardians have ceased to keep written records or acknowledge the Guardianship programme designed to ensure their network of influence. Thirdly, the Guardians are considerably more important to the preservation of the Line than simply being aware of their identity. The Guardian Line is responsible for the proper pastoral care of the Compass subjects. The Line ensures that appropriate education is administered and that the skills of the individual Compass' are put to good use so they may fulfil their destiny. Their talents are too numerous to name but go well beyond that of mere fortune telling. They are known to have inherent traits of common sense, reason, fairness, equity and justice, empathy, understanding and respect for others even when those qualities are not reciprocated. They are also thought to be truthful and conscientious, pragmatic, inherently selfless, have great courage, benevolence and generosity of spirit. As Mr Halford has already alluded, Compass subjects have also established themselves as great visionaries with accomplished powers of foresight and vision. The Compass Line have been influential at most of the gravest moments in our history including I might add, at our recent existential threat involving the

President of the United States, the Cubans and the Soviet Premier Mr Khrushchev. But for the influence of The Compass, the outcome might have been very different and Kennedy might have been convinced to send in the 90,000 troops the generals were advocating instead of imposing the blockade as he eventually did. It is my understanding the last remaining American contingent of The Line enjoys the trust and confidence of at least two of the serving members of Mr Kennedy's Executive cabinet which advised the President during the recent missile crisis.'

'From where I'm sitting it didn't take a lot of foresight to see that if Kennedy had dropped the bomb on Cuba to neutralise the Soviet weapons, Khrushchev would have retaliated' said Halford.

'Perhaps not but it did take a conscientious adviser willing to stand up to the military Chiefs who were calling for the President to escalate the blockade and send in the troops. It did take common sense and mutual understanding to convince the President to negotiate a de-escalation of the conflict by the magnanimous agreement to remove the American nuclear intermediate range ballistic missiles from Turkey.'

'And you really believe that some anonymous guy with concealed powers of persuasion, a guy that no one has ever heard of, had something to do with Kennedy's decision to move the missiles from Turkey? Have you all gone completely mad?' Halford barked, downing the last few dregs of his pint.

'There's one final thing you should know about the Compass Line' said Holbrook. 'They are not and never have been men. The Line is now and always has been entirely female.'

'Well that says a lot' mocked Halford 'I've never met a woman yet who doesn't think she knows everything, insists on the final word and is always right.'

The familiar bell rang out across the Wheatsheaf and the landlady hollered '*last orders at the bar.*' Summerfield stood up.

'This round's on me, same again?'

The others nodded in affirmation and Summerfield sauntered to the bar with the empty jugs.

Flying Officer Jim Miller came hurtling in through the back door almost knocking Summerfield over in his haste. An icy draft followed him.

'Shut that door' shouted Holbrook.

Miller glanced around the snug and realising only the Brits were in disappeared through to the public bar. The ironic sound of Buddy Holly and the Crickets on the jukebox echoed through the door between the bar and the snug as it opened. *That'll be the day eh eh when I die.*

Miller reappeared a few minutes later.

'Have you seen Commander Bill Paterson Wright, Sir?' Miller asked giving a cursory salute.

'No' replied Halford. 'I haven't seen any of them all night. They're probably packing up the remaining wagons over at Silver City. Is everything alright?'

'I take it you haven't heard the news, Sir?'

'No, I've been in here most of the evening with these reprobates, what news?'

'It's dreadful, Sir. President Kennedy has been assassinated. He was shot this afternoon in Dallas.'

'Is he dead?' asked Halford.

'Yes, Sir, like I said, Sir, assassinated, two bullet shots clean blew his head off Sir' retorted a breathless Miller.

'Oh dear how shocking, thank you Jim' said Halford. 'Try Silver City, I'm sure you'll find the remaining American off duty personnel over there.'

'Yes Sir, thank you, Sir.'

Miller disappeared back out of the door leaving another chilly gust in his wake.

'So where was your broad with her infinite powers of foresight this afternoon then?' Halford scoffed. 'Not in Texas that's for bloody sure.'

147

CHAPTER 16
WILL

May 9th 1998

Emilie Weston awoke in a cold sweat to an unfamiliar ring tone. She sat up and opened her eyes, squinting in the pitch black of night.

'Your phone's ringing' she groaned, tapping Will on the shoulder who was sleeping like a baby.

'Will' she groaned louder, 'your phone.'

He woke and answered the call.

'Yes. No. I don't see how. I tried. Yes. Ok I'll be there in thirty minutes.'

Will cut the call, climbed out of bed and began to get dressed.

'Go back to sleep' he said. 'Sorry I woke you'.

'I can't.'

'Why not?'

'I've just had a horrible dream. Not a dream, a nightmare'.

'Not another one. What was this one about?'

'It started with an articulated lorry. A consignment of flour and margarine is being loaded into the back of it.'

'Doesn't sound like much of a nightmare so far.'

'The lorry is driving uphill through the mountains. The scenery is beautiful. There are snow tipped conifers for as far as the eye can see. It passes a green and white road sign that reads;

Milan 243
Turin 182
Aosta 59

'They're all cities in northern Italy' said Will. 'What are you doing in Italy?'

'I've no idea but a thick mist descends. The tops of the trees, those higher up on the mountain side, they disappear into this foggy abyss. The HGV passes another sign. This one's digital and its flashing.

Traforo del Monte Bianco
Traffico regolare

'Traforo del Monte Bianco, traffico regolare' repeated Will. 'If I'm not mistaken, that's Italian for, *tunnel of Mont Blanc, regular traffic*. So you're definitely on the Italian side of Mont Blanc.'

'But I've never been to Italy' said Emilie.

'Trust me, you're in Italy. That tunnel is over seven miles long you know.'

'No, I didn't know.'

'It cuts right through Mont Blanc Mountain. You go in one end in Italy and come out the other in France. It still doesn't sound like much of a nightmare. What happens next?'

'A traffic light is on green. The HGV stops at a toll booth. It then makes for a small black hole in the side of the mountain. There's a huge concrete arch. The HGV drives underneath it and enters the black hole. It's dark, except for the headlights of oncoming vehicles. It feels like driving inside a never ending drainpipe. There are two parallel lines of white lights overhead that go on and on, until ultimately the two lines converge in the distance. Every so often, there is what looks like giant beer barrels affixed to the roof and the road opens up into a small recess, before it reverts to being a narrow two-lane drainpipe again.'

'It certainly sounds like the Mont Blanc tunnel from what I remember of it. Those beer barrels, they're part of the air conditioning system. They pump in oxygen.'

'Then all hell breaks loose. There's an almighty explosion. Flames spread really quickly. Thick black smoke starts billowing out at one end. It's the other end to the one the lorry entered because this

149

side has a zigzag roof structure that looks like it's been formed from the serrated edge of a gigantic cheese grater.'

'Beer barrels, never ending drainpipes and a gigantic cheese grater?' Will smiled.

'Do you want me to tell you, or don't you?'

'I'm sorry, carry on.'

'Tyres are exploding. Vehicles keep coming but they can't go anywhere and become trapped behind the exploding lorry. Some cars are being abandoned. People are …'

'OK, you don't need to go on. I get the picture. Mont Blanc tunnel eh?'

'How should I know? I've never even seen Mont Blanc tunnel.'

'I have to go' he whispered, kissing her on the forehead.

'What time is it?' she asked.

'Three thirty.'

'Where are you going at this hour?'

'There's been a flood at Fillet, I have to go and sort it.'

Fillet was one of a chain of Steakhouse restaurants owned by Will's family. Will had been busy working to increase their market share. Since the closure of a number of Berni Inns, they had opened a number of additional restaurants. This meant Will worked irregular hours and she had gotten used to him coming and going at all times of the day and night. She settled back into the pillow and listened to the raucous engine of his Maserati as it pulled off the drive in full throttle before drifting back into a disturbed sleep.

Will Weston pulled up to the car parking barrier. He waited for it to rise, drove through and found a parking space. He slipped his mobile phone into the pocket of his jacket and made his way inside the Novotel. The reception was deserted. He called a number on his mobile phone.

'I'm here' he said when the call was answered.

'Room 401.'

'I'm on my way.'

He called the elevator to the fourth floor and knocked on the door of room 401.

A middle aged man with thinning silver hair and thick tortoiseshell spectacles opened the door. Will followed him in.

Another man, much older, dressed in an expensive pin striped suit and highly polished black leather shoes sat on the edge of the large bed made up with pristinely laundered white linen and a contrasting brown velour overlay. A third man, dressed casually in blue jeans and plain sweater sporting well used training shoes sat in an easy chair in the corner of the room by the window.

'We thought it was time we talked' said the suit.

'What do you want to talk about?' asked Will. 'Where's my Father? I thought he was going to be here.'

The toilet flushed and the lock on the bathroom door sounded.

'Hello Son' said a heavily set man of over six feet, who appeared at the threshold between the bedroom and the bathroom. He had broad shoulders and the beginnings of a paunch, the result of too much good living, rich food and over consumption of beer. He was dressed in neatly pressed black slacks and a white dress shirt open at the collar with a loosened dark patterned tie.

"Hello Dad" said Will. 'What's all this about? Has something happened?'

'You could say that. Sit down. It appears we have a small problem. I'd like to show you something.'

'Who are these guys?' Will asked.

'I thought it was time I introduced you to the team. This is Bob' directing Will's attention to the suit on the bed who gave a nod.

'This is Tom' pointing to the man who'd answered the door. 'Alright?' said Tom.

'And this is Dick' patting the casually attired man on the shoulder who stood up and offered a handshake which Will reciprocated.

Tom adjusted his spectacles and lifted a large wooden crate onto the bed. He unlocked the combination and removed the lid before taking out a computer monitor and standing it on the desk. He then connected a processing unit, a speaker and a keyboard. He pressed the power button and the computer began to initialise.

'Have you seen this before?' asked Tom.

'A computer? Will asked. 'Yeah I've seen a computer, who hasn't?'
'Not any computer, this one?'
'What's so special about this one?'
'It's not the computer that's different, although it has a lot of processing power and a much bigger memory than anything you might have come across before.'

Tom sat at the desk and navigated the keyboard. He hit the return key and sat back in the chair. A moving image appeared on the screen; a large gilt framed mirror and through the mirror a reflection. A semi naked woman in black and red lacy underwear with black stockings and suspenders and black stilettos was laid out on a crumpled bed. Beside her lay a well-toned naked man. The woman mounted him and sunk her lips into his chest. The man then tossed her over onto her back, their legs entwined and he was on top kissing the woman's neck and moving down to her cleavage.

Will noticed a bead of sweat had appeared on his forehead and he wiped it away with the back of his hand. A looming sense of revulsion rose in his gut. The woman was on top again, her face reflected in the gilt framed mirror. He recognised the woman. He didn't recognise the man.

'What is this?' Will implored. 'That's my wife, that's Emilie. What the hell is going on? Is this now? Is this happening right now? What am I watching here?'

Tom turned on the volume. Moans and grunts of ecstasy resonated from the speaker.

'These are the bits I still like best' said the suit adjusting his position on the bed to get a better view.'

'You fucking pervert' Will scorned.

'He calls me the pervert yet it's his wife who's busy fucking another man' grunted the suit.

'Turn it off.'

Tom muted the volume.

'I said turn it off now.'

'Turn it off Tom' instructed Mr Weston senior.

Tom paused the image leaving a still shot of Emilie's contorted face reflected in the mirror, the unknown blonde straddled behind her, his hands on her breasts.

'Calm down Son.'

'What is it? Where did you get it? Is this what she's doing right now?'

'Yes and no' said the suit.

Will had already made up his mind he didn't like the suit. He wanted to punch him in the face and wipe the voyeuristic smirk clean from it.

'What is going on? Why are you showing me this?' asked Will.

'She's having an erotic dream' said Tom 'so in answer to your question, yes it's happening now but no, it isn't really happening because it's just a dream.'

'She's been having a lot of them recently' muttered the suit 'and not always with the same guy. Haven't you been servicing your Missus lately?'

Will wanted so much to punch his lights out.

'What you've just seen is a demonstration of Project Emilie' said Mr Weston. 'We have never shown you the technology in practise before because well frankly, we've never felt any need to, but as you have just seen for yourself, your wife has become preoccupied with things of a more let's say, primitive nature than we're happy with.'

'What do you expect me to do about that?' asked Will. 'I can't control what she dreams about?'

'How are things with your wife at the moment?' asked the suit.

Will fought the inclination to punch him in the face.

'I think Bob is asking…'

'I know exactly what Bob is asking, he's asking whether I'm fucking my wife and my answer is it's none of your business.'

'That's where you're wrong Son. It's all of our business. Project Emilie *is* our business and it's been a very lucrative business, particularly for you. It paid for that fancy school you went to. It paid for that ostentatious car you drive, it pays for your expensive suits, your all-inclusive holidays, it indulges your taste for fine wine and swanky restaurants, your private medical cover, I could go on.'

153

Will went over to the mini bar and took out a small single serve bottle of Cognac. He tipped it into a glass and swallowed.

'So what is it you want from me? I don't understand what it is you think I can do.'

'You need to help us get Project Emilie back on track' said Tom. 'Subscriptions have fallen over the last quarter for the first time in the history of the project. We need to address that.'

'I say we address it by finding a more appropriate market for the X rated stuff' interjected the suit. 'There's a lucrative market out there, we need to tap into that.'

'I hope you're not suggesting you turn my wife into a pornographic model.'

'No we're not' said Mr Weston. 'Bob, we've discussed that and decided it's not an option, not unless Will was in agreement anyhow.'

'Turning my wife into a porno actress? Like hell I'd support that.'

'I don't know why you're taking this attitude, it's not like you married the broad for anything other than the money' cursed the suit.

'She's still my wife and a man has his limits.'

'Will's made his opinion known so let that be an end to it' Mr Weston ordered.

'Then laddo here needs to sort his wife out and get her back on track and we all know this is not just about the sex.'

'What is that supposed to mean?' asked Will.

'Bring up the analysis, show Will what we mean.'

Tom navigated the keyboard. The image of Emilie in the throes of passion disappeared and was replaced by a series of charts that Will was invited to consider. They spanned the last twenty years and were divided into five titled segments;

No considerations or voids,

Big issue considerations,

Small issue considerations,

Family considerations,

Personal or selfish considerations.

The considerations were subdivided into subscription revenues.

The considerations fluctuated with each year.

The years with the greatest proportion of Big Considerations were represented with greater revenues.

The years with the greatest proportion of Personal Considerations were represented with lower revenues.

The past year had been dominated with an equal proportion of Small and Personal Considerations and as a result revenues had fallen through the floor.

'Someone will need to explain what exactly I'm looking at here' said Will.

'Let me explain' said Tom. 'It's really quite simple. This is an analysis of every thought your wife has had over the course of the last twenty years since she was eighteen. There's a separate chart that depicts years zero to eighteen but we don't need to concern ourselves with that one. The problems of that era were dealt with when we removed Emilie from the environment she was in which you know had proven to be highly unsatisfactory. That's when she entered into the relationship and subsequent marriage to you. At eighteen her mind was full of what we describe as Big Issues. We define Big Issues as matters of national and international interest, the state of the economy for instance, anything to do with national security or the health of the nation, diplomatic tensions arising both here and across the world, the onset of strange weather phenomena or environmental concerns that need national action, ideas about national infrastructure such as housing stock, road building and manufacturing centres, the education curriculum is also regarded as a Big Issue. That's not a definitive list but it gives you an idea of what constitutes a BC. Basically anything the national Government concern themselves with.'

'Collation and dissemination of the Big Issues is what Project Emilie was devised for' said Mr Weston 'and we are unanimously agreed that early on you did a damn good job focusing her mind towards these matters.'

'They are the money spinners' the suit interjected 'and without them we're screwed.'

'What are the voids?' asked Will.

'The voids are the waste of space' declared the suit 'when we're making nothing.'

'Bob is correct' said Tom. 'Even the most gifted brain doesn't process thought for one hundred per cent of the time. We've calculated that, despite some minor fluctuation from subject to subject, the Compass brain is processing data for between eighty and eighty eight per cent of the time. The voids are the twelve to twenty percent.'

'So is that when they're sleeping?' Will enquired.

'No not necessarily as you've just seen. Even during sleep the brain transmits an enormous amount of data. There are some voids during sleep but that doesn't explain them all by any means.'

'So when do the other voids occur?'

'They occur at different times during the day. Tell me, can you recall her saying that she needs to switch off for five minutes?'

'Yeah, she'll often say she needs to take five minutes.'

A vision of Emilie doing just that appeared in Will's mind.

'She'll stretch out her arms, flick on the kettle and open a bar of chocolate, or she'll pour a large glass of wine and announce she'll be taking a hot bubble bath and doesn't want to be disturbed.'

'Bath time doesn't produce voids' muttered the suit with a wry smile.

'Do you watch my wife in the bath you lecherous old bastard?'

'Of course not, it's her thoughts we see, not mine. I do like it when she stands in front of the mirror mind, then we can see her. Tell me Will did you buy her those sex toys or has she had to resort to finding her own means of satisfaction?'

Will's pride took another nose dive. He didn't know Emilie possessed any sex toys and he'd certainly never considered buying any himself. With the crushing of his ego Will grabbed the suit by the scruff of his shirt collar pulling him up from the bed and raised his fist. 'I should smash your bloody lights out.'

It took both Tom and his father to pull Will away. The suit adjusted his misshapen attire, his shoulders flapping with consternation like a disgruntled peacock.

'Cut it out Bob' ordered Tom 'this is not helpful. I need to complete my presentation. It's nearly dawn, we're all knackered, tempers are frayed and we're letting the seriousness of our situation get the better of us. Everyone needs to calm down and Will needs to be home before Emilie gets up.'

'The incompetent little runt is all yours' the suit shirked dropping back down onto the bed.

'Right then, we've gone over the Big Considerations and why they are so important to the success of the project and we've covered voids.'

The suit sniggered.

'I said cut it out' Tom hollered.

'The Small Considerations are less important, at least in so far as potential revenues are concerned. We define the Small Considerations as any matter which has merely a regional significance of public interest, which in the case of your wife, has tended to be Midlands centric. This regionalisation focus is a geographical constraint based on the location of the subject and where they live or have lived. We accept that subjects always have a particular interest and therefore generate transmissions about places that are dear to them, the Compass subjects are human after all, and they form bonds and ties. Now there is a ceiling on how much data even the most gifted of brains can compute. Historically this regionalisation focus hasn't been an issue because we've also had a subject in the north and another in the south to compensate for Emilie's Midlands centric mind. That was until recently and at this point I will hand over to Dick to carry on.'

Tom sat down and swigged the remainder of a glass of Scotch.

Dick climbed out of his easy chair and took up a position standing in front of the window. The heavy velvet curtains were open and through the nets it was possible to tell the dawn was beginning to break.

'Right I'll cut to the chase' said Dick. 'Your wife is gonna have to do much better, she's gonna have to work a hell of a lot harder if we're gonna recoup the lost revenues and you're gonna have to be the one to take care of it.'

'How do you suppose I do that?' asked Will. 'She'll say she already works long hours and I wouldn't disagree.'

'But she's wasting her time on the wrong sort of work. She needs to be refocused.'

'But she enjoys it and she won't welcome me interfering in her decisions I can tell you that.'

'What do you think we pay you for?' asked Dick.

'You pay me to be her husband. That was the deal.'

'No, we pay you to keep control of the bloody woman and see that she fulfils her transmission quotas.'

'I don't know where you've been for the last century but this isn't Victorian England. Women want control of their own lives, to be masters of their own destiny. A husband can't control his wife anymore, they have rights.'

'Then I think it's time you came off the payroll.'

'Now just a minute, there's no need to be hasty. You can't do that I have commitments.'

Dick collected a paper file from the floor. 'That you do William and quite a few commitments I see. He began to reel them off one by one.

Car payments for that ostentatious Maserati;

Two weeks at an All Inclusive resort in the Bahamas during the summer at a five star hotel, very nice;

Your expensive wine club subscription;

Receipts too numerous to go into here to cover your Saville Row tailor, regular visits to the hair stylist to the stars, cosmetic dental reconstruction, various personal trainers and life coaches. What the hell is a life coach?

Then there's your new house and a host of builders and architects fees because apparently you weren't altogether happy with your choice of new home and had it completely remodelled. Just out of curiosity, who do think owns that property?'

'I assume Fillet own it.'

'Wrong Sonny, wrong. It's actually owned by an anonymous shell company in the British Virgin Islands, set up by the executive committee and operated though a corporate services provider in

Wyoming. Your right to remain there extends only so long as you remain on the payroll. Am I making myself clear? You have premium memberships to various health clubs, casinos and gentlemen's clubs, and don't think we don't know what 'gentleman's club' is a euphemism for. There's private medical cover which I notice does not extend to benefit your wife and nor do the various lucrative life insurance policies. I see she didn't accompany you in February for the two weeks you enjoyed courtesy of the most expensive resort in the Italian Dolomites. How can après ski be this expensive I wonder? You're certainly living the high life Mr Weston.'

'Look' said Will 'I didn't say I wouldn't co-operate. I'm just saying that it won't be easy and I'm not going to apologise for enjoying the finer things in life. You all choose what to spend your dough on and so do I, just because you disagree with my choices doesn't make my choices bad ones and I resent the inference.'

'What are ominous by their absences in your expenses are any sign of school fees and associated educational pursuits for the two boys.'

'We don't believe in private education, that's what we pay taxes for. The boys are happier at the local state school where the neighbour's children go. As for extra-curricular pursuits, they do plenty and Emilie likes to take care of that. While you're busy criticising my expenditure and my life choices, perhaps you should take a look at hers.'

'I wasn't going to bring that up but since you have done, let's take a look, shall we.'

Dick picked up a second file.

'In the last year, forty per cent of Emilie's income has been paid to you in twelve separate monthly bank transactions.'

'She insists on paying her share of the utilities, like I said she's a modern woman.'

'I think you are full of bullshit William. Tom, will you bring up Article 24(c) please. I think young William should see it.'

Article 24(c) was an extract of a transmission dated six months ago. Emilie was at her computer typing figures into a spreadsheet entitled *BUDGET.* The first column of the first line of the spreadsheet read

'*MORTGAGE*'. Will glanced at the remainder of the spreadsheet. The balance shown on the last line read *NET ZERO*.

'Can you explain why your wife believes she's paying a fifty per cent share of a mortgage? A mortgage that, judging by her calculations, has fifteen years before it will be discharged, when as a point of fact, as we've already determined, no such mortgage exists?'

'Frankly how my wife and I divide our financial resources is none of your goddamn business.'

'Whilst I beg to differ, we'll continue. Twenty five per cent of your wife's income has been spent at various grocery and superstore outlets, presumably feeding and clothing the children since you have no equivalent expenditure.

Fifteen per cent has gone in car and travel related expenses.

Ten per cent has contributed to the aforementioned educational pursuits for the children and of the remaining ten per cent, two per cent is accounted for in standing orders to various charities and I can tell you she visited the Cancer Research, British Heart Foundation and MENCAP charitable shops on six separate occasions purchasing a total of four dresses, two skirts, two shirts, two pairs of trousers and a coat. She made one visit to a hair stylist and two visits to the dentist. It's hardly the financial diary of a woman enjoying all the benefits of an affluent husband, is it?' Dick threw the file across the floor.

'You are supposed to be protecting that woman so she may fulfil her destiny and let me tell you, we think you are doing a lousy job.'

'Her destiny' Will sneered 'and what is that exactly? To have her mind prostituted on your clandestine information highway.'

'Let me tell you, so you're in no doubt as to the seriousness of the situation. The direction that things are going, we're driving at break neck speed from an information highway and into the scrap heap of an information cul de sac.'

'I think we're backing ourselves into the blame game here and that's not helpful' Tom interjected. 'We need to determine whether he is with us on this and if he is, find a way forward that addresses the loss of revenue.'

'Are you still with us Will?' asked his father.

'Yes, I'm not a fucking idiot, I've come this far.'

'Good, let's move on' said Dick. 'Having established that you wish to remain an integral part of the project - we have established this, yes?'

Will nodded. 'I've just said so haven't I?'

'OK, only so that you are in no doubt, there's no going back from here.'

'We need to address the issue of having only one remaining live Compass subject, namely your wife.'

'I was under the impression there were three live subjects.'

'There were, we lost the second one three years ago in an accident.'

'What sort of accident?'

'A plane crash. The subject was aboard an Embraer on her way to Scotland when it came down shortly after take-off.'

'Why didn't I know about this?' asked Will.

'There was no need for you to know about it. Information has always been on a need to know basis and the executive committee took the decision you didn't need to know.'

'If that's the case then why are you telling me now?'

'Because the situation has changed but first you must understand this. When the Embraer came down and the second subject was killed, there was the matter of an autopsy to determine the cause of death as is mandatory in such circumstances. The Executive committee had to consider the possibility that the implant would be detected during this autopsy.'

'Was it?' asked Will.

'As far as we've been able to ascertain, no, it wasn't, which was most fortuitous. There was an in-flight break up which ruptured the passenger cabin at three thousand feet accompanied by an in-flight fuel fed fire. It wasn't deemed a survivable accident by anyone on board and as a result of the injuries sustained we believe the implant was destroyed.

'So there are two remaining live subjects?' asked Will 'Emilie and subject number three. Are you going to tell me who subject number three is?'

161

'All in good time.'

'But I think I've earned the right to know.'

Mr Weston senior nodded his head.

'There's a problem with number three' said Dick.

'And I suppose you're going to tell me I don't need to know what the problem is' said Will.

'No, in fact that's the main reason we've brought you here tonight. The third subject went offline a month ago and we haven't been able to ascertain why. The implant simply stopped transmitting a little after 2pm on 12th of April.'

'Has that happened before?' Will asked.

'No, never' replied Dick.

'So you put in a faulty implant.'

'There was nothing wrong with my implant' Bob defended curtly.

'So you bungled the operation and it was damaged during the implant procedure.'

'We don't think so' replied Dick. 'The implant had operated flawlessly for eighteen years without a single break in transmission. A fault would have been detected. We'd have expected to see some initial intermittent failure but we didn't. It's like someone just turned it off.'

'But that's not possible, is it?'

'No.'

'Is it possible it's been detected and someone has removed it?'

'Not without us knowing and there's nothing contained in any of the transmissions that might suggest that either she or someone else knew the implant was there. We've painstakingly been through every transmission for the last three months and we're all of the same opinion, she didn't know it was there.'

'What if she didn't know it was there but someone else discovered it during a medical procedure?'

'You think a neurosurgeon would remove it without first clarifying what it was doing there? Besides she's had no medical procedures, we've have known, her transmissions would have told us.'

'So how do you explain it?'

'We can't and after the risk of detection following the death of subject one, we've had to consider what was to be done with number three.'

'If it's an intermittent fault, it might come back online' suggested Will.

'We couldn't take that chance. If there's a problem with the implant it could result in neurological damage which would see the subject hospitalised and scanned. We couldn't risk the implant being detected and it falling into the hands of someone who might start asking questions.'

'Even if it was discovered it can't be traced back to any of us, surely?'

'There's always an audit trail Will, to someone who's pig-headed and intractable enough to keep looking. Someone who asks the right questions of the right people and follows the pertinent leads. The materials used, the technology involved, there are others who if asked could make a series of educated guesses that could lead right to each of our doors. The Executive committee decided that the only viable course of action would be to remove the implant, permanently.'

'How are you going to do that?' Will asked

'It's already been done' replied McDermott.

'How?'

'With two bullets to the back of the head.'

'You shot the third subject?'

'Is she dead?'

'Yes, problem solved but you don't need to thank me' said Dick.

'Thank you? You fucking psychopath. Did you know about this?' Will asked staring aghast at this father.

'Yes I knew. It was me who ordered it. Taking out the redundant Compass subject killed two birds with one stone.'

'What do you mean?'

'Bring up appendix 3 please Tom.'

Tom navigated the keyboard to reveal another chart.

'Look at this. This is analysis of your wife's transmissions. You're now familiar with the differences in the grades of transmission. Emilie was first elected to Council here, five years ago. Prior to this her Bigs were consistently over sixty percent. Look what happened to them with each passing year since she took public office. The Smalls have increased, the Bigs have decreased. This section here denotes the period following her decision to run for the office of Mayor. You can see the result is in an unprecedented downward shift of Bigs. There is a clear correlation between this reversal and her revenue stream. To reverse the trend it was imperative she was not elected to the office of Mayor.'

'But you couldn't control whether or not she was elected, that was a Council decision.'

'Indeed it was, a Council constituted of the smallest Tory majority. Remove that majority and the proposal to elect a mayor from the ranks of the Tories could not be ratified. Since the Tory majority was just one member, removing two members was sufficient to negate the majority needed and ensure she wasn't elected.'

'So you're telling me you deliberately gerrymandered that result?'

'What we did didn't actually constitute gerrymandering in the strict sense of the word but none the less it is a good word and I'm happy to use it.'

'So the third subject was a Council member?' asked Will. The blood in his veins ran cold and an awful realisation punched him in the gut. 'You killed all five?'

'Unfortunately, what we thought to be a fool-proof exercise went awry on the night' continued Mr Weston. 'We knew Wallmichaels was driving as Flatliner's car was in the garage. We didn't know the other members were going to be in the car.'

'So why didn't you call it off when you discovered the others?'

'Because we were committed' exclaimed Dick. 'It was too late to call it off when we realised, we'd already ambushed the vehicle and the occupants had already seen both our faces and the guns.'

'How many of you were involved?'

'We're all involved Will' said his Father.

'I mean how many of you were there at the scene?'

'There were two of us, me and Bob' replied Dick. 'I did the driver and the rear seat passenger behind him; Bob did the other three.'

'So who was the Compass?'

'It's probably better you don't know' said Mr Weston.

'What would be better would be for you to have not murdered five innocent people' Will fumed. 'Now tell me, which of them was the fucking Compass?'

'Dana Coxstable' said Dick 'and don't even think about taking the moral fucking high ground. I did what I had to do to save our asses, to save your ass.'

'You bastard' cursed Will. 'This meeting has just been about making me complicit in your psychotic enterprise.'

'No' shouted Mr Weston 'It's been about you bringing your wife back into line, to make sure she gets back on-board with the programme and increases her transmission Bigs'. There's to be no more tinkering in menial concerns that don't matter to the wider nation. You've got three months or make no mistake; I will pull the plug on your expenses.'

CHAPTER 17
THE DINNER PARTY

November 28th 1948

The winter chill had not abated for days. A thick blanket of frost covered everything as far as the eye could see. Ivor Newlove put on an extra sweater beneath his tailored jacket. He added a second pair of socks and went downstairs to prepare a boiled egg for breakfast. He turned on the cold tap to fill the kettle to make a pot of tea. Nothing came out; the pipe had frozen again so he poured a glass of milk from a bottle in the pantry which the frigid conditions had preserved for an extra day. There being no water to boil an egg he opened a jar of Mrs Bywater's blackberry preserve and spread a generous topping onto the remains of yesterday's bread. He had slept in, beyond the hour at which he usually woke and surgery was due to begin in fifteen minutes.

The client list of a village doctor was a small one and the only regular customers were the ladies who came to seek remedies for bouts of insomnia and various maladies brought on by having too much time on their hands to think about the faintest of symptoms. Dr Newlove's advertised price for a consultation was three guineas. No new guineas had actually been minted for well over a century but he adopted the practise of pricing in guineas as did many of his counterparts in adjacent villages. At the time of the final minting the value of a guinea was fixed at twenty one shillings. There were twenty shillings in a pound. Prices expressed in terms of guinea's had remained in the psyche of the Englishman, who were said to pay their tradesmen in pounds and their tailor in guineas. Given that the weekly salary of a labourer or farm hand was less than six pounds, a visit to the Doctor swallowed up half a week's pay rendering visits by a labourer's dependants quite unaffordable. As a result, Dr Newlove often found himself accepting the payment of a single shilling for the most deserving of cases. This didn't help put food on his own table, coal in his cooking range or meet his subscription responsibilities to the British Medical Association.

He opened the sitting room curtains of Grace Dieu cottage which doubled as his consulting room. He peered across the front garden towards the manor house. After the death of Lord Noel, the financial dire straits of the Noel legacy became apparent. The unprofitable mine was sold for a song just to be rid of its liabilities. The Noel stake in the local electrical generating company was sold to pay taxes and Ivor was forced to consider selling the Grace Dieu estate. Fate intervened in the shape of the March's, who proposed to run a dairy farm and took up a tenancy. Ivor moved out of the manor house and into the small but comfortable Grace Dieu cottage where he had spent his formative years.

He lingered at the window and attempted to extract the blackberry seeds from the preserve that had gotten stuck between his teeth. Ivy was walking towards the cottage from the manor. He waved and she reciprocated. He hadn't seen her for what seemed like months.

Lord Noel had lived with the after effects of his bout of tuberculosis for nearly two years before finally succumbing to its respiratory ravages in 1928. Ivor completed his medical studies the same year and returned home to Grace Dieu to put his Grandfather's affairs in order and arrange the funeral. It was there he met Ivy March for the first time. He saw her from across the church as she came in and was instantly captivated. Her long thick wild mass of strawberry blonde hair was loosely tied back off her face revealing a pale complexion characterised with light freckles that radiated out from a small perfectly formed soft rounded nose. Her full lips bore the luscious shine of applied polish in a hue of rose pink. She reminded him of a portrait he'd seen a few years earlier in the gallery of an American collector in Massachusetts. The picture depicting a lady crocheting had been painted by the artist Auguste Renoir in 1875 and it had captivated him in much the same way as to leave him speechless. Ivy's likeness to the goddess in the art work was bewildering.

After the formality of the funeral service, attended by hordes of folk Ivor had never met but who came to offer condolences, a gathering resumed at Grace Dieu. It was a fine day and the mourners mingled in and out of the cloistered courtyard. His good friend Hague Montgomery arrived unexpectedly that morning to offer moral support. He used Hague's presence to solicit an introduction to Ivy. She was every bit as charming as he imagined. Her tentative smile, a genuine empathy that permeated from beautiful hazel eyes and a voice as soft and as kindly as ever he'd heard, produced stirrings of a craving never experienced before. She demonstrated her superior knowledge of flowering plants without leaving Ivor embarrassed by his deficiency with regards to French Lavender species, loosely tied bunches of which she had placed at the grave of his Grandfather earlier. Ivor had been about to exhibit his knowledgeable prowess with regard to the medicinal benefits of Turmeric when Hague interrupted them. He was followed by Clementine March; Ivy's mother who thought Ivy might like to be introduced to Edwin Phillips and dragged her away. Ivor declared his infatuation to Hague who encouraged Ivor to act on his instincts before Edwin Phillips could get a look in. Hague soon changed his tune when Ivor revealed that the Goddess Ivy was in fact his Sister. Hague only departed back to Cambridge after Ivor had solemnly pledged never to act on his base instincts and Ivor remained true to his word.

Ivy married Edwin Phillips a year later. It was another decade before they produced a daughter. Holly was born on Christmas Eve in 1939, just two months after the declaration of another war with Germany. Publicly Ivor was pronounced Godfather at her Christening; privately he became the Compass Line Guardian of the new charge who was barely ever out of his shadow and much of his time was taken up in lengthy explanations, discussions and demonstrations in a bid to satisfy the child's unending curiosity about the world.

The summer of 1933 was a particularly quiet period in the surgery in which he saw only four full fee paying patients throughout the month. There were two dozen one-shilling patients, half of which were call-outs at ungodly hours of the night. He decided to use this upturn in the good health of the patients on his list and the spare time it afforded to investigate the contents of the brown suitcase left by his Grandfather. He began by cataloguing the documents into chronological order by date. Then he began the process of trying to make sense of the content, reading each document over and over until he'd gained a satisfactory understanding of how each Compass Line had progressed, who was of the Compass Line, who was of the Guardian Line, when and where they'd lived, what their achievements had been, what insurmountable problems of the time they had tried to solve, the people who had been influential, the people who'd been influenced and those who hadn't.

He read with particular interest about the prejudice faced by certain lines which included detailed accounts of the execution of two Compasses for the crime of witchcraft towards the end of the eighteenth century. They had both experienced visions of widespread sickness that went on to occur precisely as the women had predicted. Ivor was unable to find any evidence that recommendations made by them - to cease distribution of bread produced from the rye harvest - were acted upon. He concluded from the description of the symptoms described by the two unfortunate daughters of Massachusetts; blackened burning limbs that fell off, convulsions and hallucinations, that the disease was most probably Ergotism caused by the ingestion of rye infected with the fungus Claviceps Purpurea. Ivor had had an intimate relationship with this deadly fungus through the viewfinder of a microscope after being given the opportunity to study its properties in 1926 after an outbreak of Ergotism in Russia. Ivor concluded the two poor women had been ill-served by their defence counsel. He had proclaimed in their defence the gangrene was not caused by the women as vessels of the devil for which they had been charged. He maintained that the illness was undoubtedly the work of St Anthony's fire and had been brought about by divine retribution for the sins of the sufferers themselves. The explanation failed to satisfy the judicial authority and they were both convicted and duly burned to death. The account of their execution was extremely harrowing. The two young women were tied to a stake above a mound of dry wooden kindling which was then set alight. The first had been stripped of her clothes and tied naked to the stake. A large fire soon took hold. She let out three shrieks before falling unconscious within a minute. The second Compass was forced to watch the ghastly proceedings and upon the removal of the first corpse, the remaining kindling was shovelled onto to the ashes. It made a substantially smaller mound. The young woman, who was just fifteen, screamed as a man attempted to remove her garments. She went to the stake clothed in a long white dress over a petticoat. The mound was lit but the lack of kindling made for a smaller fire. Her terrified shrieks were heard over a mile away for fifteen minutes as the flames devoured her outer garments. The report left Ivor sick to his stomach and without an appetite to continue reading any further. It was another two weeks before he had chance to resume where he'd left off. A year later he had read and digested all the documents except those relating to Ivy's ancestral line. These he'd put carefully to one side to absorb later.

The autumn of 1934 brought another downturn of clients coming through the front door of the surgery. The great depression which had started across the Atlantic with the stock market crash of 1929 had at last filtered through to the small market towns and agricultural hamlets of England. Demand for iron ore had reduced with the reduction in consumerism brought about by the economic hardship. This reduced the spending power of the workers of the ironstone quarries and associated smelting works and this produced a knock on effect across all other trades. Unemployment figures were at a record high. Ivor used a free afternoon to travel into Oakham where he visited the library to select a book. He paid the librarian thrupence to borrow the recent publication of a memoir, *Burmese Days* by a new writer George Orwell and sat in the library to peruse J B Priestley's new travelogue *English journey*. He left the library at six and took a leisurely stroll along the High Street to the Cross Keys Inn on New Street which opened at half past six. He passed the time of day sitting at the bar in the company of Albert Butcher, a patient on his list. After Ivor downed two pints of

Ruddles beer he bid farewell to the publican who was engrossed in polishing one of many brass horseshoes that decorated the walls. He meandered slowly along South Street towards Simper Street and the Picture Theatre, a simple tin tabernacle that showed three pictures a week. An advertisement for a new film was displayed outside. Ivor studied the poster. *The Battle*, a wartime drama set during the Russo Japanese war of 1904 starring Charles Boyer and Merle Oberon. The letter he'd found in the brown suitcase from Monsieur Lobari written in 1899 came to mind. The young Celeste had predicted a successful career in moving pictures of a man by the name of Charles Boyer. Intrigued, Ivor paid his ten pence for the ticket and found a seat in the auditorium. When the film ended he began the long walk home through the Orchid meadow dense with leaf and spikes heralding the impending late bloom. He cut across the fields before joining the long road to Grace Dieu cottage. He arrived home a little after half past ten and changed into his pyjamas.

Unable to sleep, he got out of bed at midnight and took out the brown leather suitcase. He selected the loose bound papers he'd put aside, those relating to Ivy. As with the other documents he ordered them by date but instead of starting with the oldest and reading that first, as he had done with the other Compass Lines, he decided to start with the most recent. This was a carbon copy of the letter he himself had written to the other eleven Head Guardians informing them of the death of his Grandfather and of his wish to carry on where his Grandfather had left off. He placed the letter into a new paper folder and moved onto the next. This was a letter to the eleven Guardians informing them of the untimely death in 1920 of Ivor's Mother, Summer.

My dear friend, confidante and ally,
It is with great sadness I report to you to the untimely death of our beloved Compass Summer Newlove taken from us by the merciless influenza, the Spanish scourge that continues to blight our existence. Her final years I regret to inform you have not been happy ones. Summer lost her beloved William to the rat infested trenches of the Somme in France during the Great War which affected her disposition

171

greatly. Before her demise she predicted with all assuredness that an Austrian born German soldier will rise in Germany and wreak revenge on the western allies in retaliation for the punitive sanctions placed upon his Fatherland. She also saw the impending destruction of the German economy by the occupation of the Ruhr territory by sections of the allied forces. Whilst it appears quite impossible that Germany will ever recover from its recently enforced demilitarisation and humiliating reduction to that of a mere pastoral state I beg you to foster relations with those who retain the power and influence to halt such a turn of events as Summer so vividly envisaged during her final months.

Ivy is now a confident and beautiful young woman with a penchant for nature and the natural world. In recent months she has taken a particular interest in matters of social justice, taking up the causes of soldiers maimed during the Great War and now denied appropriate employment. I remain confident that she will ultimately fulfil her destiny,

I remain always your friend, confidante and ally,
Lord Englebert Noel

Ivor was overcome at the memory of that ghastly period. Over the course of little more than a year he received word that his Father had gone, followed by his Grandmother and just a month after that his beloved Mother was taken before her time. He considered the predictions offered by his Mother, so clearly described by his Grandfather in the manuscript fourteen years earlier. A new politician had swept into power in Germany earlier in the year. Adolf Hitler, leader of the Nazi party had declared himself Germany's Fuhrer, effectively subsuming the positions of Chancellor and President into one elite position. Confident that the peace treaty signed at the end of the Great War was regarded sufficient to have rendered Germany impotent, Ivor filed the letter and thought little more about it, content that the Nazi party would be a flash in the pan and by the very fickle nature of party politics, would disappear as quickly as they had arisen. He might have given it more consideration had the next batch of documents not have been such a profound shock. A bundle of papers from 1899 laid out in no uncertain terms the manner in which both he

172

and Ivy came into the world. Ivor was not the biological child of William and Summer Newlove, he was an interloper, compensation to the Newlove's for the deceptive sacrifice of the child that was theirs, Ivy. There was nothing that identified who his biological parents actually were, other than that she, his Mother, had been a woman of ill repute, poor character, without a hope of salvation. Ivor was stunned. He had never doubted his heritage, not for a second. He'd always felt like a Newlove and the heritage of being a Newlove was also to be a Noel. He had belonged to them and them to him. Now it appeared to have been a lie, a deceitful charade played out by those he'd implicitly trusted. What's more, it meant that Ivy, the only woman he had ever hankered after, was not in fact his sister. He could have married her. He could have seen off the advances of Edwin Phillips and outmanoeuvred him at each romantic turn until he'd been able to secure her affections for himself. A great angst for his dead Mother welled inside him. She had been unwittingly deceived and her beautiful child substituted with him, the discarded offspring of a parent incapable of love and nurture. These feelings were compounded by the insufferable knowledge that if only he'd read the papers sooner, he wouldn't have been reduced to living a life without the daily affections of the beautiful woman he loved. Ivy could have been his. Gobs of salty tears swelled his eyes and soaked the chest of his pyjama top as a tsunami of grief streamed down his cheeks.

Fourteen years had passed since the discovery of his true heritage, the knowledge of which made no real difference to his daily routines. Ivy now resided at Grace Dieu manor, her rightful place, he the interloper at the small cottage. The education that had been lavished upon him with no expense spared, he was putting to the best use he could. He watched Ivy draw nearer and when she was feet away he greeted her at the threshold of the front door.

'Good morning' she beamed.

'Good morning' he replied 'Is everything alright?'

'Yes, we are having a dinner party tonight and I hoped you'd be free to join us.'

'Dinner parties aren't really my thing' said Ivor.

'I know, but there are some people attending who I thought you might like to meet.'

'Who's that?'

'Medical types.'

'Medical types, can you be more specific?'

'A Doctor Holbrook from Nottingham and a Professor of Medicine from Leicester, Mr Billy Rubin, say you'll come. I don't know a lot about medicine, I would really like your moral support' she pleaded.

'What is Doctor Holbrook a doctor of? Ivor asked.

'Something to do with the head.'

'Not a psychiatrist? You know I can't bear psychiatry types.'

'No, not psychiatry, brains. I think he calls himself a neurologist.'

'And Doctor Rubin, let me guess, he's a haematologist?'

'No he's something to do with blood.'

'Haematology is blood.'

'Ah then, see I'll be absolutely lost without you, please come.'

'Yes alright, thank you I'll be there. I never can say no to you can I? What time?'

'Pre dinner drinks at seven and the dress code is formal' she smirked, eyeing his bobbled old sweater 'and you might want to remove those seeds from between your teeth. See you at seven.'

She turned on her heels and ran tentatively back across the frost drenched garden towards the manor house. He stood at the open door watching her, oblivious to the escaping heat of the range, until she disappeared behind the Laurel.

Ivor arrived at Grace Dieu just after quarter past seven, purposefully late since he didn't enjoy indulging in small talk. By the time he'd apologised for the tardiness, hung up his coat and collected a glass of wine people were already being seated at the perfectly dressed dining table.

'It's a political fundraiser' whispered Ivy 'they've all paid ten guineas a ticket, so don't say anything socialist.'

'Ten guineas!' exclaimed Ivor 'what are you serving roasted gold?'

'Roasted veal and Yorkshire pudding which I know will satisfy your limited palette. I've sat you between Dr Holbrook and Mr Rubin so you'll have something to talk about.'

Ivor dutifully took his seat at the table of sixteen diners. Edwin Phillips sat at the head of the table dressed in full formal attire as though he'd just arrived from a wedding. Ivy at the opposite end dressed in a wispy chiffon dress that hung in such a way so as to reveal the femininity of her narrow shoulders without being immodest. Across from Ivor sat James Heathcote Drummond Willoughby, the current Earl of Ancaster and local Member of Parliament. His wife Nancy, the Countess of Ancaster whose Mother had been the first female Member of Parliament, sat alongside. To their right sat Captain Mulberry Montgomery sporting the uniform of the Royal Air Force and his timid wife, Victoria. To their immediate left was the young bachelor Robert Halford who had just completed his degree at Cambridge and was in the process of considering post graduate study. Next to Robert Halford was Imelda Brocklehurst, a hosiery manufacturer in a khaki utility suit and her Husband, Barnaby, a veterinarian in matching khaki. Ivor who was feeling claustrophobic at the centre of the table, adjusted his stiffened winged shirt collar to loosen its suffocating grip and was wishing he hadn't accepted Ivy's invitation. Ivy sensed his discomfort.

'I hear the British Medical Association are about to issue a ballot on the Government's proposals to nationalise the health service' she smiled at Ivor.

'They already have done, I received mine this morning' interjected Mr Rubin. 'Damn foolish idea, I've already sent mine back with another stern letter telling them why their ridiculous scheme should be consigned to the waste paper basket.'

'I'm still on the fence' said Dr Holbrook.

'On the fence man, good God, mark your ballot with an emphatic *No* or the profession will be decimated.'

The two young waitresses, which Mary the house cook had brought in to assist with the dinner, served each guest with a bowl of Mary's Tomato and Basil soup accompanied with a warm freshly baked bread roll. Flour had only just been taken off the rationing list and Mary had secured a sack earlier in the week. The tomatoes had been picked from the estate's allotment, created as part of the *Digging for Victory* campaign during the war.

'How are you going to vote, Ivor?' asked Ivy.

'I've already voted. My ballot arrived yesterday. I think the idea has merit, so I've said *Yes*.'

'Merit?' Mr Rubin scoffed. 'I don't know why we're even having a second ballot. The members of the Medical Association made it clear with the last one. Eighty five percent said no. We don't want it and we'll do all we can to put a stop to it before we all become slaves to the state.'

'I'm not a slave to the state' said Dr Holbrook.

'You will be if Health Fuhrer Bevan has his way. A national health service indeed, mark my words it will stifle research and development.'

'Why do you say that?' asked the Earl of Ancaster.

'What will be the incentive for the dedicated medical professional to work all the hours God sends to develop a new technique or find a new cure or create a new drug if the prospect of him making good from his endeavours is stolen away from him?'

'But you can't think the current system works well for people surely?' suggested Ivor 'not everyone anyhow. Consider the productive hours that are currently lost due to unskilled low paid workers and labourers not being able to afford to have their condition investigated and improved. Many of the patients on my list don't visit me until their condition has deteriorated to the point where disease has progressed quite grievously. Free access to a doctor will not only improve the quality of life of the patient but the advent of his better health will improve his levels of productivity.'

'What do you think Ivy?' asked the Earl.

'I think the principle of a national health service that is free at the point of service, based on need and not the ability to pay is a noble one. I agree with Ivor, the potential gains of free access will stand to benefit both the individual and the state. The difficulty will be controlling the costs when you consider the pent up demand that must exist within the community. If Mr Rubin were to be wrong about the stagnation of research and development leading to new cures and improved management of chronic conditions, the costs will spiral upwards with the inevitable increase on the demands for the service' she replied.

'Free,' scorned Mr Rubin 'why should it be free? When are people going to learn that nothing in this life is free? You sound like the band of woefully naïve, bleeding heart student doctors at the University. Some of them have had the audacity to have started, in direct defiance of the British Medical Association, a Socialist Medical Association to counter the opinion of their legitimate professional body.'

'Whilst I might not want to make a habit of coming out in support of Mr Bevan' said the Conservative Earl 'the proposed service won't be free. Free at the point of service yes, but not free. Someone has to pay for it and the State is not taking on the liability by itself. It's a partnership, which if passed in the House, will be funded by everyone paying a contribution by virtue of a national insurance fee from their wage or salary.'

'That's where you're wrong with the greatest of respect to you Sir' countered Mr Rubin. 'The women won't pay, the children won't pay. It'll only be the men who pay because they're the ones who earn.'

'You know the solution to that don't you, Mr Rubin?' retorted Imelda Brocklehurst who was affronted. 'Let the women into the workplace. Equip them with the skills to do the jobs and pay them a wage equal to that of men, then I assure women will be only too happy to pay their own darned national insurance fee.'

'Now you're being ridiculous' argued Mr Rubin. 'A woman can't do the work of a man, what a preposterous thing to say. A woman's place is in the home.'

Each guest looked ominously at the guest opposite. Some stifled smiles or twitched nervously. Ivy knew what the ferocious Imelda Brocklehurst was about to unleash on the unsuspecting gentleman and poised herself for the onslaught.

'I think you'll find that women managed quite well during the war' Imelda barked. 'While you men were away fighting who do you think kept the factories going and the services running? Women. And a damned fine job they did of it too. Sir, your attitude is as outdated as the suit you're wearing and every bit as offensive as the halitosis you appear to want to do nothing to remedy.'

A deafening silence enveloped the room. Ivy, the consummate hostess, turned the conversation away from matters of dental hygiene and back to the less contentious topic of medicine.

'I think what happens at the outset will be very important in controlling the ongoing cost' she said. 'We all know that without the doctors there can never be a health service, since they will be the ones who will deliver it. It gives them an enormous collective power. If the doctors are going to hold the Government to ransom and only agree to take part provided Mr Bevan stuffs their mouths with gold, then I fear we'll be getting off on the wrong foot. They will insist their mouths being stuffed with gold this year, next year and every year thereafter.'

'You've been very quiet Dr Holbrook' said the Earl. 'Has anything you've heard this evening been helpful in making up your mind about which way you will vote?'

'I'm going to hold off for a few days and see how the wind blows. I have a lot of private clients. Private clients are my bread and butter. I only have to see four a day to provide me with a good living and time enough to play golf. I don't relish the thought of being tied to the hospital all day every day dealing with a never ending string of no-fee clients. I want to be able to keep my private clients and if I can keep them then perhaps I might consider seeing some non-fee paying patients.'

The soup bowls were cleared away and the two girls served the main course. Despite meat still being on ration, one benefit of maintaining a dairy herd had been a surplus of calf meat. Female calves joined the herd for their milk. Male calves that didn't produce milk were superfluous to requirements and had to be slaughtered. Mary's sack of flour came in handy again and coupled with the egg ration she'd been harbouring she had produced sixteen huge well risen Yorkshire puddings that sat atop a generous serving of thinly sliced veal. The accompanying potatoes and carrots came from the allotment. Barnaby

Brocklehurst announced he hadn't seen a Yorkshire pudding in years and asked for his compliments to be sent to the cook.

The conversation turned to rationing as most conversations tended to, once folk had run out of more important or impending things to say. Imelda expressed her frustration that the clothing ration was still in force. She had produced virtually no ladies hosiery in the last seven years as the availability of material declined. The merchant ships bringing imports into Britain had been targeted ruthlessly by the German submarines in a bid to starve the country into submission by destroying essential commodities. The issue of rationing tokens had been the consequence. Acquiring a single pair of stockings demanded two rationing tokens out of the annual clothing allowance. In 1941 the allowance was 66 tokens. By 1945 this had reduced to less than 30. Since the acquisition of a dress took care of 11 tokens, a coat was 14, a pair of shoes 5 and a single undergarment demanded 4, most women found they were forced to do without stockings. Her factory as a result had been given over to the production of utility wear to meet the needs of the uniformed forces. Now the war was over, she was clearly using up the remaining khaki.

The table was cleared once again and small portions of apple pie and fresh cream were brought out. This was followed by tea plates of homemade biscuits and a spoonful of quince jelly. Three large serving platters each with a different uncut round of cheese were laid in the centre of the table. Large intakes of breath at the sight of so much cheese carried around the table.

'I'd like your opinion on the cheese' announced Ivy. 'I've been experimenting with new formulas and recipes. You'll have to forgive me but tonight I'm ruthlessly employing you as my human guinea pigs, you'll be the first to try each of the cheeses before you.'

'You've made all this cheese?' asked Mrs Montgomery, who'd sat as a quiet as a church mouse all evening.

'I hardly ever see my wife these days' complained Edwin Phillips. 'She spends all her time in the chapel with her different cheeses.'

179

The Chapel at Grace Dieu was a later addition to the original building which had allowed it to be easily separated from the main living accommodation and Ivy had converted it into a creamery.

'The cheese at the end is a Grace Dieu Red Leicester, the paler round in the middle is a Leicester with the addition of cranberries and walnuts and this one is a Blue.

'How do you give this its vibrant orange colour?' Captain Montgomery asked slipping his cheese knife through the round.

'By adding annatto' Ivy replied.

'What's annatto?' asked Imelda Brocklehurst.

'Annatto is the seed from a tree native to South America, the Achiote. It's taken me twelve years to locate and import the seeds which thanks to Mr Newlove and his intrepid detective prowess, I did last year.'

'I'm not sure about cheese impregnated with fruit and nuts' Ivor exclaimed, examining the pale yellow cylinder of cheese speckled deep red with crushed cranberries with a disapproving eye. 'I really can't see this achieving widespread appeal Ivy. Wherever did you get that idea?'

'I think you should try it before you cast aspersions Ivor' defended Ivy.

'If I must' he said cutting the thinnest slice his knife would allow.

'I disagree with Mr Newlove' said Captain Montgomery. 'This is delicious.'

'How do you keep the cranberries fresh?' asked Imelda, surely like all soft fruits the harvest was during the summer?'

'The cranberries fruit until well into November' replied Ivy 'and what a tiresome and thankless exercise harvesting them is. After processing them with sugar they went straight into the curds a few weeks before Christmas. That particular cheese therefore has only undergone a three month maturation, which isn't ideal but I'm confident the flavour will improve. It's not often we have such a large gathering, so I thought I'd bring it out.'

Despite the general consensus of opinion being extremely positive towards Ivy's new cheese with cranberry and walnut she had already concluded that until such time as the availability of sugar increased there wouldn't be any more Leicester with cranberry on account of the fact she'd had to hoard her individual sugar ration over the course of the autumn to provide the sweetener necessary to preserve the fruit.

The supper was concluded with a speech from the Member of Parliament as was customary at fundraising dinners, followed by a period of questions.

Group Captain Montgomery, a professional airman who flew Hurricanes with Bomber Command during the war, enquired as to the fate of the many Air Force Squadrons conceived during the war for which now there seemed to be little need of. He followed up with a question about the policy to continue with a conscripted National Service for all men between seventeen and twenty one whom he saw as taking the jobs of the professional personnel. Finally he went on to question the merit of the plan to pull British forces out of Palestine now the new state of Israel was declared.

Imelda Brocklehurst asked two questions. How long the country was going to be expected to *make do and mend.* She then made a request that the Trucking Act of 1831 be repealed since her workers were using it to insist on the continued weekly payment of wages by cash rather than monthly by banker's cheque as she would prefer in order to save on administration, frequent trips to the bank to collect large amounts of cash and the bother of securing it against theft.

Mr Rubin sought to extract a guarantee from the Earl that he would support the views of the British Medical Association when the vote as to whether or not to enact the provision of a national health service was taken in the House of Commons.

Robert Halford asked how he could protect intellectual property rights to ensure they remained with him and not with the university, for any discovery he may subsequently make.

Dr Holbrook sought an assurance that the Conservatives would ensure investment into the realm of medical research particularly in regard to Neuroscience and that advancements in this field would not be curtailed by a decision of the Labour Party to begin a national health service.

Edwin Phillips asked whether there was any truth in the rumour that the Earl of Ancaster was about to abandon the constituency in favour of an invitation to take a seat in the House of Lords. He followed up with an enquiry as to whether Churchill was expected to be leader of the Conservative Party when it came to fighting to retake control at the next General Election in two years' time.

Ivy, as the hostess was afforded the final question before the vote of thanks to the guest speaker brought the evening to a close. She enquired as to the health of the relationship between Britain and America since the catastrophe with Mr Fuchs. He had run off to the Russians with British nuclear state secrets, and as a consequence, the Americans were refusing Britain access to their nuclear armament programme. She then asked whether Britain was progressing with its own nuclear deterrent and if so, where it would be tested. Ivy enquired as to the existence of the protective layer around the earth that filters the Sun's radiation. She went on to ask whether high altitude atmospheric testing was proposed and if so, what research would be carried out to determine the possible damage to the layer by the chemical release of nitrogen oxide during the explosions.

CHAPTER 18
EMILIE

January 1st 1964

The raucous rendition of *Auld Lang Syne* reverberated around the room, heralding the start of another year. Revellers joined arms and danced in a circle exchanging kisses and greetings of Happy New Year! Robert Halford produced a bottle of malt whisky to toast the occasion and poured generous measures, handing them out to his guests. When the singing had died down, Halford realised the telephone was ringing. He slipped into the hall to answer it and came bounding back in a few minutes later to look for Group Captain Montgomery.

'It's time' said Halford.

'Time?' enquired Montgomery.

'Yes time, the baby has arrived, we need to go.'

Montgomery, who was a little worse for wear, staggered to the hall to collect his coat. Halford rounded up McDermott who was in the kitchen engaged in an erotic embrace with Halford's neighbour, whose husband had passed out in a drunken stupor on the settee.

'We have to go' ordered Halford, pulling McDermott free of the affectionate woman's clutches.

'Go where?'

'The hospital.'

'Is the …'

'Yes, now come on!'

Halford surveyed the merry scene. Someone had turned the gramophone back on and was stacking a new selection of 45's. The first record dropped onto the turntable, Dominique by the Singing Nun.

As the opening bars of the acoustic guitar began to play, he concluded he would simply leave the inebriated revellers, who were already jigging along to the tempo.

Halford unlocked the car and toppled into the driver's seat. Montgomery struggled with the passenger door handle, swaying uneasily from side to side. McDermott took over, negotiated the handle and pushed Montgomery in before himself climbing onto the back seat. Halford engaged the choke and turned the ignition, revving the engine before pulling away. The car kangarooed down the road until Halford got the measure of the temperamental clutch. He fiddled in the door panel for a piece of double mint gum, removing the wrapper before slipping it into his mouth to disguise the smell of scotch.

'We'll stop off at Summerfield's on the way' he called to McDermott.

Summerfield had received an invitation to the New Year's Eve party but Mrs Summerfield had come over with one of her migraines, as usually happened when gaiety was the order of the day. Halford pulled up outside Summerfield's house, clipping the kerb and rolling into the back of Summerfield's parked car.

'I'll go' said McDermott crawling out and proceeding to fall flat on his face as he tripped over a protruding stone in the grass verge. He reappeared five minutes later with Summerfield still his pyjamas and slippers, carrying a dark suit and a freshly pressed white shirt.

'Are you drunk?' Summerfield asked as he climbed in.

'Of course I'm drunk, it's New Year's Eve for pity's sake' replied Halford.

There was no reply from Montgomery who had fallen asleep and was slumped up against the window.

'Harry had better not be drunk' retorted Summerfield.

'No he's as sober as a judge.'

'Good, he'll need to be, is everything going to plan?'

'Yes' said Halford. 'We'll stop at Headquarters so you can initiate the monitoring station. Everything OK with the Missus?'

'Yes, she's fast asleep. She'll be out until morning, she's taken one of her sleeping pills. I've left her a note by the Teasmade.'

Halford parked the car on the main road so as not to alert anyone within the hospital compound to their presence by the sound of the engine.

'What are we going to do with him?' asked McDermott, pointing at Montgomery who was still out like a light.

'We'll leave him here. He's no good to us in his condition, better let him sleep it off. He'll come and find us when he wakes up.'

Halford went to the boot, took out a picnic blanket and placed it across Montgomery's lap. They then walked the five minutes into the sprawling red brick hospital complex. Originally built as a workhouse with a separate infirmary at the beginning of the century, the infirmary had also been used as a military hospital during both wars.

Harold Holbrook Senior had been a doctor at the hospital during the Great War, treating men who came back from the front suffering from shell shock. The most severe cases he despatched to Saxondale. In retirement, Holbrook Senior joined the committee of Hospital Guardians. He retained his association with the hospital until 1948 when the committee were abolished in favour of the new National Health Service. His son followed in his footsteps. After completing his medical training, Harry Holbrook junior served at the hospital during the Second War. Two generations of experience gave Holbrook junior an intimate knowledge of the rambling site and a keen instinct, about which fascist matrons were to be avoided at all costs. The ninety acre complex of scattered detached red brick buildings, many joined together by long empty corridors, had been undergoing a substantial period of refurbishment with the addition of new departments, outpatient unit and modernised wards. The flux caused by the constant upheaval on site and the coming and going of an increased number of people, allowed Holbrook to mingle quite undetected and unchallenged. He found himself able to occupy a space adjacent to an abandoned theatre. The hospital had no Accident and Emergency Department and as a result, procedures tended to carried out during the working day. By five o'clock everyone had gone home and Holbrook found he was able to occupy the space quite unhindered.

Montgomery had recommended Doctor Holbrook to his goddaughter, Holly Phillips. Dr Holbrook, he assured her, could be trusted implicitly to guarantee absolute discretion as to her condition and unwed state.

U.S airman James Wingfield had been gone for months without so much as a letter. Holly had shed untold tears enduring the heartbreak of his cruel and sudden departure. To avoid the shame and indignity of being an unmarried woman with child, she left her home at Grace Dieu and had taken up temporary residence with the Montgomery's. Their lifelong relationship was one of absolute trust. Holly allowed her Godfather to make whatever arrangements he felt were right and proper given her unfortunate circumstances. The last thing Holly wanted was to bring disgrace onto the family and for her reputation to be irrevocably tarnished. Montgomery had made no bones about it. Secrecy was the key unless she was reconciled to being brandished an Airman's trollop and her child a bastard for all eternity.

Holbrook set about the delivery of Holly Phillip's infant. The moment the baby was born, he covertly exchanged the Entonox cylinder for a general anaesthetic and Holly fell unwittingly into a welcome oblivion.

'I still get lost in this place' whispered McDermott, in a drunken stupor fumbling to find his way in the dark and stumbling off down the wrong path.

'It's this way' hissed Halford quietly opening the door to the abandoned theatre and going inside. McDermott followed and let the door swing behind him. Halford caught it just before it could bang into the doorframe and cause an echo that would reverberate through the empty corridor.

'Don't be a bloody fool' Halford quietly scolded.

'Where have you been?' Holbrook cursed as Halford and McDermott slipped into the theatre. Holbrook was cradling the new born in one arm and had a bottle of milk in the other.

'Here' said Holbrook 'take this' offering the infant to McDermott.

'Me?' exclaimed McDermott 'I don't know what to do with a baby.'

'You feed it' commanded Holbrook, thrusting the bottle towards him.

'Not me. I'm no good with babies, make him do it.'

'He can't do it he needs to assist me, now take the bloody baby and keep it quiet.'

'Where the hell have you been?' whispered Holbrook.

'We got here as soon as we could' replied Halford. 'We had to wait for Summerfield.'

'Where is he?'

'HQ.'

'What about Montgomery?'

'He's pissed up and asleep in the car.'

'You left him in the car?'

'He's better off in the car, believe me he'd be no use in here, not in the state he's in. Besides we don't need him until she wakes up. By then he'll be ok.'

'Right we haven't got as long as I'd hoped. I had to administer the general anaesthetic nearly half an hour ago. We need to make haste.'

Halford washed his hands, switched on the microscope and sat at the bench. He rifled in a small drawer and took out a compartmentalised lidded tray. He opened the lid and gently removed the first tiny microchip with a pair of fine surgical pliers before placing it under the microscope to inspect. Satisfied, he transferred it to a surgical tray and passed the tray to Holbrook.

Holbrook, already in full scrubs, positioned Holly onto her side. He added a pair of surgical gloves and a face mask over which he placed a pair of powerful magnifying lenses. He collected a scalpel and proceeded to make a small incision in her scalp, before using a fine bit to drill the first hole.

McDermott paraded back and forth across the floor rocking the baby in an attempt to stop it from wailing.

'I take it it's a girl' said McDermott.

'Yes of course it is' confirmed Holbrook.

'What's her name?'

'I suppose that will be up to the Morris'' replied Holbrook.

'I disagree, I think she should already have a name before we deliver her to the Morris'' said Halford.

'Then what do you suggest?' asked Holbrook.

'She was conceived during project Emily' replied Halford, transferring the second chip onto a plate and selecting a third. 'Perhaps she should be called Emily.'

'But our project isn't Emily. Emily was just a lie we employed as a cover to disguise what we were really doing.'

'There you have it then,' said Holbrook 'she's not Emily, she's Emilie.'

CHAPTER 19
THE ONE WITH ALL
THE BLOOD

May 9th 1998

The six o'clock alarm sounded with Sonny & Cher, *I got you Babe.* Emilie reached over, hit the snooze button and sank back into the pillow. Nine minutes later it came alive again, it was still Cher but singing *Bang Bang, my baby shot me down.* Emilie initiated the snooze to invoke another blessed nine minutes. At its third attempt to rouse her from the bed, the clock read 06:19. This time Merseybeat band The Searchers were singing the closing bars of the 1964 number one hit *Needles and Pins.* The disc jockey informed his listeners that that concluded the Sonny Bono tribute, who in addition to having been one half of pop sensation Sonny & Cher, had also been a United States Congressman and past Mayor of Palm Springs. He had died following a collision with a tree whilst skiing in January. Without opening her eyes, Emilie fumbled for the buttons on the top of the digital radio and silenced it once and for all by pressing the *stop* button. She swept her arm across the bed to prod Will, who as usual, hadn't woken through any of the alarm calls. His side of the bed was empty and it was cold. She called towards the bathroom, no reply. She climbed out of bed and peeked inside, it was empty. Slipping a satin robe over her short pyjamas, she ventured downstairs to prepare breakfast expecting Will to be in the kitchen but he wasn't. It was only then she recalled him going out in the middle of the night and concluded he must still be dealing with the flood at Fillet. She thought about calling but guessed he wouldn't appreciate the interruption if he was busy. Instead she placed two glasses of orange juice and two bowls of cereal on the breakfast bar leaving the carton of milk in the centre before switching on the kettle to make coffee. She collected the strong mug of coffee, headed into the hall and hollered upstairs to wake the boys. The daily newspaper had been delivered by the paperboy and was sticking through the letterbox. She checked the front page expecting to see a large spread on the life of Frank Sinatra but there was nothing so she dropped it on the stairs and made her way into the study. Her desk was in its usual disarray. She removed the overflowing ashtray, an assortment of cold coffee cups, the contents of her make-up bag and the remnants of yesterday's packed lunch then set about going through the pile of papers. She slipped the planning papers, the budgetary monitoring bundles, the draft corporate plan and the minute book that arrived in yesterday's post into her Pending tray. She came across a note scribbled in Sam's hand writing that stopped her in her tracks. It read *Ring Dana Coxstable ASAP*. She heard Sam thumping down the stairs and met him at the bottom.

'When did this arrive?' she asked thrusting the yellow post-it note in his direction.

He studied the piece of paper.

'The other night.'

'Which night?'

'The night you went out, Thursday.'

'What time?'

'I dunno, just before you came home.'

'Why didn't you tell me about it?'

'Because you say I should write messages down and leave them on your desk so that's what I did.'

'What exactly did she say?'

'She said she needed to speak to you urgently and you were to call her when you got in.'

'And that was it?'

'That was it.'

'She didn't say what she needed to speak to me about?'

'No, can I go now? I'm not used to being interrogated at this time of the morning.'

'I'm not interrogating you. She's dead you know. Dana was one of the passengers in the car accident. This phone call must have been one of the last things she did before she got into that car. It might be important; I might need to tell the Police about it.'

'Why? What's a phone call wanting to talk to you got to do with the Police?'

Emilie had taken the decision not to tell the boys her five colleagues were actually murdered and not the victims of a tragic road accident as she'd initially been led to believe.

'Never mind' said Emilie. 'Your breakfast is in the kitchen. What time do you have to be at the Paintball Centre?'

'Nine. Phoebe and Layla will be here at eight fifteen.'

Emilie was just going out of the door with her car load of adolescents when Will's car pulled onto the drive. He slammed on the anchors, the wheels slipping and churning up the gravel, before coming to an abrupt halt.

'Everything OK?' she asked, pecking him on the cheek.

He nodded.

'Can't stop, we're off to shoot the hell out of each other.'

'What?'

'Paint balling. Hopefully we'll be back by lunch, unless, now that you're here, you want to take them and I can get on with some work. Shooting's more your thing than mine.'

'What makes you say that?' he asked defensively.

'Someone's a bit tetchy this morning Mr Grumpy. Are you sure everything is OK?'

'Yeah, I'm just exhausted. I need to get some shut-eye. Wake me when you get back and if the kids survive the morning, send them all next door for an hour, we need to talk.'

'Sounds ominous, what about?'

'Later.'

Will disappeared and closed the front door.

The teenagers changed into the obligatory gear; camouflage jumpsuits, bullet proof vests, kneepads and full face masks by which time they looked more like a Special Forces brigade expecting a gas attack than a group of rampant teenagers. Emilie struggled to pick out her own two offspring from the other armed gung-ho combatants. Once satisfied they'd understood the rules of combat and surrender, the instructor led them away. Emilie made an excuse to leave, announcing she'd be back at midday to collect them and they were to wait in the reception without leaving the facility.

She drove north for half an hour through Ilson and on past the abbey ruins to the sleepy rural hamlet of Dual Abbey where Dana Coxstable had lived with her mother. A middle aged woman still in her nightclothes answered the door. Her hair was matted and unkempt. Swollen bags of skin hung below her red sunken eyes. Emilie's senses were met with the unmistakable stench of stale alcohol and marijuana.

'Hello Mrs Coxstable' said Emilie. 'I wonder if I might ask you a question about Dana.'

'My daughter is dead' she replied.

'I know that and I'm so very sorry for your loss.'

'What do you want?' asked Mrs Coxstable.

'I was hoping you might be able to help me. I've only discovered this morning that on the night Dana died, she called me at home. It would have been just before she left for the Town Hall. I wasn't home unfortunately but she left a message with my son. I was hoping you might be able to tell me what she was calling about.'

'I've no idea, I'm sorry I can't help you. Now if you'll excuse me I'm expecting the vicar to discuss the arrangements for the funeral and as you can see I'm hardly attired suitably to receive him.'

With that, Mrs Coxstable stepped back and abruptly closed the door. Undeterred Emilie knocked again but there was no answer. She knocked again, still nothing so she sank to her knees and peered through the letterbox from where she detected the unmistakable smell of freshly burned hash.

'If you should recall what it was about, I'd like you to call me on this number' Emilie shouted through the letterbox. She pushed her business card through the opening and waited for a response. There wasn't one. Frustratingly she got back into her car.

As she sat at the junction to the main road, she noticed a white van parked half way down the street. It looked like the same van she'd seen twice that morning, first parked down the street at home and then again pulling into the car park at the Paintball Centre.

Don't be ridiculous she thought. *There are thousands of plain white vans. Half the tradesmen in the country drive small white vans. What on earth has made you paranoid about this one? The chances of it being the same van are infinitesimal.*

She couldn't shake the irrational paranoia so took a mental note of the registration number through the rear view mirror before turning into the flow of traffic.

Emilie stopped at a Drive thru to pick up a sausage muffin and coffee before heading back to the Paintball Centre. She considered calling the detective who had questioned her at the Town Hall but thought better of it. The message from Dana Coxstable may have been nothing of consequence and she didn't want to be thought of as a time waster or worse still neurotic. She decided she'd wait and see if Mrs Coxstable called later in the day when she'd sobered up.

Just before noon she pulled into the car park at the Paintball Centre. She entered the front door. Phoebe and Layla were sitting down until they saw her, at which time Layla became hysterical and starting sobbing. The instructor appeared.

'Where are Sam and Miles?' Emilie asked.

'I'm afraid there's been a terrible accident' said the instructor. 'Please sit down.'

'I don't want to sit down, where are my boys?'

'I don't want you to panic Mrs Weston but Sam has been involved in an accident. The ambulance has only just left. Your other son Miles has gone in the ambulance with him.'

'What kind of accident?'

'I didn't see it but apparently he ran across the road and was struck by a van. Unfortunately, the driver of the van didn't stop.'

'What was he doing running across the road? They were told not to leave the building until I came back.'

'I'm aware of that, as were the children. When I left them, they were sitting here where I told them to remain until you arrived. I had to go and prepare for our next intake.'

'Did anyone get the registration number?' Emilie asked.

'No I'm afraid not, all we know is that it was a white van.'

'We told him not to leave Mrs Weston' sobbed Layla 'but he insisted he wanted to go and get some crisps from the shop over there.'

'No, you wanted him to go and get crisps' accused Phoebe. 'He wouldn't have gone if you hadn't have kept going on about it.'

'I'm sorry Mrs Weston' sobbed Layla. 'I didn't know this would happen.'

'Stop crying' Emilie shouted over the teenage hysterics 'it's not helpful, I can't hear myself think. How badly is he injured?'

'I'm not a trained medic of course but we believe he was unconscious for some time although he had regained consciousness before the ambulance left.'

'Which hospital has he been taken to?'

'Queen's' replied the instructor 'we tried to call your husband at home but all I've been able to do is leave a message on your answering service I'm afraid.'

'I think it's serious Mrs Weston' whispered Phoebe 'there was a lot of blood.'

'Right then, Queen's it is. Have you called your parents? Can one of them pick you up?'

'No, Dad's gone fishing and he's taken the car, he won't be back till teatime.'

'Great, then you'll have to come to the hospital with me and you can call your Mum from there. There's a bus between home and the hospital, she'll be able to use that.'

'Can I check we have your correct contact details before you go please?' asked the instructor. 'The Health and Safety Executive will no doubt want to conduct an investigation and they may well want to speak to you.'

Emilie gave him her business card, apologised profusely for the trouble and raced off frantically with the girls in the direction of Queen's.

The multi storey car park at the hospital was jam packed. She eventually found a space on the top floor and hurried on foot to the Accident and Emergency Department, stopping numerous times along the way for Phoebe and Layla to catch up. She was asked to take a seat in a side room and told a Doctor would be along as soon as possible. She called Will but got his answering service so she left a message. She then gave her mobile phone to Phoebe to call home, initiating the speaker function so she could hear both sides of the conversation.

'Mum, it's Phoebe'.

'Where are you, I told you to be home for one o'clock.'

'I'm at Queen's hospital with Layla and Mrs Weston.'

'But it's gone one thirty, you're supposed to be home, your dinner's drying out in the oven.'

'What is it?'

'Fish finger and chips. What time will you be home?'

'Can you come and pick us up?'

'Where from?'

'I told you, Queen's hospital.'

'What are you doing there?'

'We're with Mrs Weston. Sam has had an accident.'

'Didn't you tell her you were needed home for one o'clock? Couldn't she have brought you home first?'

'No, we came straight here from the Paintballing Centre. Can't you come and fetch us?'

'No, you know your Dad's not here.'

'Can't you get the bus?' Phoebe asked.

'What, all the way to Queen's? Is Mrs Weston going to reimburse the bus fare?'

'I don't know.'

'I bet she won't, not a full fare return and two half singles. Can't she bring you back?'

'No'

'Why not?'

'She's waiting to see the Doctor.'

'Well I'm sure the Doctor won't be long, she can bring you back after she's seen him but I won't be here so she'll have to keep you until your Dad gets back.'

'So you won't fetch us?'

'I'm just about to go to Bingo; Mrs Perkins is waiting for me. I'm already late which means we'll probably miss the first game, which is why I specifically told you to be home for one o'clock. This really isn't good enough Phoebe. If Mrs Weston can't have you back on time then I'll have to think about you going anywhere with Mrs Weston in the future. It's most inconvenient and she should know better than to put folk out like this.'

'She couldn't help it.'

'Look, I've got to go we'll miss the entire first sitting at this rate. You behave yourself and I'll see you when I get back tonight around eight.'

'OK, see you later.'

Emilie took the handset and cut the call.

'Mum says …'

'I heard what your Mum said.'

'I'm hungry' said Layla. 'I never got me crisps.'

'Well you'll have to wait, I haven't got any money' replied Phoebe.

Emilie took out her purse. She had two notes, a ten and a five and a selection of coins. She removed the ten pound note and handed it to Phoebe.

'Take this' said Emily 'and go down there to the elevator. Go up one floor and follow the signs to the Main Entrance. There you'll find the WRVS café; you'll be able to get something to eat there. It might not be fish finger and chips but you'll get something hot, a baked potato with beans or cheese and salad, you can bring me a cup of coffee back if you don't mind.'

'Thank you Mrs Weston' said Phoebe 'we won't be long.'

Emilie waited for the girls to disappear into the elevator and tried calling Will again. She left another message. After the girls had been gone for half an hour she went in search of a Doctor but found only a nurse who told her to sit down and that a Doctor would be along shortly. Another thirty minutes passed before the girls returned, each armed with handfuls of vending machine products that occupied the seating capacity of two chairs.

'I thought you were going to have a hot meal, none of this looks very nutritious' said Emilie surveying the veritable array of crisps, chocolate bars, and packets of sweets, snacks and fizzy drinks.

'We couldn't find it' said Layla.

'But you found the vending machine round the corner?' asked Emilie. 'Did you get me a coffee?'

'Oh no sorry, like we said we couldn't find the café.'

'There's a hot drinks machine next to the machine you got that lot out of.'

'Oh sorry, we didn't see it, besides there was no money left. If you give us some more money we'll go back and have another look' suggested Layla.

'It's OK, the doctor will be here any time now.'

Another hour passed before a Doctor did emerge. Sam had lost a lot of blood, was still haemorrhaging and needed blood they didn't have.

'His blood group is O negative' said the Doctor. This means he can only receive donated blood from supplies of the same O negative blood and unfortunately there's a national shortage.'

'I thought O blood was the most common' Emilie responded 'and there was a lot of it.'

'For patients whose type is O positive, there is a good supply, well a better supply at least. Unfortunately, your son's type isn't positive, it's negative. He is one of just thirteen per cent of the population who have it, unlike O positive which is shared by thirty five per cent.'

'So why can't he be given O positive blood if it's the same type?'

'Because of something we call the Rh factor and the probability of a transfusion reaction. There are a number of different reactions to a transfusion that can occur where incompatible blood is given, so it's vital we transfuse the correct type or we risk haemolytic reaction.'

'What's a haemolytic reaction?'

'This is where the patient's own antibodies attack the cells in the transfused blood causing them to haemolyse or break open releasing harmful substances into the bloodstream. Such a reaction can cause many difficulties including kidney damage which leads to renal failure and is life threatening.'

'So what's the difference between positive and negative blood?' she asked.

'Positive blood has additional antigens which sit atop the surface of the red blood cells. Negative blood doesn't have these D type antigens. If we transfuse positive blood with the D antigens, Sam's body will initiate an immune response to fight off the invading cells, just as it does to fight infection. As I explained, the consequences can be fatal.'

'What about another negative blood type?' asked Emilie.

'It's a similar picture I'm afraid. Type A blood has A type antigens, type B blood B antigens, AB type blood has A and B antigens. In much the same way, Sam's immune system will likely trigger an antibody response to destroy the invading antigens his body doesn't recognise. He can only have Type O negative blood which has zero antigens.'

'Can I give him my blood?' asked Emilie. 'I'm his mother surely my blood will be compatible.'

'Yes indeed it might. Sam has also inherited alleles from the genes of his biological father so if your blood isn't a match, his father's might be. Do you know what blood group you are?'

'No I'm afraid I don't. Perhaps I did once when I was pregnant, but I've forgotten. Can I take a test?'

'Yes of course. I'll have a nurse arrange it. Two batches of Type O negative have been located at a bank in another part of the country. One of our dedicated blood couriers is on his way to fetch it so please don't worry.'

'I think my Husband is type A negative. He donated blood a few times and I'm sure I remember seeing it on a card they gave him. Why are you so low on supplies of blood?' Emilie enquired.

'As I have already explained, it's not a common type therefore there are fewer people to donate it but this isn't the only reason. Because type O negative lacks the antigens we've talked about, this makes it suitable for use in emergency situations for all patients, regardless of their blood phenotype. It's what we call a universal blood. It's the age old problem of supply and demand. Not enough supply coming in and too much demand going out. Perhaps when Sam is fully recovered and comes of age he will consider joining the blood donation scheme.'

'How long will it be before the blood gets here?' asked Emilie.

'About two hours' replied the doctor.

'How is my Son? How serious are his injuries? Can I see him?'

'He's very poorly I'm afraid but he is conscious now. He's had an ultrasound and a CT scan which shows us he has some internal bleeding and unfortunately some damage to his spleen. He's undergoing an MRI scan which will help us to determine the extent of the damage but he is going to need an operation either to remove or to repair his spleen.'

'Can he live without a spleen?'

'Yes he can go on to have a fairly normal life, the spleen isn't essential. Without it he will have to be careful of bacterial infections but this can be managed with monitoring and vaccinations. I'll have a nurse come and find you when he comes back from the MRI.'

'I apologise for keeping you, Doctor, but my younger son Miles came in the ambulance with Sam. Where is he?'

'Oh yes young Miles. He's stolen the heart of all my nurses I don't think they want to let him go. I'll have someone bring him to you and try not to worry we're doing everything we can.'

'I'm bored' Layla announced at three o'clock. 'There's nothing to do here. Can't we go home?'

'No I'm afraid not, we have to wait.'

'But I'm bored, what can I do?'

'What would you like to do?' asked Emilie.

'I'd like to go home so I can watch the TV.'

'Well we can't go home I'm afraid. Phoebe, why don't you call your Mum again?'

'There's no point, she won't be back from Bingo for hours.'

'She might have come back early, you never know. Shall I try?'

'You can if you want to but unless she's had a win, she'll be there until seven. She never comes home early.'

Emilie dialled Mrs Moore's mobile phone, initiated the speakerphone and passed the phone to Phoebe. It answered on the sixth ring. The sound of the bingo caller could be clearly heard in the background, two fat ladies…

'Mum, it's Phoebe. Layla wants to come home, she's bored.'

'Well what do you expect me to do about it? I'm at the Bingo.'

'Can you leave Bingo early and come and fetch us?'

'No I can't. Why can't Mrs Weston bring you home?'

'She's waiting for a blood test.'

'What's she doing having a blood test when she should be looking after you girls? I thought it was Sam who'd had the accident.'

'Yes it is. Mrs Weston might have to give him some of her blood.'

'Then she ought to bring you home before the blood test. It can make you feel proper dizzy having your bloods taken, she shouldn't be driving straight afterwards, not with you girls in the car. Tell her you want to come home now.'

'There isn't time the nurse could be here any minute. Why can't you just leave the Bingo and get on the bus and come and pick us up?'

'I can't afford the fares all the way to the Queen's and back and I'm not giving up my winnings to hand to a bus driver. By the time I get there Mrs Weston will have had her blood test, so you might as well stay until it's done.'

'Eyes down' the Bingo caller announced.

'I have to go or I'll miss my game. I'll see you later and you make sure Mrs Weston buys you some tea if you're still there at teatime and make sure you have a pudding, it's the least she can do for all the inconvenience she's put us through.'

The phone fell silent, Mrs Moore had cut the call. Phoebe handed the phone back to Emilie.

'Mum's not coming' said Phoebe.

'I heard' replied Emilie.

'But I'm so bored' complained Layla.

Emilie rifled in her handbag for her purse and removed her last £5 note.

'I know you couldn't find the café last time but next door to it is a newsagent and gift shop. Do you want to go and have another look and see if you can find it? You might be able to get yourself a magazine or a puzzle book or something?'

Phoebe took the £5 note and the two girls trundled off down the corridor.

It was just after half past three when a middle aged nurse with wild afro hair, tamed with a sturdy hair clip, approached with Miles and took her into a side room. She was barely five feet tall and not much less widthways, with a huge bottom and penguin feet that made her waddle as she walked. She had a beaming smile and brilliant white teeth that would have brightened the darkest of days.

'Here she is young man.'

'Mummy' beamed Miles racing over to Emilie and throwing his arms around her waist.

'Hello little guy, I hear you've been busy.'

'I have and I don't think you can call me little guy anymore not after today. I wanted to be sick and pass out from all the blood but I didn't. I did what you always told me to do. I stuck with it because Sam needed me.'

'I'm very proud of you. Are you alright? Have you had something to eat and drink?'

'He's eaten us out of house and home he has and he's particularly susceptible to Jaffa cakes. I'll take your bloods now my lovely, if that's alright with you?'

Emilie rolled up her sleeve.

'How's Sam doing? Is he back from the MRI yet?'

'Aye, he's just come back up, Doctor's with him now. You'll just feel a little prick.'

The nurse removed the needle and attached a ball of cotton wool and sticking tape.

201

'This will go off to the lab now to see whether Mum's blood is good enough for your big brother. Someone will be along to speak to you soon.'

When the nurse had gone Emilie called Will and left her eighth message.

At four thirty the nurse came back and announced that the children might like to visit the Day room where there was a television. No sooner had they gone, the Doctor returned with news that shook Emilie to the core.

The blood bike courier bringing the two units of O negative needed for the operation to save her Son's life, had himself been involved in a road traffic accident. The rider had been killed instantly and the blood he was carrying was lost.

Emilie composed herself and the Doctor announced he wanted to repeat her blood test.

'Is there something wrong with the sample I've already given?' asked Emilie.

'I'd like to take another one just to be sure' he replied. 'You said earlier you didn't know your blood group. Have you thought anymore about it?'

'I have, but I'm sorry, I simply don't know. It sounds very irresponsible now, given the circumstances, not to know, and I'm sure it would have saved you a lot of time and trouble if I did know it, but I don't.'

'Not to worry, lots of people don't know their blood type. It wouldn't have saved any time so please don't worry about that. Your blood will still have to go to the lab to be tested for Hepatitis B, Hepatitis C and HIV. You are Sam's biological Mother yes?'

'Yes, why?'

'I can't apologise enough but it would appear there has been a mix-up in the Haematology lab because the sample that's been labelled as belonging to you is not what I'd have expected to see'

'Why is that?'

'It is a phenotype that would mean irrespective of your Husband's blood group, it isn't possible for you to be Sam's biological parents.

202

According to the label on the blood sample you provided, you have blood type AB negative. As a group it's rarer even than O negative, less than three per cent of the population.'

'I don't understand. Why do you say it's not possible, what do you mean?'

'I'll draw you a diagram, it might be easier to explain that way.'

	I^A	I^A
I^A	$I^A I^A$	$I^A I^A$
I^B	$I^A I^B$	$I^A I^B$

	I^A	ii
I^A	$I^A I^A$	$ii\ I^A$
I^B	$I^A I^B$	$ii\ I^B$

'Parent one let's say, your blood group, **AB**, is written vertically to the left of the punnet square. **AB** is expressed as $I^A\ I^B$. See?'

'Yes.'

'The blood group of parent two is written horizontally, above the punnet square. To understand how this is expressed, it's important to know that a person inherits two alleles from their parents; one from each parent. Blood has two alleles. Your alleles are *A* and *B*, assuming this is your blood. We say you are heterozygous because there are two different alleles, *A* and *B*.

Now let's look at the second parent. Parents two's type is represented horizontally across the top. There are two possibilities here. The parent can be homozygous for *A*. This means they have inherited two *A* alleles, or they can be heterozygous for *A*. This means that of the two alleles they have inherited, only one allele is *A*. The other could be *B* as in your case, or it could be *O*. You need to know that type *A* and type *B* are co-dominant. *O* however, is considered to be a regressive or a non-dominant allele. This regressive *O* allele is usurped by the dominant allele. A dominant *A* type and a regressive *O* type will simply be expressed as *A*.

You'll see that **O** is expressed in the second punnet chart as **ii**. To predict an offspring of **O** type, we need to be seeing two sets of **ii**'s in a square. Where we see **ii** coupled with an **A** or a **B**, the **A** or **B** as the co-dominant allele, takes precedence. Am I making myself clear?'

'Yes, I think so. Then I must have Will's blood type wrong' said Emilie. 'He must be **O**.'

'Perhaps so. Let me draw you another diagram. Let's for arguments sake, assume that your husband is homozygous for **O**. In other words, both his inherited alleles are **O**.'

	ii	ii
I^A	I^A ii	I^A ii
I^B	I^B ii	I^B ii

'Do you see that even in this scenario, we don't see two sets of **ii**'s? There's still a dominant **A** or **B**.'

'So what are you saying exactly?'

'I'm saying that if this sample is indeed your blood, then I'm sorry, but it's not possible that you are his Mother.'

'That's preposterous' she exclaimed. 'I can assure you, I am his Mother. I was there at the birth, I remember it well. It was a difficult labour. I was told at the time I wouldn't be able to conceive again, although I did try. Alas it wasn't to be. Our younger son Miles, he's adopted, although he doesn't know. I'd like it to stay that way until he's older. I assure you Doctor, Sam is our son! He is our biological child.'

'Like I say, I apologise, sometimes mistakes do happen. If there's been a mistake, it's easy to rectify with a second test.'

'How long is all this going to take? And how is my son? I'd like to see him now please' insisted Emilie. 'I've been here for hours,' the frustration welling up inside her like a pressure cooker about to blow its lid.

'Just a little prick. Well done. The nurse will be back any minute and she'll take you up to see Sam. He's very sleepy but he has been asking after you. Some of his injuries are superficial but he is going to need surgery as soon as the blood arrives. Is Sam's father able to come in for a blood test? I'm sure it won't be necessary but it might give us another option.'

'I've been trying to call him all afternoon. His phone is switched off. Is my Son going to die without this blood?'

'We are going to do everything we can to prevent that Mrs Weston. My colleagues are trying to source additional blood supplies as we speak and we are carrying out cross-matching on other bloods to see if we can find any compatibility.'

'I thought you said only O negative would work.'

'Sometimes the samples get mislabelled, we are checking as fast as we can.'

The nurse came back in.

'They're happy as Larry in the Day room' she said. 'I've found a video of The Nutty Professor. That will keep them occupied for a couple of hours. I'll take you up to Sam now, if you're ready?'

'Yes please.'

Emilie called Will again and was forced to leave her eleventh message.

An hour later and the Doctor reappeared. Emilie was sat at Sam's bedside. Sam had drifted off to sleep, waking only once to acknowledge his doting Mother's presence.

'Can we talk?' the doctor asked.

Emilie wiped away her tears with a soggy, crumpled tissue and followed the Doctor to the end of the bay.

'I have just received the results of your second blood test. You are type AB, there's no doubt.'

'I don't understand' wept Emilie, unable to contain the bewilderment. 'I am his Mother. Sam is my son. Have you been able to source any blood?'

'Not yet, but we're not giving up.'

CHAPTER 20
NEW YEAR'S DAY

January 1st 1964

After five gruelling hours, Holbrook emerged and announced Holly's implants were complete. The hospital was waking up to another day with nurses on a shift change coming and going. Even so, the hospital was quieter than usual due to it being New Year's Day and there being no routine procedures to bring in the hordes of doctors, nurses and out-patients. Holbrook announced he was too exhausted to countenance the possibility of carrying out the infant's implants and despite the risk of a return visit they would have to come back later to carry out the procedure.

McDermott was despatched in a taxi to deliver the new-born. He settled the fare, walked up the garden path and rapped on the door. Morris eventually answered, attired in pin stripe pyjama bottoms and an old string vest.

'Here she is' said McDermott. Your new daughter, her name is Emilie.'

'You'd better come in' replied Morris who called for his wife, who was still in bed, to come down at once.

Mrs Morris appeared a few moments later.

'What's all the urgency?' she chastised her husband. 'It's only eight o'clock.'

'The baby has arrived.'

'What today? But it's New Year's Day. There's a film I wanted to watch on the tele later. I wasn't expecting it to arrive today. Do you like our new tele Mr McDermott? It arrived just in time for Christmas. It's been a Godsend what with not being able to go out and introduce myself to our new neighbours. I'd like you to thank Captain Montgomery for helping us to get this house; you will tell him how grateful I am won't you?'

'Yes I will.'

'As you can see, we've not yet quite settled in and there's still some unpacking to do, but you can't do everything at once can you?'

'I suppose not' answered McDermott looking around at the numerous packing containers being used as resting places for yesterday's empty beer bottles, dinner plates, cups, saucers and overflowing ashtrays.

'Is this it?' she asked, surveying the tiny bundle tightly wrapped in a white woollen blanket, locks of jet black hair peeking out from the sides.

'It is indeed. I'd like to introduce your new daughter. Her name is Emilie' McDermott said, handing the baby over, relieved at having empty arms back again.

Mrs Morris took the baby and had a good look.

'Is it alright?' she enquired. 'Everything in working order?'

'Yes, she's perfect. Ten fingers, ten toes and a fine set of lungs. She's ready for feeding and changing I think.'

'And a fine head of hair. I've never seen so much hair on a new-born baby before.'

'Where are the supplies?' asked Mr Morris.

'Supplies?' asked McDermott.

'Yes, the bottles, the milk, the nappies. Have you brought them with you?'

'Don't you have them already?'

'No.'

'But you were given the money to buy everything you needed.'

'There wasn't enough money to buy everything. There was the pram, the cot and the clothes. Babies need a lot of stuff and it's expensive.'

'Yes I'm aware of that and I thought you'd been amply compensated. That rusty old thing over there, is that the expensive pram you're talking about?'

'There's nothing wrong with that that a little lubricating oil won't fix, but we are going to need some more start-up money. You did say you'd cover all the expenses or I'd never have agreed to it.'

'Forgive me Officer Morris, but I thought you'd agreed to take the baby in exchange for having your various misdemeanours buried, which otherwise would have resulted in your dishonourable discharge from the service, with the consequential loss of your commission and your military pension.'

'Don't take that tone with me laddie. I can just as soon change my mind and hand the ruddy thing back to you.'

'You'll do no such thing' interrupted Mrs Morris. 'Ignore my husband Mr McDermott; he got out of bed on the wrong side this morning. We can manage. Help me, will you please? There's a large suitcase by the French window.'

McDermott opened the suitcase to reveal it packed full with used baby products, most of the hand knitted white woollen products were now grey and misshapen from repeated laundering.

'If you feel around in there, I know there's a bottle somewhere.'

McDermott found a bottle but the teat perished in his hands when he tried to brush away the dirt. He ferreted around for second one and his finger caught on a corroded old nappy pin which pierced the tip of his finger.

'Find a nappy as well if you will please Mr McDermott. Mr Morris took me to the local church jumble sales before we moved. I couldn't believe how much I was able to get. Some of it is passed its best but most will suffice.'

'When can we expect to receive the first weekly payment?' asked Mr Morris.

'You'll receive the payments as per the arrangement with Captain Montgomery, weekly in arrears from the day you take parental charge which is today. Now you must remember to register the birth with the local registrar as a home birth as has already been discussed. I will collect the baby one week from today to be taken for a thorough examination by Dr Holbrook to make sure she is thriving.'

* * *

When Holly had recovered from the effects of the anaesthetic, Holbrook transferred her to a wheelchair. He administered a sedative in case she became hysterical on realising her child had already been taken away and given over to the adoptive parents. It was imperative they made it off the campus without bringing attention to themselves. A hysterical woman was the last thing they'd need. Halford was sent to find Montgomery who was still sleeping off his hangover in the car. He'd keep her calm, she trusted Montgomery implicitly. Holly was transported to the Montgomery house to convalesce. There she could be kept quietly under sedation until the wounds in her head were sufficiently healed.

Summerfield spent the next three days monitoring the implant's outputs around the clock. A never ending supply of cups of strong black Camp coffee and Embassy cigarettes kept him awake when it was all he could do just to keep his eyes open. He'd fallen asleep sitting bolt upright in the chair on a number of occasions. As a result there were gaps in his recordings.

'You look like shite' said Halford who brought four rounds of cheese and onion sandwiches wrapped in brown paper and dropped them on the desk.

'How's it going?' asked Halford.

'It's wild, we're getting far more data than I ever expected. I knew there'd be an uptake from the output we got from the Macaques and the rodents but what we're seeing is beyond anything I ever thought possible.'

The door opened and McDermott came in with Holbrook.

'Jesus, what's all this?' McDermott asked, rifling through the pages scribbled in Summerfield's handwriting, strewn on every surface, across the floor and pinned to the wall.'

'That's the content of your subject's head' replied Summerfield. 'For God's sake, don't move anything, its carefully catalogued and ordered.'

'This is ordered? I'd hate to see the havoc you create when you're not being orderly' McDermott quipped, picking up a pile of papers from the floor.

'I said leave it' shouted Summerfield. 'Don't touch anything.'

'Is everything being recorded?' asked Holbrook.

'Yes, onto those tapes over there. We need to make a decision whether we're going to tape over data after a given time.'

'Surely that depends on whether there's anything worth keeping' replied Holbrook.

'Ok, then we should define what's worth keeping.'

'Anything significant. Have you discovered anything significant?'

'Define significant' replied Summerfield. 'I think you might be interested in this. I've noticed that the outputs go into overload when there's no external task performance and reduce when there is, so perhaps you're onto something with your default mode network theory. I've also noticed a distinct drop in communication between the posterior cingulated cortex and the medial prefrontal cortex in the early stages of sleep but it doesn't last long and then the outputs are back up again.'

'Would someone mind translating that into something I might actually understand?' McDermott asked.

'That pile of papers is an account of the output when she's not doing anything specific, when she's just thinking. Those smaller piles were taken when she was engaged in some conscious effort of some kind.'

'What was she engaged in?' asked Holbrook.

'Here she was baking. Here she was reading Wuthering Heights and here she was building a chicken coup.'

'What's happening now?' asked McDermott. 'This may all be very interesting on a scientific level but you need to give me something I can sell. I can't sell do-it-yourself chicken coups.'

The tape got to the end of its reel and stopped. Summerfield installed a new one.

'Here,' he said, offering McDermott the chair and turning the monitor round 'see for yourself. I need a coffee and a breath of fresh air. Don't forget to write it all down as it happens. Sometimes you can't make sense of it straight away and things move on very fast. If you write it down it's easy to refer back to.'

Summerfield lit a cigarette and disappeared outside with Holbrook.

McDermott collected a pen and a notepad and begins to write down what he sees.

Sporadic violence is erupting on the beaches of Margate, Brighton, Clacton and Hastings. Gangs of youths on Lambretta scooters clash with motorcycle riders clad in leather.

The image disappears and another series of images appear.

A man enters. He is introduced as Luther Terry, the Surgeon General of the United States. He briefs a group of journalists on the newfound link between smoking, chronic illness and death. The American research corroborates the work carried out eighteen months earlier by their counterparts at the British Royal College of Physicians.

A mechanic is scraping the word Marlboro from the vertical tail of a red single seater sports car. McDermott is then transported to an empty sports stadium. Camel cigarette advertising hoardings are being covered over.

This image gives way to one of a factory floor with men in overalls on a production line. The door of an adjacent office opens and a group of men in pin stripe suits are sitting around a long table. A contract is being signed for the sale of four hundred Olympic buses to the Communist regime in Cuba.

Another image appears, the Red flag of China with its five gold stars is flying. China is taking delivery of a quantity of Uranium 235. Plans to build a nuclear fission bomb are unveiled.

The Americans are launching a white bodied Thor-Agena rocket carrying the satellite Echo2.

American firms Boeing, Lockheed and North American Aviation are all submitting plans to produce the world's first supersonic aircraft, much to the chagrin of the Supersonic Transport Advisory Committee at the Royal Aerospace Establishment and the British Aircraft Corporation who have still to perfect their own delta wing model. The British team are being told the future of the British aeronautical industry rests on beating the Americans to supersonic travel.

Robert Kennedy is posing for a photograph as Idlewild is re-branded as John F Kennedy International Airport in tribute to his dead Brother.

McDermott is then taken down a dreary High Street. It's not a familiar place. Ornate red brick Victorian buildings below slate multi hipped roofs mingle between square flat roofed brutal structures of grey concrete. The streets are empty apart from Styrofoam, tin cans and crumpled paper blowing on the breeze. Cigarette butts litter the shop doorways. Half the shop fronts have metal shutters pulled down and padlocked. Some are emblazoned with hastily painted symbols or daubed with words he hasn't come across before. Empty shops without shutters have broken windows. The remaining shops have large signs in the window that read CLOSING DOWN SALE or EVERYTHING MUST GO.

The screen changes to the image of a crying baby. It's somewhere hot. Sunlight is streaming in through the window illuminating uneven walls. The doors and windows are thrown open to catch a breeze. A woman is perspiring in the heat. She addresses the infant with baby talk and calls him Jeff. A young man comes in. She calls him Mr Jorgensen. They discuss the cost of the textbooks she needs to complete her studies.

The sunny arid place gives way to a grey dull day. There are architects plans laid out across a large oval table. Men in expensive suits are chewing on cigars. A small man comes in and is introduced as Minoru Yamasaki. He produces a three dimensional scaled model in white. Two tall skyscrapers soar 110 floors upwards, overshadowing the other buildings in the model, swamping what looks like the Statue of Liberty at the periphery. The two towers then crumble into dust as quickly as they had appeared.

The bespectacled American Secretary of Defence, Robert Strange McNamara, sporting greased perfectly combed dark hair parted unnaturally to the left, appears on the screen. He is announcing 1000 additional troops per month are to be sent into Vietnam to assist the 16,000 already deployed. Groups of Mothers sit huddled together sobbing remorselessly. A body bag marked number 216 heralds the return of the last serviceman to die before the end of the year.

British soldiers are being taken hostage by the 11th battalion of the Kenyan Rifles.

The Warren Commission are reporting on the assassination of President John F Kennedy. Someone is calling out whitewash and for Duran and Duran to be questioned.

The screen goes blank for the first time prompting McDermott to stop writing. A few minutes passes before he finds himself transported to the Yorkshire Moors with an impetuous Catherine Earnshaw and the vengeful Heathcliff. Holly is reading. He puts down the pen and is soon captivated by Holly's unique visual interpretation of Bronte's ill-fated lovers.

McDermott was rudely interrupted from his voyeuristic trance when Summerfield and Holbrook returned. He made a mental note never to be beholden or so obsessed by a mere woman since it could only ever lead to grief he could well do without.

'Have you seen anything interesting?' asked Summerfield.

'I don't know about interesting, it's mind blowing' replied McDermott.

'It is that. The primitive instincts of the macaques in the lab were easier to read, eh? They're complicated creature's, women.'

'So what exactly have I been seeing?'

'Why are you asking me? You're the one who's been watching.'

'How the hell do you make sense of it? The outputs never stop. God knows what it must be like being in that mind of hers. I found it impossible to keep up.'

'The important thing for us at this stage is to be able to clarify the accuracy of what we're seeing' said Holbrook.

'How do we do that?' asked McDermott.

'We study the transcripts and verify what they are telling us.'

'So what does this tell you?' asked McDermott, thrusting his notebook at Holbrook. 'Are we seeing events that have already occurred?'

'No, well there are some memories sure but most of what we're seeing hasn't happened yet.'

'How do we tell what are memories and what aren't? It's not memories we're interested in, they're worth nothing.'

'You soon get into a rhythm' replied Summerfield.

213

So if these things haven't yet happened how are we supposed to verify the accuracy?'

'We look for events with an imminent outcome.'

'How do we know an event is imminent?'

'You look for clues. Let's have a look at what you've recorded. This sporadic violence on the beaches for instance. Tell me exactly what you saw.'

'I saw bikes. Lots of bikes, not just big bikes like Norton's and Triumphs, there were also loads of scooters. The bikes congregated west of the pier, the Scooters to the east.'

'What else?'

'Studded leather jackets, denim jeans, brothel creepers.'

'Go on.'

'Suits and drainpipe trousers, long khaki jackets with fur trimmed hoods and what looked like archery targets.'

'Did you see anything that might date when this was?'

'Like what?'

'Advertised prices can be a useful guide as to a date or a location. If you see something advertised in pounds shilling and pence then you know the location is more than likely in Britain. If you see beer advertised at less than 10 pence a pint, you can say it's not too far into the future; likewise the price of petrol might give you a clue. Are you on a newly built road that doesn't yet appear on a map? What about date bricks in buildings or the style of architecture. Look at the clothes people are wearing. Types and models of car or car registration numbers are a great source. People reading or carrying newspapers, what are the headlines? Theatres and cinemas, what films or shows are they advertising?

'The Odeon' exclaimed McDermott. I saw the Odeon on Brighton sea front.'

'And did you see what was advertised?'

'Yes, Elvis Presley in Viva Las Vegas.'

'A telephone call to the Brighton Odeon will confirm if it's a film on their schedule.'

Summerfield replaced the telephone receiver.

'Viva Las Vegas. It's due to be shown at the Brighton Odeon in May. It'll be the main feature over the Whitsun holiday.'

'So that violence will erupt over the Whitsun holiday?'

'Yes.'

'I need more than one example if we're going to whet the appetite of any large groups.'

'I'm working on it. Give me another couple of days and I'll have a tape full of verified events. When will the second implant be carried out?'

'Easter' replied Holbrook.

'That's three months away' said Summerfield. 'Why so long?'

'It's too risky to do it any sooner. If we leave it until Easter when the hospital will be working on a skeleton staff, there's much less chance of us being caught in the act.'

'But I thought you said we needed to do it sooner rather than later.'

'By sooner I meant within the first seven years of life before unutilised synapses start to terminate. Until then we need to concentrate on developing the business case for the first subject.'

CHAPTER 21
CHAMPAGNE SUPERNOVA

May 21st 1998

It was five minutes to midday when Emilie Weston moved to the threshold to wait for Sam's arrival. Miles stood silently at her side fidgeting with the new black tie around his neck. The black hearse and its accompanying limousine turned into the street and drove slowly along the road before coming to a dignified stop outside. Emilie climbed into the back of the limousine after her young son to begin the laborious journey to the crematorium. Neighbours who weren't already making their way to Wilford Hill stood respectfully at their gates as the cortege passed. This was Emilie's sixth funeral in as many days but none of the others had prepared her for this.

Will Weston had disappeared. He hadn't been seen since the morning of Sam's hit and run. His personal belongings had been cleared out as Emilie discovered when she came home from the hospital. His mobile phone had not been answered since. He'd left a note propped up against the kettle which read simply *I'm sorry*. She longed to speak to him if only to be able to ask what it was he was sorry for. A Police search for both Will and the white van that killed her son had so far proven fruitless.

The cortege meandered slowly up the winding hill through the cemetery, memorial stones and flowers in varying degrees of life littered the grounds on each side stretching out until the horizon ran out. The car came to a halt outside the chapel at the top of the hill. Emilie adjusted the netting to her small black hat, took a deep breath and stepped out, turning to help Miles out after her. She glanced around but could see neither Will nor her in-laws. Sam's classmates dressed in their school uniforms stood obediently in a long line. Opposite were a number of young Air Cadets from 2195 Squadron in their smart blue-grey uniforms, obligatory berets and highly polished shoes.

Four pall bearers, made up from the ranks of the adult officers of the regiment, removed the casket from the hearse. The Cadets saluted as the casket was carried past them on the way into the chapel and people began to filter quietly in after it. All the seats were soon taken until there was standing room only at the back. Emilie was directed to take up a seat on the front row with Miles. She glanced toward the door hoping to see Will. There was no sign of him. Late arrivals were still peeling in. She regretted not having requested the bigger chapel to accommodate everyone. She recognised most of the faces but there were one or two she didn't. An odd man she didn't know shuffled into a tight space between two cadets. With folds of sagging skin under his eyes, a large growth at the side of his mouth and a long hook nose, the thought crossed Emilie's mind that the poor man had probably never been fortunate to find himself at the front of any of God's queues.

The service began and she turned to face the front, taking hold of Miles' hand and squeezing it tightly. Sam's form tutor gave a touching eulogy citing examples of her son's academic successes, his sporting prowess on the football field, his sense of humour and his popularity, reducing most of the girls in the congregation to swells of tears. The congregation was invited to join in with the two hymns Emilie had chosen. A young cadet gave an unexpected and impromptu rendition of The Last Post, at which point Emilie finally lost her composure. The service was brought to a conclusion with the closing of the curtains before the casket and Sam disappeared for the final time. Emilie calmed herself, wiped her eyes and prepared to lead the congregation out of the chapel to Sam's favourite song - *Champagne Supernova* by Oasis. She took up the obligatory position outside to receive the long line of well-wishers who had come to offer their commiserations and read the messages of tribute attached to the many floral arrangements that had been sent. Emilie had requested that in lieu of sending flowers, people should instead go along to the Donor Centre and give a pint of blood. Nonetheless there were still a lot of flowers. The biting wind tore through her black dress as she thanked each mourner in turn for coming, extending an invitation to attend the wake. The line finally came to an end with another man she didn't recognise dressed in a smart black suit. He had an unnatural mop of jet black hair she presumed to be a toupee. He clutched her hands firmly in his own, pecked her once on each cheek and offered his condolences. Before he walked away he took a small white envelope from the inside pocket of his jacket and slipped it into her hand before disappearing around the corner. She studied the blank envelope and opened the flap expecting to find a sympathy card. She'd had so many. Removing the contents she was confronted not with a greeting card but with a single sheet of Green Shield Stamps to which was attached a small note that simply read *A FRIEND*. Emilie ran in the direction of the mystery man but he was nowhere to be seen. When the congregation had filtered past the floral display she meandered over to look at the tributes herself. At the back was a red helium balloon anchored in place by a length of black ribbon tied to a football fashioned from red and white roses, the colours of Nottingham Forest. Emilie lost her composure for the second time, took Miles by the hand and led him back to the car.

The limousine chauffeur saw them coming and opened the rear door. Everyone had dispersed and the last few cars were heading downhill back towards the main road. Back at home people came and went all afternoon. The bottles of wine and trays of ham and egg sandwiches Emilie had helped to prepare that morning slowly evaporated. A little after six o'clock the final guests left.

'Is it ok if we take these sandwiches?' asked Phoebe who was looking in the fridge. 'I doubt Mum will be making any tea tonight.'

'Yes alright,' replied Emilie 'just transfer a few rounds onto a plate for Miles.'

Her words fell on deaf ears. Phoebe removed the cling filmed tray, rummaged in the salad crisper drawer, helped herself to a bag of apples and scurried out of the front door.

Emilie put the kettle on and made two strong mugs of coffee, passing one across the breakfast bar to Miles.

'I didn't think I was allowed to drink coffee' he said.

'I'm making an exception today, you're a man now. Have you had anything to eat?' she asked.

'No, but I'm not hungry.'

'I've got a ghastly headache' she said reaching for her handbag to find a packet of paracetamol.

The white envelope she'd been given earlier that day fell out. She picked it up and took out the green stamps with the accompanying note from *A friend*.

'What are they?' asked Miles.

'These? They are Green Shield Stamps.'

'I've never seen them before, what are you supposed to do with them?'

'I don't think you can do anything with them these days, but when I was a little girl, shops and petrol stations used to give them away every time you brought something, a bit like a store loyalty card. Each book contained 1280 stamps and if I remember rightly, you had to spend six old pence to get one stamp.'

'What did you do with them?'

'You stuck them into a book and when your books were full you could take them to the Green Shield shop and exchange your books of stamps for one of their products. Seeing these has reminded me that on my birthday every year and each Christmas I used to receive a large envelope stuffed full of books of Green Shield Stamps. The week before my birthday I'd take the catalogue off to my room and imagine all the things I could exchange the stamps for. When I was six I wanted a scooter; that was four and a half books. When I was seven I yearned for the desk and chair; that was fourteen books. At eight, it was a doll, at nine a transistor radio and at ten I imagined I could be the proud owner of a Fidelity record player for twenty four books.'

'You got all those things with your stamps?'

'Actually, no I didn't.'

'How come?'

'Because your Grandmother would take the books that arrived on my Birthday and treat herself to something from the catalogue that took her fancy. Your Grandfather would take the books I received at Christmas and do likewise.'

'That's not very nice, not if they were intended as a gift to you.'

'No, perhaps not. They'd tell me every time the books arrived that food needed to be paid for and that the books didn't go near enough to offsetting the expense of feeding me and that I should consider myself lucky to be fed at all.'

'You don't eat much now' said Miles 'did you eat so much as a child you got bored with food?'

'No you daft thing. I didn't eat very much at all. I was always hungry, except on the last Sunday in the month when I'd be invited over the road to take tea with old Mrs Cohen who'd feed me all the chocolate spread sandwiches I could eat and open a can of peaches for dessert. Then we'd listen to a record on her old gramophone. Jim Reeves on a 33rpm or a very scratchy Marlene Dietrich on an old 78. They were the only two records she possessed. I really enjoyed the last Sunday in the month.'

'So you never got to have anything with all your stamps?'

'No. Not a thing.'

'How come I've never heard of Green Shield Stamps?'

'They don't exist anymore. The shops stopped giving them out. The catalogue still exists though. You make your Christmas list from it every year.'

'No I don't.'

'Yes you do. That laminated book of dreams you know as the Argos catalogue. Once upon a time, that was the Green Shield Stamp book.'

'Who used to send the stamps to you?'

'That's the oddest thing. I never knew who they came from. By the time I was ten, I'd grown accustomed to them arriving on my Birthday. I'd worked out the postman didn't bring them because there was never a postage stamp on the envelope. On my tenth birthday, I remember I sat at the window all morning waiting for them to arrive. When a dark green Jaguar pulled up outside, I raced downstairs but by the time I got to the door the envelope was already wedged in the letterbox and the man was running back to the car. I ran after him but he was driving away so I never got to see who it was, or speak to him, or thank him.'

'Didn't you ask your parents who sent them?'

'Yes but I always got the same answer, that curiosity killed the cat. I'd then be reminded that children should be seen and not heard and would be sent to my room.'

'So do you think it's the same man who gave you those stamps this afternoon?'

'I don't think it can be. It's been over twenty five years since I saw the man in the green Jaguar and whilst I didn't get a good look at him and it was a long time ago, I had the impression he wasn't a young man back then. The man we saw this afternoon wasn't old enough to have been the same person.'

'So why did he give them to you?'

'I've really no idea Miles.'

'Do you think Dad will come back?'

'I doubt it.'

'Do you think he's alright? What if something has happened to him? What if he has been run over like Sam and is lying dead in a ditch somewhere?'

'Whoever put that idea in your head?'

'Phoebe.'

'Well, Phoebe talks nonsense most of the time, you know that. I'm quite sure your Dad wherever he is, is perfectly ok. He left a note didn't he? He couldn't have done that if he'd been dead in a ditch now could he? Believe me; your Dad is absolutely fine.'

'How do you know that?'

'On account of the fact he packed all his clothes and his personal belongings then cleared the safe and emptied all the bank accounts.'

'Does that mean we have no money?'

'Not a lot no, but we'll survive.'

'Will we have to sell this house?'

'Yes, but we'll buy a smaller house somewhere else. We don't need a big house like this for just the two of us, do we?'

'I suppose not. I've been wondering.'

'What about?'

'I've never heard you talk about your Mum and Dad. Are they dead?'

'I'm not really sure, I don't think so. They moved to Spain many years ago.'

'Why haven't you ever taken us to visit them?'

'I suppose because we've never had an invitation.'

'But they're your parents, my Grandparents. Why do we have to wait for an invitation?'

'Because to tell you the truth Miles, I don't actually know where they are. I used to send a Christmas card until one year, many years ago, when you were just a baby. The card came back stamped with *Return to sender, no longer at this address* and I've not heard from them since.'

'But don't you miss them?'

'No not really. I know that technically they are your Grandparents but trust me Miles when I tell you they weren't very nice people.'

'Why not?'

'I don't know why not, but you're not missing anything not having them in your life, you have to believe me.'

'Why? What did they do that was so bad?'

'I'm not saying they were bad, they were just indifferent. I don't think they really wanted me. I was a bit of an inconvenience to them, quite a big inconvenience actually if I'm being honest.'

'Do you want me? Am I am inconvenience?'

'Don't be ridiculous. Of course I wanted you, I love you with all my heart and I'd do anything for you.'

'So when did you last see them?'

'The day after my sixteenth birthday. I came home from work to find a suitcase packed and waiting for me in the hall. They told me their contractual obligation towards me had expired and that it was time I was on my way. When I tried to explain I had nowhere else to go your Grandmother suggested I threw myself at the mercy of the Salvation Army.'

'So what did you do?'

'I picked up the suitcase and left.'

'You said you'd come home from work. You went to work when you were sixteen?'

'I'd been at work for almost a year by then. I went to work when I was fifteen.'

'But weren't you still at school?'

'Not in those days.'

'Will I have to go to work when I'm fifteen?'

'I sincerely hope not, no. I hope you'll get an education and will go to University and earn your degree.'

'So where did you go?'

'I stayed with a friend who let me sleep on her sofa until pay day when I took a room in a house with a group of university students.'

'So you had to live with strangers?'

'Yes and it wasn't half bad. I had a ball. For the first time in my life I had a new dress and was able to buy a new pair of shoes straight from the shop, not a tatty old pair your Grandmother picked up at a jumble sale. I saved up and did all the things I'd always longed to do. I acquired a library card. I took piano lessons and dance classes. I went to a restaurant and a hairdressing salon. I took day trips to the seaside and ate fish and chips straight from the newspaper. I learned to drive and I finally bought not only the record player I'd always hankered after but a TV as well. I wouldn't have been able to have done any of those things had my suitcase not have been waiting for me on my sixteenth birthday.'

'Why not?'

'Because the wages I earned were paid straight over to your Grandfather to cover my board and lodgings as he called it. Expensive board and lodgings they were too, considering the gruel your Grandmother used to pass off as supper. So you see Miles, even though things may appear to be very bleak, with hard work, determination and a little bit of luck and optimism, even the darkest times give way to brighter days and new opportunities. You must always look forward and keep going. Everyone has memories. Some we cherish forever but memories should be stored where they belong, in the past.'

'So you never received any more Green Shield Stamps once you left home?'

'No.'

Miles picked up the green stamps and studied them.

'What do all these numbers and letters mean?' he asked.

'That'll be the batch number I imagine, for security. Blow me down' she exclaimed.

'What?' asked Miles.

'Look at the letters and the numbers. EM 1164, my birth initials Emilie Morris and 1164, that's my birthday, 1st of January 1964. I'll be damned.'

CHAPTER 22
THE BUSINESS CASE

1971

The cork from the bottle popped and flew like a bullet ricocheting off the ceiling causing Holbrook to instinctively take cover. Champagne oozed from the neck of the bottle.

'This is indeed a cause for celebration' said Montgomery pouring five glasses. 'To the 100,000th subscriber' he toasted, raising his glass and clinking it with Holbrook's.

'The 100,000th subscriber' echoed Holbrook.

'100,000' repeated Halford.

'To the next 100,000 subscribers' added McDermott.

'I always said you were a greedy bastard who'd never be satisfied' laughed Halford, his flute clinking against McDermott's.

'It's not greed, its optimism.'

It had been seven years, seven gruelling years, travelling back and forth across the counties of the United Kingdom, into Scotland, Wales and Ireland, then across to mainland Europe and on into the America's. Each of them had played host to thousands of clandestine meetings in quiet corners and back rooms, in toilet stalls, elevators and dark corridors, by lavish swimming pools, on deserted beaches and windy rooftops.

Between them they'd found 100,000 gullible punters. Their confidential client base spanned the globe and with each month that went by, the subscribers increased. They'd created the ultimate pyramid scheme. It had started with just a single contact which led to two contacts which led to four which led to eight and on it went until they were wholesaling the greatest secret in town - access to the mind of The Compass. Each punter willing to pay for the privilege of being selected to witness history in the making, before the protagonists who would play out that history had the slightest notion of what would come to pass. Each punter signed a contract of non-disclosure. Each one having had their fragile ego massaged and their wilful arrogance manipulated into believing that they were somehow special to have been selected, making them and only them deserving of the gift that was being extended. Montgomery's repository team weren't actually gifting anything; the subscribers were paying every month for the privilege.

The punters came in many forms, from many different walks of life. The investors and the money market men were interested in information that afforded them the foresight to get in on the ground floor before the clamber of the masses brought the accompanying and inevitable diminishing returns. Some used it to beat their competitors at their own game, to be able to anticipate the right time to bail before the bottom fell out of the market.

The media men needed to be ahead of the next big headline, to see it coming before their competitors did. They were interested in the minutiae of the human condition in all its sordid splendour. When it came to selling copy, sleaze appeared to matter more than truth. Meteorologists were interested in floods, philanthropists the next worthy cause; ambitious head hunters sought evidence to determine which prospects were worth their time and investment and which of their protégé to dump into the mass market of mediocrity. The defence lawyers developed covert ways to circumvent the conventions of the taxi cab in favour of defendants who were destined to be found not guilty, whilst the prosecutors looked for the guilty verdicts to sure up their tally of success.

While McDermott and Holbrook were selling subscriptions to the hardened and professional gamblers, Halford and Montgomery were selling to the Bookmakers, calling their duplicitous interventions a balanced portfolio of risk. The subscribed gamblers won, but at such negligible odds, the status quo wasn't unduly altered and the

Bookmaker's weren't bankrupted. Everyone was getting something and the money was rolling in.

The repository team weren't often surprised and were usually able to second guess the interests of their potential punters. They got it wrong with the politicians. The primary focus of the politician was not to be able to judge the unintended consequences of new policy decisions as McDermott thought it would be. The ambitious politician wanted to be sure of backing whoever was going to be first past the post, the next leader and an assurance they'd end up victorious at the ballot box. Being able to see the unforeseen consequences of the policies they rolled onto the statute books might have been a bonus, but in order enact new polices, it was more important to be mandated the power to do so. That meant winning.

The punters may all have been looking for something different from their subscription - the acquisition of wealth, domination in their field, notoriety, power, success - but they all had one thing in common. Each one revelled in the prophetic supremacy their subscription endowed. In an era of cold war, information reigned supreme and access to information sourced from within the mind of the indefatigable Compass was King.

The Compass Cabal, as Montgomery had coined the group, were enjoying their success and it was reflected in the bank balance. Manipulating the mind of The Compass had made them rich men by any standard as monthly subscriptions continued to roll in and there appeared to be no end to the limit of it.

Wealth so far had been founded on the use of one Compass subject, Holly, who Montgomery as Guardian, continued to control. He learned to engage her in specific topics of conversation. These carefully chosen topics initiated triggers that focused her conscious mind. Quite unbeknown to Holly, the Cabal had discovered the trickle-down effect whereby her conscious deliberations acted as a catalyst to her subconscious thought, where the lion's share of outputs lay. She did very little from day to day, aside from cultivating a small cottage garden and carrying out mundane chores around the house. Montgomery always had a freshly laundered shirt pressed to perfection and she soon learned how to prepare his favourite meals. She saw very few people to distract her attentions. This gave free reign to her neural default mode network to remain open to the business of foresight, even though she didn't realise that was what she was doing. Through Montgomery's manipulation, she remained content at doing very little and was blissfully unaware she was in fact being manipulated. The dramatic increase in neural output during periods when she was sleeping persuaded Montgomery to encourage she took frequent naps following their topical discussions. Consequently, Holly found she could, provided she was comfortable, often sleep sixteen hours in a day. She nevertheless remained in a perpetual state of mental exhaustion. Her life was a far cry from the descendant members of The Compass Line, who were encouraged to hone their thoughts into actions and using their gifts of reason and fairness, to offer workable solutions to the most insurmountable of problems. Montgomery didn't need her equitable her solutions. This would only have detracted from her money generating outputs concerned with foresight. This was what the punters were paying for. If Holly ever felt any dissatisfaction to the sheltered existence Montgomery forced her to unwittingly endure, she never expressed it.

The second Compass subject had reached the age of seven. Holbrook had insisted that Emilie be encouraged to study during these formative years. Numerous books, encyclopaedias and an assortment of daily newspapers and magazines had been provided to the Morris' specifically for this purpose. A huge row ensued when it was discovered that the Morris' had sold the encyclopaedias through the personal column in the local newspaper and had cancelled the newspaper and magazine subscription with the newsagent in favour of cigarettes. The encyclopaedias were replaced, although unbeknown to the group, Emilie had been denied access to them by the Morris'. They intended to sell the second set in pristine condition at the first possible opportunity.

The Cabal had been monitoring Emilie's outputs for five years. Holbrook had had a change of mind and refused to carry out the procedure until her second birthday. As yet the Cabal had not offered her outputs for sale, much to the chagrin of McDermott and Halford. Over the second bottle of Champagne, a disagreement erupted as to when the right time to do this would be.

Halford was satisfied the modifications he had made to his closed circuits between the implantation of Holly and Emilie were good. As far as he was concerned, Emilie's implants had been tested sufficiently and been proven to be highly satisfactory. He thought she should be entered into service forthwith, potentially doubling their subscription rate.

McDermott, who exclaimed himself the King of the Patter having negotiated more subscriptions than the rest of his colleagues added together, agreed with Halford. Emilie's outputs were not the innocent ramblings or imaginings of a child's mind but showed pragmatism, logic and great astuteness. McDermott announced he would quite happily sell her outputs with confidence tomorrow alongside her adult counterpart.

Montgomery declared he was as usual, sitting on the proverbial fence. He would be content to be advised on the best time for Emilie to be taken into service.

Summerfield saw no reason why she shouldn't be put to work straight away. He'd spent ample time cross checking her outputs against fact and accuracy. She had consistently demonstrated the necessary attributes that would render her visions saleable in the market.

Holbrook was the dissenting voice. He disagreed, insisting Emilie should spend at least another year engrossed in study, practical activities and physical exercise.

'It's been my expertise and my theories on the functions of the brain that have made this project possible' he argued. 'I am telling you, if we remove the stimulus now, we risk premature decay of the neurons and the failure of important synaptic triggers that could have negative repercussions later on.'

'How many times do we have to have this conversation?' asked Halford. 'When she was five, you said one more year. When she was six you said one more year. I seem to recall that when she was two you stated quite categorically that by the age of seven her brain would be developed significantly enough to warrant removal of stimuli.'

'We're not at liberty to remove all stimuli, she still has to go to school' interrupted Montgomery. 'We can't do anything about that until she's at least fifteen. She'll receive stimuli in that environment. I suggest therefore we remove all extracurricular stimuli, monitor for three months and then make a decision.'

'That sounds good to me' said Halford. 'Are we agreed? We instruct the Morris' to remove all non-statutory sources of stimuli including books and magazines.'

'Yes' replied McDermott. 'She spends far too much time indulging herself in children's picture books in the library. Her library card should also be confiscated.'

'Agreed' said Summerfield.

'Thank God' added Halford. 'We can't prevaricate forever. She doesn't need to think for herself. She needs to think for the Cabal.'

'It looks like you're out-voted old man' said McDermott. 'We take her live in three months.'

CHAPTER 23
THE ANDERSON SHELTER

May 25th 1998

Miles Weston bounded out of the house like a frustrated prisoner on day release. He ran down the front garden towards the road. The front gate was open.

'Stop running' shouted Emilie. 'Stop, be careful the gate's open.'

'Mum, I'm not a baby, stop treating me like one, ok?'

'I'm sorry, I know you're not a baby but the roads are busy.'

'I know the Green Cross Code. We've been over it a thousand times. Stop. Look. Listen.'

'I know you do but ....'

'So stop treating me like I'm still a baby.'

Phoebe appeared from next door dressed in chunky platform heeled boots and thick black tights under a tight black skirt. The skirt barely covered her bottom, already showing the signs of the high calorie, high fat, sedentary lifestyle in which she indulged. Layla wasn't far behind, dressed more appropriately for school in black slacks and pumps.

'Are you sure you don't want me to drive you?' Emilie appealed.

'For the last time, no.'

'Ok, but you will be careful, won't you? Don't mess around at the roadside, keep your eyes open and your mind on the job.'

'Don't worry Mrs Weston, we'll see he gets to school ok' called Layla. 'We'll be fine.'

It was Miles' first day back at school since the funeral. He appeared to be coping with the prospect of being out alone for the first time far better than she was. In another term he'd be moving up to the local comprehensive where it certainly wasn't cool to be brought into school on your mother's coat tails. She watched them disappear around the corner and went back inside to look for her mobile phone. She'd give him fifteen minutes and then call school to make sure he'd arrived safely. The school secretary knew to expect her call.

Satisfied that Miles had arrived at school in one piece, Emilie brewed a coffee and sat at the computer to compose a number of letters. She was disturbed by the doorbell. The postman had a Recorded Delivery packet that needed a signature. She signed for it, closed the door and took the packet into the kitchen where she used a carving knife to open it. Two books full of Green Shield Stamps, a plain cassette tape and a single un-inflated red shiny balloon fell out. Stapled to one of the books was a type written note.

Don't be alarmed Emilie,
Come quickly to the address below the moment you open this packet.
Do not delay, your life depends on it.
Come alone, it is imperative you do not stop along the way,
don't tell anyone where you're going,
come now and play this tape as you are driving, play it loud.
And here is a red balloon, I think of you and let it go
A friend.

Emilie read the note again. The address she'd been given, across the county line, was a good twenty miles away. Below the address was a map showing the route she should take. As she read the note for a third time, her blood ran cold.

And here is a red balloon, I think of you and let it go.

It was the closing line to the song *Ninety nine red balloons* and it held great poignancy. The song had been playing the night she met Will. He'd coined it their song soon after, which displeased her intensely since it was most definitely not a love song. It was about war. She'd have much preferred for *their song* to have been something by Billy Joel, Lionel Richie or George Michael, who were all singing about romance. Ninety nine red balloons had been cemented into perpetuity as *their song* on honeymoon. Will had filled their rented cottage on the Yorkshire Moors with ninety nine red balloons and they spent the next five days releasing them one by one. She had never told anyone about the balloons, fearing it would have sounded far too cheesy a thing to have done and had no intention of being ridiculed.

She considered the request to come alone, mindful that the assailant who shot her colleagues at close range in cold blood just a few weeks earlier, was still out there. No arrests had been made. What's more, the hit and run driver in the white van who'd killed her son was still on the loose as the Police had drawn another blank. Driving to an unknown address to meet someone alone, having told no-one where she was going stood at odds against her better judgement. She thought about the stamps and the unknown benefactor who had delivered them on her birthday and at Christmas every year. He'd had plenty of opportunity over the years to harm her if that was the intent. She thought about the old veteran at the Town Hall protesting with the placard demanding Green Shield Stamps be brought back. He'd been a harmless old man, bent double with the ravages of age. He couldn't possibly be a threat. She thought about the man at the crematorium who had approached her after everyone else had gone and with whom she'd been alone behind the chapel. He could have done her in there and then if he'd wanted to.

She set her better judgement to one side, got in the car and as instructed, inserted the tape into the player. The hiss of empty tape soon gave way to the opening bars of the testosterone fuelled nine minute operatic rock epic that was *Bat out of hell* by Meatloaf. She turned up the volume, lit a cigarette, pulled off the driveway and headed for the motorway. Meatloaf gave way to *one two three four* and the dulcet melodic whistle of Axl Rose and *Patience*. She stopped at a red traffic light before joining the queue to head south on the M1. Wilson Picket's *Mustang Sally* was followed by The Eagles and their dark satanic ballad *Hotel California*. By the fifth track, Elton John's *Goodbye Yellow Brick Road*, Emilie realised only someone who knew her intimately could have made the tape. Each track was a link in what she had termed her musical nirvana, her most favourite songs, songs

233

she couldn't help but sing along to. Her very own Desert Island Discs. Richie Valens and *La Bamba* gave way to Chubby Checker and *The Twist*. For the first time in weeks, Emilie found she was actually enjoying a moment free from grief, shock and sadness. This realisation brought her temporary elation to an abrupt end. She approached junction 23, filed into the left hand lane and signalled to leave the motorway. She followed the instructions and continued along the Ashby Road before looking for a left turn. She arrived at a junction not shown on her map, so signalled to pull into the side of the road to recheck the directions. She concluded she must have turned too soon. She pulled back out into the road and looked for a place to turn around. A break in a row of houses opened up at the side of an old stone built Inn, The Man in the Compass. It was far too early for opening time and the front door was closed. The sign above the door, depicting a silver haired old man in a peaked cap, swung gently in the breeze. Signalling right she manoeuvred the car and did a three point turn in the empty car park, re-joining the highway to go back the way she'd just come. Dusty Springfield, with her soulful rendition of *Son of a preacher man* came on.

Emilie caught sight of the ten chimney stacks it had been suggested she look out for and turned into a long winding driveway. The uninterrupted view across the undulating green fields down to Whitwick in one direction and Belton in the other was spectacular. She came to a pair of old stone pillars that once would have held a wide gate and drove through, finding herself in the shadow beneath the canopy of an avenue of mature leafy trees. The mix tape fell silent. The tarmac ran out so she parked at the side of the road and stepped out of the car. She removed her Raybans to get a clearer view of her shady surroundings. There didn't appear to be a soul about. She was considering getting back into the car and driving out of there when she heard the distinctive sound of a twig snapping underfoot. There was someone behind her. The hairs on the back of her arms stood up. She turned around. There stood Will, unshaven, uncharacteristically unkempt and haggard.

'This way' he whispered.

'Will!' she exclaimed, 'what are you doing here?'

'Don't talk, just follow me' he ordered.

'Not before you tell me what the hell is going on' she hollered, unsure as to whether she wanted to hug him or slap him as hard as her shaking arms could muster. 'Where have you been? I thought you'd left me. Our son is dead and not a word from you.'

'Not now Emilie. Come on, quickly, we need to get you indoors. Did anyone follow you?'

'No.'

'Are you sure?'

'Yes, I'm sure. What are you doing here? What am I doing here? What is this place?'

'I can't explain yet but I will. For now it's important you focus on something. Think about the time we let off all those red balloons, keep thinking about that, nothing else, just that. Don't let it out of your mind. Did you listen to the tape?'

'Yes.'

'Did you sing along?'

'Of course, you know I can't help myself when those songs come on.'

'I thought you would. Mercifully for me at least I didn't have to listen to it.'

'What do you mean by that?' she smiled.

'Well let's be honest, you can't sing. I just wanted to give you something I knew would keep your focus during the journey.'

'And the motorway wasn't enough of a focus? You know I hate driving on the motorway.'

'I know but it was the quickest and most direct route here. I know how easily you get lost. You didn't get lost did you?'

'Just the once, I took a wrong turn and ended up at the junction of The Oaks and Loughborough Road so I turned round in the pub car park.'

'The Man in the Compass?'

'Yes.'

'That's ironic.'

'What do you mean?'

'I'll explain later, we need to make haste.'

Emilie followed him around the back of an old sprawling Victorian house. The original footprint and its stone façade had been embedded within a host of enormous malformed and unsympathetic extensions.

'Whose house is this? It's huge.'

'No one, its empty, it's just been sold. Will you keep up?'

The heels of her shoes sank into the soft grass with each step so she removed them and increased her step to a canter to keep up with his brisk pace. The old manor house was now behind them and they were crossing a substantial, yet woefully neglected, overgrown garden. A small ivy covered cottage came into view. Will continued past the cottage and onto a path which led between two ornate but derelict greenhouses. Most of their panes were smashed or missing, broken glass and pieces of terracotta pot were lying strewn across the ground. Emilie was overcome by sadness that what once would have been such a beautiful and enchanting place had been allowed to wither to such a sorry state.

Will came to a halt just beyond a wall.

'After you' he said, directing her with his arm.

A set of steep narrow stone steps led down to a small door underneath a large mound of earth which gave the impression the door led to an underground room.

'I'm not going down there' Emilie exclaimed. 'What is it?'

'It's an Anderson shelter' Will replied. 'It was built to withstand bombing during the war.'

'I know what an Anderson shelter is and this doesn't look like any Anderson shelter I've ever seen.'

'It's an expensive one, Army surplus from the war, the real McCoy.'

'The war? Then it's sixty years old. Are you sure it's safe?'

'It's actually Cold War not Second War, so it's only thirty years old and yes I assure you, it's quite safe. In fact it's the only safe place for you to be right now so can we get a move on please.'

Will led the way and beckoned Emilie to follow him. Reluctantly and for the second time that day, she set aside her better judgement and did as he asked, following him down the steps and into the underground bunker.

CHAPTER 24
THE OIL WELLS

1978

Dick McDermott threw down his heavy, black Samsonite and poured a mug of black coffee from the percolator. He lit a cigarette and offered the packet to Tom Summerfield who looked like he hadn't slept for days.

'How was the flight?' asked Summerfield.

'Delayed' McDermott replied. 'How are things here?'

'Much the same as they were when you left. See for yourself.'

McDermott sat down, swivelled the chair into position and adjusted the angle of the screen.

'Jesus, it's like the gates of hell. This was what we were seeing when I left.'

'I know and believe me there's been no let up. Three weeks without a break.'

'Have we got ourselves a faulty chip do you think? Are we just seeing repeating visions, the same thing over and over again?' asked McDermott.

'That's what I thought for a while but no, I don't think they're recurring. We never get repeat visions, it never happens, once a vision's gone, its gone.'

'Yeah I know which is why I'm wondering if we have us a fault.'

'I'm quite sure there's no fault and we're only seeing the same area once. If you study the images, as I've done for days, you soon see there are minor differences. The presence of buildings - or ruins as is the case in many of the images, the plants and landscaping, the positioning of pipes and other structures, the lay of the land. You have to look for them but the differences are there.'

McDermott stubbed his cigarette into the ashtray and studied the screen some more. Dense black smoke billowed outward from the ground churning ferociously across a tarmac road then cascading with the wind into the distance. Abandoned vehicles lay strewn about, some looked as though they had been parked, some were upended and on their roofs. Others were no more than burnt out wrecks.

'Is it night time?' McDermott asked.

'No, there's just so much thick smoke, it's blocked the sun.'

'Like we'd see in a nuclear winter?'

'Maybe, but there haven't been any mushroom clouds so I don't think we need to concern ourselves we're looking at the aftermath of a nuclear detonation.'

The image changed. A small boy was being cradled in his mother's arms, his head burrowed into her shoulder. The boy turned around revealing his little face. He was weeping black tears. The woman's head was covered with a black hijab. Whether it was black when she put it on was anyone's guess but now it was. It was hard to tell where the line of the hijab stopped and her unnaturally blackened face began. She used the fabric of her dress to wipe her puffy red eyes, spreading lines of soot and sweat, ingraining the texture of the fabric into her smeared cheeks. The little boy drew up his knees to his chest just as he'd probably done in the confines of his mother's womb, clinging with all his might to his Mothers neck and burying his face into her breast.   A new image appeared; a long distance view giving McDermott the feeling he was peering through the view finder of a camera that had suddenly zoomed out. On the horizon, seven columns of raging fire funnelled vertically upward into an obliterated sky. Thick swirling black and grey smoke emanating from each inferno was being carried westward on the wind. The scene changed again, more fire, this time the flames were a huge fireball rather than a ferocious vertical funnel. The acrid black swirling smoke was the same, rising into the heavens like an angry volcanic pyroclastic cloud of ash. The scene changed again and again and again. Each one a similar example of the one before, fire and smoke. If McDermott had any imagination as to what arriving in hell might be like then this was it.

'Do we know where it is?' asked McDermott.

'No, not yet but I've got people working on it.'

'Who?'

The telephone rang before Summerfield could reply. He leaned across the desk and picked up the receiver. McDermott continued to watch the catastrophic images. A new scene, smoke blackened the sky for as far as the eye could see, like the darkest storm clouds. This image was different, there were no flames. Instead a highly pressurised fountain of black liquid spewed hundreds of feet into the air before raining back down to ground. The rain had created an ebony lake.

Summerfield replaced the receiver.

'Look at this' said McDermott 'a lake of black water.'

'It's a lake alright but it's not water' replied Summerfield. 'That's oil and we now think we know where it is.'

'Where?' asked McDermott.

'Kuwait.'

'Where's Kuwait?'

'It's in the Middle East, a small country at the head of the Persian Gulf bordering Iraq and Saudi Arabia. It's also a short distance to the border with Iran. We're looking at the Kuwaiti oil wells on fire.'

'All of them? How many have they got?'

'A lot, Kuwait is thought to have nearly ten per cent of the world's entire oil reserves.'

'Do we have any idea *when* this is happening?' McDermott asked.

'No.'

'So what do you think we're looking at here? A natural disaster? A volcano perhaps? What about an underground fire that's consuming all the oil in its path?'

'No, I don't think so because the fires don't appear to be contained to within a single oil field. All the oil fields appear to be affected.'

'What about methane burns? Don't they burn off the gas that rises with the oil?'

'Yes they do, but it's highly unlikely there would be so many simultaneous methane burn-offs. A tally I did this morning suggests there are over six hundred separate wells either on fire, have been on fire and are now smouldering, or spewing oil, which suggests the well heads have been damaged. You don't get damaged well heads from a methane burn.'

'So you think we're looking at deliberate sabotage?'

'Think about it. Six hundred wells alight and that's just the ones we've seen so far. They've been burning for three weeks. Who's to say how much longer they'll continue to burn? Whatever it is, I think we can safely say it isn't an accident or a freak of nature. You've got to say sabotage looks highly likely.'

'By who?'

'I've just been informed those wells collectively produce one and half million barrels of oil a day. Over the course of three weeks that's thirty one and a half million barrels of oil up in smoke and most of them are still burning.'

'But why?'

'It looks to me like the result of a scorched earth policy by belligerent retreating forces in the aftermath of war.'

'Have you seen any evidence of that, aside from the burning wells? Any soldiers? Artillery? Tanks? Barracks?'

'No soldiers but I have seen abandoned heavy artillery and armoured vehicles.'

'Whatever, it's not our concern' said McDermott. 'Switch it off. I've had enough, it's depressing. The subscribers have access to the images. Let them do what they want with the information. It's up to them what they do with it. It's not our responsibility to analyse the data, we just provide the access to the information.'

'It doesn't bother you we might be seeing the consequences of a war that's still to occur?' Summerfield asked.

'No, a war in the Middle East doesn't bother me at all. If they wanna blow each other to smithereens then let them get on with it, it doesn't concern me one iota. I won't be losing a minute's sleep over it and neither should you.'

240

'It might concern you when the price of petrol for that gas guzzler you call a car goes through the roof or worse still, petrol gets rationed, think about that. What do you get, seventeen miles to the gallon?'

'I wish. I might get fifteen on a good day with a favourable wind and I choose to drive like a Nun.'

'Which Compass is having these visions?' McDermott asked.

'Emilie, poor kid. No one should ever have to witness this hell.'

'Don't get sentimental old man. Besides, she's not witnessing it. The visions are coming from her subconscious, she's not aware of them.'

'That's what we've always thought, I know' replied Summerfield. 'I hope you're right, but Montgomery got a call from the Morris' this morning. That's where he is now or he'd have been here. I should have knocked off hours ago.'

'What do they want?' McDermott enquired.

'Compensation.'

'Tell me something I couldn't have guessed. For what?'

'It appears young Emilie has been having nightmares. They started about three weeks ago, just as the fires of hell exploded onto our screens. Apparently she wakes up screaming in the night.'

'So?' McDermott scoffed.

'So we have some concern that the visions have crossed over into her conscious mind and haven't remained buried in her subconscious as we thought.'

'No, I mean so what do the Morris' expect us to do about it?'

'They want compensation for sleep disturbance' Summerfield went on. 'Can you believe it? They're also asking for an additional sum, payable to take account of the toll it's taken on Mrs Morris' mental health, having to deal with a hysterical teenager night after night.'

'That's what they damn well get paid for' McDermott jeered. 'I hope Montgomery is going to tell them to get stuffed.'

'He's going to use the opportunity to broach the subject of extending their Guardianship contract. It expires in eighteen months. We've never given much thought about what is going to happen with her when she reaches sixteen.'

'I assumed she'd stay with the Morris' until such time as we find her a husband' said McDermott. 'We'll just extend the contract until then.'

'It's hardly been what I'd call a satisfactory arrangement' said Summerfield. 'I've yet to see any evidence of that woman having a single maternal bone in her whole body.'

'I've got more maternal instinct than that rattle snake of a woman' replied McDermott 'and as for Mr Morris, he's just a lazy bastard, but I don't see any alternative, do you? I suppose a menial job could be arranged for her. Something not too taxing that will interfere with Holbrook's neural mode network.'

'She doesn't want a menial job, she wants to go to college,' said Summerfield.

'That's out of the question' stated McDermott.

'Why?' Summerfield questioned.

'Because we don't want her wasting her capacity on fanciful academia' said McDermott. 'You've seen what happens to her outputs when she studies. They reduce.'

'I don't see how we can stop her going to college if that's what she wants to do. She's a bright kid.'

'I don't care how bright she is, she isn't going.'

'It's not your decision to make' Summerfield countered. 'It'll be a decision of the committee and I for one will vote for her to be allowed to continue her education. An education might actually improve the quality of her outputs in the long term. Have you thought about that?'

'It won't.' McDermott assured.

Just as Summerfield and McDermott were about to debate the subject of Emilie's further education, Montgomery came in, silencing them both on the issue.

'How was your trip?' Montgomery asked. 'Fruitful I hope.'

McDermott had been on a sales trip into mainland Europe pushing Compass subscriptions.

'Not bad. Three hundred monthly subscribers have signed up for a year - journalists, editors and politicians mostly. The University campuses proved to be a surprising and highly lucrative bonus. It's a market we need to tap into. I could have sold more, but I depleted the entire stock of Compassnet devices. I hope Mr Halford is going to be able to replenish the stock faster than he did last time, I've got a waiting list.'

'He'll be joining us at five, as will Dr Holbrook. There's a matter we need to discuss.'

'What about?' enquired Summerfield. 'Can't it wait, only I've been here for nearly eighteen hours. I was hoping to go home.'

'It's about Emilie and her future but I suppose we can make the decisions without you Mr Summerfield.'

'It's alright I'll stay' Summerfield responded curtly.

'You don't have to stay' chimed McDermott, 'we can make the decision without you.'

'Thank you Mr McDermott but if it's all the same with you, I'll stay. We need the five of us here or there may be a problem with voting if two of the committee agree and two don't. We've always said that no one of us has the authority to exercise a casting vote so I'll stay to make up the number.'

'Has there been any change in Emilie's outputs?' Montgomery asked.

'No, just the same' replied Summerfield. 'My contact has confirmed the location of the fires though.'

'So where are they?'

'Kuwait, the oil wells.'

'I thought that might be the case' said Montgomery. 'So which ones are burning, those in the south in the neutral partition zone with Saudi Arabia or those in the north near the border with Iraq?'

'What difference does it make?' Summerfield asked.

'It might suggest who set them ablaze. The Saudi's are very astute. It would appear to be the case they have entered into cooperation with the Kuwaitis over resources that sit in the partition zone. They'd hardly torch the very oil fields from which they were deriving an economic benefit now, would they? The same arrangements don't appear to exist with oil fields that span the border with Iraq.'

'You're very well informed.'

'I did some research. I was here late one night about six months ago doing some paperwork so I watched Emilie's output's on screen for a while.'

'Hoping to find her masturbating were you?' asked McDermott.

'Don't be vulgar' Montgomery hissed. 'I found myself the passive spectator at a meeting in which an interpreter was translating between British and Arabic. The conversation centred on an accusation of illegal drilling. The Iraqi contingent at the meeting was accusing the Kuwaiti's of slant drilling into the Rumaila oil field located just north of the Kuwait border in southern Iraq.'

'What did this meeting conclude?' asked Summerfield.

'The Kuwaiti's denied the accusation of course, and made a counter accusation that the Iraqi's were simply looking to plunder the wealth of the Kingdom of Kuwait and they were having none of it. The Iraqi's then laid out a second accusation for which they were seeking financial recompense from Kuwait. Iraq blamed Kuwait for the drop in the price of oil, claiming the reduction was the direct result of Kuwait over producing, in contravention of the OPEC quotas. The Iraqi lawyer present, I assume he was a lawyer, he certainly looked like a lawyer, produced a very long report. Do you want to know the date, which was clearly visible on the front cover of that report?'

'Yes' insisted Summerfield 'of course I want to know the date.'

'December 1989.'

'Whilst none of that is conclusive enough to be able to say we're seeing the policy of the Iraqi's at work, it might suggest the Kuwaiti's have a little over a decade to learn how to extinguish multiple well fires if they're going to avoid the climatic catastrophe we're currently witnessing.'

'I would say so' replied Montgomery.

'I'll call my contact tomorrow.'

'What about Holly? What has she given us today?' Montgomery asked. 'Anything of note?'

Summerfield swivelled his chair to reach for his notepad.

'Eleven submarine fitters at Chatham Dockyard have gone out on strike looking for an additional craft allowance.'

'Yes we know that, they downed their tools this afternoon.'

'But what you don't know is that another sixty are about to walk out in support. Talks between the Argentines and the British I think, about the sovereignty of the Falkland Islands, wherever they are, are about to come to nothing and oh, here's a good one, the Conservative Party are about to select a woman as their Leader.'

'A bloody woman?' McDermott exalted 'that would explain why they're in opposition. I'll believe that one when I see it, eh Captain?'

'I might remind you Mr McDermott that over fifty per cent of the voters in this country are bloody women' replied Montgomery.

'Aye, again thanks to the ruddy Conservatives. Giving women the vote, equal franchise indeed, the most stupid thing ever to seep out of that palace of feckless incompetents, self-indulgent and pandering whimsies they call Westminster.'

'And for your information gentlemen, The Falklands is an archipelago in the South Atlantic' added Montgomery, ignoring McDermott's misogynistic slur. 'The two main islands lie east and west of a stretch of water known as Falkland Sound and they have been under British Protection since 1833. Really gentlemen your ignorance of geopolitics never ceases to astound me. Is that it? That's all she's given us?'

'I can tell you a horse by the name of Rubstic comes in ahead of the pack at next year's Grand National but I haven't been monitoring Holly's outputs very much today. I've been concentrating on Emilie's fire and brimstone. We've got a few minutes to kill if you want to have a look now.'

Summerfield turned on Holly's monitor and adjusted the volume. Hordes of loud fervent protestors filled the streets, marching in chaotic unison, fists clenched, hands rising and falling. A synchronized chant of *almawt li'amrikana almawt lilshaah* resonated from the unruly throng. The flames of small fires in makeshift braziers along the route were being fed with American flags.

'Isn't that the Shah of Iran?' asked Summerfield, as a large wooden picture frame splintered under the cosh of a hammer. The picture was tossed into the roaring brazier. Other portraits of the Shah followed into the flames. Protestors without access to a brazier used matches to ignite their portraits of Reza Pahlavi, the self-styled King of Kings of Iran, throwing them to the ground once the flames had taken hold of the portraits and they could no longer be held. Some protestors could be seen carrying banners which read *almawt li'amrikana or almawt lilshaah.*

'What the hell does *that* mean? McDermott asked.

'I believe it means death to America, death to the Shah' replied Montgomery.

'How do you know that?' asked Summerfield.

'I'm from a long line of serving members of the British Army. I spent enough of my formative years in the Arab world to know Arabic when I see it.'

The image changed. An old man sporting a black turban and long black caftan sat crossed legged on a Persian rug in silent contemplation. The room he was in had no furniture. Liver spots were apparent across his cheeks and nose. His brow was heavily furrowed, his dark eyes sat in deep wrinkled bags below thick black bushy eyebrows. A long silver beard, like an oversized brillo pad, dangled from his chin. The picture changed again. The cabin door of a white bodied *AIR FRANCE* aeroplane opened. The old man just seen in the previous image was being escorted slowly down the steps on the arm of what looked like a uniformed pilot.

'And that's Khomeini' stated Montgomery. 'A fervent Shiite Muslim who has been in exile in Ponchartrain in France for thirteen years since the Shah threw him out of Iran.'

Another new scene depicted a large crowd gathered in a square. Khomeini appeared on a raised platform surrounded by a preying colony of mullahs. The revolutionary guard stood obediently in rows to the sides. Alternate soldiers were attired in the white shroud of martyrdom. The crowd threw themselves to their knees in reverence of the Ayatollah and kissed the ground. Nowhere to be seen were the brightly coloured fashionable dresses worn by the progressive women of the Shah's Iran. All the women, without exception, were dressed like nuns in long black robes, their heads covered in black veils.

246

'And that's the Azadi Tower in Tehran' continued Montgomery. 'The Shah built that in 1971 to commemorate two and a half thousand years of Iran becoming an imperial state.'

'By the looks of it, I don't think Iran is going to be an imperial state for much longer' exclaimed McDermott.

'It's not possible' exclaimed Summerfield. 'Even a philistine of geopolitics such as myself knows the Shah of Iran is beloved, not just by his own people but people and governments all over the world. A revolution in Iran, I don't believe it.'

'I agree it's almost impossible to imagine' said Montgomery 'but we know The Compass never lies. I suppose it was only a matter of time.'

'Why do you say that?' asked Summerfield.

'The Shah's rule has hardly been what a reasonable person would have called legitimate. Still, I wonder what the straw that broke his camel's back was.'

'Why do you say he was illegitimate?' asked Summerfield.

'I think you'll find that the current Shah only became Shah after a coup by the Americans. They deposed his father in 1953 after he'd nationalised Iranian oil in 1951, thereby denying the West their investments. The West put Pahlavi Junior on the throne after the coup. To the groups who oppose his secular administration or his right to absolute rule - the Communists, the Nationalists, the Leftists, the fervent Islamists - he's seen as little more than a puppet of the West. He hasn't helped his case by doggedly refusing to move away from a one party state and introduce a proper democracy.'

'So he's a crook?' asked McDermott 'a dictator.'

'That's not what I'm saying, no, although it's probably fair to say his rule has been punctuated with accusations of corruption by some.'

'His Secret Service gets a bad press' Halford interrupted 'on account of the supposed mal treatment of dissidents and anti-loyalists who speak out against the Shah.'

'The Secret Service of every country gets a bad press' Montgomery argued. 'He's spent more money buying British weapons than any other country in the region and has built up quite an arsenal. You have to wonder why, when his national guard is so well armed, they haven't put down an uprising.'

'So he's a crook with a lot of guns' scoffed McDermott.

'No I don't actually believe he is a crook. He's done many good things for Iran. You're doing the man a disservice.'

'Really, what exactly has he done?'

'He's increased literacy. He's improved the country's wealth by exploiting the oil reserves and mechanising industry. He's embarked on a series of reforms to the land laws to do away with the feudal system. He's crowned a queen; the first Shah ever to do so and he's given women the vote.'

'What use is a vote in a one party state?' enquired Summerfield.

'Perhaps the term *one party* is a bit of a misnomer. Here I think we'd call the system they have in Iran a coalition. There may be a single party, but my understanding, limited as it is; is that there can be multiple candidates vying for a position within that single party such that the result is a coalition of opinion.'

'So it's back to the ruddy women again' said McDermott. 'I tell you it all goes belly up when you give women the bloody vote, they're a goddamn liability.'

'I really don't think giving women the vote will have amounted to the Shah's undoing, if that is indeed what we're seeing unfold. Like Mr Summerfield, I find it extremely hard to believe. I know the Compass never lies but perhaps we're misinterpreting what she's trying to tell us.'

The scene changed again. Three young Iranians sit behind a long table. A woman in the centre, with a headscarf tied tightly in a big knot under her chin and wearing no make-up is reading from a script. The script is unequivocal in its denunciation of America. She announces that unless the Shah is returned to Iran to stand trial for his crimes against the country, the sixty six American hostages taken from the Embassy will be put on trial in an Islamic court in his place. A British speaking journalist informs the young women she must be mad if she thinks the Shah will be returned to Iran and enquires as to what crimes the Shah is charged with. The young woman replies that the Shah has turned the country into a ruin, martyred or tortured tens of thousands of opponents and allowed the Americans to exploit the countries natural resources.

'I must be stupid. There was me thinking the West actually bought their goddamn oil' scoffed McDermott 'who is this stupid bitch?'

She went on to state there were no qualms on the part of the Iranians loyal to Ayatollah Khomeini, about carrying out any sentence an Iranian court imposed on the nest of spies at the Embassy. She herself would pick up a gun to carry out the executions if necessary, even if it resulted in her own martyrdom. Oppression and tyranny she exclaimed, must be destroyed. She informed her audience that bullets couldn't kill faith, humanity or martyrs.

'I'd like to put a bullet in that bitch and see whether she still agrees with the utter garbage she's spouting' McDermott cursed.

'At least it tells us the Shah fled the country before they could execute him' said Summerfield 'which no doubt they'd do. Who do you think we should call about this?'

'We call no-one, that's not our remit' Montgomery commanded.

The door swung open and in walked Halford followed closely by Holbrook.

'Now we're all here I suggest we convene the meeting of the committee' said Montgomery, taking up a seat at the head of the table. Halford poured a mug of lukewarm coffee from the jug and sat down next to McDermott.

'As you know I visited the Morris' this afternoon' said Montgomery. 'They've asked to be compensated for the disruption they've suffered by the young Compass experiencing nightmares and breaking their sleep.'

'How much compensation do they want?' asked Halford.

'Enough to pay for a two week holiday here' Montgomery replied, throwing a glossy brochure into the centre of the table. Halford collected it and studied the open page.

'Five stars in Benidorm, nice.'

'I hope you told them to bugger off' suggested McDermott.

'Yes and no' replied Montgomery. 'They've made it quite clear that unless we acquiesce to their request, the contract of care will not be extended beyond the current term. The current term as you know expires when Emilie reaches sixteen years of age. That's less than eighteen months away.'

'Let's not be hasty' said Holbrook. 'The child has never had a holiday. She's had no experience of life beyond the confines of the Morris house. I think we should consider it. Perhaps there's some room to negotiate a three star hotel.'

'I don't think I made myself clear' said Montgomery. 'There's no suggestion by the Morris' that Emilie will be accompanying them. In fact they've made it quite clear they don't intend to take her.'

'So what are they proposing to do with her?' asked Holbrook.

'They are proposing to send her to stay with old woman Cohen over the road.'

'But she has to be knocking on ninety years old'

'She's actually ninety four.'

'I agree with McDermott' said Halford. 'Tell them to bugger off. We already pay them handsomely for their services. Too handsomely if you ask me. Let them pay for their own five star holiday and their own initiation into the jet set.'

'I don't disagree with you' interjected Holbrook 'they've been taking us for a ride for years. There's no-one who will be more pleased than I to see the back of them. Their care has been wholly inadequate from the beginning but I thought we agreed we needed to secure a two year extension on the contract until she's eighteen.'

'You agreed we needed a two year extension' McDermott groaned 'I didn't. I think we should terminate the contract in eighteen months.'

'And do what with her?' asked Holbrook.

'She can get a job, there's work around if you look for it. There are plenty of factories.'

'And where will she live? It's imperative she doesn't come to the attention of the authorities.'

'There's accommodation available, she can take a room somewhere.'

'And how much do you think an unskilled sixteen year old can command in the labour market? She won't be qualified to do anything.'

'Qualifications aren't needed for menial work.'

'That's what you want to reduce her to is it? One of the greatest minds in the world; confined to some factory floor assembly line by day and flea pit of a bed sit by night, trapped within an eternal circle of poverty.'

'Do you have a better solution Dr Holbrook?' asked Montgomery.

'Yes. I say she should stay at the Morris house until she's at least eighteen so she can continue her education for two more years at the very least.'

'And are you going to give the Morris' the money they want to go to Benidorm and pay their over inflated contract for two further years?' asked Halford.

'The Executive committee will continue to pay it, as it has done for the last fourteen years. We've all done very well out of this scheme, none of us need the money.'

'Speak for yourself' said McDermott. 'Not all of us were born into money, some of us have had to pull ourselves up by our boot straps and start from nothing.'

'And how well you've done Mr McDermott, or are you planning to trade up from your luxury penthouse?'

'It may be luxurious but it still has an outstanding mortgage which I intended to clear as soon as we rid ourselves of those insufferable bloodsucking cockroaches.'

'Perhaps if you gave the Casino a wide berth, your situation might improve.'

'Gentlemen, we're going off at tangents, please can we bring the matter of Emilie back to the fore? Mr Summerfield what do you think should be done?'

'Whilst I too will be happy to be rid of the insufferable bloodsucking cockroaches, so eloquently put by Mr McDermott, I have reservations. The Morris' have continually used the dubiousness in the legality of our agreement to drain and exploit every last ounce of goodwill on our part to service that agreement. I can't however, without compromising the last of my integrity, render the child to a life such has been described by Dr Holbrook and as Mr McDermott would have us render upon her.'

'Cut to the chase man, stop dilly dallying and waffling on with your gibberish. What do you think we should do?' barked Montgomery.

'I think we have a duty to extend the contract for two further years so the young lady can continue with her education. If that means we have to pay for the Morris' and their five star luxury hotel in Benidorm then, as much as it pains me to agree to it, so be it.'

'You're a goddamn bloody fool' Halford protested. 'Their continued demands are outrageous. We already pay them twice what Morris makes in his mechanic's job, and that's before all the extra demands. Benidorm this month, a new bed last month; we know a King sized bed, as was clearly described on the invoice they supplied, won't fit into that box room the child occupies. Clothing allowances when we know she's dressed in hand-me-downs and rags from jumble sales. Uniform allowances when we know she's dressed in whatever Mrs Morris finds in the school's lost property box. Hot school dinners when we know she eats a single jam sandwich every day. Piano tuition, not to mention the piano and the sheet music, ballet classes, tap classes, ballroom classes, trips to the theatre, the cinema, Goose Fair, school field trips, activities at the Youth Club, Brownie & Girl Guide's uniforms and subscriptions, Christmas gifts, birthday parties, outings to the seaside, hairdressing costs, art materials, bicycles, toys and games too numerous to mention. None of these things the child has ever had or ever done, yet we keep paying. They are taking us for fools. Enough is enough. They have failed in every way a dutiful guardian could be measured by. We should be threatening to sue them for dereliction of duty not stuffing their pockets some more.'

'So what would you have us do Mr Halford?' asked Montgomery. 'You know that suing them for dereliction of duty is not an option.'

'Then at least we cut our ties at the earliest possible opportunity.'

'Right, I think we should take a vote' suggested Montgomery 'unless anyone has anything else they'd like to add?'

Silence reigned.

'Those who wish to terminate at the end of the current contract period on January 1st 1980 and deny the Morris' latest demand?'

McDermott raised his hand and was followed by Halford.

'Those who wish to extend the contract until 1st January 1982 and pay for the Morris' to go to Benidorm?'

Summerfield raised his hand, followed by a reluctant Holbrook who only managed a half-hearted attempt with the raising of a single index finger.

'We have a tie which means it falls to me to make the decision. I think we should extend the contract for a maximum of two years beyond the existing agreement but on the condition that the child passes her examinations next summer and achieves the necessary grades to be accepted at an establishment of further education. Should she for any reason not be accepted at such an establishment, then I propose we terminate the contract forthwith and we see she is engaged in some menial paid employment sufficient to cover her living expenses until we can find her a suitable husband. That concludes the matter for this evening gentlemen. I will revisit the Morris' tomorrow and give them the good news.'

***

Fifteen months later

The bell sounded signalling the end of another school day. Fifteen hundred pupils scurried out of their classrooms and crossed the school playground towards the gate of freedom. A man squeezed past the crowd of adolescents exchanging football cards and headed to the school office. The Secretary saw him coming and renewed her lipstick with the aid of a compact in her handbag. A foray into the new world of video dating following a brutal divorce had manifested in a date with the self-proclaimed charming and handsome self-made businessman Dick McDermott. She couldn't believe her luck. Ten years her junior and he couldn't seemingly get enough of her. He rapped on the door and without waiting to be invited to enter, he marched in.

'I wasn't expecting to see you until tonight' she said.

'I couldn't wait that long' he replied adjusting the window blind so it was almost closed with just a narrowest slit to see out. She was at the filing cabinet. He sauntered over and wrapped his arms around her waist before shuffling her towards the desk and pushing her onto it.

'What are you doing? Someone might come in.'

'I can't help it' he replied unbuttoning her blouse. 'Who's going to come in? Everyone's gone home.'

'Not everyone, there's still an exam going on in the hall.'

'If everyone's in the hall, they're not going to be coming in here then are they?' he said lifting up her skirt, thrusting her down onto the desk and removing her knickers.

'No we can't, not here, the exam is about to finish. The invigilator will be along any minute' she feebly protested pulling him down on top of her and fumbling with the buckle to release his belt.

'Yes we can. You said we couldn't yesterday. Nor the day before and you said it last week, but we did' he whispered, smudging her red lips as he kissed her, before inching down slowly to her neck and into her cleavage.

'You are wicked' she teased, undoing the button to his trousers.

'I know and that's just how you like it' he moaned turning her over and penetrating her forcefully from behind.

Powerless to resist his violent thrusting she grabbed a hold of the edge of the desk to steady herself and surrendered to his will. Moments later it was over. He released his hold and tucked himself back into his trousers.

'You'd better go and freshen yourself up' he said pulling her into an upright position 'you look like you've just been fucked.'

'This is getting to be a habit' she replied.

She collected her knickers from the floor and her handbag from the hook on the wall, as she'd done on each previous occasion and disappeared to the ladies.

The outer door banged. McDermott crossed the room, sat himself in a chair in the corner and picked up a magazine from a table adjacent. The examination invigilator came in with a pile of papers.

'Hi' said McDermott.

'Hi again' said the invigilator. 'Where's Cynthia?'

'She's just nipped to the ladies. She said if you came in to leave them on the desk.'

'She's always in the ladies that one.'

He set the pile down onto the desk and disappeared. McDermott quickly got to work rifling through the pile until he found the paper he was looking for, Emilie Morris. He removed three loose sheets, folded them twice and slipped them into his pocket before returning the remaining front and back sheets back into the pile.

Cynthia came back.

'What are we doing tonight?' she asked.

'That's partly why I'm here now' replied McDermott. 'Something's come up, I have to work.'

'That's a shame I was looking forward to it.'

'I know I'm sorry, the wheels of commerce and all that. Don't worry, I'll make it up to you' he said, sidling up beside her, running his hands through her long mousy blonde hair and scrunching it into a pile on the top of her head.

'You should wear your hair up. It makes your face look less fat.'

With that parting shot, he pecked her on the cheek and made for the door.

'I'll call you' he uttered on the way out.

She certainly couldn't call him. He'd never given her his number.

CHAPTER 25
THE REALISATION

May 25th 1998

Emilie stepped hesitantly into the bunker. Will closed the heavy steel door behind him, depriving the room of any natural light. She studied her surroundings and was overcome with a sense of claustrophobia. The room was about eight feet square. There was no window, the only light coming from a battery powered lamp on a small table on the back wall. A folded out camp bed with an unzipped sleeping bag lay on top. She recognised the sleeping bag to be Will's, bought for their camping trip a few years ago. A second camp bed, still boxed, was propped up against the opposite wall. Next to it sat her sleeping bag.

'Have you been sleeping in here?' she asked.

'Yes' he replied 'when I've not been working.'

'But you haven't been working. I've been into Fillet four times and no one has seen you.'

'I didn't say I'd been working at Fillet did I?'

'So where have you been working?'

'Here and there, but mostly here preparing for today. Emilie, sit down please' he pleaded, unfolding a slatted chair and setting it by the lamp table.

His tone was one she hadn't heard before.

OK I'm sitting down. Start talking and this had better be good. I'm not in the mood for..'

'You have to believe me' he interrupted, cutting her off mid-sentence. 'I never intended for any of this to happen. I know who killed your colleagues, that night on the way to the Mayor Making. I know who shot them. I swear on my son's life, I had nothing to do with it, but I know who did.'

'Which one?'

'Which one what?'

'Which of our son's lives are you swearing away?'

'That's cruel and not like you.'

'I'm cruel? You weren't at your own son's funeral and you accuse me of cruelty.'

'I was there, you just didn't see me. Well that's not altogether true. You did see me but you didn't recognise me. I came in after everyone else and stood at the back and I snuck out just before the end when the Oasis song came on.'

'No, you weren't there. I looked for you. If you'd have been there, I'd have seen you.'

'You did see me. You turned around, looked me right in the eye and gave me your pitiful look. Then the vicar started prattling on about a child he clearly didn't know.'

Emilie thought back to the day.

'I did tell the vicar he was Sam, not Samuel. Hook nose man?'

Will nodded.

'That was you?'

'Yes, that was me.'

'Did you leave the red balloon and the football?'

'Who else would have left a red balloon?'

'But why all the secrecy, I don't understand.'

'You will. I'm hoping that when you know the truth, you'll find it in your heart to forgive me because I love you. You have the biggest heart of anyone I've ever known. If anyone can forgive me it's you and only you.'

'What have you done Will?' Emilie asked, a sense of dread establishing itself in the pit of her stomach.

'Do you remember the night we met?'

'Yes, of course I do.'

'Our meeting wasn't an accident. I'd been sent to meet you. I went there with the intention of bowling you over and getting you to marry me.'

'But we'd never met, how could you have known you wanted to marry me?'

'I didn't, but that didn't matter, I'd made a contract.'

'A contract? A contract with who? And why?'

'A group of men, they call themselves the Compass Cabal. I've been on their payroll ever since. I'm going to be arrested and I'm probably going to go to prison but the only thing I ever did was to fall in love with you I swear it.'

'Are you saying you were paid to marry me?'

'Yes, but …'

'And you knew you were going to do this before you ever actually met me?'

'Yes, but …'

'So you'd have married me irrespective of whether you loved me?'

'Yes, but I did love you. I do love you. I loved you the second you spoke to me.'

'But why?'

'Because you are beautiful and kind and smart and …'

'I'm not asking why you love me, if indeed you do. I'm asking why were you sent to marry me?'

'Because I was to be your handler.'

'My handler? What the fuck is a handler?'

'Please calm down and listen. I know this is gonna sound way out there and it's gonna be hard to believe, but when you were two, a set of implants were put into your brain. These implants have allowed the Cabal to monitor your brains activity ever since.'

Emilie's fingers began to probe her head frantically.

'You can't feel them, they're embedded.'

'What do you mean by monitor my brain activity?

'Your thoughts.'

You're telling me someone can read my mind?'

'In essence yes, but not just someone.'

258

'Then who?'

'Anyone who pays the Cabal. Last I heard there were over one hundred thousand subscribers.'

'You're telling me one hundred thousand people are able to read my mind?'

'I think the numbers have dwindled lately but yes, pretty much.'

'I don't believe you. Have you gone mad?'

Emilie eyed the door and considered whether to make her escape from the confines of the underground coffin in which he'd imprisoned her. She no longer considered it a bunker. Suddenly it had become a coffin and one she found herself sharing with a mad man.

'Believe me, I wish I had gone mad. I know how preposterous this sounds but you have to believe me. Why would I lie?'

'Prove it' she ordered.

'I can prove it, but that would mean leaving this room. The second you do, your thoughts will no longer be shielded and the Cabal will know something's not right. Believe me Emilie, they will kill you before you can do anything about it.'

'But surely, if what you're saying is true, this Cabal are already reading my mind?'

'Not as long as you're in here?'

'How come?'

'Because we've been modifying the structure to block the HF waves your neurons transmit on. At least we hope we have. We're not exactly sure what frequency they are using.'

'What?' said Emilie looking perplexed, 'so the Cabal might be reading my mind now?'

'We don't think so.'

'How can you be so sure?'

'The transmitter, that's one of your implants, emits a high frequency signal. We know the frequency of this signal is somewhere on the radio wave sector of the electromagnetic spectrum. We think somewhere at the top end between High Frequency and Very High Frequency.'

'I don't know what the electromagnetic spectrum is' she said.

'That's not important.'

'It is to me' she hollered.

'OK, it's the range of electromagnetic radiation. Different types of waves sit at different places in that spectrum of radiation, from say Gamma rays and X-rays at the top end, to infrared, microwave and TV, down to radio and at the bottom, submarine communications.'

'What kind of waves am I transmitting?'

'Like I said, we're dealing with high frequency radio waves'

'OK, carry on.'

'This signal sends a skyward radio wave that refracts off the ionosphere back to a receiver which the Cabal control. We can make an educated guess about the frequency based on data known about the lowest and the maximum useable frequencies for successful refraction to take place but we can't say for sure.'

'Why not?'

'Because the sun's an unpredictable beast and its behaviour has an effect on the ionosphere.'

'What in God's name is the ionosphere?'

Will took a paper and pen from his holdall.

'I'll draw you a picture, it'll be easier. He drew two circles.

'This is the sun. This is the earth. The ionosphere is in this area. It's the upper atmosphere just before space. It begins about thirty five miles from the earth and stretches to two hundred and fifty miles or so from the earth. It's the layer above the stratosphere here, which contains the ozone layer. The atmosphere closest to the earth below the stratosphere is the troposphere where all the weather is formed.'

'How do you know all this?' asked Emilie.

'You'll be surprised how much a man will be prepared to learn when his wife's life is on the line. Can we please stop digressing?'

'Carry on then.'

'The sun gives off rays of ultra violet radiation that penetrate the atmosphere of the earth. These rays cause electrons to form by a process of ionisation. Electrons are simply electrically charged particles, before you ask. Lots of things can affect this ionisation process and change the lowest and maximum useable frequencies.'

'Such as?'

'Coronal mass ejections or solar flares. Do you know what a coronal mass ejection is?'

'It's when the sun spits at the earth.'

'Yeah, the sun spits at the earth, that's pretty much it. God, I love your innate ability to cut through all the bullshit and just nail something as it is. Well, when it spits, it ejects a huge burst of radiation which increases ionisation as more neutral particles get converted into electrons. The most regular changes in the makeup of the ionosphere occur between day and night time. At night the charged particles, the electrons, start to recombine with the negative particles and reform into neutral atoms but this process doesn't occur uniformly throughout the ionosphere. Now, this is where it gets complicated so bear with me. At the bottom, the bit nearest the earth, the atmosphere is much denser and the particles are more tightly packed. This lower section is known as the D Layer. There's an E layer and, in the upper realms on the edge of space, where the atoms are less densely packed, is the F layer. This recombination of electrons into neutral atoms occurs at a much lower rate and they hang around. This F layer is subdivided into F1 and F2.'

'This is all very interesting but how the hell does any of this explain whether or not my mind is being read?' Emilie shouted.

'I'm trying to explain how we have figured out that in here you are safe and your transmissions are being blocked.'

'Well I don't understand, and who is *we*?'

The door to the bunker suddenly opened from the outside. Sunlight streamed in making it impossible to see who was at the door. Squinting, Emilie took to her feet and looked for something with which she might defend herself. The first and only thing she saw was the pen on the table. She picked it up and held it out as if to spear the first person to approach. As she instinctively tried to step backward to increase the distance between herself and the intruder, the chair folded in on itself and concertinaed to the concrete floor landing with a thud.

'I thought you might like a cup of tea' said the intruder. Will closed the door.

'This is my wife Emilie' said Will. 'Emilie, this is Dr Wingfield. He's a friend.'

261

Emilie lowered her weapon of mass blue ink and studied the man carrying a stainless steel tea service on a tray.

'Are you *The Friend*?' Emilie asked.

'I like to think so' he replied.

'Thank you Mark' said Will. 'I'm parched. I was just trying to explain to my wife how we are quite certain she isn't transmitting from in here.'

'You've had a demonstration of the radio test have you?'

'Radio test?' Emilie enquired.

'I was getting to that' replied Will. 'I hadn't actually got beyond an explanation of the theory because someone wouldn't stop asking questions.'

'What's the radio test?' she asked.

Will rummaged in his holdall and removed a portable radio.

'If the bunker is successfully blocking radio waves then we won't be able to get a reception on any of the bands of the radio, short wave or long wave.'

Will demonstrated by switching on the power to the radio and slowly turned the dial. The radio gave out nothing but a hiss.

'So that's conclusive is it?' Emilie asked.

'Not quite' replied Dr Wingfield. 'I assume your husband has told you we don't know what frequency we're dealing with.'

'Yes but if the radio won't work…'

'Mobile phones work on a similar wave length, but on a different place on the spectrum. When we carried out a mobile phone test, those signals were still getting through. We discovered we were able to convene a call between a mobile phone outside to one inside the bunker.'

'So I could still be transmitting on a mobile phone frequency?'

'No my dear, please don't alarm yourself' said Dr Wingfield. 'We've made the bunker secure.'

'How?' asked Emilie.

'With the addition of many layers of metalized polyethylene terephthalate.'

'What's that?'

'A polyester resin coated with aluminium. The stuff shiny balloons are made with essentially. It's the reason the walls in here are red. Your husband insisted it had to be purchased in red. Damn stupid colour for a faraday cage if you ask me, but it does appear to have worked. Let me demonstrate. Mobile phone at the ready Mr Weston?'

Dr Wingfield keyed in Will's mobile phone number and waited. No call arrived. They waited some more, still no incoming call. Dr Wingfield placed his mobile phone on the table, picked up the teapot and poured strong tea into three fine china cups, placing the cups onto matching saucers and handed one to Emilie.

'Perhaps you'll step outside and complete the demonstration Will.'

Will disappeared outside returning a minute later with his mobile phone now displaying the missed call.

'See, no matter the frequency, you're quite safe in here. The call couldn't be received so long as the phone was in here. Will had to leave the bunker for it to pick up the signal.'

Emilie studied Dr Wingfield as he sat on the middle of the camp bed sipping his tea. Something about him was familiar but she couldn't place him.

'Have we met before, only you seem familiar to me but I can't place where we might have met?'

'Indeed we have, twice. The first time was outside the Town Hall in Aitone, then again at the cemetery. I was very sorry to hear about your son.'

She still couldn't recall him.

'The guns d'ya ear em?' said Dr Wingfield, contorting his stature to one side, bending himself over and speaking with a different dialect. 'Bring back the green shield stamps' he continued in the same manner.

Emilie recalled the old veteran outside the Town Hall in the wheelchair with the placard calling for the reinstatement of the Green Shield Stamps.

'You were the old man in the wheelchair with the medals and the placard?'

'Yes, guilty as charged Ma'am.'

'But why were you there?'

263

'To plant a seed without you realising it was being planted. I knew about your history with Green Shield Stamps. I hoped you'd recall the kindness of the benefactor who used to gift them to you and that it would make you amenable to trusting me when the time came.'

'I thought you were a senile decrepit old man.'

'As you can see I'm anything but. I'm into amateur dramatics. I make the prosthetics. That day I had my Richard III head on.'

'When was the second time?' Emilie asked. 'You said we'd met twice.'

'At the cemetery. That day I was sporting my Edmund Blackadder head. I had intended to use Quasimodo but someone else insisted on wearing it' he said looking across at Will.

'You gave me the Green Shield stamps printed with my birthday?'

'Yes.'

'But you can't be the person who gifted them to me all those years ago, you're far too young.'

'No, that wasn't me. It was my mentor, confidante and closest friend in the world, Dr Ivor Newlove.'

'Ivor Newlove? I've never heard of Ivor Newlove. Who is he?'

'He's dead now, I'm sorry to say. To understand who Ivor was, you will have to study some documents. We can go through them together, we have some time to kill.'

Dr Wingfield rummaged on the floor below the camp bed and brought out three cardboard boxes along with a long worn leather cylinder tied with frayed ribbon.

'But why me?' asked Emilie. 'Why has this happened to me?'

'I think the answer to that question will become clear when we've studied all the documents. Before Ivor died, he entrusted me with these documents. In so doing, he sought a guarantee that I would protect and defend you. Ivor loved your Grandmother, Ivy Newlove, with all his heart and through that lifelong bond, evolved a natural affection for Ivy's daughter, your mother Holly.'

'You're mistaking me for someone else. My mother isn't Holly.'

'Yes Emilie, she is. I assure you, Holly is your biological mother. Any doubt I may have harboured in that respect was finally quashed the day you gave a blood sample at the hospital. I work in the haematology department and quite by chance, I happened to be on duty that day. You have the rarest of blood phenotypes. Your blood carries the Compass antigen. Dr Newlove retained a sample of it, taken from Ivy, and he allowed me to study it. Less than fifty people around the world are known to carry this antigen. I'd never seen it again until the five victims of the shooting arrived at the morgue and then you turned up.'

'You're saying that the victims shared this rare blood type with mine?'

'One of them, yes.'

'Which one?'

'The young Coxstable girl, Dana.'

'I don't understand, what does that mean?'

'It means that Dana was your biological child. Dr Newlove was meticulous with his record keeping. It's all in here. The Morris' I'm afraid, were not your biological parents. They adopted you illegally. They were a part of the Cabal's conspiracy. They were also a pair of freeloading blackmailers as it turned out, who saw an opportunity to hold the Compass Cabal to ransom. When the Cabal refused to pay them anymore money they simply discarded you.'

Emilie's memory shifted back to the day she came home from work to discover her suitcase waiting in the hall.

'You should also know that I am the son of James Wingfield. I was just a boy when my Father was seconded from the United States Air force to serve in England during the deployment of the Ballistic Missiles in the sixties. It was during this time that Ivor and my Father met and they became friends. They remained in touch over the years by the regular exchange of letters. James Wingfield was your Father. He and Holly had a fling. She was pregnant with you when he was sent back to the States. It means that I am your Brother and you are my Sister.'

Will announced it was time he left the bunker for the drive to collect Miles from school. He bent down to retrieve a fourth box from under the bed.

'What's in there? Emilie asked.

'Photocopies of salient documents the Police will want to see' replied Will.

'Have you read all these documents?' she asked.

'Yes'

When? Before we met?'

'No, I've only seen them for the first time this week, I swear it. I'll come back with Miles, there's a bed for him over there. Then I shall go and turn myself in for the part I've played in all of this. If the Police don't let me out, Dr Wingfield will look after you. You can trust him.'

'Like I trusted you?' Emilie asked. 'Like I trusted the Morris'? Like I trusted those who told me Sam was my son? Don't you dare dictate to me about trust William Weston.'

Will was taken aback. She never called him William before, ever. His father was William. He was and always had been, just Will.

Emilie filed away one stack of papers, reached for a new pile and checked her wristwatch. It was four thirty.

'Don't worry' said Dr Wingfield. 'They will be here soon'.

Emilie continued reading and Dr Wingfield answered her questions, as best he could. They were both startled at five minutes to five by a frantic rapping on the door.

'See,' said Dr Wingfield, climbing up from the bed. 'They are here'.

'What if it isn't Will?' Emilie asked.

'It is' he replied.

'How can you be so sure?'

'Listen to the tapping.' Tap tap tap in quick succession, then three more taps but slower followed by three quick taps again.

'It's our code, the international Morse code signal for S.O.S. Dot dot dot, dash dash dash, dot dot dot. Listen again'.

Tap tap tap, three spaced taps then tap tap tap.

Dr Wingfield opened the door.

'Come in, quickly' he said.

The young Miles, his arms full of books and his favourite threadbare teddy bear, came in, followed by Will.

266

'Sorry we're late. Someone insisted he couldn't countenance a camping trip without something to read, so we had to stop at home on the way'.

'It's cool in here' said Miles. 'Why are the walls red?'

'It's a long story' said Will. 'I'll explain later. This is Dr Wingfield. This is his bunker and he's very kindly offered to let us camp here for a few days.'

'It's very nice to meet you, young man. Your Father has told me a lot about you. You're interested in the solar system I see,' said Dr Wingfield, eyeing the top book of Mile's collection.

'Not really. Dad thought I should bring it. A Bunker, this is really cool. There's not much room though. Where are we all going to sleep?'

'I'll leave you to it,' said Dr Wingfield. 'It's time I started to prepare dinner. How does Hamburger, chips and salad grab you? Your Dad tells me that's your favourite.'

'I'll have mine without the salad if you don't mind,' replied Miles.

'Just as you like. Perhaps while I'm doing that, you might like to study this card?'

'What is it?'

'It's Morse code. Have you heard of Morse code?'

'Yes, I've heard of it. I've never used it though.'

'What, never?'

'No, never.'

'Well, there's no time like the present to learn a new skill, so I'll leave it with you. See if you can learn how to say S.O.S in the time it takes me to make your hamburger.'

'I have to go on a few errands' said Will, 'so I'll be leaving with Dr Wingfield. You stay here with your Mum and I'll see you soon, okay?'

'Where are you going? Can I come with you?'

'No, I'm afraid not Son. Your Mum has something very important she needs to talk to you about.'

'Use the bolts' said Will, on his way out. 'Keep the door shut. Lock yourselves in when you're here alone. Don't let anyone in without the code and please don't leave until Dr Wingfield tells you it's safe to do so.'

He blew her a kiss. The door closed and Emilie slid the three heavy duty bolts into place.

'It looks like it's just the two of us then' she said. 'I have to do some reading and you have to practise your Morse code before dinner, so we'd best make a start.'

Half an hour passed slowly. Miles' incessant tap tap tapping was driving her to distraction but she carried on reading. Half an hour became forty five minutes. Forty five minutes became an hour. A loud bang outside caused them both to look up.

'That must be Dr Wingfield with dinner' said Emilie, getting up from the camp bed. She moved to the door and waited to hear the code.

A few seconds later, a second ominous bang, louder than the first, rang out.

'Open the door then' said Miles. 'I'm starving.'

'I'm not sure I should. Dad said not to let anyone in without the code. We haven't heard the code have we?'

A third bang, louder again, resounded just outside the door. It sounded distinctly like gunshot. Emilie froze. She willed the tap tap tapping of Dr Wingfield's code to commence. All she heard was silence. Deadly silence. A fourth shot, and the door to the bunker vibrated.

'That sounds like a gun' said Miles.

Emilie checked the bolts on the door.

'Mummy, I'm scared' whispered Miles. 'I want to go home.'

'So am I' she replied.

'Can we go home?'

'No, I'm afraid not. Not yet.'

'Why not?'

'Because there are some bad people that Daddy thinks might want to hurt me. He's gone to the Police station to tell them about the bad people. We have to wait in here until he comes back and tells us it's safe to go out.'

Why do the bad men want to hurt you?'

'It seems that when I was a little girl, these men put a micro-chip in my brain. This chip tells them what I'm thinking.'

268

'They can read you mind?'

'Yes.'

'Cool.'

'Cool? It's not cool, Miles. It may be many things, grievous bodily harm, criminal invasion of privacy, what it most definitely is not, is cool, ok.'

'But why do they want to hurt you?'

'Because I've found out about the micro-chip. They want to stop me from reporting it to the authorities.'

'You said Daddy has gone to the Police. If he's gone to report it, then everything will be alright.'

'Yes, but the only evidence of this chip is in my head. The bad men need my head to get rid of the evidence.'

'What if it's the Police outside and they haven't been given the code?' Miles asked.

'Dr Wingfield has the code. He'd have given it to them, wouldn't he?'

'I suppose so. So what do we do?'

'I don't know, but I think we should wait a little longer to see if Dr Wingfield comes as he promised.'

'Have you got your mobile phone?' asked Miles.

'Yes.'

'Then I think you should call for help.'

'I can't' she replied, collecting the phone from her bag. The RECHARGE BATTERY message had been flashing since she left home in a hurry that morning. 'Dad and Dr Wingfield think the chip in my head works on similar wavelengths to those used by mobile phones. The reason I'm safe in here and why my mind can't be read is the same reason that a mobile phone won't work. The signal is blocked.'

Emilie considered her surroundings. There was just enough room to swing the door outwards to ninety degrees, about three square feet. Then nine concrete steps to the top of the dug-out. If someone was waiting at the head of the stairway, she'd be a sitting duck the second she ventured out. They were trapped. She looked around. The small bunker was little more than eight feet square. She'd been told it was

269

sealed. How long it would be before the two of them extinguished the breathable air? Sooner or later she was going to have to open the door.

Another sixty torturous minutes passed. Emilie used the time to explain to her young son, in terms a ten year old would understand, about the Compass Line, at least as much as she knew herself.

'I don't think Dr Wingfield is coming' she eventually announced. 'It will be dark out there now. Take off your sweater'.

'Why?'

'Because I'm going outside and I need to be wearing something dark. I'll stick out like a sore thumb in this white shirt. I'm also going to need your shoes. Before I open the door, I want you to turn off the lamp. It will be very dark in here but it's important the light doesn't seep out and give us away. You're going to have to be very brave. Can you do that?'

'No, Mummy, I don't want you to go.'

'But what if Dr Wingfield needs help? He's been very kind to us. You'd want me to help him wouldn't you?'

'Yes, but…'

'No buts, it's going to be fine.'

'No, it's not. What if they've shot him and they shoot you too?'

'Your Mum's a tough old bird. She can look after herself, provided she knows that you are safe. As soon as I've gone out, you must fasten this centre bolt. Come and show me you can do it.'

Miles unlocked and relocked the bolt. She collected the lamp from the table.

'Now show me how you switch the lamp off and on again.'

It went pitch black. Miles switched the light back on.

'Good. Now I want you to get down on the floor and stay as low as you can.'

Emilie tipped the camp bed onto its side, tugging the centre W shaped leg free from the canvass frame. She grasped the metal leg at one end with both hands, stepped into the corner of the bunker and swung it with all her might. The pointed end of the leg, the end she imagined would do more damage if it were to strike an assailant, swizzled a hundred and eighty degrees in her hand, finishing up on the opposite side she intended. She gripped it tighter and swung again. This time, the lethal point remained at the required angle. She swung for a third time, just to be sure.

'Are you ready?' she asked.

'No, but I imagine you're going to go anyway' replied Miles.

'Don't worry. Dr Wingfield has probably just burned the burgers and he's had to go and get some more. He doesn't strike me as a man used to being in the kitchen. I'll be back soon. So it's light out, door open, door closed. Bolt on, light on. Got it?'

'Yes, I know what to do.'

'And on no account, open this door without the code. What is the code?'

Tap tap tap, tap – tap – tap - , tap tap tap.

'Excellent. You've got it' she said, pecking him on the cheek, silencing her mobile phone and slipping it into her pocket. She slowly unlocked the bolts.

'Now'.

The light went out. She grasped the handle and slowly opened the door, pausing when it reached forty five degrees. She slipped outside and closed the door behind her. Furtively, she made her way up the steps, staying as low as she could and maintaining a firm hold of the camp bed leg, keeping the pointed end to the left in the direction she'd have to swing. When she got to the top, she scurried to take cover behind a large shrub. The light in the cottage kitchen was on. She watched for a sign of activity. There was none. A bedroom light upstairs was also on. The silhouette of a man crossed the window. Unsure whether the figure was that of Dr Wingfield, Emilie instinctively tucked herself into the thicket and looked around. She took out her mobile phone. She had ten missed calls and a number of unread text messages. She dialled Will. His voicemail came on. Her fingers scrambled to send a text message.

Wingfield missing. Gunshot? Help.

The figure upstairs crossed the window a second time. A loud crash resonated from inside the cottage. There was nowhere else to take cover between the shrub and the cottage, she'd have to run across the lawn and hope no one saw her. About half way, she stumbled upon Dr Wingfield. He was lying face down in the long grass. Kneeling at his side, she attempted to rouse him. There was no sign of life. She forced him over onto his side, fumbling for his wrist in a bid to discern a pulse. He was alive.

'Dr Wingfield' she whispered 'please wake up. Don't be dead. Please God, don't die.

There was no response. He was out cold.

'I'm going to find help' she continued. 'Please, hang in there. I'm sorry I've been so long, please just hold on, help is coming.'

She took her phone and dialled 999. The digital display went black. The battery had died.

'No,' she cursed. 'Not now.'

She collected the leg of the camp bed and continued running, keeping one eye on the upstairs window. She'd done twenty frantic paces when a security light, affixed to the cottage wall, came on, illuminating the garden and her place in it.

'Shit' she cursed breathlessly, still running.

The figure appeared at the upstairs window. He'd seen her and was making his way out of the room. She knew he was on the way down. She had to get away. She had to get to the car. If she could just get to the car, she had a chance.

'Here' a man's voice boomed. 'The bitch is here. We've got her.'

The man sprinted towards her, blocking her path. She'd crossed the length of the lawn and had almost made it to the driveway. Now there was no way to escape. She couldn't see a way past the shadowy figure. He came closer. Fifty feet, forty feet, thirty feet, he was almost upon her. She stood firm, gripped the leg of the camp bed and prepared to strike. He raised his arm. She guessed he was about to shoot. She was in his line of fire, like a helpless, terrified rabbit caught in a headlight. Darting to the left, she heard the discharge of the gun. The bullet tore passed, grazing her right cheek. He fired again. By some miracle, the second bullet also missed. She began screaming like a banshee and made off at full steam for him. She swung the leg of the camp bed at his head with all the strength she could muster. His arm went up defensively and the metal leg caught his wrist. He winced and the gun toppled from his hand.

'You bitch' he cursed, lunging forward and punching her right in the centre of her forehead with his clenched fist. She recoiled and fell backwards into the border. He bent down to retrieve the gun. This was it. In seconds she'd be dead. He couldn't miss from this distance. An image of Sam came to the forefront of her mind. He was singing. *You gotta roll with it....* For a split second she was reconciled, both to her defeat and to the surety that she'd be with her son again very soon. The gun was pointing straight at her. Survival instinct kicked in. She rolled to the left. The bullet punctured the soil. Her roll was broken when her hip caught on the sharp edge of a rock. The rock moved. With both hands, she fought vigorously to free her new weapon, unleashing it in her assailant's direction. It struck him right between the eyes and he fell into a bloody heap. Emilie got to her feet, retrieved the leg of the camp bed and made for the car. Hot on her heels was a second assailant. He came bounding out of the front door of the cottage. She reached the car and delved into her pocket for the keys. They weren't there. They must have fallen out in the tussle on the lawn.

'Help' she yelled. 'Help.' She knew her plea was futile. There was no one to hear it. The only house, the big house, she'd been told, had long since lain empty. The second attacker neared the car. He marched to the driver's side. She scurried around, towards the bonnet, then on to the passenger side. He came after her. She knew she wouldn't be able to keep the car between them for long. This man was older but he still looked fit. She doubted she could outrun him. Where would she run to? They were in the middle of nowhere.

'What do you want?' asked Emilie.

'You know what I want' replied the attacker.

'No, I don't. Tell me'.

'We know you know about the implant Emilie. You know it has to be destroyed. We won't stop until it's destroyed. Make it easy on yourself and I'll kill you quickly. You won't feel a thing, I promise.'

'Get away from me you psychotic bastard.'

273

'Make it easy and we might be inclined to spare your son. We know he's in the bunker. Will, he's told us where he is.'

'No, he hasn't. You're lying'.

'I'm not lying. How else did we know where to find you?'

'You read my mind. I told you where you'd be able to find me.'

'Think about your son. Give it up, for the sake and the life of your boy. Will doesn't want to have to come here and kill you himself, but he will, if he has to. He follows orders. He's a loyal member of the Cabal.'

'Lying bastard. Will would never kill me.'

'No? Then why did he bring you here?'

The assailant made a sudden dash and he almost caught her. She twisted, and slipped out of her jacket. He was left holding the empty cuff. The car was between them again.

'You've tried my patience now, you stupid fucking bitch' he cursed. 'I'm going to kill you and when I've killed you and bashed your head in, I'm going to do the same to Miles. I gave you a chance to save him.'

Emilie became terrified at the prospect of what lay ahead. She was tiring. Why hadn't she kept up her fitness training? She was hungry, she hadn't eaten since yesterday. She was angry. The moment came. It was now or never. She couldn't keep running. He came at her again. This time, she didn't run. She stood her ground, gripping the leg of the camp bed with both hands. She wielded her weapon, just as she had done in the bunker. The pointed end embedded itself into his neck. She yanked it out. Blood began to gush and he collapsed to the floor. A moment later, he was on his feet again, the palm of his hand stemming the blood, before collapsing once more. He was still.

Emilie's instinct was to go to Miles. She tossed the leg of the camp bed in her wake and sprinted back across the garden towards the bunker. Her presence triggered the security light. The first assailant had disappeared. His body wasn't lying where she'd left him. Panic took a hold and she froze in abject horror. What if the other guy in the expensive suit had been telling the truth? What if Will had been in on it all the time? What if he had lured her here to kill her? He couldn't have picked a better place. What if he had given the Cabal the Morse

274

code to get into the bunker where she'd left Miles? Why hadn't she changed the code to one only she and Miles would know? She had to get to him. She didn't get very far. The assailant she'd smashed in the face with the rock lurched at her from behind a shrub. The same shrub she had taken refuge behind when she came out of the bunker. Why hadn't she seen this coming? She toppled backwards and he was on top of her. The gun was in his hand. She fought and kicked and screamed and he dropped the gun. Distracted by retrieving it, she got the upper hand. She pulled both feet up to her chest and released them, kicking him with all the force she could bring to bear in his balls. He doubled over, cringing in pain. Emilie retrieved the gun first, pointed and fired. Somehow, in spite of the nearness, the bullet missed. She pulled the trigger for a second time. The barrel was empty. The assailant regained his composure. Through the glare of the security light, he looked her in the eye with an evil grimace. She guessed he was enjoying himself. It was then she recognised him. He was the man she'd seen in the white van, on the day of the paint-balling. He'd been parked at the bottom of the street when they left that morning. Then again, when she left the house of Mrs Coxstable, he'd been there. She'd only seen him from a distance, through her rear view mirror but was sure it was him. She wanted to kill him. She lunged, screaming, punching and kicking, like a devil possessed. She bit his hand when he tried to grab her, again he cursed. No matter how hard she fought, he was stronger, much stronger. He soon took the advantage. Struggling, Emilie fell to the floor and he had her pinned on her back. He was heavy. His weight was overpowering. She was trapped. His hands were around her throat. Once more, Sam came to mind. He was playing air guitar. *Baby, you're gonna be the one who saves me, cos after all, you're my wonder wall.* She could feel herself slipping away. The sound of sirens approaching and the sight of blue flashing lights produced in her, a final rush of hope. She fingered the grass, frantically searching for the gun. There it was. She could feel it. Bit by bit, she inched it towards her until she had a good grasp on the barrel. She brought it up and tried to whack him on the side of the head but his arms were too long. He was too far away. She was drifting away, she couldn't hold out any longer. I'm coming home to you Sam.

'Put your hands up' hollered a voice. 'Armed Police, put your fucking hands up'.

EPILOGUE

Emilie finally emerged from the bunker in which she continued to shelter, three days later, after the five members of the Cabal, Halford, McDermott, Montgomery, Summerfield and Holbrook, had been taken into custody. They were charged with numerous offences ranging from unlicensed broadcasting, grievous bodily harm, attempted murder and conspiracy to commit murder. The Cabal member Emilie had speared with the leg of the camp bed turned out to be Bob Halford. The son-of-a-bitch survived. The Cabal member, who had been trying to strangle her when the Police arrived with Will, had been Dick McDermott. Apparently, Emilie and her rockery stone had given him one hell of a headache and a mild concussion, but nothing more. Dr Wingfield spent a month in hospital recovering from multiple gun-shot wounds. Mercifully, none of them had penetrated his vital organs and he did eventually make a full recovery.

McDermott and Halford were also charged with five counts of murder for the shooting of the four Councillors and young Dana Coxstable. The Cabal of five soon became six when William Weston Senior was indicted. It emerged that he had bankrolled the venture after the Ministry of Defence stopped paying the illicit bills. Alerted by the arrest of the five, he'd had time to destroy all the details held in files, including the identities of the subscribers and no-one had come forward voluntarily to admit they had been on the client list of the Cabal. All six were denied bail.

During the trial, it came to light that McDermott had also murdered the Morris' in Spain. The Cabal had taken them off the payroll and they had threatened to inform the authorities about the illegal activities of the Cabal. Two further counts of murder were added to his charge sheet.

No one was charged for the hit and run that had killed Sam. Emilie knew it had been McDermott, his way of trying to keep Will in line but, in the absence of sufficient material evidence, the Crown Prosecution Service wouldn't charge.

She sat in the public gallery to witness the sentences being handed down. The Cabal were each jailed for life. A life sentence didn't mean life of course. It could mean less than fifteen years if they kept their noses clean, stayed out of trouble and were able to convince a parole board they were no longer a threat to society. Emilie surmised they were each wily and clever enough to be able to do just that when the time came. McDermott caught her eye from behind the screen where he'd been throughout the trial. It was the same eye he'd given her in the garden of Grace Dieu manor that horrible night. From behind the screen he ran his index finger along his throat and grimaced. The only saving grace, McDermott and Halford were handed multiple life sentences with a recommendation from the Judge that they never be released. Will didn't get away scot-free. He was sentenced to two years on lesser charges including conspiracy to commit illegal broadcasting, for the part he played in the chain of events that began sometime during the autumn of 1963 when he was just a baby. She didn't blame Will. She'd already forgiven him for the part he'd unwittingly played in the Cabal's elaborate conspiracy. He'd been manipulated, just as she had. Still, whether she wanted to remain Mrs William Weston she hadn't yet resolved. She hadn't ruled it out. He had saved her life after all. She had at least a year to make up her mind.

Scans had revealed the presence of the implants but no surgeon could be found who would agree to remove them so for now, they remained in situ.

Emilie left the court and drove home. She pulled onto the driveway and applied the handbrake. A *For Sale* sign had been erected in the front garden and a single metallic red balloon had been tied to the front door knocker. She sat in silence and thought about whether anything would ever be normal again, whether she'd ever feel normal again. She doubted she'd ever feel entirely safe or secure again. She turned off the ignition. There was no radio to be silenced. She didn't listen to the radio anymore. Her mind wondered back to the last time she remembered what normal felt like. The night of the Mayor Making, when she had arrived home full of expectation about what her year in office would hold. She'd parked the car that night just as she had done now. She'd noticed all the lights in the house were on and she'd turned off the radio just as the presenter had asked; *If someone could tell you what was going to happen before the end of the day, the week, the month, the year, would you want to know?*

The End

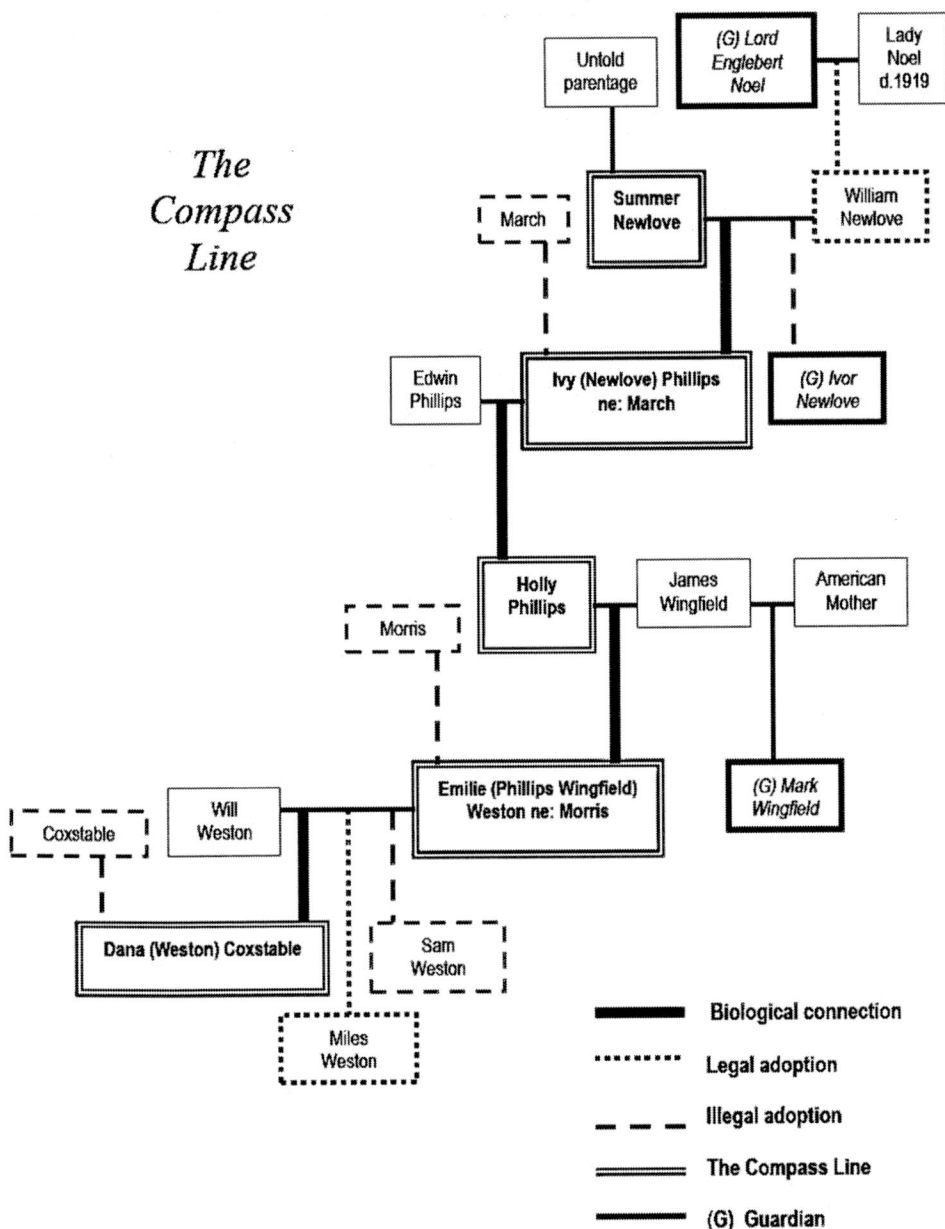

The Compass Line

Legend:
- Biological connection
- Legal adoption
- Illegal adoption
- The Compass Line
- (G) Guardian